BLOOD MOON

Cambridge Murder Mysteries

by Charlot King

First published as an ebook 2018
Published by: Beautiful Day Cambridge Ltd
ISBN: 978-0-9934083-2-8

Illustration: Robin Howlett

DEDICATION AND THANKS

I would like to thank my son for his continued encouragement. I am truly in his debt and would not be writing were it not for him. To Penny, a dear friend, for reading this story ahead of publication. I would also like to thank Robin Howlett again for another beautiful illustration. And finally a big thank you to the readers of 'Poison' and 'Cursed'. Writing 'Blood Moon' was so much more fun knowing there might be a genuine audience out there who love Elizabeth Green, Inspector Abley and Godric as much as I do! Thank you to all, it means a great deal.

PROLOGUE

Apples have always been my favourite fruit, ever since I was a boy. I remember scrumping in the orchards at the back of the lane near my childhood home. Must have been only seven or eight years old. A small gang of us, neighbourhood kids, would compete to see who could reach the highest, reddest and juiciest. We'd take turns at winning, sometimes letting the smallest kids have their moment in the sun in those joy-filled days. I was always the biggest, strongest and best at everything then, my pockets bulging with the most apples. I feel small now.

I can't see anyone here, but I know I'm not alone as I can hear breathing. The embers still burning in the brazier and the pungent mud around my head clogging my nostrils. The cold has travelled into my back and down my legs though I've been numb to it for a while now. My breath shallow like a popped balloon. I wonder who I'll see on the other side. My thoughts are crowded by a searing pain, which rumbles in waves and burns my belly. What's left of me feels sick and panicky.

It's a bitingly cold autumn night. I try to reason in my hypothermic stupor that if only we'd fallen ill inside, perhaps we could have phoned for help. But alcohol and the riverbank... I take my last look at the sky, all bright and shiny. A shooting star sparkles as if with an urgent message, telling me to let go and become part of this infinite beauty. I remember the card I meant to post to my Mother still on the side. I think of my Father's death and hope to see him soon. I'm scared. I can taste apples in my mouth. Three slices of pie. I take my last breath, there is no space here for me anymore, and so I fix my eyes on the moon.

1
HORSES OF STOURBRIDGE COMMON

It is an early Sunday morning in Cambridge. A thick autumn mist hangs under the willows on Stourbridge Common. Everything and everyone are asleep along this inky stretch of river. All but a man walking his dog and a solitary sculler up way too early for even breakfast as the darkness finally begins to lift. Lock-keeper Ed's wellingtons crunch frosty turf, Clive his large Old English Sheepdog huffs and sniffs local pee-mail, while twenty-five-year-old burly American postdoc Brad's rollocks creak under the weight of his long strokes as his oars dip and drip cutting through the water.

Then quick as a blink, harmony is broken by Brad bellowing "Get outta here!" at horses drinking at the old ferry-boat slipway. Ed shouts, "Leave the ruddy horses in peace!" Clive pays no attention, continuing to cock his leg, knowing full well this isn't the men's first exchange and won't be the last. Brad rolls his eyes as Ed picks up a handful of mud and hurls it straight at the American's head, who then threatens to come over and, "Shove it where the sun don't shine!" This altercation is soon swallowed up again by the quiet in this vast expanse of nothingness, just a mile or two out of the historic city centre.

After a while and further along Stourbridge Common towards the gates through to Riverside, old Ed rubs his eyes in case they are fooling him. Clive has already picked up a trot to investigate. A hundred or so yards ahead are two large dark brown mounds strewn across the path which Ed swears look like horses, something which makes him anxious. The closer he gets, the more suspicious he grows as to their health. "Better get the vet quick," he says to his loyal friend, "they look rotten." Ed scrambles for his phone while cursing himself for leaving his glasses at home. Warm horse breath hangs in the cold air, but Ed's is shallow and frantic as he holds his phone as far away from his eyes to dial.

Further up the path, as Ed's conversation is ending with the vet he says, "Hang on, there's a young woman here on the bank, she's on the ground?" and, "Oh, here's another, and oh my—" Ed doesn't finish his sentence, instead rushes to the woman who isn't moving, to feel her pulse. More bodies are lying in the grass. There must be four, no five he can see. He stands up and looks behind him and spots another, and another. They look like boat dwellers, some with dreadlocks, some in multicoloured jumpers. Canal boats just feet away, with doors wide open and lights still on. Clive sniffs the woman, as Ed tries to pull him away while hanging up on the vet and dialling 999. "I can hear some moaning, but I think they're dead", he says into the phone. They ask him to stay on the line, but Ed drops his phone on the grass as he notices apples everywhere beneath his feet, dozens maybe a hundred of them scattered in the grass, and a huge barrel containing more apples tipped over with apples below, bobbing between a canal boat and the riverbank. He kicks an apple under his feet as a brazier, still burning low from the night before outside one of the boats, emits its last heat. A black cat sits on top of one of the boats, watching Ed suspiciously. Ed bends down, unsure which person to help first. They all look dead.

2
NO MORE VALENTINO

About a mile away, closer to the spires of Cambridge Colleges where students and Fellows are just waking up, breakfast is being served in Foxes Haven super early. Professor Elizabeth Green brings a fresh pot of tea into her drawing room and places it on the table beside her grandson, Godric. Wearing striped pyjamas, Godric is thoroughly committed to doing as little as possible this Sunday, an approach Elizabeth knows he applies to every other day of the week. And he hasn't so much woken up very early to eat breakfast with his nanna as gotten in very late in the early hours and not yet gone to bed. If he thinks slipping deftly into his pyjamas is fooling anyone, then he should have brushed his teeth, as Elizabeth can smell a Scottish distillery on his breath… even Bertie has turned away.

But Elizabeth is happy this morning. She has just come back from walking the Afghan Hounds across Jesus Green, her boots and coat out in the hallway still steaming by the radiator, her messy brown curls squashed from their time under her brand new autumn duffel coat. Now in cosy slippers and her favourite chunky cardigan of Gerald's, which she loves to wear when it gets cold, she has lit a fire. Elizabeth has also unpacked boxes of pastries and pancakes from the bakery and is looking forward to a nice sit-down with a peppermint tea and conversation with her favourite (and only) grandson. She watches as Godric finishes raspberries on a pancake in no time before stuffing a whole pain au chocolat into his mouth, her beady eyes passing judgement, but this morning she lets it go.

Elizabeth perches and tickles Bertie's head as he sits on the table in a perfect spot with the weakened sun streaming in. Bertie's new companion Soot is stretched across the back of the sofa above an upside-down Monty with his legs akimbo. Monty's brother Hector is beside the fire, chasing rabbits in his dreams. Godric chews his pastry as he scrolls through some recent text messages on his phone. Elizabeth pours him a fresh cup of tea, leans over and spots a photograph of Valentino posing against an Italian wall with climbing jasmine and an ice-cream sign for vanilla cones. He is clutching his heart, and the picture message reads "Miss You." Godric hits 'delete'. Elizabeth breathes in sharply.

"I can't believe you can so casually toss away such a handsome young man, and from San Gimignano – think of the holidays," she booms as tea spills from the teapot she's still pouring into his cup and now saucer.

"Oh, he was just too romantic, Bunny. Bit dippy, drippy. I couldn't breathe." Godric huffs through a full mouth of pastry. His nanna wouldn't understand as he positions his cup more directly under the spout.

"I don't see the issue. Valentino walked the dogs, cooked delicious broccoli rigatoni, put the hose on the roses, what's not to love?" When Godric ended it, Elizabeth remembers how hard it was not to offer Valentino the spare room and a job as her chef. She hinted at it to Godric but the look he gave, there were daggers.

"He did a lot more than you do." Elizabeth is full of smiles, thinking about Valentino, who lit up the room. About his broad grin and easy temperament, which on some level reminded her of her late husband. "A quiet and gentle spirit and yet also so much fun, always so generous with his time." And now he is back in Italy, pining after Godric. Her smile falls away as she adds, "You had to go and choose a cold, pompous, arrogant Englishman. Sometimes I truly wonder, Goddy."

Godric replies, mildly irked at his nanna questioning his taste, "Wonder? Wallis is great, so delicious." Godric slurps his tea, all starry-eyed and looks to his nanna to wait for her to break into a smile, which she doesn't so he adds defensively, "I accept he may be a tad pompous, but he's *my* new ever so slightly stuck up but an incredibly handsome pompous boyfriend. And if you invite Valentino to stay, then you will have one less grandson living here." Godric stares at Elizabeth remembering her offer. "You may drool over his food, well I drool over Wallis's—"

"Stop," Elizabeth interrupts.

"He's such a beautiful man. Everyone else thinks so." Godric looks at her as earnestly as he can on no sleep and with a hangover which would kill off weaker humans. Hector breaks wind loudly behind them.

"I'm clearly not alone in my opinions," Elizabeth replies flatly.

Godric then spots his new beau through the French windows, right at the bottom of the garden clinging onto Elizabeth's lawn, one oar flat on the water about to go sculling on the river. Elizabeth sees too and sighs, her tranquil morning now broken. Godric opens the French doors, letting the draft in which makes Elizabeth shiver and mumble about letting all the heat out. The dogs aren't keen to leave the warmth of the drawing room either, nonchalantly looking up at the movement and activity, but dipping their heads again in slumber as she shuts the doors up tight. Bertie jumps down to sit even nearer the crackling fire, right between Hector's legs. Meanwhile, Wallis waves at Godric who is now walking to greet his new lover.

"I will never understand the speed with which my grandson falls in and out of love, positively nauseating, Bertie." Elizabeth utters as she peers at the two men embracing, Godric now bent down on his knees to reach Wallis who is still in his scull, bobbing a little on the water. To Elizabeth, Wallis looks like a deliberate throwback to the 1920s, with clipped blonde short back and sides, bright blue eyes, wealthy bone structure. When Godric briefly introduced him at her front door for the first time a couple of weeks back, Wallis called Hector "A disgusting perve", just for sniffing his groin? Then added, "What's this, a zoo or something?" just because Bertie and Soot happened to be sitting on the stairs watching him. And when Wallis and Godric departed before she shut the front door she distinctly heard Wallis scoff, "Your nanna's place stinks. Is she some mad old cat lady?" No, this young man was her least favourite from Godric's stable.

As Elizabeth watches with disappointment at Godric now laughing, a welcome interruption comes from the telephone trilling from the hallway. It is her best friend, Emily. Can Elizabeth come to dinner this week? "Who will be there?" Elizabeth pulls a face. This day is rapidly going downhill. "Do I have to? I'd really rather not. Last time I had supper at Victoria I got stuffed vine leaves, which I'm sure they bought over the road."

Elizabeth walks back into the drawing room with the phone to her ear and can't resist checking on Godric again. She pulls another face of disappointment at her grandson, who is now doing some kind of funny walk around the lawn just to make Wallis laugh. She shakes her head. "No, I won't end up like—" Elizabeth is constantly interrupted by Emily, talking at her on the other end of the phone. "Yes", and, "No, that's not going to happen", until finally, she sees Godric say goodbye to Wallis, who is thankfully now rowing away, much to Elizabeth's pleasure. “No, I haven't heard from him in weeks. I know. I don’t know.” Elizabeth listens again to Emily as she watches Godric walk back up the lawn in his wet slippers. She smiles at Godric, who asks to be let back in the French doors. Elizabeth points at Godric’s feet, then points at the back door. She watches her grandson look down at his now muddy feet and then walk around the back to come back in through the kitchen. Elizabeth then interrupts her friend, mildly irritated by what she hears, responding, “I don’t care what you think, Emily, he’s a good policeman.”

3
FLASHING BLUES

Ed, the Jesus Green Lock Keeper, is taking the weight off his feet. For the past twenty minutes, he has sat on a bench facing the River Cam. About fifteen feet away to the left, two ambulances have driven up onto the grass after Ed had earlier opened the gates to Stourbridge Common. Sitting with a medical silver blanket wrapped around him, he is still in shock after being told by a kindly paramedic that he has probably saved lives this morning. Ed thinks of all the people he could have saved, only the rowers would have been a worse bunch. The dirty boat squatting scroungers with their litter and diesel choking up the riverbank were not those he much cared for. Clive is still sniffing about, curious to know what's going on and getting occasional strokes by the paramedics. Ed stares at a duck swimming about in different directions on the river, trying to ignore the fact that various bodies are being placed on stretchers and fitted with drips while being tucked in under blankets. None of them speaking, none of them moving.

To the right, Ed hears the winch whirring as it pulls up

one of the horses and transfers it into a large medical horse truck fifty yards back on the Common behind him. Ed watches as the lifeless animal hangs awkwardly in the harness. He kicks something and looks down, another apple beneath his feet.

Soon after the SOCOs arrive in their white all in ones, stretching the police tape and starting to piece together the jigsaw in front of him. Not ten feet away from Ed, a Constable briefs Sergeant Lemon. Ed can hear the whole conversation.

"How many?"

"Eight, Sir," the Constable replies.

"Any fatalities?" Lemon asks.

"No."

"Good," Lemon replies.

"Do you want to know about the horses?" the Constable asks.

"What about the horses?"

"The vet says he can't be sure until he gets them back to the vets, or whatever you call a vet hospital," the Constable says. Lemon nods for him to continue. "But he said it looks like they ate something, Sir." The Constable looks at Sergeant Lemon, who couldn't be less interested in the horses. Instead, he watches the paramedics carrying people to the ambulances.

"Make sure the bikes don't try to break the tape this morning. They'll just have to find alternate routes," Lemon instructs the Constable, knowing the track record of cyclists ignoring crime scenes as if they are somehow outside the law, it annoys the hell out of Lemon. "Book them if they cross it. And knock on all the boats if you haven't already. See if anyone is in or left along this stretch up to The Green Dragon, okay?"

"Where's Inspector Abley?" The Constable asks. Lemon glares at the Constable.

"Just get on with it," Lemon replies, before walking over to Ed. "Hello sir, Ed is it?" Lemon looks at his notepad. The Constable has already given Lemon the man's full name. "I hear you were the one to call for an ambulance, is that right?"

"Yes."

"What time did you find these people here?" Lemon kneels, to get closer to Ed. Ed continues to stare back at the duck on the river, still changing direction for no apparent reason. Ed is still unsure about everything. Lemon can see Ed's mind turning over, trying not to remember.

"I know I woke around four thirty. Don't sleep well these days. Brain just gets up before my body wants to get out of bed. Then Clive here sees I'm awake and that's it." Ed pats Clive who has come over to join them and is now sniffing Sergeant Lemon's face and nearly toppling him over. "Down the stairs to let him out and then he wanted feeding." Ed's answer is coherent but lacking the concise response for which Lemon was hoping. But it doesn't stop Ed. "Then I thought about porridge, but Clive wouldn't let me sit. Fidgeting he was, so I thought poor sod needed to go back out. So I put my boots on, and off we came. Must have been not far past four forty by the time we left the Lock House.

"So you were here when? Four fifty?"

"Who d'you think I am, bionic man, with my ticker?" Ed pauses, both men aware of the irony of the shock Ed has just had. "It takes a good twenty minutes from the lock. Old Inspector Abley would know that. Where is he?" Ed stops and looks around. Lemon is annoyed with Ed for being dismissive about his detective skills, but also mildly amused that this much older man is calling Abley old. He knows the Inspector would have chuckled and then been affronted.

"Please go on."

"I was walking back when I saw them. Been over the Science Bridge to Logan's Meadow, thought I'd walk up to the church in Chesterton. Came back over the Green

Dragon Bridge. Otherwise, I'd have seen them on my way out. Maybe they'd have been in better condition. That means that Brad would have seen them too when he went past earlier. Huh, he didn't stop, did he?" Ed glances up at Lemon and gives him a worried look.

"Nothing suspicious? No one you saw who you think might have done this? Who is Brad?"

"I walk along here every day, twice a day and the only thing I can think of is the rowers. Brad, he's one of them. Don't know his other name, just hear them shouting to one another, you know, 'Brad!'. They don't like the horses. He was out here this morning like I say shouting at them for drinking the river. I mean, he doesn't own the river and where does he think they are supposed to drink? I wouldn't put it past them to cause suffering to the poor creatures. Toffee-nosed brats don't like anything that lives unless it has a silver spoon in its mouth."

"Right, right, and you think this Brad might have knocked out these people?" Lemon asks.

"Is that what you think happened?" Ed looks at Lemon, adding, "Well, he's a bit of a bruiser. D'you think he was checking to see if his antics had worked?" Ed stands up and throws an apple for Clive to chase, but Clive has already sniffed them earlier and doesn't fancy apple this morning.

"Can you not do that please Sir, everything is evidence here now."

"Apples?"

"Yes."

4
HELLO MY WIFE

"It's so good to see you." Inspector Bob Abley says. He has come down from the shower and is surprised to see his wife standing in the kitchen of their home in Park Parade. A little self-conscious, wearing his green checkered golfing trousers and pink jumper and about to leave for the golf club, he tries to hug his wife. But Maureen moves away to fill the kettle.

"Just let me get my bearings." Her bags around her feet and still wearing a summer dress, she looks out of place. Her suntanned arms on show, now with goosebumps.

"It's cold," she says.

"It's autumn," he replies smiling, the crinkles on his kind face now showing, unsure what to say next. Her having been gone since early summer. He wants to grab her in his arms and tell her how much he missed her. That he forgives her for everything, for that thing she had with the man next door. Instead, he just says, "Summer wasn't all that this year."

"The house is a bit of a bombsite," she says.

"Ouch," he replies, grabbing his jumper near his heart trying to lighten the mood, but his wife doesn't react. So Bob Abley scratches his hair, then starts to pick things up and tidy up. He makes quite a racket.

"Stop!" Maureen shouts. Abley freezes on the spot and twists his head to look at her, waiting for her next word. But she says nothing.

"Look I know—," but Abley can't find the words to tell Maureen what he's thinking. He reaches out to put his hand on the arch of her back but feels her flinch.

"I just need time to acclimatise, that's all. I need a long sleep, get used to this place again, before…" She trails off. Her words throw Abley, as he thought she wanted to come home to him. He's nervous about speaking, nervous of hearing what else she might say. But he doesn't have to say anything, she says it for him. "Can you go, just to give me some space to settle in?"

"Go?" Abley can't help it. The word spills out of his mouth. He hears it bounce off the walls.

"Just a day." She says, looking at him hard, cold. "See you tomorrow?" She stares away. This isn't a discussion. He is just pleased that she's back, pleased this is a start. Of course, she needs a rest.

"You must be tired. Of course, no problem. I'll go and see a friend. And see you tomorrow."

"Thanks." She replies, opening a kitchen drawer.

"Everything is going to be all right, I promise." He says, trying to make her feel better, feel less stressed. He can see her back is stiff, and her hands are rubbing the teaspoon a little too hard between her fingers. He knows her so well. "I promise, love, it will be okay."

5
BOAT DWELLERS DOWN

Following the 'incident' on Stourbridge Common, that's what Ed hears the police call it, Ed is a little wobbly on his feet when he gets up from the bench. A paramedic says it is most probably shock and to be on the safe side it's best that he "come in and have a cup of tea so we can check everything is okay." Ed tells them he is always wobbly in the morning, but the paramedic is having none of it. The vet who has by this time loaded both horses into special veterinary horse boxes offers to take Clive for a bit, so Ed reluctantly agrees to get a ride in an ambulance to Ripplewater Hospital.

After doctors and nurses have listened to Ed's heart, taken his blood pressure, peered into his eyes, and after he's drunk two cups of tea with two sugars, Ed has had enough of sitting about and being fussed over by nurses thank you very much. Even though they are not his favourite people, Ed is curious about what happened earlier he decides to pay a visit to the boat people. Standing outside the ward, it feels a little strange visiting people he doesn't know. But Ed gets past the nurses' station, perhaps ignored because he's still wearing a hospital blanket around his shoulders. He opens the door to a side room and sees a row of boat people in beds on drips, with sicktrays, sick on some pillows. Most look asleep, but one man with a shock of red hair, red beard and bright yellow T-shirt is more alert than all the others. He greets Ed.

"So that happened." Ed hears the man say from his red beard Ed can't stop looking at. He has seen this man before, wandering about on his boat at the Common. The man tries to sit up but is too weak.

"You were all on the floor. It was early. I didn't see you on the floor." Ed replies.

"Must have been some party." The man says, looking around at his surroundings and then at the drip attached to the back of his hand pumping in the fluid from a bag above his hospital bed.

"The horses are at the vet's." Ed says, feeling like he has to update this man, like a helpful neighbour imparting gossip across the garden wall.

"Right, right… what horses?" The man asks.

"Two of them. Stallions, maybe geldings. They must have gone down with a whack. I'm Ed. I called the ambulance. I mean two ambulances came, but I called 999," Ed says.

"Oh thanks. I'm Joe," the man introduces himself.

"Vet thinks they were poisoned, the horses. Strange goings on." Ed says, curious about these people to whom he has no affinity. "It's those bloody rowers, I'm sure of it."

"It's true. They do hate us." Joe looks around and for the first time sees other boat people in the beds beside him. "Tom, Sarah, oh my god. What happened?" As Joe asks Ed, who is about to say he doesn't know, Ed sees a rather glamorous woman enter the room. Unlike those in the beds, who are still wearing rather shabby clothes, this woman has painted nails, shiny black six-inch heels and red lips.

"I wasn't sleeping and heard it on the radio. What's happened?"

"I don't know, oh Talya." Joe and Talya embrace, then Talya walks over to Sarah and squeezes her hand, causing Sarah to moan. Perhaps the squeeze was a little too tight. Talya looks at Sarah carefully and sees that she is still out of it. So, she turns to the next bed, where Tom is lying.

"Should he be this white?" Talya asks Ed, mistaking him for someone who might know. Ed just shrugs, feeling more like an imposter now.

"Well, I must get back and let the chickens out," Ed says. "They need feeding." Ed decides to leave. He sees that they are all alive in this room, at any rate, and with his curiosity fed he now wants to pick up Clive and give him a big hug.

"Apparently on the news report it said horses were poisoned? A vet up at Molton Street said he had to give them something for it. Is that what happened to you?" But Joe doesn't answer. He lies back down. It has all been too much too soon and is more poorly than he first thought. Talya goes back to sit next to him and strokes his brow. "If I find who did this I will kill them!"

6
JUST FOR THE NIGHT

Sergeant Lemon is standing outside Inspector Abley's house on Park Parade. He looks out towards Jesus Green at a man walking a German Shepherd. Lemon drove here from Stourbridge Common after spending time with the SOCOs collecting evidence from the earlier incident. He was hoping to pick up the Inspector on his way to Ripplewater Hospital, and perhaps be invited into the kitchen for a coffee and warm up a little after the early start this morning. But instead the two men are now standing out in the cold, neither able to share the pastries the Inspector bought and left out for breakfast ahead of his game. Lemon cannot help but notice Inspector Abley's green checkered trousers sticking out from the bottom of his coat and an overnight bag on the wall open to all who glance to see his toothbrush and various shirts stuffed inside. He thinks how forlorn his boss looks, as if out of ideas.

"Golfing weekend?"

"Maureen just got back this morning from abroad. All sun-tanned. No warning. I can't believe it."

"Is that good?" Lemon looks at the bag again.

"She asked for a bit of space today – you know women – so I'm not under her feet while she unpacks, sorts out her autumn wardrobe and no doubt puts the vacuum round. Says I'd let the place go." The Inspector tuts. "Not that bad. Women have such high standards, don't they?"

"Where would we be without them, Sir?" Lemon says.

"Knee deep in carpet fluff apparently," Abley replies, crossing his fingers, although his face looks a bit more worried than it should. "Fingers crossed it'll be back to normal tomorrow."

"She's given that no-mark the heave-ho then?" Lemon asks. Abley doesn't answer. This is all getting a bit too intimate and revealing. So instead Abley grabs his bag and starts to walk along Park Parade, Lemon following. Up ahead, some tennis players are taking advantage of the dry day on Jesus Green, while cycles are toing and froing along the criss-crossing paths to their right. But Abley wanders aimlessly with nowhere to go. He just needs to get away from the conversation about his wife and her ex-lover as it makes the whole broken thing far too real. He still hopes he might wake up one morning and find out it has all been a horrible dream.

"You can stay with us, Sir, tonight I mean?" Lemon offers. "We have a new duvet cover in the spare room. I've recently been dragged to the Beehive Centre to spend all my money on scatter cushions, throws and stuff, enough to make a base camp in the Antarctic. Put my foot down on the colour though. Midnight blue. Very tasteful."

"Ah, that's very good of you. It's okay. I've got plans." Abley is not about to take Lemon up on his offer, as he can't face talking about what's going on. "In fact, I need to be somewhere now. Do you want anything?"

"Just came to see if you wanted to come to the hospital," Lemon asks.

"I'm fine, just a bit tired. Don't fuss over me, Lemon."

"Picked up all these ill boat people. Nothing's been

confirmed." Lemon replies. Abley realises his error and feels terrible for thinking Lemon was talking about him needing the hospital.

"Anyone dead?" Abley asks.

"No, but looks like they've been poisoned, as there were two horses as well, fell down too and the vet has already deduced as much. All happened on Stourbridge Common earlier this morning. They are likely related."

"Facts?" Abley asks.

"Eight down, all in hospital. Two horses down within a hundred yards. No witnesses, no evidence of foul play. No weapons recovered."

"What was it, a chemical mist off the river? Something they ate?" Abley asks.

"We don't know yet," Lemon replies.

"What have you done? Eliminate those closest. Who owns the horses? Are any boat dwellers well enough to interview?" Abley goes through the obvious questions.

"We interviewed the man who found them. Says he thought it might be the rowers having caused it. Must find a Brad, a rower to interview. We don't have his surname yet."

"Good, and?" Abley adds.

"And that's it," Lemon replies, wanting to tell Abley to get off his arse and come back to work. But he can't bring himself to be insubordinate.

""Sounds like one for our favourite Professor Green," Abley says swinging an imaginary golf club and then looking up at his imaginary shot. Lemon realises this means he's not coming back yet and tries not to show his disappointment. Surely it's time, and the Super can stop twisting the knife now. The suspension has run its course. Lemon is nervous about his next words, as the last thing he wants to do is make the Inspector uncomfortable. But curiosity gets the better of him.

"How did the meeting with the Super go?" Lemon asks.

"Not been in. Read the health warning. Thanks for picking up my clubs for me. If you get the chance, I think I left a putter?" Abley replies.

"You know they are talking about Pober as permanent?" Lemon mentions, looking at Abley directly in the eye.

"Ha!" Abley laughs bitterly. "Yes, well, he's one of a kind."

"Sir?" Lemon replies, hoping the Inspector will be persuaded to do something, or say something about the situation at the station. But instead, Abley just turns his back to Lemon and walks off, with a casual goodbye wave without once looking back.

"That's it?" Lemon says under his breath to himself before shaking his head, walking back over to his car and getting in. Inside he rubs his hands together in the cold, picks up an empty drink in the holder and holds it to his mouth, hoping for something. Disappointed, he tosses it on the floor and drives off to Ripplewater Hospital.

7
A NIGHT ON THE STARS

The Department of Galileo at the university is always quiet at the weekend, and so an excellent opportunity to come in and get things done without being disturbed. Which is why the Head of Department, Professor Nigel Crowhams likes to spend the night with the love of his life, his telescope. It isn't it any old telescope. The twenty-foot beauty resting on a brick plinth in a small circular wooden building with a dome roof opening up to the sky is the perfect companion for stargazing. Professor Crowhams loves to shine and polish this marvellous instrument, to remove all traces of dust or any chance of contamination or interference, which is why he has been doing it for over an hour now. No one else is allowed to clean her, as her marvel needs to be cherished. She has given him countless evenings of joy no woman ever could, and for that, with love, he works his duster along her girth.

On a day-to-day basis, the Professor keeps this small domed building housing his prize beauty locked to maintain the absence of any overly enthusiastic undergraduates, who as far as Crowhams can tell know very little about either astronomy or learning. And while perhaps they know a little more, Professor Crowhams also does his very best to discourage his colleagues from popping in either, dropping all kinds of not so subtle hints that its use is the privilege of Head of Department alone. He tells them, "It comes with the office", and "Oh, I have it booked this week", and similarly regular comments he uses to manipulate his solitary time. So much so that with persistent unpleasantness, he has all but successfully driven away any others from sharing his most sacred of places. Subsequently, he often spends solitary evenings without interruption, viewing Jupiter and all her Galilean satellites in their sparkly splendour. A stickler too for the old-fashioned pencil and squared-paper notes, his work is neatly piled up on a stool, full with private discoveries he's unlikely to share with the rest of the world, who just don't deserve them.

Professor Crowhams looks up through the roof and can see Sunday morning has finally broken, disappointed that another clear night of stargazing is over. He knows it won't be long before a colleague comes looking for him even on a Sunday – this is Cambridge after all. At that prospect, his stress levels begin to rise. He stops to open his flask and pour out the last of his French onion soup before inevitably having to leave his favourite place. But as the last of the soup tips into the cup, his body is suddenly catapulted forward by a hard blow to the head. His papers fly up into the air and slowly begin to float down until strewn across the floor. Sticky brown soup spills all over the telescope as Crowhams is now flat on the floor. A nasty cut to the head oozes blood as he lies motionless on the bricks below, onion soup now dripping onto his face from the telescope above.

8
A CALL FROM LEMON

Having changed out of his slightly damp pyjamas after larking around in the dewy grass earlier, Godric has sat back down at the table with Elizabeth in the drawing room and is now sipping his fourth cup of tea, in no rush to get on with things on this particular or any Sunday morning.

"You seem to go through men like those pigeons eating my bread." They both watch a pigeon currently attacking a slice of wholemeal on the bird table outside on the side lawn. Bertie, now sitting on the back of a sofa near the window, puts his paw up to the pane of glass hoping to reach its grey feathers and is slightly confused at hitting the see-through barrier.

"I like a fresh slice now and then." Godric reaches across to the toast rack, picks up a triangle to make his point and spreads it with marmalade. Hector spots this and comes across and puts his head on the table, being quite partial to marmalade. Godric pulls off a corner crust and gives it to Hector, who starts to munch. Monty sees this and can't help himself, getting up to come for toast.

"Poor Italian stallion." Elizabeth tries her hardest not to say she thinks Wallis is bad news but is finding it harder to drop the conversation.

"I was growing fat. All that pasta and good loving were turning me into a blob," Godric says. "Wallis's making me want to row again after my knee thing keeps me on my toes. He's smart. I thought you'd be pleased? You're always telling me to work harder."

"I'm always telling you to work. Harder would be a bonus. Anyway, you said Valentino was smart," Elizabeth replies.

"Drop dead gorgeous-smart, not smart-smart." Godric gives Monty a piece of toast.

"Stop feeding them, Goddy."

"Nanna?" Godric wonders why she said this. She's usually so soft on them.

"I've had a lot of things to do this morning."

"Walk the dogs, and?"

"Do you have any projects to finish today?" she says, picking up some toast.

"It's Sunday." Godric smiles. "Nothing happens on a Sunday. Just how God wanted."

"You're an atheist." Elizabeth picks up the marmalade.

"Today I'm agnostic, hedging my bets," Godric says. Elizabeth loves her grandson so much that she pours him a top-up tea and spoons out some fresh mango into a bowl, pushing it towards his plate for him to eat. "Well, if you are going to pray today, make sure you wear a vest, it's chilly out there this morning." Godric pulls the mango closer to him while crunching into his toast.

"Are you going to College today?" Godric asks. "I can pop in, have lunch? It will be nice and quiet, how you like it."

"Not if I can avoid it. I might get caught in conversation with Kendall about the wonky library water stand, the moss on the bench in the Fellow's garden or something equally banal about the size of the notice board." The new Master of Granta, Anthony Kendall, has been driving Elizabeth mad.

"Just think, it could have all been yours," Godric says.

"Yes, well your degree can be yours if you try and read a book or two. That's generally how it works Goddy," Elizabeth replies, giving him an 'eat up and get on with it' look.

"Where's that Inspector friend of yours? Haven't there been any murders recently or doesn't he want your help anymore?"

"You know he's suspended, and that the Super says I can come in anytime," Elizabeth replies.

"Want me to go out and poison someone?" Godric jokes. Elizabeth shakes her head at Godric. She can't admit that without Inspector Abley it doesn't quite feel right to just pop into the police station. She was his consultant, not some roaming nomad.

"Cambridge is not awash with murders involving poisons Godric. Perhaps there is a lull?" Elizabeth booms, biting into a piece of marmite toast.

"That Inspector always had a soft spot for you."

"Utter drivel. You'll say anything to get out of talking about your studies."

Both Elizabeth and Godric are pleased at the interruption when the telephone trills from the hallway. Godric looks at his plate of mango and puts the largest slice in his mouth to make the point that he can't answer. Fed up with cold marketing calls, Elizabeth has stopped repeating her number and saying hello like she used to when she picks up the receiver. Instead, she puts it to her ear and says nothing.

"Sergeant Lemon, how lovely to… yes. No, don't worry, this isn't early for me. Have been up hours. Yes." Elizabeth's face reveals the pleasant surprise when she hears Sergeant Lemon's voice on the other end of the line.

"Long time, no speak?" She listens for a while, then says, "Yes, well, no one knew. What is Superintendent Raynott thinking?" Elizabeth listens again. "Okay, I can, happy to, yes of course. See you shortly. Right, bye." Elizabeth replaces the receiver and walks back into the drawing room and having grabbed her coat from the hallway pegs she locks the French windows. The dogs get excited, thinking they are going back out already for a second walk. "No, no. Not this time."

"Well?" Godric asks, but Elizabeth is already out the back door like a flash and opens the garage with the electric switch to reveal the Talbot Lago, all clean and shiny. Elizabeth picks up the driving gloves that Gerald gave her. Godric appears, his blonde locks all tousled, two Afghan hounds at his legs. "Bunny?" He watches his nanna get in the car and start the engine. She looks at him and then back at the dashboard, checking she has enough petrol for her journey, and putting on her driving gloves. Godric is nonplussed, standing, watching.

"I have to go to Ripplewater. There's been a suspected poisoning."

9
RIPPLEWATER

It is still early morning when Elizabeth parks her car at the back of the hospital. She negotiated long ago with the administration to use a space. Nobody questions this as the cream curves of the Talbot take any parking attendant's breath away, too fearful of spoiling the windscreen with any naughty ticket. It is not long before Elizabeth is making her way into the busy main reception where other visitors are meeting for cups of tea or buying things from the small selection of shops and newsagents. She looks at the note of the ward details she had written down earlier and makes her way along the myriad of corridors, trying not to bump into people on crutches, in wheelchairs, or merely struggling along.

Elizabeth opens the doors and cannot escape the sight of eight people in their beds in a row, the curtains pulled back so the nurses can keep an eye on any common symptoms. They all look so pale and ill, and the room is silent in marked contrast to outside. She spots Sergeant Lemon, who is currently speaking quietly with a nurse who has brought him the contents of the trousers of a few of the boat people, as well as a couple of mobile phones. Lemon is placing them in evidence bags and then passing them to a Constable standing quietly by his side. Elizabeth stands beside them and interrupts.

"Sergeant Lemon." Elizabeth smiles and nods.

"Professor Green, thank you for coming." Lemon passes the last bag to the Constable and turns his back on the nurse and Constable.

"You mentioned you'd like my help with something?"

"Yes, yes please." Lemon walks a little further away from the nurse, Constable and patients. The nurse leaves the room. "These people, all eight of them, and two horses who are not here for obvious reasons." Lemon looks at Elizabeth to see if she's keeping up, but she looks back at him irritated to get on with it. "Well, exactly. The nurse spoke to me earlier and thinks something has poisoned these boat people, and we don't know what, why or by whom. I need your help to look into it."

"Is Inspector Abley about?"

"No." Lemon replies, mildly irritated now by people asking him that, and yet him having to deal with everything. "It's just me I'm afraid."

"Where is he?"

"Right now? No idea." Lemon replies, looking back at the patients.

"Is he coming back?" Elizabeth looks to Lemon, hoping for the answer she wants to hear.

"It was me who phoned you," Lemon now says, irked. Elizabeth realises she owes Lemon for the call and doesn't want to blow it.

"Enough said, we will solve this ourselves. The Inspector's not still drinking is he?" she asks, but Lemon just ignores her and continues with the case.

"Because there are so many of these boat people ill at the same time, we're pretty sure it is poison," he says, "and the hospital is keeping a close eye on them. They're waiting I think for a shift change. Short staffed."

"Who's we?" Elizabeth asks.

"The paramedics, obviously, but also the vet treating the horses, and that nurse. I'm waiting for them to wake up so I can take statements. Joe here was awake earlier. I spoke to him for a bit but has gone back to sleep. He wasn't making any sense for the nurse, to be honest. This woman is a friend, who wasn't at the incident."

"So the hospital, what have they done?" Elizabeth asks.

"The nurse says they are looking for symptoms," Lemon replies. "They've checked them for rashes and palpitations. I think they were talking about pumping their stomachs. The consultant is apparently on his way. It's been a crazily busy shift, but they've told him it's urgent."

"Right, I'd like to talk to the man who was awake. Joe, did you say? Then the consultant if you can find him please."

"Yes." Lemon double-checks his notes, a little flustered. But Elizabeth doesn't wait for him to confirm and walks over to the bed he had pointed to earlier, where Joe is lying.

"Hello, Joe." Elizabeth shakes him. "Joe?" Joe stirs, having been asleep.

"Hey!" Talya tries to object, but Elizabeth's presence stops her.

"Joe, what are you feeling?" Elizabeth asks.

"Like nothing before," Joe replies, trying to open his eyes.

"Apparently there is a chance you've been poisoned. What did you eat?"

"I remember drinking, a lot." Joe groans and moves in his bed onto his side. "We were all drinking cider and shots," he says.

"You seem to be okay?" Elizabeth looks at Talya sitting on the other side of Joe's bed, who gets up to shake Elizabeth's hand. But Elizabeth leaves her hanging and just nods. So Talya frowns a little and sits back down.

"I don't live on a boat. Maybe it has something to do with the brazier they lit or something? I've been fine." Talya replies.

"So what were your first symptoms?" Elizabeth persists in asking Joe.

"I've already told the Inspector here." He replies. Elizabeth smiles and raises her eyebrows at Lemon, who doesn't escape the Inspector reference either, but decides not to correct Joe and nods, encouraging Joe to repeat what he told him earlier, as Lemon has already said Joe was making very little sense before. Joe looks at Lemon and then back at Elizabeth and sighs, having to repeat what happened all over again. "I remember feeling dizzy and kind of confused, unable to breathe properly, like this biggest fatigue. I threw up, lots, I threw up for over half an hour, just apple mainly. Then my heart pounded, and I got a terrible headache, and I just remember passing out."

"Have you told this to the doctor?" Elizabeth asks.

"I can't remember." Joe replies.

Elizabeth presses the big red emergency button for a nurse to come back, and within a few seconds, one appears.

"Can you administer the antidote for cyanide poisoning as a matter of urgency to these patients." She looks at Joe, "How many apples did you eat? Did everyone eat apples?"

"I don't know." Joe looks very worried.

"Get the doctor." Elizabeth asks the nurse calmly. "These people need amyl nitrite, sodium nitrite and sodium thiosulfate straight away."

"But doesn't it take hundreds of pips to cause cyanide poisoning?" the nurse questions Elizabeth.

"That it may, but these people have been poisoned with cyanide. If you don't do this immediately, most likely they will die," Elizabeth says matter-of-factly.

"But the doctor—" The nurse tries to suggest they wait. But Elizabeth interrupts.

"Two to six hours from ingestion and they may be

dead. You might want to do it if I were you," Elizabeth booms.

The nurse rushes over to a doctor in the corridor who listens, comes in and looks at one of the patients, then another, then gives the nurse the orders to get some antidote packs. She rushes back in. Joe looks very worried and gets the first smelling salts of amyl nitrite, and then a drip is then attached to him of sodium nitrite.

"What do you mean cyanide poisoning?" Lemon looks very worried, and Joe even more so. A female patient lying the other side of Talya wakes up as the nurse puts amyl nitrite under her nose. She looks terrible and is struggling for breath, as another nurse finds a vein to puts in the drip.

"It can be a quick death or a slow one. But it's always painful." Elizabeth walks over to look at a man in the far bed. There is something about his face, Elizabeth thinks, something grey about him. "Nurse." And the nurse rushes as Elizabeth holds his wrist to read his pulse and shakes her head. The nurse shouts for crash paddles, and everything goes into slow motion as the nurse pulls the curtain around the patient. Elizabeth steps out and stands with Lemon once more.

"Do you think someone was trying to kill the horses? There was a big barrel of apples near the gates of Stourbridge Common," says Joe weakly across to Sergeant Lemon. "The man in here earlier thought it was the rowers."

"People hate the horses," Talya says, "even more than the boat people. The horses knock people off their bikes sometimes and try to steal the food in their baskets, chasing after them. Maybe someone tried to poison them?" she says frantically.

"We will be investigating every avenue," Lemon replies as a Constable comes back into the room.

The crash team with resuscitation paddles rush into the room and behind the curtain. Everyone is quiet outside as they hear words like "Clear" and "Stand back", and then hear the charge and wump of the electrical discharge, trying to save the man.

"Oh god, oh god," Joe says.

"It's Tom," Talya says quietly to Elizabeth.

Elizabeth already suspected it was too late when she saw Tom in the bed. He had slipped away, and she was pretty sure from a coma brought on by cyanide poisoning. Joe tries to get out of bed to rush to Tom, but Talya stops him. While a doctor and some nurses try to bring Tom back from the dead, Lemon is in quiet conversation with the Constable at the back of the room as Elizabeth walks over to Talya. There is a pause in conversation in the room, as everyone listens to the medical team trying to save a life.

"How did you know your friends were ill, here?" Elizabeth asks Talya, cutting into the silence.

"It was on the news. It sounded too much like Tom, Sarah, Joe and the others. I can't believe this. It's like a bad dream, I'm going to wake up, and we'll all be somewhere else," Talya says, staring at the drawn curtains around Tom's bed.

"So you were there last night?"

"Must have gone home about two, maybe earlier." A single tear rolls down Talya's face as she clutches Joe's hand. "When they start partying, sometimes they stay up until it gets light," Talya almost whispers.

"It's gone very quiet in there?" Joe says, looking very worried at the curtains around Tom's bed.

"So you woke early and heard the radio?" Elizabeth persists with Talya.

"Yes, a vet was being interviewed, saying he took in two horses, but there were people on the ground too... that he's treated the horses for poisoning."

"He shouldn't have said that on the radio." Elizabeth replies.

"Maybe he was stressed like the rest of us." Talya says

to Elizabeth, "Who are you? A mum of someone here I haven't met?"

"A police consultant," Elizabeth replies.

"Is Tom going to be okay? Is this food poisoning?" Joe asks.

"Hard to say at this stage what caused it," Elizabeth replies matter-of-factly, then, like the others, turns to Tom's bed. They all watch as the doctor and the extra nurses leave Tom's curtained cubicle with the crash kit, leaving the curtains now open as a nurse is covering Tom's face with a sheet.

"No!" Joe screams, realising Tom has passed away. He tries to get up to go to his friend but is too weak. Talya stands up and rushes over to Tom and pulls back the sheet. The nurse tries to stop her, but Talya succeeds and then just stares.

"Is he dead?" she asks. The nurse nods and holds her arm. Elizabeth watches Talya standing by Tom's bed motionless. At that moment Lemon beckons Elizabeth.

"There's been an attack up at the Department of Galileo." Lemon whispers in her ear. "Will you come with me? I have no idea if it's poisoning too." He looks at the wallets in the evidence bags at the Department of Galileo staff cards. "Look." Lemon holds up the bags containing the belongings of the people from the boats on Stourbridge Common that he had given to the Constable earlier. Both can see that at least three of the personal effects bags have university entrance cards to the department.

"They worked at the Department of Galileo?" Elizabeth asks.

"Looks like it."

Both Lemon and Elizabeth leave the ward and start to walk towards the exit.

"Is Raynott going to put Inspector Abley back, especially now we have a death on our hands?" Elizabeth asks as she and Lemon step up their pace.

"No one at the station knows what's going on. I just hope I don't get Pober. He's—" Lemon badly wants to say how terrible Pober really is, but something inside stops him, especially given this is the wrong time to rake over the seriousness of Abley's suspension. From Lemon's reticence, Elizabeth worries that Bob has gone too far, left it too long, made so little effort to reform his behaviour and drinking that there is nothing to save him now.

"Spit it out," Elizabeth says.

"Mrs Abley is back," Lemon replies. "Just hope that changes things. Worked with Inspector Pober a few weeks ago on a burglary." Lemon shivers as both of them now step outside the hospital and walk towards the cars. "Made us all get back in our cars when we turned up at a break in, just to park in straight lines parallel to each other. Said if we park crooked then we looked crooked to the public. Left the burglar laughing all the way as he buggered off I'm sure." He stares at Elizabeth, who is looking wide-eyed at him, and continues. "Just the other day he made me go out and come back into a room because I hadn't addressed him at the top of the conversation as Inspector Pober." The two of them have now arrived at their cars. "So Inspector Abley can't come back too soon, I told him as much this morning."

"What did he say?" Elizabeth asks.

"He just walked off," Lemon says.

The two walk briskly to separate cars. Elizabeth follows the Sergeant, who puts on his flashing lights, despite it being Sunday morning. The whole of Cambridge can be woken up by now, he rationalises, as he's already been up since five-thirty this morning. But he decides not to put the siren on. He has a heart.

10
NOWHERE TO GO

Not quite Sunday lunchtime. Inspector Bob Abley has been wandering the Petersfield area of the city, up and down the long terraced streets with door numbers running into the hundreds, occasionally catching a glimpse in a window of a young family sitting around the a table for elevenses, or of a cat looking out on the street at something magical but invisible to human eyes. Abley feels an overwhelming sense of being shut out, separated from happiness.

He has butterflies in his stomach that Maureen is back, along with a dull ache at her instruction for him to clear out. He hadn't expected it, but then again he didn't know what to expect. He didn't dare imagine she would run into his arms and beg forgiveness, but a little bit of him hoped she would, or thought at the very least that after her affair that was what he was owed. But he knew her too well and was accepting that they may just have to move on. He was prepared for that, ready for making everything feel normal again like nothing had happened.

Abley's stomach is empty. He rectifies this by stopping at a local bakery and buying himself two pastries and a piping hot coffee. He realises he's getting close to Parker's Piece, as he has just turned into Melbourne Place, past The Cricketers and The Elm Tree pubs, both annoyingly still shut as it is a little too early. Somehow a cosy corner bench in The Elm feels like just what he needs. Instead, Abley decides to take his breakfast and eat it on a bench on the Piece before determining his next steps. But as he continues up the narrow path running alongside a secondary school, he sees a homeless man walking towards him. The man eyes Abley's breakfast, then tells Abley that he doesn't have anywhere to go and it's cold out this morning. Abley looks at him. They are the same.

"I'm sorry about that." Abley gives the man his breakfast and takes off his coat and hands it over. Now cold himself, Abley wanders out into the middle of Parker's Piece at a loss of purpose. He knows that he is near the police station and turns to look up. Once his second home, he casts his eyes across the windows of his office. He stares up, thinking how detached he feels from it all. But then he spots the Super at the window. They both lock eyes. Not wanting to give the Super the satisfaction of looking away first, Abley quickly turns his back on him and walks over to the corner of Parker's Piece to the little café which can't be seen from the station because not enough autumnal leaves have yet to fall. Inspector Abley buys a second breakfast and a paper and sits in on a chair outside in the cold. Despite being in a busy spot, Abley feels invisible as people walk by, caught up in their own lives.

For a short while Abley stares at a group of students playing football, their breath evident in the cold air, their rosy cheeks beaming out as they shout to each other to pass the ball. Eventually, Abley opens up the back pages of the *Cambridge Herald*, hoping to read golf or cricket news. But he knows it is the wrong time of year for that. There is a piece about yesterday's game at the Abbey Stadium, where Cambridge United scored in the last minute.

Then he flicks through the rest until he gets back to the front page. He sees the headline "Horse Apocalypse" and thinks what a terrible title, then reads on about how two horses were found ill on Stourbridge Common. Eight people are in hospital of whom one is now dead, with a photograph of apples strewn on the grass and a photo of the river from Stourbridge Common and some boats with healthy looking horses eating the grass.

He reads an interview Lemon must have given to the reporter. Lemon is quoted as saying, "Police are investigating probable causes," and "will be making a further statement when we have investigated more fully. In the meantime, we would ask anyone to come forward if they were on Stourbridge Common last night or in the early hours, and if they have any information they think might be relevant to the case." Finally in the interview, Lemon says, "We think it might be poisoning, but we will know more soon."

Abley screws up his face, realising Lemon has nothing to go on yet and shouts out loud at the paper.

"You don't say that Lemon! Facts, stick to the facts!" At an adjacent table, a woman looks up from a crossword at Abley, who is for all intents and purposes talking to himself. Abley folds up his paper, throws it down on the table then looks up at the sky. He knows Lemon would be better off with him and has also heard the rumours that the Superintendent is grooming Inspector Pober to take his place. Abley feels sorry for Lemon. But there is nothing he can do, so he bites into his apple and cinnamon brioche then dips it straight into his coffee. As he is about to take his second bite of pastry his phone rings. Thinking it might be Maureen and without looking carefully at the number, he answers.

"What do you need?" Abley says in his chirpiest voice, balancing his now dipped breakfast over his coffee cup. At the other end of the line, he hears Lemon's voice, so he launches in. "Why did you say poison if you don't know for sure? No, no, no." Abley listens to Lemon, "Yes, I know, it says that in the paper." Abley listens again. "What am I supposed to do? Just seen the squirmy creature at the window. Yes, I'm on Parker's—." He listens again, clearly having been interrupted. "No, I'm not... Have you asked Green? She'll be all over it." Abley hangs up, now doubly stressed out by Lemon. He watches his tasty brioche fall into his coffee.

11
NOT MY TELESCOPE

Sergeant Lemon and Professor Elizabeth Green arrive in their separate cars at the Galileo Department of Astronomy, up off the Madingley Road. The department is eerily quiet, with no one to guide them to the incident. Lemon tries the front reception door, but it is locked. They decide to walk around the back of the big glass building, hoping that perhaps there will be a back entrance. Elizabeth has been here before, but she doesn't know the department well enough to lead Lemon anywhere.

As they walk along a path, they see a woman running towards them. In her fifties, with blonde hair that sticks up in the sunrise illuminating her head and heels far too high, and having heard Lemon's siren she beckons.

"Are you the police?"

Lemon nods. All three now running up a path then some steps, around a corner and behind some other buildings until they then have to hop across some stepping stones on dew-soaked grass to reach an old white round building made entirely of wood, with a domed roof and a little red door. They walk inside, already feeling the temperature go down and noticing how dark it has become. Lemon and Elizabeth see that a motorcycle paramedic, his crash helmet by his side, is already treating the injured victim. The man is down on the cold brick floor, motionless.

"I just found him here, he's not responding. So I called for an ambulance. I'm not sure what's happened." The woman looks at Elizabeth.

"When was this?" Lemon asks, showing her his badge.

"About an hour, maybe less?" she replies.

"And you are?" asks Elizabeth.

"Cynthia. Cynthia Hatman. I work here, research. He made me come in. It's Sunday you know. To go over some papers."

"Yes, we are well aware of the day, Mrs Hatman," Sergeant Lemon replies.

"Oh, I'm not Mrs, just Doctor," Cynthia says.

"Him being?" Elizabeth asks.

"Professor Nigel Crowhams." Cynthia replies.

"Did you do this to him?" asks Elizabeth.

"Of course not." Cynthia shakes her head. "It's a good job for the Professor that he did force me to come in, or he would've been like this until tomorrow." All three of them watch the paramedic place a mask of oxygen over the victim's face, his skin like an overripe plum. Professor Crowhams starts to wake up, which is a good sign, and the paramedic shines a small torch into one of his eyes, which makes him shout "Get off!" And he punches the paramedic. Sergeant Lemon springs into action, pinning down Professor Crowhams as the paramedic groans from the pain and shakes his head.

"What are you doing here?" Crowhams shouts at Lemon. "Get off me."

"You have a head injury. If you try anything like that again—" Lemon is tussling with the man. "I'll have to arrest you if you don't stop this. Keep still, will you?" Lemon says, struggling.

"Are you police?" Crowhams asks.

"Yes! And you've just assaulted a paramedic!" Lemon shouts. Professor Crowhams shakes his head and winces as he moves his neck, then gestures that he won't punch anyone else. So Lemon lets go. Professor Crowhams stands up, his head bloody, his face white as a sheet, moaning about the pain in his head. The paramedic stands up, wiggling his nose to check the Professor hasn't broken it.

Professor Crowhams wails as he looks at what has happened to his best friend, his telescope. Lemon and Elizabeth can see what the man can see, all this sticky mess of soup, bits of salad and dressing and coffee tipped over an intricate link in the scope's neck, two large flasks and a plastic sandwich container on the floor below.

"If I catch who did this, I'll kill them!" the Professor screams, as he takes out a handkerchief from his pocket and tries to start cleaning away the soup and coffee and balsamic vinegar off the instrument before it has a chance to seep past the nuts and bolts.

"Did you see them, Cynthia?" But Cynthia shakes her head

"Step away from the telescope, Sir." Lemon says. The paramedic is still wobbly. He doubts if he gets paid enough for this. He's not about to wrestle the man into treatment, and so just looks to Lemon to sort this situation out.

Lemon himself knows he should not be left alone like this and wishes Inspector Abley was here before the threat of Inspector Pober becomes a reality. He would know what to do, how to talk this man down. He tries to channel the Inspector into his own voice, with varying degrees of success.

"Now come on, it looks like you've had a nasty blow.

Let's get you fixed up so that you can have many more days stargazing or whatever it is you do in here. Head injuries are not to be ignored. Let's get you seen to." Lemon nods at the paramedic, to indicate that it is his turn, time to walk over to the man and start joining in with the situation.

"This is not stargazing you, idiot, this is finding out new things about Ganymede that no modern telescope could ever tell us," Crowhams spits. "This is pure science, not your newfangled computers!" Crowhams stumbles backwards, his head injury a little more severe than he anticipated.

"Professor, let this man take your vitals, get you oxygen now," Lemon says. The paramedic has an oxygen mask in his hand. "You need to sit so that we can properly assess what you might need," Lemon continues.

"It's nothing! Bugger off!" The unwilling bloody-headed and rather ungrateful Professor Crowhams pushes away Lemon's efforts. He is not going to the hospital for a CT Scan.

"I shan't get in any ruddy ambulance so you can tell that to turn around straight away or it'll be a wasted journey." The paramedic looks at Sergeant Lemon.

"You should do what emergency response tell you, Professor." Cynthia chips in wearily. "For your own good. Head trauma, primary or secondary, is very serious. We want to get you to hospital in one piece."

"I'm not going to hospital. I need to clean this. Oh, my." Nigel looks at his telescope and sees all the goop running down the barrel. "This is one big headache!" he shouts. Sergeant Lemon pulls a face, already irritated by this unpleasant and ungrateful man, but then realises that he's probably in shock, and from somewhere finds a little more patience.

"That's exactly why you need to be treated. Now if you just sit down and let the paramedic tend to your head, then everyone will be out of here sooner than you think. But I do have a couple of questions. Did you see who did this to you?"

"No of course not, or I would have said. This is deliberate vandalism."

"It probably looks worse than it is," Elizabeth says, irritated by the Professor's overly dramatic response to a bit of soup on a telescope.

"What do you know? Just get out," Crowhams says.

"Who do you think did this? D'you have any enemies?" Elizabeth continues. Lemon is pleased for the help. The paramedic walks over to his bag, deciding to put away all his equipment.

"His name's Joe. He's the gardener here. Always looks very untidy, dirty clothes. Lives on one of those Stourbridge boats. Not the image we want to project to visiting Fellows. I'll throttle him if he did this." Nigel looks up at his telescope, the goo still dripping down the barrel.

"Joe who?" Elizabeth asks.

"How the hell should I know? I don't bother myself with gardening." Professor Crowhams scoffs. "Just Joe, boat Joe. You'd have to ask the Department Administrator. He never does anything I ask him to do. He never tends the garden around this telescope hut. I've seen him eating his sandwiches in here and hiding instead of working. So I locked him out. He's probably just cross." The paramedic starts to phone in a report.

"Isn't that a bit over the top, to hit you because he can't eat his sandwiches in here?" Elizabeth says.

"Professor Crowhams is talking about Joe Grader, Inspector," Cynthia adds helpfully. "But I don't think Joe did this. He's a good man, wouldn't harm a fly. It'll be someone who knows how much you love this telescope. Looks like someone trying to get to you, perhaps an academic rival I wouldn't be surprised," She adds.

"Do you think he meant to hit you?" Elizabeth asks. "Or did he want to take something and stumbled across you? Did you have anything else in here?"

"How the hell should I know?" Crowhams turns and looks at Elizabeth. She watches the blood running down his ear from the cut on his head. "No, I didn't have anything. Apart from my research." Crowhams looks at all his papers scattered on the floor, covered in onion soup. "My research." Crowhams starts to pick up the wet paper frantically, his notes destroyed. "It's Joe I tell you! He doesn't like me. He's always glaring at me through the window like he has me marked or something."

"Glaring?" Lemon asks.

"And he doesn't cut the grass, around the telescope building," Crowhams adds.

"I don't think that will stand up in a court of law as motivation, grass cutting." Elizabeth is impatient with this man.

"He's got one too many chips on his shoulder if you ask me. Doesn't like academics, jealous, clearly messed up his own small life." Crowhams says about Joe.

"We have just come from a Mr Grader, who lives on a boat as you say. He's in the hospital," Lemon replies.

"Red hair red beard?" Cynthia asks.

"That matches the description," Lemon answers.

"Oh dear!" Cynthia replies.

"Why's he in hospital?" Crowhams asks, mildly interested.

"It's likely he's been poisoned," Elizabeth says. "One of his friends has died. Should we be looking to see if this was deliberate?" But Nigel turns towards the door.

"I need to get some proper cleaning equipment. I can't leave this like it is." Then the Professor rushes out. As Elizabeth and Lemon chase out after him, they see he has already got quite a lead on them. The Professor turns back as Cynthia comes out of the telescope house and shouts over his shoulder.

"And another thing Cynthia, I need you to redo it all. That paper didn't make any sense! You and Tom need to get your act together."

"What a charming taskmaster. He thinks he can dictate Tom and my research? Not on your nelly," Cynthia says. "He's always moaning that one, no idea how he made Head of Department."

"I think he's cross because his telescope has got soup on it. He's been hit on the head," Elizabeth says, looking at Cynthia.

"That was waiting to happen. The man's got enemies coming out of every crack in the pavement," Cynthia replies.

"He seems pretty certain this Joe did it?" Elizabeth asks.

"Professor Crowhams is the most annoying man I know, a proverbial pain in the arse. I'm sorry, are you an Inspector too?" Cynthia asks.

"No, Dr Hatman. I'm a police consultant," Elizabeth replies.

"Well, then you should know that that man is a ticking time bomb," Cynthia says. "The only thing I'm surprised about is that he's not dead. Whoever did this is a rubbish killer."

12
THE LOCK KEEPER

Ed, the Lock Keeper, is back home at the Lock House on Jesus Green, in the garden cleaning out his chickens. On the other side of his garden wall, tourists queue for boat trips on the River Cam while shutterbugging the life out of the swans and ducks, who are themselves hoping for dropped snacks and being very vocal in the process. Ed mutters over the wall to a passer-by who looks local, battered briefcase and copy of *The Cambridge Herald* under his arm.

"Gets busier every year down here." Ed rolls his eyes at him, wondering why can't people leave him in peace and not congregate near his home.

In truth, Ed loves living in the Lock Keeper's cottage. He feels most at home with the river, having spent his formative years in the Merchant Navy. It is a shame that he doesn't like boats, or rather other peoples' boats. Ed hates how they drive too fast and disturb nesting creatures along the bank and spit out a film of diesel onto the water. But at least being the Lock Keeper he has space for animals, and only has to step out onto the Green to walk Clive. Ed collects up all the chicken droppings, used hay and dirt in a metal bucket and walks over to the compost heap where he drops them. Then he walks over to a sunny wall in his back garden where under a shelter he has stored two bales of fresh hay.

He pulls out some hay and spreads some in the chicken run and into the chicken house. Then he shoves some more in a different bucket, opens his back gate onto the Green and starts to walk towards Midsummer Common. Clive follows, wagging his tail and jumping about, enjoying another chase of imaginary squirrels. Once through the gates by the cattle grid on the Common, Ed taps the side of his bucket with a key and watches the horses come running. They know Ed will appear every day with a tasty treat.

Ed also has a few apples in his pockets. Just like the apples he saw scattered earlier this morning on Stourbridge Common. Ed's mind flashes back to the dead man lying in a hospital bed. He smells a couple of apples the man on the market gave him yesterday free for the horses. They are local drops, a bit bruised, but nothing wrong with them otherwise. Ed breathes in the fresh air. He knows he is a lucky man. In the short time Ed's mind has wandered, he has become surrounded by horses sniffing his jacket for goodies. Ed pushes their noses back until he has space to cut one of the apples, and makes sure every horse gets a slice. Then, once the apples are eaten, he lifts the cover on the bucket and hands them all a mouthful of hay, patting their shoulders and stroking them until the last one runs way, happy with their tasty interlude.

Ed decides to walk back to the lock along the riverside path. In the distance, a couple of boats with groups of female rowers push off the side, and Ed knows all too well that Sunday is a busy day for this sort of thing. Closer to Ed, he spots three scullers pulling out from one of the boathouses.

"Don't you have anything better to do?" Ed shouts at Brad, the rower he saw earlier this morning, who now appears to be leaving for his second row of the day.

"Err, you're the one stalking us?" Brad replies, standing at the water's edge with Godric and Wallis, both of whom are also dressed to head out. Brad bends down and helps Godric into his scull, and then walks over to his own. Ed can see two swans swimming down the river towards them.

"You'd better not hit these two, or I'll skin you," Ed shouts.

"Hmm, tasty," Wallis shouts back. "Might these be the two on our plates this week at Victoria?" Wallis climbs into his scull. He kisses his fingers then throws them out into the air like a gourmet chef gesticulating over his favourite dish.

"Don't." Godric looks at Wallis, unimpressed at winding up the old Lock Keeper. Wallis's marble eyes widen, and his face shows mock shock at being reprimanded by his new boyfriend.

"Swan for din dins!" Wallis continues, shouting at Ed, pushing out and starting to row towards the swans. "It's not just St. James's that cooks up swan these days. Must be catching. You must dine at Victoria this week."

"You're disgusting," Ed shouts back. "You don't deserve to share this planet with such beautiful creatures."

"Piss off old man," Wallis continues, as Godric shakes his head behind Wallis.

Ed starts to feed the ducks with some seed he has in his pocket, but Brad, now in his own scull, pushes out into the centre of the river and disturbs the ducks with his oars. So Ed rolls up bits of hard bread and throw them at Brad.

"Can't we leave poor Ed alone?" Godric shouts to Brad, who flicks his oar at the ducks.

"He makes it impossible. It's like he's asking for it," Brad replies as he gets hit by what feels like a stone rather than bread. "Stop it you crazy man, before I do something to shut you up!" Brad shouts.

"Ed is birdman," Wallis replies to Brad and Godric, "Loves his chickens, always up to 'fowl' play. Get it?" Wallis rows closer to the swans. "Hey, birdman. I'll get your birds. I'll get your birds!" Wallis starts to splash the swans with his oar. One of the swans decides he has had enough of this, hisses and raises himself out of the water. Wallis decides probably best to leave the swans alone, but can't help shouting a parting word to Ed.

"We'll pluck these two for the top table this week. You should join us. They are a particularly succulent dish."

13
PUB LUNCH

The sun is as warm as it will be today this Sunday lunchtime, streaming through the trees on Victoria Avenue and falling onto the tables outside the Fort Saint George. Professor Elizabeth Green, Monty and have Hector have come to meet their friend Inspector Bob Abley. She spots him first, dozing on a comfortable outdoor wicker sofa. She stands above him, shading him from the rays. A lick from Monty makes him stir.

"Professor Green, if I live and die. I got your message." Bob Abley sits up, rubbing his hands together to keep warm but also as a sign of his pleasure of her arrival. They haven't seen each other in a while. The Afghan Hounds remember Bob Abley and jump up to sit on him, hoping for crisps, which they remember he fed them last time. "Hello, hello. Get down. I won't need a bath if you slobber anymore." He laughs, "Get down." The dogs calm a little, while she continues to stand, happy to go to the bar to get a warm beverage.

"Bob. You look terrible. Haven't you got a coat?" she

asks, very glad to see Abley, but not keen to give him the satisfaction of knowing. "Lemon says you've been kicked out. What's she up to now?"

"No he didn't, don't put words into his mouth. She's back, don't spoil it," Abley replies.

"Has he dumped her? She's come crawling to you again?" Elizabeth asks.

"I am led to believe it was mutual. So stop. She looked like she has missed home," Abley says.

"This is why you're cold and outside?" Elizabeth quips and she points inside the pub, indicating that she's happy to purchase Abley a drink.

"I've missed you," Abley replies sarcastically as he gets up, picking up his empty.

As they walk in from outside, the dogs follow and do the rounds. Sniffing under the tables and picking up dropped snacks from the floorboards. A crackling fire roars in the corner as Abley points to a table by the window overlooking the river for Elizabeth to sit while he orders something at the bar.

Elizabeth says, "Peppermint tea please," to the barman.

"And a pint of this." Abley points to a lager on tap, "and a couple of menus please." He raises his eyebrows at the barman, who starts pouring the pint while leaving it alone to go and fill a cup with a teabag behind him. Abley pays and walks over to Elizabeth.

Elizabeth has bribed Monty, and Hector with dog treats from her pocket, and they are now both sitting quietly on benches at the table on either side, leaving only one chair left for Abley.

"It's like having lunch with three beautiful women," Abley says, smiling at his friend and her dogs, shaking his head with pleasure.

"I'm the only female here," Elizabeth reminds him, thanking the barman who has brought over her tea. "Lemon says you're not at home tonight?"

"Stop. She just needs her sleep, jet-lagged," Abley says.

"Jet lagged?" Elizabeth questions.

"It's all been a bit of a shock. She's acclimatising." Bob Abley tries to convince Elizabeth, less sure he's convincing himself.

"Have you been in to see him?" Elizabeth asks, changing the subject.

"That marsupial, have I heck. Raynott needs a rocket up his jacksie." Abley says.

"That's all very well, but Lemon needs you. You can't leave him to Inspector Pober."

"Pober's all right, in small doses," Abley replies.

"Is that right?" Elizabeth says. Abley knows he's lying: Pober is terrible.

"When you called I thought you just wanted a friendly lunch. Should have known." Abley looks at the dogs, and then at the menus the barman just put down with his pint.

"So you're not going to help Lemon with the attempted murder of a Cambridge Professor?" Elizabeth asks.

"Attempted murder? Lemon called and gave me the facts. I heard it was an assault, possibly a theft, so let's not exaggerate it." Abley raises his eyebrows at Elizabeth.

"To the back of the head? There was nothing to take, just a room with a telescope. All his papers were on the floor. They didn't take his wallet. It looked pretty personal to me," Elizabeth replies.

"So, at worst, he could have been hit for his research, jealous colleague or something. Not attempted murder." Abley shrugs his shoulders and sips his pint.

"I think something is fishy in all this," Elizabeth says.

"You hypothesise too much." Abley doesn't want to hear more about the case, enjoying his pint too much. But Elizabeth won't leave it.

"Who would try to kill a man who spends most of his time not even in this world, but with his head so far above the clouds? As far as I can tell from talking to colleagues, he doesn't do anything else. He doesn't even drink tea in the department breaks apparently – always too busy working on his plan for his next all-night watch, looking up at the stars." Elizabeth then continues, as an aside to herself, "He must be a very intelligent man indeed to make Head of Department without mixing with his peers."

"So Lemon called you in. I did suggest you. I'm glad." Abley lifts his glass and cheers Elizabeth.

"I do have college work Bob, and I might remind you that the Super invited me to have a wider brief after helping you solve that last case. But I can understand why you may have forgotten, the police seemingly not being your priority right now. Would you like me to talk to the Super on your behalf? I'm sure if you both say sorry to each other. The male ego—"

"Don't you dare." Abley interrupts Elizabeth; just thinking about the Super is enough to make his blood boil. He downs half his pint. "Just get to the bottom of the horses and people poisoned."

"First impressions from the vet's findings, which can be much quicker and cruder… apples poisoned them." Elizabeth says.

"Exactly, how hard is that?" Abley replies.

"Very, but it was surely meant for the horses? More people hate those horses than anything else on these Commons. I think they are beautiful and deserve the right to be left in peace. What do people expect, leaving all their fast food litter about near the benches? Eating and walking, a horrible habit. Show me a horse who doesn't like a bit of sugar, and I'll eat my hat." Elizabeth replies.

"Eating and walking?" Abley pulls a face, "Whatever sin will people commit next? Anyway, I thought you couldn't get poisoned by eating apples."

"If it was the apples that poisoned them, then they were tampered with. I will be checking this afternoon," Elizabeth replies.

"Tampered?" Abley asks.

"Well, you need to chew open a fair amount of apple seeds to be poisoned. I wouldn't try it, as evidence varies on the number of seeds it takes to cause harm, as it depends on the individual's metabolism," Elizabeth says, "It's much easier to be poisoned from fruit like plums or apricot stones or even smashed up cherry pips."

"Right." Abley says.

"Might not even have been cyanide, or could be cyanide from another source added in." Elizabeth looks at the river, sparkling in the sunshine outside. She gives Hector and Monty another biscuit each.

"How do you add poison to an apple?" Abley asks.

"I don't know," she replies, "What do you think I spend my time doing in my lab, injecting fruit?" She shakes her head "I suppose someone could have injected them or soaked them? There must have been quite a few apples tampered with to bring down so many."

"Sounds more suspicious than someone being hit over the head? Leave the academic to fend for himself. Look into the apples and poisons." Abley says.

"What if the boat people weren't poisoned at all? And it was just the horses? It could be something else that got the boat dwellers? And you should have seen Professor Crowhams. He's saying someone deliberately threw his food all over his telescope. He was obsessed with it."

"What?" Abley asks, a little confused.

"Soup," Elizabeth replies.

"I'm not sure what it is, might not be vegan. Let's check the board." Abley looks at the board behind the bar.

"No, they'd poured soup all down the barrel of his old telescope. He'd been looking at Jupiter's moons. And yes, the butternut squash looks good." Elizabeth looks at the board and sees a vegan sign against the soup of the day.

Abley's phone rings; this time he looks at the caller I.D. It is Lemon. He puts it down on the table, unanswered.

"Aren't you going to get that? Oh give it here. How do you work it?" Elizabeth snatches her friend's phone.

"Leave it," Abley orders. The two tussle with the mobile and Elizabeth manages to figure out how to speak with Lemon before Abley can cut the call. She listens intently, with some “Uh-uhs” and “rights” and some beady looks at Abley.

“What is it?” Abley asks impatiently.

Elizabeth finally says goodbye to Lemon and puts the phone down. She looks out the window and strokes Monty looks up at the board behind the bar and says.

“I’ll have the butternut squash soup please,” Elizabeth says to the barman.

“Bloody hell, woman, what did he say?” Abley asks.

“You don’t want to work. Best you don’t know,” Elizabeth teases.

“Tell me,” Abley raises his voice, not pleased with Elizabeth’s games, “or I’ll ring him back myself.”

“The dead man was an academic at The Department of Galileo. Dr Tom Mirren. He was quite high up, a Reader.”

“So perhaps you'll take the boat people more seriously,” Abley says.

“Or perhaps you’ll see this was no ordinary burglary of the Head of Department. I think this might be another case with your favourite kind of people, us academics.” Elizabeth smirks.

“Another reason not to come back,” Abley huffs.

“It’s been two months now, hasn’t it? Lemon says your suspension ends this week,” Elizabeth says, observing the dogs watch a sculler go by and nearly hit a swan.

“I’ve already said, you won't get me in a room with that snivelling little man.” Abley shakes his head.

“So what are you going to do?” Elizabeth asks, staring at her friend.

14
JESUS GREEN LIDO

Not a spit away from the Fort Saint George pub where Professor Elizabeth Green and Inspector Abley are eating lunch, Ed, the Lock Keeper pushes open the big gates to the Jesus Green Lido and closes them behind him. A hundred yards of glittery water surrounded by tall trees create a suntrap for the sparkly pool. Already now closed to the public for the winter, Ed has a key from the managers and is asked to check now and then against vandalism and make sure all is shipshape and how it should be in these quiet months. Just an extra layer of security as he only lives next door, and made the offer many years ago when there had been a spate of break-ins.

One of the perks is that Ed is allowed to take a dip before the frosts come. Swimming is the last thing Ed wants to do. All those verrucas and unidentified objects floating in public pools are enough to drive him well away. But it has been hot in late summer, which bled into all of September and half of October, so the water is still warm for this time of year. And Ed does have a friend, a very special friend, who likes to swim here. In fact, it is one of her favourite places as she misses the sea air, having moved from Wells-Next-The-Sea many years ago. Ed likes making peoples' wishes come true, especially Cynthia's.

This lunchtime Ed has decided to bring a picnic of tomato and cress sandwiches. When he turns into the secret oasis, he spots Cynthia's lithe body in a bright red swimming costume cutting through the water. He stops and smiles to himself. He has known Cynthia as a friendly companion since his wife died over six years ago. He didn't think he'd find someone else to share happy times with, but Cynthia came into his life like a whirlwind and changed everything. Now he wants to shave, watch what he eats, wants to share his passions and make her happy.

Cynthia finally gets to the end of the pool, about to turn around and go back again when she spots him and a big smile breaks out from one side of her face to the other, and she waves then points that she will get out. Ed walks over to her lounger and places the tin of sandwiches on the table and picks up her towel. They kiss, and Cynthia shivers. Ed is not surprised; although the sun is hitting the wall behind them and bouncing back, it isn't as powerful as it was just a month ago.

"When will we run away together?" She coos in his ear.

"Hello, my love," Ed says and kisses Cynthia. "Let's fly to Capri tomorrow." The two of them always joke about leaving their 'boring' lives. But the truth be told, Ed doesn't hate his life as much as she hates hers, and he worries that she means it.

"What's the matter?" She asks.

"Nothing," he replies.

"Come on. It's me you're talking to. I can tell when someone is riled about something." She leans in to him.

"Those scullers, make my blood boil. From your place, Victoria, as well. Rowed at the swans this morning, and that Wallis lad." Ed fumes.

"No," she says in disbelief.

"Yes, and I saw them shouting at the horses. Did you see those people as well, taken to hospital? I saw it. Called the ambulance. Just been a stressful morning." He shakes his head.

"That's terrible. Apparently one's dead," Cynthia says. "Do you know who?"

"Dead?" Ed looks very worried at the news, and he has to sit down on the lounger.

"You all right? I know you're not mad on the boat people," Cynthia replies.

"They disrupt the river for the wildlife. Go too fast back up to the pump to change their water. But dead?" he says.

"I know you don't hate them enough to harm them," Cynthia states, reassuring Ed she knows he wasn't to blame. "Radio was talking to a vet about the poisoning of the horses."

"What if it had been the ponies on Midsummer? Too close to Clive and my chickens," Ed worries.

"Where is Clive?" Cynthia asks, guiltily pleased he's not with Ed, as she's allergic to Ed's dog and chickens.

"At home indoors, by the burner. Why, d'you think he's not safe?"

"Of course, he's fine there," Cynthia replies. "I'm sure he's exhausted if you walked over to Stourbridge this morning and been back to feed the horses."

"Oh, he'll be sleeping. He's got a bit of a dodgy tummy. Made him some rice and scrambled egg for lunch." Ed says. Cynthia doesn't want to talk about dogs, even the dog of her boyfriend. She tries to change the subject, with other more important things on her mind.

"Can you believe that man made me go into the department today?"

"It's Sunday," Ed says.

"Tell me about it. Crowhams wants to read our latest paper, Tom and my joint one. I'm sure he's determined to try to ruin my private life." Cynthia leans up and kisses Ed on the lips.

"Over my dead body," Ed says.

"Is it bad to say that I'm glad his telescope has been vandalised." Cynthia looks guilty.

"Vandalised?" Ed asks.

"Yes, and Crowhams was hit over the head. Whoever did it didn't hit hard enough."

"I'll do anything to get him out of our lives," Ed says, screwing up his eyes.

"Maybe it won't be just a bruise and a few stitches next time. I called Tom about the public astronomy nights, but I've heard nothing." Cynthia says.

"They're this week, aren't they?" Ed asks.

"Yes. I'm involved, but Tom takes most of the glory." Cynthia opens the tin of sandwiches. "Tomato and cress, Yum."

15
BOTANIC GARDEN

After Elizabeth leaves Inspector Abley, she heads to the Cambridge University Botanic Garden. She knows that the Head of the Galileo Department has a connection with the boat people, but she can't fathom what. One thing waiting for her to examine are the apples. Fruit lying all over the floor by the boats, nowhere near apple trees, makes them very suspicious objects indeed. The vet had already jumped to this conclusion as a precautionary measure and she finds that he has also sent her samples to her laboratory here. She would telephone him later to thank him.

Elizabeth's mind starts to stray back to lunchtime with Bob. She tries very hard not to pity her close friend. It seems clear to her that there is nothing good about Maureen kicking him out, and equally nothing right about his attitude towards Superintendent Raynott. She is sure that if nothing changed, he is going to lose his job. Bob must go in and talk to the Super. She feels more bound to this case, knowing that if she helps Lemon solve it, then

Raynott might not bring in Pober, and there might still be a chink of light through the door for Inspector Abley to walk back in. If she could only make a connection between Professor Nigel Crowhams and the boat dwellers, perhaps that would be a start. What is it that they all share, apart from a department?

Elizabeth unwraps the apples and the contents from the horses and human stomachs to examine in her favourite laboratory. She puts the sealed tubes in a stand on the side. Protocol would have it that she should perform this research at Parker's Piece Station with the police pathology laboratory. If Leedham knew what she was doing here, he would undoubtedly start fussing for her to bring them straight over. But the pathology lab at the station is a dark grey room, overlooking the squad car park, the cold, sterile overhead lights a match for Leedham's slow, plodding interruptions. No, she has tried before and found that her own laboratory is the only place she can properly concentrate.

Here, she can work in peace, while looking through windows at the vast redwood trees on sweeping lawns and watch the multitude of oranges and auburns in the afternoon sunshine shimmer and flicker just outside her window. The only thing which makes no sense is working on this case without Inspector Abley. Without him, the whole thing feels off kilter.

Elizabeth pours liquid into a test tube on the holder and then extracts a couple of drops and looks at it under the microscope. She finds that the apple has much more cyanide in it than is natural. Elizabeth wonders if the apple was soaked or injected with cyanide.

Along with the papers and sample, the SOCO's also sent Elizabeth a dozen or so apples. She slices an apple in half and examines the skin. She can see under a light, many small incisions. Perhaps from small needles piercing the apple's skins. She finds abnormal amounts of cyanide present in the apple. The horses' stomachs had thirty times the safe dose. She examines the concentrations from the human sample, and they are higher.

The vet's suspicions were right, and he was wise to give the horses the correct antidote in time. She reads the vet's note accompanying the samples, which states that both horses are making a speedy recovery. A shame that can't be said of the hospital patients. But then all the boat dwellers were unconscious at the time. There was nothing to go on, and it is impossible to take gambles with human lives in the way the vet could chance it with the horses.

It takes Elizabeth no time to surmise that there is too much cyanide in the apples for this to be a coincidence, that there is definite evidence of tampering. So, they are looking for someone who meant harm to either horses or people, or both. Sergeant Lemon told her there were apples scattered everywhere, including a tipped over barrel full as well. Perhaps it was only some boat dwellers who saw a free meal who accidentally cooked apple crumble. Lemon says the apple barrel was found by the gate. Who would leave that, thinking it likely that people would not eat them? Elizabeth takes a bite from one of the apples in an evidence bag and chews it. It is a cooker. She spits out the piece of apple in the bin a sharp taste and pops in a hydroxocobalamin pill to counter any possible traces of cyanide.

She wonders if this could be a murder. If you were trying to kill people, you'd put out a sweeter dessert apple? Or even deliver a pie wrapped up in a bow. No, something is confusing about this. It doesn't add up. Someone is dead, another attacked and left for dead. Could it just be a coincidence that some have the Department of Galileo in common? According to Lemon, the man who is dead, Dr Tom Mirren, ran a project called the Public Understanding of Science at the department. Did that have anything to do with it?

A colleague pops his head around the door in the laboratory. "This one is for you." The phone in the department starts ringing. Elizabeth picks it up.

"Hello?" Elizabeth hears her dear friend Emily on the other end of the call. "Yes, I can come, although I don't know that music that well." Then she listens "Why didn't you tell me? Yes, it is a good job you sing so well, you can mask my notes." Elizabeth hangs up and looks at the clock. Then she stares out of the window at the oak trees in the gentle autumn breeze outside. The leaves drop in the sunshine, floating down like paper onto the lawn below. Oh, what she would give for an hour to wander around the gardens, to take in the lake and the glasshouses. That will have to wait for another day. She looks at the clock again. She just has time to check her findings twice more before she goes, just to be on the safe side.

16
UNFORGIVABLE WALLIS

After some time on the river, sculling down past Fen Ditton, Godric and Wallis hang up their oars, say goodbye to Brad and go back to Foxes Haven. Godric decides he wants to replace exertion with relaxation, and Wallis tentatively agrees to enter Elizabeth's home, although he already has doubts. Professor Elizabeth Green has a fierce reputation. Were it not for Godric's effervescent personality, Wallis is sure Godric would have been blackballed from fresher's term for fear of any new friend incurring her wrath.

"What's it like living with the esteemed and notorious Professor Green?" Wallis asks entering the home, genuinely curious about this enigmatic academic figure, wondering how she survives amidst all the tradition and ways of doing things.

"Never boring," Godric says, not keen to share any of his family secrets, but more interested in getting to know Wallis a lot better. "Why don't we take these coffees out into the garden?"

"Isn't it a bit cold?" Wallis asks.

"No look." And Godric points to a ball-shaped garden room standing on a rotating plinth. "It's this brand-new pod Bunny bought, to lengthen the summer she says, spend more time outside. It has all these groovy gadgets. Solar heat. We can listen to music." Godric picks up his coffee and opens the terrace French windows for Wallis to follow.

"Groovy." Wallis says sarcastically. Hector and Monty follow, sniffing his crotch. Godric runs ahead and opens the pod.

"Hang on, not the—" But before Godric can stop the dogs, they jump into the pod and leave their muddy footprints all over the new cushions. Godric knows this is Bunny's pride and joy and gets them to climb down.

"Mmm, now it's stinky in here too," Wallis says.

"Perhaps we should leave it. It is a little chilly, you're right. Let's go inside," Godric replies.

"Nonsense." They both hear the doorbell go. "That's the takeout," Wallis says.

"Pizza in the afternoon. Why do all men insist on trying to make me fat?" Godric shakes his head.

"I'll get it, you stay here and keep things warm." And Wallis gives Godric the biggest kiss, which makes Godric forget the muddy prints and stretch out in the pod while turning on the funky lighting and music.

Wallis walks back to the front door, with the dogs following in case food is involved. He opens it to the delivery man, then turns to get his wallet from his jacket while the man waits. Wallis doesn't see, but Hector slips out the front door while the delivery man picks up the pizzas from the back of his moped. Wallis shuts the front door with Hector outside on the pavement and comes back in with his hands full and throws himself down in the pod. Wallis shuts the door of the pod on Monty, leaving him out in the cold. Godric pulls a face at Wallis's meanness, but Wallis replies "No muddy paws." And kicks off his shoes.

When Elizabeth arrives home, she finds it strange that Monty comes rushing towards her and Bertie and Soot also arrive at the top of the stairs to greet her. She says hello to them all, but there's no Hector. She looks for him, calling, walking through the drawing room, study, kitchen, opens the back French windows, everywhere. She walks into the garden and spots the pod all steamed up and rotating. Perhaps Hector is in there. But when she opens the door, she gasps at the sight of her grandson in a state of in flagrante delicto.

"Where's Hector?" she asks.

"Is he not in the garden?" Godric replies, scrabbling for his shirt.

"He is nowhere. Nowhere!" Elizabeth shouts at them.

"I don't know. He was here. Oh." Godric looks at the pizza boxes, with tomato ketchup stains now on Elizabeth's cushions. She guesses and looks at Wallis. She drops everything and runs to the front door. She shuts it tightly behind her, so the other animals are safe before bolting up Castle Hill, asking people if they have seen an Afghan to blank stares, then skips down towards Magdalene bridge, panic in her step. Trying to think at least he isn't on the road run over with people staring. She crosses the path back up to see if Hector made it to Alexandra Gardens on Carlisle Road. A place she takes him if pushed for time, not two minutes from home. Nothing. She feels even sicker. She meets Godric, who has come out to help her look.

"You haven't left that bloody imbecile with the animals have you? Go back!" Godric sees the horror on her face so runs back to the house. Elizabeth carries on across Jesus Lock Bridge, blowing her dog whistle continuously, and calling. What if he's taken himself off to Jesus Green? She knows he likes the smells that come from all the food people leave in the bins. But there are no tall long-haired blonde dogs that she can see, and there is quite an open view of a lot of the Green. Nothing. She blows the whistle. She calls, looks in every direction. She feels sicker. Hector is nowhere. Desperate she asks in the ice-cream kiosk, looks in the tennis courts, dares to look below the weir. Nothing. She's about to go back and retrace her steps when in the far corner she spots a man – with Hector!

She runs towards him, Hector now straining on the collar having seen her, but the man has a belt around him, and is not letting him go. Elizabeth is very apologetic and explains where she lives. The man is very insistent, however, that he checks she is who she says she is. How does he know, she could be a thief? He's a beautiful dog, after all. Elizabeth cannot help feel the irony blowing strongly in the wind, as the man tightens his belt. But after a few moments, he explains curtly to her that he called the phone number on the collar, but no one picked up.

They wander back to Elizabeth's house, Hector oblivious to the trouble he's caused. The man has to come in and check her phone number against the one he dialled. But, the photograph of the two dogs in a frame on the telephone table and the presence of Monty is the final proof he needs before he smiles, saying you can't be too sure these days and declines a cup of tea, that he'd better be getting back home himself. After all the kerfuffle, Elizabeth is impressed with the man, but after he has gone and the front door is shut tight, she is still visibly shaken.

So it is with some distress that she walks out into the garden with Hector and Monty to recover from all the running she has done in the past half an hour and to cool down and spots the steamed windows of her new summerhouse. She revisits the takeaway spilt on her cushions and the muddy paw prints – oh, and Wallis still sitting in there with Godric. Granted both a little sheepish, but also seriously not sorry enough for the crime.

"Someone left the front door open. Hector could have been killed on the road or taken by someone." Elizabeth delivers her words very quietly. Godric knows this is serious and sits up immediately. "Please show your guest out."

Wallis is not happy. She has interrupted his enjoyment for the afternoon and he does not understand some mad old lady's concern about a dog, who seems to be fine after what sounds like a minor ordeal. Wallis huffs and stands up, only to reveal that under a blanket he was naked from the waist down. He puts his trousers on.

"When you invited me back to this quaint old cottage I thought you promised an afternoon of passion, not a lecture about inconsequential concerns from an elderly relative." Wallis scoffs to Godric, who looks at his nanna apologetically.

"You have outstayed your welcome," Elizabeth replies.

"Not my cuppa here anyway, kind of cramps one's style… all this chintz," Wallis says. Elizabeth knows there is not a scrap of chintz in her home, which is an elegant combination of eclectic pieces of art deco and art nouveau furniture.

"Well, you know your style. Best you go and find somewhere more appropriate." Elizabeth replies.

Wallis leaves, and Elizabeth follows him out, making sure she firmly shuts the front door this time. Then she goes back out to her summerhouse pod, to review the mess. She finds Godric picking up the takeaway boxes. Thankfully her new cushions appear to be waterproof.

"They could have been killed," she says quietly.

"I'm sorry, I didn't know," Godric says.

"You should have known,"

"I've said I'm sorry, all right? It was an honest mistake. And now he's probably never going to come back,"

"Good. He's not a patch on Valentino." For the first time in ages, Elizabeth is cross at Godric, cross that his carelessness nearly cost a life in the family. But it also makes her cross at men, as she's also residually cross at Abley for letting her down, and cross at Gerald for not being here. All in all, right now, the only males she's not cross at are the four furry creatures who share their home with her at Foxes Haven.

She goes back inside to be with Hector, Monty, Soot and Bertie. She turns on the radio in the kitchen. It's tuned to BBC Radio Three. Gerald used to listen to it sometimes, and it has become a solace to her, keeping him alive through the little things. Unfortunately, she has caught the two o'clock news. She listens with a heavy heart to the headlines. Some member of Parliament is involved in a sex scandal, a television chef is opening a new chain of restaurants, a leading academic has produced a report about why drinking coffee may be just as good or bad for you as drinking beer, depending on twelve criteria, which is causing all kinds of furore. "And finally there will be a blood moon this week. Over to the weather woman to update us on where it will be clear." Elizabeth pricks up her ears, "A blood moon?"

17
VICTORIA COLLEGE

Elizabeth watches the day fade, despite it still being mid-Sunday afternoon. The autumn colours in her garden are so beautiful from her kitchen window. She puts her cup in the sink and glances back at the dogs finishing a snack after their ordeal…

Not wanting any other surprises, she decides she will pop over to Victoria College to make sure chef knows her dietary requirements, and that meal Emily has invited her to this coming week isn't going to be another big fat scene in her day like the one Wallis was responsible for just now. She is also using it as an excuse to get away from Godric before she says something she'll regret. At least Godric's men last as long as a sunny spell in England, and Wallis will get his cloudy day. The more she says against him, the more she knows Godric will dig in his heels.

As Elizabeth walks back across Jesus Green down the avenue of London planes, this time alone, she wonders why Emily bothers. Her friend knows how Elizabeth finds communal eating at the very least a strain. Listening to overweight, heart-diseased diabetics defending their meaty feasts was one of the least enjoyable obligations of being a Cambridge Fellow. And one has a minimal choice with College Formal Hall dining who one might sit beside and opposite. When accused of having no sense of humour on the topic – thankfully very rarely to her face now – she'll ask them if they would have liked to be put in a blender at birth for being male, stunned with a bolt to the head or perhaps castrated without anaesthetic and would proceed to laugh out loud. But apparently, her humour isn't the same as those with the blood in their mouths.

The particular meal this coming week, according to Emily, is an All Saints Day celebration. Elizabeth does wonder the timing, as All Saints is on the 1st of November. For some reason the College is not doing it on the actual day, probably to fit with the Dining Hall's busy schedule. The day is supposed to precede the Nativity fast of forty days leading up to December 25th, where Victoria College opens its doors to Fellows from other colleges for a feast to remember.

Inside the gates, Elizabeth spots Cynthia Hatman, the lady she saw earlier in the Galileo Department.

"Hello again."

"Is he all right?" Cynthia asks.

"You mean Professor Nigel Crowhams? I've no idea. You didn't have any good words to say earlier," Elizabeth replies.

"Yes, but I wouldn't want him hurt, I mean physically. A bit of verbal taking down a peg or two, that's different, he needs that. You're not at this College, I mean I'd know you if you were. Although your face is familiar. You said you are a police consultant?"

"Elizabeth Green, and no. I'm Granta," Elizabeth replies.

"Not Professor Green?" Cynthia asks.

"Yes."

"I've read about you. You were in the University Echo."

"Don't believe everything you read. Can you tell me what you know about Professor Crowhams?" Elizabeth says.

"What is there to know? Apart from the fact that he's the most unpleasant man to work for on the planet," Cynthia replies.

"Surprised you only said planet, given where you work," Elizabeth smirks.

"Good point, let me revise to the universe," Cynthia says.

"You're not surprised he was attacked?"

"As I say, the only surprising thing is that it wasn't done sooner," Cynthia replies.

"You think it was a deliberate attack on him, rather than on any research that he might have been working on?" Elizabeth asks.

"I don't know what you mean," says Cynthia.

"He had papers with him. They were destroyed, some of them," Elizabeth mentions.

"I'm not his secretary, although he treats me like one," Cynthia says.

"So this was not a theft?" Elizabeth asks.

"With the greatest of respect, there's no way anyone would steal his research from that telescope. It is severely lacking and unreliable. It just doesn't compare to other equipment we have elsewhere in the department," Cynthia says, adding, "He has other projects which win awards. But not his little hobby up on the hill."

"How has he become Head?" Elizabeth shakes her head.

"He burns the candle, Professor Green. He's all work, no wife, no family. Nothing outside the department. You know the type, Cambridge Professor so far up his own..." Cynthia stops herself. "I suppose he's a purist. Perhaps that's why nobody likes him. He's so exacting, unforgiving."

"I take it you're not a fan then," Elizabeth says.

"When it comes to people, he's got no small talk whatsoever. A total bore, just talks about his research." Cynthia replies.

"So you think it was him someone was trying to hurt?"

"Take your pick – the police's problem will be finding who didn't want to whack him," Cynthia says.

"Did you?" Elizabeth asks.

"Sure, really hard too. But I value my freedom more. He's not worth it."

"Do you know the people in the Department of Galileo who live on boats?"

"I know some of them. There's Sarah Robertly, a junior lecturer, she's young and going places. Crowhams hates her," Cynthia says, "Joe, our gardener, adorable fellow, always brings me flowers for my office. Crowhams can't stand Joe either. Tom, a Reader here, always organising things, you know events for the public, stargazing and things like that. Getting people involved. I've been helping on that project. And we are writing a paper together," Cynthia adds, "Not like Crowhams. Crowhams always belittles other people, tries to separate himself from others. Are you coming to the lunar eclipse night? Should be a lovely event later this week with the blood moon. I'll be there as I'm working at both."

"Are you aware of what has happened to those boat dwellers?" Elizabeth asks. "More specifically, one of them?"

"The radio news said something, that one of them has died? Terrible. But not anyone I know, right? Or, I'd have heard," Cynthia replies, looking at Elizabeth for news.

"Perhaps you should sit." Elizabeth points to a bench in a courtyard outside the library of Victoria, in the sunshine. Cynthia looks at it. It seems a little damp from the autumn dew, which the sun hasn't entirely burned off today.

"No, I'm okay thank you, Professor. There are a lot of people living on boats in Cambridge." Cynthia waits.

"It's Dr Tom Mirren. We're not sure if he died from eating poisonous apples or from natural causes yet."

"Oh god." Elizabeth walks Cynthia over to the bench, and they both sit.

18
A GOOD FRIEND

Elizabeth enters her front door at Foxes Haven. The dogs greet her, but all the lights are turned off and at this time of year it makes the house feel dark. She wonders where Godric is, but given their last encounter decides not to call out. Instead, she walks into the drawing room, patting the dogs' heads as she goes. A melancholy hits her as she looks around. Elizabeth sits at the piano, still in her coat, and just stares for a while as the dogs nudge her arms and get no response. Things aren't sitting right in her head. Her being mad at Godric. Bob Abley intent on destroying his career. This case is making no sense.

The day started off so well, but she misses Gerald more than anyone understands. She can still feel him in the house, his laugh, the crinkles around his eyes. In the gloom she can almost feel Gerald sitting beside her, with a whisky, turning the page of her score. Elizabeth doesn't need the score though as she starts to play Chopin's Prelude op. 28 no. 1 in C Major. The darkness around her somehow helping her hide from the reality that he has gone, that she is alone, but the piece is over too quickly, and she sits again quietly slumped until she finds another in her head… Prelude op.28 no.15 'Raindrop' in C Minor. But as the piece is finishing the doorbell cuts through. Immediately Elizabeth's apanthropy is broken, her desire to wallow abruptly interrupted by her friend. Emily is at the door with cake and drinks to thank Elizabeth for letting her rehearse here this afternoon. She bustles in, turning on lights left, right and centre.

"You know my eyes aren't like rabbits, unlike yours, Liz. I'll trip over your menagerie of animals." Emily laughs as she pats Hector and Monty, who can smell Pepper and more importantly, cake.

"Come in," Elizabeth says, as they both walk into the drawing room and Emily can see where Elizabeth has been sitting at the piano in the dark. Emily says nothing, but just puts on a couple of lights in the room and adds, "Haven't we had such a lovely day today, such bright blue sky? I do love these crisp autumnal afternoons. Nothing like coming home to a lit fire. Shall I?" Emily looks at the log basket by the fire.

"Are you cold?"

"A little." Emily looks at Elizabeth who is still in her duffel coat, and who only just notices the French windows are wide open. Emily puts down the cake on the dinner table at the other end of the room and hands Elizabeth a hot chocolate before shutting the doors. "It's made with vegan milk. I just fancied a hot chocolate. The sugar probably."

"Thank you." Elizabeth passes Emily the matches from a side table and watches as Emily deftly places some firelighters, kindling and a couple of logs on Elizabeth's fire, having done it so many times before. Before long, a fire is crackling, and Emily has sat down and sliced up the cake, and they're drinking their hot chocolates.

"I do like double chocolate vegan cake. It's the little walnut pieces he puts in the icing. You know, I envy you that bakery on the corner. They always seem to be open. Mine is always shut. Where's Godric? Would he like some?"

"I don't know. I chucked his boyfriend out earlier." Elizabeth replies. Emily can see that Elizabeth looks very sad indeed, but also knows how she hides it to the world.

"I know it's today," Emily says as Elizabeth looks at her. "Gerald's birthday."

"I started off so determined to have a happy day, for him. But—" Elizabeth can't finish her sentence.

"That's what the cake is for." Emily hands Elizabeth a slice of cake and they both eat it in silence, or at least with the only noise being the dogs trying to get as close to their plates as possible. Bertie walks in to see what is going on, followed by Soot. They have followed Godric down, who bounds in.

"Cake!" Godric hones in on the cake and cuts himself a slice.

"Plate," Elizabeth says. He quickly glides out and back in with a plate and sits at the table and devours a slice. Elizabeth wonders why he can't move as fast to lectures.

"More cake?" He offers another slice to Emily and his nanna, who shake their heads as he cuts himself a huge piece.

"So, I'm very grateful. When I heard I've been asked to sing instead of play the piano I nearly fell off my chair. Many people are on holiday in my singing group and it will be a one-off, especially when they hear me."

"Nonsense. You have a lovely voice," Elizabeth replies.

"But it was written for a man." Emilly is doubtful.

"Tools down immediately then," Elizabeth replies, placing her cake plate on the table, out of reach of the Afghans. "Come on. That's why you came, isn't it?"

"Be kind. I have my own unique style," Emily says.

"Aren't I always?" Elizabeth knows she can be blunt,

but she loves her friend dearly and cannot be more grateful to her for sticking with her through the past year. Emily starts singing an unrecognisable song with a tuneless voice. Bertie and Soot soon walk out, as Monty and Hector ignore everything but the cake on the table until Emily's voice grows louder and more confident.

"Shall we try a key lower?" Elizabeth booms, as Emily's voice pierces her ears and the dogs start to howl. "Godric, come and join in," Elizabeth says. Godric waves back a polite decline. He has a mouthful of cake, and quickly cuts another slice as another line of defence. It's going to be a long afternoon.

19
HOLIDAY FOR MAUREEN

"Where do you suggest? I thought the Canaries, but apparently, everyone's going to Malta," Inspector Abley says.

"The Canaries are nice, and Malta." The travel agent says in the empty office about to close for the evening.

"Have you been?" Bob Abley asks.

"No, but people tell me they are," She replies.

Inspector Abley looks at the travel agent, wondering if she can hear the irony in her words. But then it is the end of her working day. Perhaps she just wants him to choose quickly.

"Would you like me to look and see what hotels they have available? What sort of budget were you thinking of spending?" the travel agent asks.

"Oh, I don't know, what kind do I need?" Inspector Abley says.

"Well, if you're looking for something comfortable..."

"Yes, comfortable would be good. We just want a bit

of sun. Or rather, I'd like to surprise her," Abley adds. "She's just come back you see, and already says how cold she is. We've, she's, we've been through a lot recently. She hates the autumn, the onset of the dark. Me, I like all the leaves changing, conkers, roasted chestnuts and jacket potatoes, fireworks. What's not to love?" Bob Abley pauses. "I still remember getting out the shoe polish for back to school at this time of year. Dusting off coats from the closet, finding things in pockets from last year. That train ticket, or favourite golf tee." Inspector Abley is aware of his own rambling and stops himself. He just wants the holiday to be perfect. Anything to make this travel agent get him the best place. "So yes with the comfort. Let's go high end."

"Ooh, splashing the cash. Bet you've got a good job." She says.

"Something like that."

"Well, let's see what we can find. Oh, look," and the travel agent turns her screen around as much as she can, which means Inspector Abley has to lean across her desk. He can see an expensive looking hotel and is about to say yes when he notices it has a golf course attached. It looks pretty good too. His blood levels rise with excitement.

"No, nothing with sports attached. We just want to spend time together," Bob Abley says.

"Oh, okay. Let's keep looking. I'm sure we can find you something."

"Must be nice to be able just to go when you like. Your boss must be nice?" The travel advisor asks.

"Good god no, I'll probably lose my job for trying to save my marriage. My boss is a nightmare." Abley looks up to the polystyrene ceiling and wonders if that is legal in a public building. The advisor looks around to check she's the only one in the empty travel agents. She opens her drawer and pulls out a voodoo doll. She pulls out a pin that was sticking in the side of the doll and stabs it in the eye.

"Oh." Inspector Abley is a little shocked.

"Stuck pins in her stomach the other day and my boss went home with food poisoning. Of course, it left muggins here on her own. But better than with that old crow. You should try one," the travel agent says.

"A voodoo doll?" Abley asks.

"I have a spare one," She replies. "Two ninety-nine they are over there." She points to a closing market stall. "But I'll let you buy mine for three."

Abley picks out his money and hands it to the travel agent. He rips open the packet, sticks a pin in the new voodoo doll's heart and says, "Super."

20
SOMETHING'S ADRIFT

The dogs can be spotted by their luminous collars as they run across Midsummer Common in the dusk. After their sing-song session, Elizabeth has come out with Emily, her dearest friend, to walk the Afghans with Emily's dog, Pepper. Having dogs has surprised Elizabeth just how much she enjoys walking these days, especially at the weekend. The three dogs run about, flashing bright yellow as they play and sniff.

"You've invited me to a banquet where they are going to serve swan?" Elizabeth mentions what she's heard.

"Don't be ridiculous," Emily replies. "It's illegal. Only allowed at St James's and then only once a year."

"I'm telling you. I was there earlier." Elizabeth says, "They wouldn't deny it when I asked the Chef. He's doing me these wonderful pomegranate pastries with roasted carrots and parsnips. And swan if I want it."

"So what are you complaining about?" Emily says.

"The swan!" Elizabeth remarks.

"You need to get out, leave all your menagerie. I

thought it would be nice. Godric won't be there forever. Then what?" Emily says.

"A quiet life?" Elizabeth replies.

"Wear something glitzy, dress up a little," Emily orders her friend.

Elizabeth opens her eyes wide but lets it go. She's more interested in getting to Stourbridge Common and keeping the Afghans away from the bicycles.

"So you're keeping them?" Emily nods to the Afghans.

"She's still in America. My only worry was the cats, but they all seem to be friends," Elizabeth says.

"So you're opening a zoo."

"Zoos are cruel and pointless. I like to see it more as finding my kind of friends to share a home with."

"Hmm," Emily says.

"And as for Godric, you should see his latest conquest. All the charm of rotting rubbish."

Emily nods supportively, avoiding saying anything to upset Elizabeth today.

"How's the department?" Emily asks.

"Fine."

"College?" Emily asks.

"Fine, though Professor Kendall is hardly a calming influence on the Fellows. Upsetting them left, right and centre. I'm eating in much less this term, which is why I agreed to this Victoria banquet." Elizabeth glares at Emily again.

Both women leave Midsummer Common and meander along a very quiet Riverside. Hardly any cars or bicycles about. They both walk a little way in silence, peering at the boats moored alongside, some with smoke flowing out of chimneys. Some with lit-up windows, others dark and cold. Elizabeth opens the gate to Stourbridge Common, and between some willow trees Emily can now see that Elizabeth has brought her to the spot where the boat dwellers were picked up by the ambulance.

"Oh, that's why you wanted to come to Stourbridge Common, rather than head out to Grantchester as I suggested. I should have known." Emily rolls her eyes, then kicks an apple. "Gosh, there's a lot of dropped fruit around here. Should've brought a bag." And she then looks at the police cordon.

"Not a good idea. Surprised they haven't picked them up," Elizabeth replies. A huge Old English Sheepdog comes bounding up to her. Elizabeth is so pleased to see this dog. She bumps into him now and then.

"Oh hello, Professor Green." Elizabeth and Emily see Ed the Lock Keeper walking up towards them. He's had the same thought as Elizabeth. "Why are all the apples still lying about? Aren't they poisonous?" Ed asks. Emily drops an apple she's just picked up and was about to eat.

"I suppose they're behind the cordon, Ed. How are you?" Elizabeth asks.

"Hello, Ed," Emily says, only sometimes seeing Ed when out walking Pepper, and not best pleased that Clive, his Old English Sheepdog, is now jumping up at her costly cream coat. "Oh, haha, he's a big boy. No, get down, get down, there's a good boy."

"I just don't understand why someone would poison the horses like that? I mean I have my suspicions, but—" Ed's dog Clive leaves Emily in peace and pads up to say hello to Hector and Monty, then the three run madly around the common, with Pepper watching and looking back at Emily, asking if it is entirely necessary to join in, then trotting off a little to half run too.

"Who exactly do you suspect, Ed?" Elizabeth watches Clive. "Magnificent Clive," she utters under her breath to herself.

"Professor Crowhams is always shouting at the horses. I'm sure he's put poison down in his front garden before, to keep them away," Ed says.

"People shout at horses every day." Elizabeth can't be clogging up her mind with slander. "Although like you I think that's a crime, it isn't yet."

"His next-door neighbour, Mable, ninety-two she was when she died. Lived there for years before that young couple came. She told me he poisoned one of her cats, Milly. Rat poison or something. She was convinced of it, as he hated them coming into his garden. He was always shouting at her cats. I can't remember. Her other cat never crossed the fence apparently after."

"What happened to Milly?"

"Dead from the poison," Ed replies.

"So you think this was Professor Crowhams?" Elizabeth asks.

"Could have been." Ed looks at Brad, rowing towards them in his scull. "Or him!" Elizabeth watches as Brad hits one of the boats with his oar as it is far too dark to be rowing. Elizabeth is confused. Two suspects in one minute; is Ed just blaming everyone? She's about to say, he's just a rower, when from nowhere a man shouts back at Brad.

"You do that again, and you'll regret it!" Joe pops out behind them. Now he's out of the hospital bed, Elizabeth can see just how much of a thin, wiry frame he has, his shock of red hair and beard sticking out in the dark, wearing a multicoloured striped wool jumper with a big orange heart on it in the middle of the front. Elizabeth watches Joe jump on the boat that has just been hit and make fists at the rower. She watches the rower laugh, which feels odd, given the anger he's facing and the possibility of the bearded man jumping in.

"I don't think you should be doing that. You should stay this side of the rope," Ed shouts, walking towards Joe.

"That's pretty hard seeing as I live here, and this has come away from its moorings." Joe looks at the boat out in the river, now a little too far. "And I've nowhere else to go unless you have a big house and lots of food to share?" Joe challenges. Ed frowns, he's not opening his home for rowers, he can't think of anything worse. Elizabeth doesn't offer as she doesn't like his tone. Emily just stares at the man's appearance and helpfully suggests, "They have showers at Parkside Pool. You could try there, get clean and dry?" Emily brushes dog hair from her coat. Elizabeth looks at her quizzically, grateful that Joe didn't hear as she remains the right side of the cordon with Emily and Ed. She looks up into the tree beside them and can see a black cat watching proceedings.

"They've loosened the boats. Look, oh god." Joe can see a dinghy that has been untied as well. "Ruddy rowers. They've done this. Go to hospital for five minutes and—"

"You sound sure?" Elizabeth says.

"You were at the hospital, that's right," Joe remembers Elizabeth's questions from before.

"Should you have left the hospital?" Elizabeth asks, "You look quite ill."

"I'm fine," Joe replies, dismissive about a semi-stranger's concern.

"Well Joe, you are not the only one here who thinks that the rowers might be guilty of something." Elizabeth looks at Ed, remembering what he said.

"Well, there you go. More evidence," Joe replies.

"And Professor Nigel Crowhams?" Elizabeth adds.

"What, are they are in cahoots?" Joe asks, "Old Crowhams?"

"Might be. All them academic types always are, aren't they?" Ed replies pointing at the rower, now a little too far away to hear. Joe looks at the rower.

"Well, he's one of ours. Post-doc." Joe says, looking at Brad rowing away.

"At the Department of Galileo? You're the gardener?" Elizabeth asks.

"Head Gardener," Joe replies. "Yeah, I wouldn't be surprised if they did this." Joe looks at the apples, picks one up and throws it in the river, aiming for Brad. "Poisoned us along with the horses."

"Don't do that lad. The birds will be poisoned," Ed

says, crossly.

"We narrow their path, less river for rowing. They complain. Think they own the bloody place. Now they're murderers, but they won't get away with that. I'll make sure of that," Joe says.

"So you think it is murder?" Elizabeth asks.

"Maybe, or maybe they wanted to scare us. Make us all clear out, and it went wrong?" Joe continues to stare at Brad, who is getting further away. But Elizabeth doesn't reveal her own thoughts on the matter.

"Is this your boat?" Emily asks Joe about the boat nearest the crime scene. It looks a little nicer than the others and she is about to ask where he got his flower boxes.

"Tom's. The innocent victim in all this." Joe is very gloomy, thinking about his dead friend.

"I'm sorry for your loss." Elizabeth leaves a moment before asking a question, "Tom didn't like Professor Nigel Crowhams did he?"

"Who told you that? It was the other way around." Joe says, "Crowhams made his life hell. Tom was an amazing bloke, a proper hero to everyone." Joe rubs his eyes. "Whoever did this…" Joe looks up at the trees, in seeming despair.

"Oh my god, is this the boat of that poor man, who died?" Emily asks Elizabeth quietly, just catching up. Elizabeth nods, just realising this herself.

"How are the rest of your friends?" Emily asks Joe, now feeling guilty about not offering her home to him for a shower and warmth. "You know I think I have space at home if you would like a warm bed?" Emily asks genuinely.

"Nah, you're all right." Joe says, "Thanks, but I better stay here and watch the boats."

"I'll bring back a basket of food for you later. Leave it outside." Emily offers.

"No offence, but presents of food outside the boats is

not my favourite thing right now," Joe replies.

"I was thinking more a hamper of pies and olives, sun-dried tomatoes, ciabatta, wine," Emily suggests.

Joe looks at Elizabeth to ask if her friend is for real.

"That sounds nice," Ed replies, thinking how he'd like such a hamper.

Joe throws a rope from the boat a little way into the river to Elizabeth. But Ed can see she is not about to catch it, so he slips under the cordon and catches it himself, pulling the narrow boat back to its moorings as Joe walks down to the other end of the boat and jumps back on shore. "Bloody rowers," Joe says.

"My grandson rows. He's really rather good," Elizabeth says though she's also not a huge fan.

"You know what their latest good deed is?" Joe asks rhetorically, "Pouring oil on the swans' eggs, so they don't hatch. Did it this spring, do it every year I'm sure."

"Will you show me where?" Elizabeth asks.

"I can show you where they've done it in the past. Might be washed away," Joe replies.

"They want a fight? They've got it," Ed says. He's confused, as this man seems nicer than he thought boat dwellers could be.

"They want an animal-free, peasant-free zone." Joe scoffs.

"Maybe it's the same person poisoning the horses as poisoning the swans?" Emily asks.

21
SWANS AREN'T SWIMMING

Like a dog with a bone, Elizabeth can't just go home after Joe has told her about the swans' nests; instead she frog marches him to the spot, dragging Emily behind her. Ed has come along, because he is nosey and worried about the animals.

"See?" Joe says. They stare at an old swan nest, still with traces of black oil poured all over it, despite the months that have passed.

"Oh dear," Elizabeth says.

"What have they done?" Emily isn't sure what she's looking at.

"Even in November we can still see it, so imagine how much oil these birds came back and found last spring – even with all the rain it's still baked in," Joe says. Emily can see broken shells in the nest. "This isn't the only one. It's all up to Horningsea, though I don't know why – they don't even row up that far," Joe adds.

"It would get in the feathers or prevent hatching. That's so hateful." Elizabeth pokes about in the nest and finds more cracked shells. "People never fail to disappoint, the depths to which they'll sink." Hector comes up and sniffs, quickly joined by Clive. Elizabeth uses her knee to push them out of the way. "Get back, go on."

"If they do this to the birds, you have got to ask yourself, what else?" Ed says. "I mean between you lot and these rowers, what chance has the wildlife got?"

"I think we were supposed to feed the horses those apples, Professor. A big barrel at the gate?" Joe says, "We don't get left gifts, more likely to have abuse hurled at us. They were clearly meant for the horses." Joe looks at Elizabeth, raising his eyebrows.

"Wouldn't be surprised if you lot poisoned them. Wanting the Common all to yourself," Ed huffs at Joe.

"Maybe you tried to poison us, Ed. I noticed you left before Tom died this morning. Maybe you were disappointed!" Joe raises his voice at Ed, not willing to take his stirring this morning. "You're always moaning at us."

"For all your littering, all that pumping out your old fuel into the river. You drive too fast, disturbing the riverbank. Maybe you had it coming," Ed replies, but Joe has turned his back on Ed.

"Hmm," Elizabeth says to herself as she walks up over into the farmer's field and sees a swan with something caught in its wing. "Emily, can you keep the dogs back? Do you have a mobile phone?" She asks Joe, who shakes his head. Between them, only Emily picks one out of her purse.

"You need to get one of these," Emily says to Elizabeth, straining to pass her phone while holding too many dogs. Ed helps, grabbing Clive and Monty.

After half an hour, the four of them and their four dogs watch as a vet with a van turns up, throws a net over the injured swan and then puts it in a sack after tying the beak. Elizabeth isn't sure she did the right thing, as surely they could have held it and pulled out the wire. But the vet says the bird looks dehydrated and lucky they found it.

As they walk back to Stourbridge Common, Elizabeth thinks that Joe looks tired and pale.

"Are you going to be okay?" Emily asks, "My offer still stands."

"I just need sleep. Better on the boat. As I say, someone has to watch them."

"If I catch those rowers doing anything like this, well—" Ed says of the swans. "Even if it's your son!"

"Godric wouldn't stand for anything like this," Elizabeth replies.

"Hooligans, the lot of them," Ed says.

"Were you good friends with Tom?" Elizabeth asks Joe out of the blue, not wanting to get into an argument about rowers with Ed.

"He was my best friend," Joe replies. "It's such a tragedy. I can't believe it."

"Hmm," Elizabeth replies.

22
A DIRTY MUTT

Elizabeth, Emily and Ed left Joe on his boat to sleep, and are now standing by the Fort Saint George Bridge. Ed spots Cynthia sitting outside the Fort Saint George pub on Midsummer Common with the Bonfire Society committee. Cynthia spots Ed, smiles and taps her watch. Ed mouths "Sorry," having completely forgotten he was supposed to be here an hour earlier. She pats the seat next to her and he points to the bar, but his heart sinks.

Emily waves goodbye and heads off across Jesus Green for home, leaving Elizabeth watching Hector, Monty and Clive in final sniffing mode before doing the same. She and Ed hear Cynthia and Professor Nigel Crowhams raise their voices.

"Another happy group of people," Elizabeth says to Ed. "Right, I'll be off. Bye Ed." Elizabeth starts to gather her dogs.

"I'm not sure I want to join this meeting," Ed replies. "I might throttle the Professor." The two of them listen while the dogs drink water from a bowl put out for dogs on the Common. Elizabeth wonders why Ed is so reluctant and then sees how Professor Crowhams touches Cynthia's hand. Maybe he's jealous.

"The holograms are very advanced now," Cynthia argues, leaving her hand under Professor Crowhams for what Elizabeth thinks is just a little bit too long before pulling it away. She wonders what Ed would do to frame the Professor for Tom's death, if he were jealous about this. He has already told Elizabeth he thinks the Professor poisoned the horses. And now Ed must also clearly see what is happening here. Elizabeth wonders if there is a spark between Crowhams and Cynthia in that moment.

"We must stick to what Cambridge does best! The Catherine Wheel, the Coconut, the Fish, the Falling Leaves. These are what I grew up with as a boy. These are what the families come out to celebrate. They don't want to walk down an avenue of trees lit up. That's a Christmas decoration," Professor Crowhams replies, disagreeing with Cynthia. There are a lot of hear hears among those sitting around the table.

"All I'm saying is that we could have both for a while. Try the new. They will come eventually. It's the future," Cynthia argues back. "We don't want to be stuck in the 1970s."

"Can you keep that dirty mutt away from me?" Professor Nigel Crowhams turns and sees that Clive, who has wandered over to say hello and is now licking his knee with the surplus water from his drink. Ed calls Clive back closer to him.

"He just wants the crisps," Ed replies.

Professor Crowhams picks up his crisps and teases Clive with them. This makes Ed's blood boil. Elizabeth has put both the Afghans on the lead, realising everyone knows she's eavesdropping. As she turns to climb the bridge, she spots Wallis in a scull. She can't believe how many times this young man has been on the river today, but then Godric told her he was trying out to be a blue for the university.

"Hey, you!" Wallis, shouts at Ed from the gloomy river. "Stop throwing stuff at us. You could take an eye out." Wallis throws something and hits Ed on the head. Ed flinches.

"Ow!"

"Come on Wallis, what are you doing?" Brad shouts back from his scull. "Let's go back in, it's dark now. I'm tired."

"Hey, stop that!" Elizabeth shouts at Wallis. She cannot believe it when he just blanks her. Does he not remember the crime he just committed in her home not a few hours before? She sees Wallis pick something up and throw again at Ed. He misses and picks up another object, which looks like a piece of gravel from inside his scull and throws it. This time it hits Ed's back. Luckily Ed has a coat on, but it still hurts.

"Arghh," Ed screams.

"Yeah, you don't like it when someone does it to you!" Wallis throws again. Elizabeth wonders about Wallis's words. Who started this war between Ed and the rowers? She looks at all of them and then worries for Clive in case he gets hit.

"Can you keep your dog away from me?!" Professor Crowhams shouts at Ed, pushing Clive away.

"I think Cynthia is right," Ed says, trying to support Cynthia about the lights and rubbing his head. "All these fireworks, they go on for ages. It's not just one night anymore. Holograms and light festivals are much kinder and quieter. We can combine it with an early winter solstice." Ed is hit again and flinches.

"Wallis!" Brad starts to row across to the Fort Saint George, unsure what Wallis is doing but wanting no part of it.

"Stop right now!" Elizabeth shouts at Wallis again. But she sees no reaction from Wallis, so marches down to have a closer word. Professor Crowhams is also raising his voice now to Ed about Clive. "Can't you control this beast? I'll report him to the dog warden."

Cynthia stands up and starts to fuss and try to help Ed who is clearly in pain. But she's allergic to Clive, who is excited to see her, which is subsequently causing Ed more stress trying to keep Clive away from her.

"I'm fine. Sit down, or Clive'll ruin your nice coat," Ed says to Cynthia, but as he turns to try to put Clive on the lead Wallis hits him right in the chest with a small stone. It takes the wind out of Ed, who leans on a piece of furniture and clings to his chest. Brad flicks water at Wallis in disapproval.

"Did you not hear me? I say you need to control that dog. And you can't just pick a date out of the sky and call it winter solstice. Winter solstice is typically the twenty-first of December, when the Sun reaches its most southerly declination of 23.5 degrees. When the North Pole is tilted farthest – 23.5 degrees – away from the Sun, delivering the fewest hours of sunlight of the year." Professor Crowhams drones on, utterly dispassionate about Ed's current state of health.

"All right, can you stop for a minute?" Cynthia tries to halt the conversation so she can attend to Ed, who is looking very clammy all of a sudden.

"Ed, Ed?" Cynthia says.

"Hurling stones and abuse is completely unacceptable behaviour from a student at the university." Elizabeth shouts at Wallis, "And you can count on me reporting you to the police, and your college."

"For what?" Wallis says, shrugging.

"There are witnesses!" Elizabeth booms at Wallis again, but behind her, she hears Cynthia shout.

"Ed!" As Ed falls to the ground, clutching his heart. Clive nuzzles and licks his best friend's face as Cynthia shouts, "Somebody help!" Cynthia takes out her phone and dials, while Elizabeth takes off Ed's jacket and listens to his heart.

"We need an ambulance." Elizabeth says.

23
ASK THE STARS

Monday morning, and Elizabeth Green and Sergeant Lemon have decided to pay Professor Crowhams a visit. As Ed the Lock Keeper was collapsing yesterday, Elizabeth noticed Crowhams get up from his seat and leave. Elizabeth was particularly concerned that Crowhams didn't even look back. Sergeant Lemon, still unable to get any sense from Inspector Abley and knowing Inspector Pober is perhaps hours away from turning up and making this whole experience ten times worse, is pinning his hopes on Professor Green. He has watched the way his boss works with her, so when she suggested the visit to the Department of Galileo this morning, he was more than happy to go along with her instincts on what was a baffling case. It also got him out of the station and away from the Superintendent, who was apparently searching for him to ask about Inspector Abley's whereabouts.

"Old Ed is going to be all right, in case you were wondering. It was just an attack of angina as it turns out," Elizabeth explains to Crowhams as they stand in his rooms at the department. Crowhams keeps his back to her and Sergeant Lemon while he rifles through papers on his desk.

"I hear you don't like the horses, Professor." Sergeant Lemon asks Crowhams, finishing a pain au chocolat he picked up on his way to the case.

"A stallion at the racetrack can prove lucrative, I don't personally go in for dressage, but I hear it keeps a lot of people in work and out of trouble," Crowhams says. "And horses have been pulling carts for centuries. The clip-clopping on the road is quite evocative."

"Some say you are cross about the horses on the Commons in Cambridge," Sergeant Lemon replies.

"Some say? Hmm, well if you're referring one particular man, it turns out spreading rumours about people appears to be bad for one's heart, no?" Crowhams scoffs. "And as to whether I think it a good idea to put two dozen horses on Midsummer or Stourbridge Common to do whatever they ruddy well like, including eating the flowers in my front garden and terrorising all who cross let alone sit there, then I fully admit it. Midsummer Common has neither the size nor the facilities. Now if they were to be harnessed to those ruddy awful boats to tow them away, that might finally be a proper use for them!"

"So you are in favour of the enslavement of the poor horses to do your bidding indeed. Why am I not surprised. And remove all the boat dwellers to boot. You're not bothered about making friends, it appears, neither human or animal. Have you ever poisoned the horses?" Elizabeth asks directly.

"Professor Green, you do seem to be everywhere." Crowhams looks at Elizabeth with disdain.

"Professor Green is helping me with the investigation into the death of Tom Mirren," Lemon says.

"Right," Crowhams replies.

"Would you know anything about that?" Elizabeth makes use of her legitimate position.

"Er, I think I was being attacked at the same time if the news reports are anything to go by?" Crowhams says.

"You were attacked two hours after they were found poisoned. So you had plenty of time to drive down to Stourbridge Common and poison them, as the poison had to have time to work," Elizabeth says.

"I live on Midsummer Common, why would I drive to Stourbridge Common if I was going to hurt Tom or anyone else?" Crowhams replies. "Come now, if you're going to help the police, you should at least know your geography. And as for the horses, it's reasonable not to want large horses outside my front window. What's the beef with that?"

"Metal railings are stopping any large animals from getting near the front of your garden. If you are going to attack the horses at least be accurate about the geography outside your front door," Elizabeth says. "Do you walk to the department? No, I didn't think so, we saw your car outside just now. And no one said anything about attempting to hurt anyone. We were talking about the horses. So you think someone deliberately attacked the boat dwellers, and murdered Tom?" she asks.

"No, of course not." Professor Nigel Crowhams looks worried for the first time, looking at Sergeant Lemon with his notebook out and pen scribbling furiously.

"We have heard that you didn't much care for Dr Tom Mirren," Elizabeth continues. "In fact, a little dicky bird said you disliked him and were against some of his practices at the department, even jealous?"

"This dicky bird has been busy, hasn't Joe?" Professor Crowhams scoffs.

"I didn't say it was Joe." Elizabeth replies.

"Tom had some strange ideas," Crowhams admits, adding, "Thought we were here to serve the public, set up an overly ambitious programme of public stargazing. Wanted to let the public into regular lectures for heaven's sake! Took far too much of the department budget and time. Thankfully, one of the benefits is that we can now close that down."

"One of the benefits? A man has died, Sir." Sergeant Lemon asks.

"It was costly and wasteful. We are not running a charity," Crowhams says. "We are a department of excellence. If people want to see the stars, they should turn their lights off. Stop looking at the television and look up. We are not some entertainment venue for the ignorant to gawp and forget everything we tell them less than thirty minutes later."

"So you know nothing about the death of Tom Mirren?" Sergeant Lemon asks Professor Crowhams, turning the page in his notebook and licking his pencil.

"Look, if you want to find out what happened to Tom why don't you speak with Dr Sarah Robertly and Joe, they're in this morning, Sarah's just down the corridor," Crowhams says. "I'm sure Joe is planting weeds somewhere. One lived with him, the other next door. This is what happens when you have departmental fraternising."

"Ok, well—," Lemon replies, looking behind him into the communal reception area of the department to see if he can see them.

"That seems a little quick to be back here after their ordeal?" Elizabeth asks the Professor.

"How the hell should I know? I don't whip people to come in, that's not my job." Professor Crowhams then explodes, "What are you doing about catching my attacker? That's who you should be looking for. I'm still alive, but if they attack again, maybe I'll be dead too."

"You said earlier you thought it was just someone trying to sabotage the telescope before?" Lemon asks looking through his notebook, "Why have you changed your story?"

"Well, now a man is dead. Perhaps I should be more concerned for my safety," Crowhams replies.

"Don't go wandering about at night in the department again while the investigation is ongoing," Sergeant Lemon says.

"I'm Head of Department here, how am I expected not to?" Crowhams questions.

"Well, if we think it warrants it, we may come back and offer you an officer for protection purposes. At the moment, we are treating it as a break in and an isolated incident," Lemon says.

"Good to know," the Professor says sarcastically, adding, "Now if you'll excuse me. I need to crack on."

Elizabeth and Lemon leave Professor Crowhams alone, not satisfied with their chat.

*

"Good morning, Dr Sarah Robertly, is it?" Elizabeth peeks her head around the door and walks in, with Lemon following.

"Hello," Sarah replies.

"I'm so sorry for your loss. I'm Sergeant Lemon, and this is Professor Elizabeth Green. Would you mind if we ask you a few questions?" Sergeant Lemon asks.

"Yes, that's fine." Sarah winces a little.

"Last time we saw you, you were very unwell?" Elizabeth questions Sarah, who still looks a little grey and is clearly wearing the clothes she had on in hospital, a bit hippy Elizabeth thinks, a green jumper and jeans with multicoloured flowers on the hems.

"Yes, they weren't happy I discharged myself this morning," Sarah smiles, "but there is nothing I can do. I have to be here. I'd already stayed in that bed and ward for all day yesterday, near where Tom—," Sarah can't finish her sentence 'where Tom had died'. Elizabeth can see more evidence that Sarah is still suffering from toxin poisoning, with clammy near white skin and drawn eyes.

"You just walked out? You should be in hospital,"

Elizabeth replies.

"I have to finish this." They watch as Sarah drops laser pointers and binoculars in a big wheeled suitcase, as well as portable headphones and laminated cards. "Tom was working on an event for tomorrow evening, I know he was coming back this afternoon to finish it, send out the reminder invitations, get the equipment ready, remind the city council to let the police know. Tom would have wanted it to go ahead." She looks up to Elizabeth. "I can't let him down." Elizabeth thinks of Gerald and understands what it is like to lose someone special and want to honour their memory.

"I told her I could help," Joe chips in from around the door.

"The swan is going to be okay, I phoned the vet. Thank you for showing me that evidence from the nest. We will get to the bottom of it," Elizabeth says, looking at Joe still wearing the same stripy jumper. Adding, "You're looking much better today, but I didn't expect you to be back to work either."

"When friends tell me they're jumping in a taxi," Joe says pointedly to Sarah, "What can I do?" Joe smiles at Sarah.

"Where is this taking place?" Lemon chips in, "This event you are organising?"

"Stourbridge Common." Sarah hands Sergeant Lemon a leaflet.

"Right by your boats?" Lemon asks.

"Yes, exactly. I'm not sure how I'm going to get all the telescopes there," Sarah replies, "Tom didn't tell me everything I should take, but—"

"Don't worry. You've got me now." Joe interrupts Sarah. "We can do it together."

"So you're talking about Dr Tom Mirren. He was a lecturer here?" Elizabeth asks.

"Had just been made a Reader." Sarah replies, "For his work on Black Holes."

"He was brilliant," Joe adds. Sarah looks at Joe, and Elizabeth realises Sarah is upset by Joe's use of the word 'was'. She remembers all too well how that sounds.

"Do you have any reason to believe that his death was anything but an accident?" Sergeant Lemon asks Sarah.

"I cooked the pie. It's my fault. I did it," Sarah replies.

"Don't be silly," Joe says, stroking her arm.

"He always had seconds. He loved my pies." Sarah breaks down into tears. "And now he's dead." Sarah collapses into a chair, as Joe walks over to comfort her.

"It wasn't your fault," Joe says, hugging Sarah.

"You think it was the pie?" Elizabeth asks.

"It was something we ate, and we all ate my apple pie," Sarah says, convinced, looking straight at Elizabeth.

"You said you thought it could be the rowers earlier?" Elizabeth asks Joe again.

"You've asked me this already. I can't remember much about that night, but yes, I think the rowers are the most likely suspects. They hate our boats and the horses," Joe replies. "Ed agreed, didn't he?"

"We are just trying to build a picture of what happened," Lemon says.

"Why Tom Mirren and not you?" Elizabeth looks at Joe. "Seems a bit random if it was the pie?" Elizabeth looks at Sarah.

"I don't know," Sarah replies.

"We haven't found a pie dish?" Lemon says.

"That's odd. It was round. It has a bird in it, to let the air out of the pastry." Sarah looks at Sergeant Lemon.

"How did you meet Tom?" Elizabeth asks Sarah. Sarah is happy to tell Elizabeth about better times.

"We met here, in the department. I was always very particular about wanting green tea. This was back before it was readily available. And I'd run out. And so at teatime, there was none. He came that afternoon, he'd been to the shops and bought a box. He always said after that what a cheap date I was because all it had taken was a cuppa." Sarah looks at Elizabeth. "And now I've poisoned him." And she breaks back down. Joe strokes her shoulders.

"There, there. You didn't know. None of us knew. I'm here," Joe says.

"And how did you meet Tom?" Elizabeth asks Joe. Joe pauses before answering Elizabeth's question.

"At the Strawberry Fair. I was running a stall one year where you have to throw a balloon full of water to hit a teddy bear off the stand. He spent so much money, trying to win a teddy bear. That was for you, wasn't it?" Joe says. Sarah nods. "Anyway, I took pity on him, and I pulled the string," Joe adds.

"The string?" Lemon asks.

"All the bears were weighted down, so it was virtually impossible to win them. But if there was a crowd, we'd pull an invisible bit of string to make them fall to get more punters. And I pulled it for him. I think he saw, but you didn't, as he laughed. Later on, he came back and said he was going to the pub. I went with him, and we played pool. I told him how I loved Cambridge. He said he was living on the river. I confessed that was my dream. He mentioned that he was looking for someone to live on his boat as he was moving into Sarah's. I took it. Then these two lovely people found me a job here, as the gardener." Joe smiles at Elizabeth, but then remembers Tom is dead.

"Are the horses okay?" Sarah asks Sergeant Lemon.

"As far as we know," Lemon replies, trying hard not to tell her that he's not a vet and there are more pressing issues at hand.

"Do you think they were meant for us? The rotten apples I mean?" she asks him.

"We're looking into that," Lemon says.

"Surely it was meant for the horses?" Joe adds.

"You heard the Sergeant, the horses are not dead, so what does that tell you?" Sarah looks at Joe straight in the eyes. "I've always fed the horses. They are so beautiful."

"Were you with each other all evening?" Elizabeth asks Sarah.

"You mean on Saturday night? Before?" Sarah asks.

"Yes." Elizabeth says.

"I was with Tom. We were talking about Tom's cat, Midnight." Sarah starts to ramble through tears. "He rescued the cat from a shelter. Something about black cats never being rescued because people can't take good photos of them. Tom had bought this new plug-in which can help reduce pet stress, as the fireworks are coming up. He'd just bought it. We were going to move the boat much further down the river on Bonfire night so as not to be near the display on Midsummer. Fireworks seem to go on for two weeks these days. Is he all right?" Sarah asks Joe.

"Midnight's fine. Don't worry," Joe replies.

"Were you with him all night?" Lemon asks.

"Yes, we were listening to music. Just by the stove. People came over for a drink after dinner. I'd made this pie, and we all sat by the brazier. It was quite beautiful under the trees," Sarah replies.

"You've got me now. I'll protect you." Joe kisses Sarah's head.

"Perhaps you could bring Sarah a cup of green tea?" Elizabeth suggests to Joe, who nods and leaves.

"Do Joe and Professor Crowhams get along?" Elizabeth asks Sarah.

"No, but then nobody gets on with Professor Crowhams, he doesn't seem to have any friends." Sarah replies.

"How can he be Head of Department and yet be so unpopular?" Elizabeth says, shaking her head.

"He's just so prolific with publishing papers," Sarah says matter-of-factly.

"Why doesn't Joe like him? Joe's the gardener." Elizabeth pushes, not understanding what is going on in the Department of Galileo.

"He's the only one who complains about what Joe

does. Joe planted all this lavender along the paths last summer, for the bees," Sarah says. "Professor Crowhams said we weren't living in France and ordered him to remove them all. That bees nest in walls, and he doesn't want them burrowing into his precious telescope building."

"Is Joe a jealous man?" Elizabeth probes.

"What do you mean?" Sarah wipes fallen tears from her nose.

"He likes you a lot. Would he have been jealous of Tom?" Elizabeth asks.

"Joe? No, Joe is our best friend." Sarah is convinced. "The one who was jealous of Tom was Professor Crowhams. Caused Tom a lot of stress about this event. Didn't want him to hold it. That's why I want to do it. To make sure he doesn't win. I expect he thinks it's cancelled now. Well, it's not. We will do it for Tom." She says.

Joe comes back in with a cup of green tea from the tea urn station, as well as a coffee for him and two pastries.

"Voila!" he says.

24
PARK PARADE

Elizabeth decides to pop in on Inspector Abley after her and Lemon's visit to the Department of Galileo. This is far too serious a case now for her to work on without him. Lemon has dropped her off thinking she's gone home and she waves and then double backs across Magdalene College Bridge on Castle Street and down the boards to Park Parade. It isn't long before she is standing outside Bob Abley's home, a home she knows well, or at least the front garden and door. She can count only on one hand how many times over the years Mrs Maureen Abley has invited her over for dinner. It doesn't take a genius to work out that Inspector Abley's wife doesn't much care for Elizabeth. Bob has admitted when a little drunk that Maureen finds Elizabeth a little too acerbic.

Elizabeth hopes for Inspector Abley to answer the door in the circumstances but it is not to be. Instead, she is greeted by a frosty Maureen still in her dressing gown.

"He's not here."

"Hello, Maureen," Elizabeth says.

Maureen folds her arms and waits for Elizabeth to go.

"Do you know where I can find him?" Elizabeth asks.

"No," Maureen replies.

"Has he called you?"

"What do you want?" Maureen is not interested in listening to Elizabeth.

"I want to speak with your husband. You seem remarkably uninterested in his whereabouts. It looks like you've been awake all night worrying."

"You always were a snooty cow. Thinking you're better than me."

"I'm not snooty, I'm concerned. And I think you meant sarcastic," Elizabeth says. "How's the lemon tree doing?" Elizabeth asks after a present she gave the Inspector for his last birthday.

"Excuse me?" Maureen frowns.

"I just wanted to check that you've brought it into the conservatory from outside. They don't do well in the cold." Elizabeth says.

"Huh?" Maureen replies, flabbergasted Elizabeth is talking about a plant in the circumstances.

"I can look after it for a while if you like. Can take it with me now – shall I come in and pick it up? Just for the winter, while you are—"

Maureen slams the door on Elizabeth. Elizabeth stands facing the door for a while before turning.

Elizabeth is cross at having the door shut in her face, and frowns up at the windows before marching off. "You might kill your marriage, but you won't kill my lemon tree."

25
NOT ON YOUR NELLY

Inspector Abley spent Sunday night in the bed and breakfast beside the Cambridge Police Station, the one that the station usually puts up any visiting guests. Perhaps he did this because he knew he'd see some of the lads, and wanted to hear what they had to say about his future. He knew it was time to face his demons.

This particular B&B is a favourite haunt with coppers as it has a great bar, not too busy that they will run into trouble and have to come off duty to arrest drunk people, lively enough to have an atmosphere with its jukebox and dartboard. But most importantly, with a discreet barman and owner, who has never sold any secrets to the local press. For when police officers go out for a drink, they like to know that no one is paying attention to their small talk.

As it turns out, last night Inspector Abley learnt that he is sorely missed, and his colleagues repeatedly ask - now he has been seen in the flesh - when he is coming back? Can he get rid of Pober? Is the Super leaving? Has Abley heard about Lemon? And, how they miss his banter. Advice followed in the shape of how no woman was worth it, don't blow everything just because of a bit of skirt. After every round of drinks, the calls for Inspector Abley's return to the station grew louder. His men wouldn't let him go to bed either. They all had work in the morning, but some of them were worried that this might be the last time they saw him, so they were throwing everything but the kitchen sink to persuade him to return. So much that in the end, he promised he would talk to the Super in the morning.

Now it is Monday morning Abley is beginning to regret that promise. He has put it off for as long as he can this morning, eating his breakfast as slowly as possible and reading the paper from cover to cover; and wishes only this morning that he was a broadsheet and not tabloid reader. But it's now or never, as his suspension ran out yesterday. Monday morning now, he had better get on with it. Still, it is with much trepidation that he walks through the glass doors of Cambridge Police Station public entrance, showered and shaved, like a schoolboy going to see the headmaster. There is no one he would less like to meet this morning than Superintendent Raynott.

Abley finds only smiles from every policeman and woman he meets, pleased to see him, welcoming him back, doing mock salutes and offering him chocolate in one case, which he can never refuse. He climbs the stairs to the Super's office and peeks around the corner, but it is empty. He wasn't expecting that. He knows Raynott is always there.

"Abley." It makes Inspector Abley jump as the small tarsier-like Raynott creeps up from behind.

"Superintendent," Abley replies.

"Doing a bit of nosing about in your spare time?" Raynott asks.

"No, actually I came to see you."

"Oh, to what do we owe the delight of your company here? Getting bored of playing golf?" Raynott smirks.

"What? No, never." Abley hesitates, unsure where to start. "I've come in to have a word."

"Resignation?" Raynott asks. Abley stares at Raynott and the two men lock eyes, neither blinking until Raynott looks away and adds, "Well, I suppose you'd better come in. Don't shut the door. I haven't got long."

The two men walk through into Raynott's ample room. Like Abley's it overlooks Parker's Piece and sunlight floods in and onto Raynott's empty desk. Unlike Abley's there is no hint of Raynott's character, save for a map of Africa. Before joining the force, Raynott was in the army, serving in Kenya in a training unit. Abley glances at the map, preparing himself for some repeated anecdote about how Raynott always had a tough nut to crack in his training days.

"So, you've come to ask for your job back?" Raynott asks.

"Apparently I've been suffering from a very low level of Vitamin D," Abley says. "It can leave you feeling depressed. Who knew?"

"Let me get this straight. You've been drinking on the job, going AWOL and playing golf when you should be at work due to a vitamin D deficiency?" Raynott asks.

"I've been feeling unwell, yes." Abley tries to be positive, hating every minute of standing in this small man's office. "But I've booked a holiday for the wife and myself. Canaries. Therapy to top up the vitamin D that is. And then, yes, I'm ready to come back."

"Supplements not good enough for you?" Raynott says.

"I haven't had a holiday for two years, Sir, so I think I'm owed." Abley replies.

"And what do you think you've been doing for the past two months? Did you not think you could have booked it in that time?" Raynott shakes his head. "Ridiculous. I've never heard so much poppycock in all my days in the army."

"I only just found out about the deficiency," Abley

says.

"That's convenient," Raynott replies. Abley watches Raynott sit down behind his desk. Raynott opens a drawer and pulls out a notebook. "If, and I mean *if* I am to consider your reinstatement, I would need to be convinced of your motivation to do the job to the best of your abilities. Swanning off to get some sun is hardly a good indication of how you intend to start. My boys have been working their damnedest to fill the hole left by a man down. And quite frankly, I see nothing to indicate that anything has changed. You roll up at the eleventh hour expecting to pick up where you left off. I've seen no record of you attending any of the rehabilitation courses the police force provide for coping with stress." Raynott shows his notebook, with evidence of missed appointments. "You're unshaven, you look like you slept in your clothes." Raynott can't help himself as he looks at the picture of Africa. "We don't have space for half-hearted attitudes here. People can get killed. Vitamin deficiency. I thought I'd heard them all. Well not on your nelly."

Raynott starts to write something. Inspector Abley walks over to the window and watches a young boy run onto Parker's Piece with his football, his father a few feet behind. Raynott's voice drones on again behind him. "It's all about the team," Raynott adds.

"I'm a team player." More so than Raynott, thinks Abley. Abley sees this meeting not going the way he expected. He realises Raynott is going to try to kick him out. He reaches for desperate measures, so he turns and looks Raynott in the eye. "I might lose my marriage, my home, everything… if I lose this job. I need it."

"Well, you make it very easy for me to say that I don't want you on my force," Raynott replies. "I've signed the paperwork I had ready, as I suspected this would be the case. And I shall be recommending that your position here is terminated when I post this today." Raynott shows

Abley a letter from his desk, then rises on his toes, continuing, "Now if you don't mind, I'm very busy."

Inspector Abley feels sick. He knew this might happen, knows what a horrid little man Raynott is. But didn't expect the knife to sink in and hurt so much. Abley realises he was hoping for the best, hoping there would be some humanity in this man he was now staring at in front of him. Hoping for change. But there it was, the news hit him like a train, the air fell out of him and all of a sudden he felt pathetic but also angry. Raynott was now walking towards the door, hoping Abley would leave without a scene. Abley had not prepared a plan or smart word. He has been outmanoeuvred. He looks around at Raynott's pristine room.

"You sad old fuckwit," Abley says. In shock, Inspector Abley storms out, so angry at himself and Raynott. He has walked right into Raynott's trap. He'll never get his job back now. Abley rushes out of the police station, but not before bumping into Lemon.

"Sir?" Lemon says, as they brush shoulders in the corridor.

"Sergeant," Abley replies.

"Are you back?" Sergeant Lemon asks.

"Not yet, just sorting things out, but I will be soon. Hang in there." Abley pats Lemon's arm and walks off, leaving Lemon confused and a little irked.

26
AN INSPECTOR CALLS

Elizabeth Green has come back home. "Hello Bertie, hello Soot!" she calls. She closes the door, and everything is quiet, apart from the dogs fussing at her feet. Bertie comes to the top of the stairs, pleased to see her, now staring intently. She feels for Bertie, having to share his home with the Afghans. He walks down to Elizabeth, swiping Monty out of the way and starts to brush himself up against Elizabeth. She walks to the kitchen and shakes the treats. Immediately the two dogs sit, and Bertie jumps up on the side, and Soot rushes in too. All the treats are dished out, and a state of milling about returns to the animals' behaviour.

Elizabeth walks into the drawing room, followed by Bertie, Monty, Hector and Soot, half expecting to find Godric asleep under a blanket, his new favourite pastime it seems this Michaelmas term. But the room is empty. She wants to talk to him about Wallis, and what he did letting Hector out. That boy just cannot come into the house in future.

She picks up two glasses from the table and hears laughter coming from Gerald's study, then a smash. Elizabeth walks through and opens the door. Wallis is swinging Gerald's oar around the room and has hit a framed photograph, now lying in pieces on the floor. Elizabeth is frozen, looking at the image half under Wallis's feet a photograph of her late husband enjoying a moment in Paris up the Tour Montparnasse, with the Eifel Tower sparkling in the background. She watches in horror and spots Godric's face change from laughter to guilt, as he looks at what Wallis has done and immediately runs to pick up the photograph, broken glass now in the carpet. Elizabeth just stares at Godric.

"It's only a photograph," Wallis says, "Here, give it here." Wallis grabs the photograph from Godric and is about to wipe it with his sleeve, trying to make things better, but Elizabeth can see it is grubby from rowing and slightly overreacts.

"Stop. Give it here!" She grabs the photograph. "Get out! Get out!" Elizabeth screams at Wallis, the photograph of her late husband creased and scratched. Wallis is shocked and looks at Godric, then starts to leave.

"Don't leave." Godric says to Wallis, then looks at his nanna. "Bunny, he didn't mean it. Come on. It would be lovely if everyone could be friends. I'll buy a new frame." But before Elizabeth can calm down, Monty and Hector rush in, and immediately she is fearful they may tread on the glass. She quickly leaves the room holding their collars and shuts them in the kitchen. Then comes back with a vacuum cleaner and starts to hit at Wallis's feet with the end.

"I'm going," Wallis huffs.

"You thoughtless, unpleasant young man!" Elizabeth raises her voice.

"All right grandma, keep your wig on." Wallis raises his eyebrows and leaves, dropping the oar on the floor, so it bounces. Elizabeth rushes over to the oar and picks it up. She stands in the broken glass. "I can't deal with this," Wallis says as a parting gesture to Godric, "too much drama," and Elizabeth hears the front door open then slam as she is lifting the oar.

"I'm sorry about the glass," Godric says. "Grandpa wouldn't have minded Wallis looking at his oar." Godric takes the oar and puts it back.

"Why are you being like this?" Elizabeth says.

"What?" Godric replies.

"Why are you doing this to me?" Elizabeth replies.

"I'm sorry. He's my boyfriend, and you seem intent on ruining it."

"You've just had a boyfriend staying here for the best part of two-and-a-half months."

"Only because he was a good cook and walked the dogs!" Godric raises his voice at his nanna.

"You don't exactly volunteer," Elizabeth reminds her grandson.

"This is like I'm hearing my mother right now!"

"The animals could get their feet cut. Sometimes I wonder, I don't know, what your plan is?" Elizabeth says.

"What?" Godric can't believe what he's hearing.

"Fooling around," Elizabeth replies.

"Maybe it would be better for everyone if I move out and live in college," Godric says quietly, shaking his head.

Elizabeth stops what she is doing for a moment as does Godric. Godric's last words are hanging in the air. She doesn't know what to say. She doesn't want him to move out. Why would he be so ridiculous, so dramatic? But she cannot bring herself to stop him, to tell him he's being stupid, as maybe he wants to leave. Perhaps he's been looking for an opportunity to bring it up, and she's just been blinkered, ignoring the signs. She doesn't want to force him to stay if he doesn't want to, so she turns the vacuum back on and pushing it across the study floor beneath Godric's feet.

The doorbell goes, so she leaves Godric with the vacuum

and goes to answer, Godric's words still ringing in her ears. What did he mean, where did that come from? Elizabeth opens the door. It is Inspector Abley, looking worse for wear. Godric slips out the gap in the front door, not bothering to say goodbye but instead putting on his aviator shades and jacket and bumping into the Inspector, leaving Elizabeth perplexed. But Inspector Abley leans against the door frame, very drunk. He doesn't notice the departure of Elizabeth's grandson. Elizabeth is aware the dogs are shut in the kitchen and are scratching the door down.
"Come in then. I was looking for you earlier," she says impatiently. Smelling like a brewery, the Inspector staggers into the dining room and straight onto the sofa.
"I just need to sleep. Then I'll be gone," Abley slurs a little.
"What?" But before Elizabeth can ask him why he is not at home or isn't there a friendly hotel or friend where he can stay, Inspector Abley has sat down on the sofa and is now stretched out its full length. "You can't sleep there. I have come home to think about the case, which is what you should be doing." But as she finishes her sentence, Bob Abley rolls away from her and starts snoring. So Elizabeth knows there is only one thing for it. She goes to the kitchen and releases the dogs. Almost immediately Hector and Monty rush out and over to the Inspector. They start to lick Abley's face. Abley raises his shoulders, but there is no stopping them. In the end, he sits up.
"Bravo," he says, rubbing the spit from his cheeks.
"You should be on this case. Lemon is no closer to finding the person who hit Professor Crowhams. And neither am I," Elizabeth says.
"Oh, we're not on that again are we?" Abley puts his head in his hands.
"Well if you will pop by," Elizabeth replies.
"I just want to sleep." Abley groans.
"Home, hotels?" she asks.
"You have the best beer." He looks towards the kitchen.
"At ten-thirty in the morning? Oh no, no. We've been here

before."
"Just a nice cold one, you pour them so well," Abley replies.
"If you're staying here, then I'm going to the department." Elizabeth picks up her coat and keys.
"I asked him for my job back, and he said no," Abley shouts to Elizabeth who is now in the hallway. She stops what she is doing and comes back.
"What? You spoke to the Super?" she asks. "Lemon was saying today was the last day. I knew you'd go in, can't keep away eh?" Elizabeth smiles, relieved.

"You're not listening. He said no." Abley replies quietly. Elizabeth pauses, not sure she heard correctly.
"He can't. You're only suspended," She says. "Did you turn up to all the sober check-ins and counselling?" Elizabeth sees Abley's face, indicating that he did no such thing. She can also see that he is clearly drunk and wonders if he went in drunk. "You didn't go to him like this?"
"Of course not," Abley slurs, frowning.
"Well then, they can't sack you for that. They weren't compulsory."

"He insisted that my motivation is not genuine, that I'm only doing it for my wife."

"That's not true!" Elizabeth is cross at hearing this.

"Isn't it?" Abley says, defeated by it all.

"What, you're a rubbish copper who only takes cases involving knitting and baking that she'd be interested in?" Elizabeth says sarcastically.
"Apparently Raynott can suggest my contract is terminated." Abley flaps his arms in the air.
"On what grounds?" Elizabeth asks.

"He's got the power."
"He's got no heart or soul," Elizabeth replies.

"No." Abley tries to smile, but his face falls again.

"He has no wife," Elizabeth reminds Abley.

"Mine isn't answering my calls," Abley replies.

"But I thought she was just getting her bearings?"

Abley just shrugs, so Elizabeth passes Abley his shoes and adds, "Well, he can't sack you. Here, come." Elizabeth drags Abley into the study, making sure the dogs don't follow because of the glass, and she sits down at the desk and opens her email. Abley looks at the mess and wonders if he is seeing things.

"It was good to meet you this morning, and confirm that I will be back at work in the next two days—" Elizabeth writes. "If I email this to you, you can copy and paste it into one from you to him," she says to her friend.

"I can't. I'm supposed to be in the Canaries with Maureen," Abley says, a little more upbeat. "I'm going on holiday."

"That's a silly idea." Elizabeth frowns at her friend.

"I've made my choice," Abley says.

"Does Maureen know you are jeopardising your career for a week in the sun?"

"Two weeks." Abley looks sheepish.

"Does she know it will conflict?" Elizabeth asks.

"How can she?" he replies.

"You haven't told her… about the holiday?" Elizabeth is aghast. "What if she—"

"Don't jinx it," Abley says.

Elizabeth shakes her head as she writes a draft email from Bob to the Super. "… I will be back at work this month. I will confirm a date with you by tomorrow. Best wishes, Robert Abley."

"No one calls me Robert, I don't call myself Robert," Bob says.

"No one writes letters to their friend's boss for their friends. Here, send that from your email account. They switch seats. "I don't trust Raynott as far as I can throw him. If your deadline is today, you want to get in writing that you told him you were coming back. The ball is now in his court to fire you. Smoke him out, call his bluff. Keep a record of everything. And get back to work. A man has been murdered. Lemon needs you." Elizabeth picks up her keys and walks to the front door.

"No, he needs you," Abley says quietly, but Elizabeth hears.

"We are investigating a possible murder case. And this Professor Crowhams, from the break-in, he's the main suspect in my mind. We need a good Inspector."

"Oh yes, it's always a bloody academic who kills someone. He's bound to be guilty, with his stuck-up toffee-nosed ruddy self-important prat guilt. Bloody murderers the lot of them. What's a bunch of academics at the bottom of the Cam, a ruddy start that's what." Abley gets up, walks into the kitchen and opens the fridge to help himself, something he has done many times before. "Bingo." Abley spots a large pie, with crusted pastry nipped around the edges. It's clearly not one of Elizabeth's but still in its box from the shop. He takes it out, gets a knife to slice into it. His phone goes, and he takes it out in case it is Maureen as he picks up a slice to shovel into his mouth. But he sees Lemon's number and cuts the call. "Good dog." Abley tastes the pie. Monty and Hector are now both begging. Just as he is offering them both a little piece of pie each, Elizabeth comes back in and finds him stealing from the fridge. She says nothing, just picks up the leads puts them on Hector and Monty and then walks towards the door.

"Use a plate!" She shouts before slamming the door.

27
COMMON RIGHTS

It seems Elizabeth cannot find a minute to herself. Everything is off kilter. She's never been keen on Mondays... And with this one, if it isn't Godric's love life, it's Abley drunk in her home. How can she think, it all swirls around in her head in one big mess, with Emily badgering her every few hours, reminding her to dress smartly for dinner this week and being so cryptic about the whole thing? But Elizabeth has to think about the case before any sense from it slips away. Walking the dogs on Jesus Green is all she has left to find a quiet place before she has to head into the Department of Plant Sciences to give a lecture.

Monty and Hector trot over Jesus Lock Bridge and then run full pelt across the Green. They find a playmate in the shape of a greyhound, and they are off. Elizabeth tries to turn her mind to the case, but just as she starts to think through everything she hears sirens. Not again. She wonders where they are going. At least Midsummer Common is peaceful this lunchtime as she crosses onto its grass from across Victoria Avenue and walks under the trees, some of the largest among the two hundred and forty thousand in the City, each one with a different story. She passes the people sitting by the river on benches spaced along the path: lovers stealing a moment, gentlemen watching the rowers in the boathouses, and young women reading novels about heroes. But as she approaches Riverside, she hears more sirens.

It doesn't take Elizabeth long before she's on Stourbridge Common and sees where they have come to a halt. The gate is open, and two police cars are pulled up on the towpath. Further along from that, there is a vet's horsebox, and three horses are down on the Common. The vet and his assistant are listening to the heart of a conker-coloured mare.

"Lemon." Elizabeth greets him.

"Professor Green, we meet again." Lemon turns and nods.

"More poisoning?" She asks.

"He hasn't said. He's called for two more horse boxes and a winch," Lemon replies.

Elizabeth puts both Afghans back on the lead and gives them to Sergeant Lemon to hold for a moment as he stands by the police taped cordon, before walking over to the vet.

"Decreased heart rate?" The vet says to his assistant. "Panting and runny eyes?" the vet continues.

"They're panting too, bright pink gums, a witness saw them stumbling about with dizziness before calling the police apparently." The vet finishes speaking to his assistant then looks up and sees Elizabeth.

"Elizabeth Green," Robert Likeley says.

"Robert Likeley," Elizabeth replies, pleased it is Robert helping these poor creatures.

The vet puts a couple of fingers up at Elizabeth for her to be quiet. He goes back to listening to the heart, before making a decision and beckons his assistant.

"If we can get a drip into this one, sodium nitrate, and the oxygen. I'll come back for the car." He says to his assistant, "Please ride with him." As he finishes the winch arrives and two more horse boxes, to help transport the horses back to the vets. The other two horses are well enough to stand and are put straight in the boxes by assistants. The vet flags the van with the winch over to the most unwell horse.

"Cyanide?" Elizabeth asks.

"Can't hurt, until we're sure. Don't want to take a chance on this one. His vitals are falling. How are you?" Robert Likeley says, smiling at Elizabeth.

"Yes, good thanks." Elizabeth looks at Robert, her local vet. She has always liked vets more than most and likes Robert very much.

"How's that black cat of yours? Soot?" he asks.

"Fine now, seems to be adjusting. Not skinny anymore," she replies.

"He's a lucky fellow." The vet smiles. Elizabeth nods.

"Well, I'd better get on," Robert says.

"Thanks for the samples. I found them thirty percent over normal concentrations too. What d'you think happened?" Elizabeth says.

"Someone was trying to harm them, maybe kill them most probably. You're the detective. Right, I'd better—" Robert Likeley stands up and starts to walk over to the winch, but not before looking back at Elizabeth. "You look good," he adds.

Elizabeth watches Robert walk away. She wants to correct him, tell him that she's a scientist, not a detective. But somehow he doesn't give her the opportunity.

"Professor." Elizabeth turns and sees Sarah.

"You're back?" Elizabeth says.

"Yes, I just needed to pick things up. Are they going to be okay?" Sarah says, upset, looking at the horses.

"Did you see anything?" Elizabeth asks, now spotting Lemon still holding the dogs behind her.

"No, we've just got back from the department," Sarah says. Joe appears from behind Sarah.

"Inspector," Joe says.

"I'm not an Inspector, Joe. Just call me Professor Green." Elizabeth doesn't much like this man, who appears to be everywhere. Elizabeth watches Joe stroke Sarah's arm and spots the tiniest flinch from Sarah.

"You should be resting. Cyanide poisoning is not a walk in the park. Your body needs sleep," Elizabeth tells Sarah.

"Yes, I think you're right," she replies. "Will the horses be okay? Is this the same thing all over again?"

"It looks like it," Lemon says as he walks over.

"So someone was trying to hurt the horses then?" Joe asks.

"Nothing is clear yet," Elizabeth says. "Is someone trying to harm the horses or people? Was this meant for you, Sarah?" Elizabeth asks as she sees that someone has left Sarah some baked goods with a get-well card.

"You're not eating that!" Joe says and throws it in the water. Elizabeth rolls her eyes and shouts to Lemon.

"Think you might need to get in the water and recover some evidence," she says.

"While I'm holding your dogs?" Lemon asks.

28
SABOTAGE

Professor Nigel Crowhams peeks around the corner of a corridor in the Department of Galileo to see if he can see anyone. When the coast is clear, he sneaks into his colleague's room, where Elizabeth and Lemon had been interviewing Sarah and Joe earlier this morning. The place is empty, but the computer is still on. He hears colleagues or students walk by the door, and cannot risk being spotted, so shuts the door behind him.

Professor Crowhams sits down at the computer and starts to open software spreadsheets, searching for something. He clicks on different documents and grows a little frustrated, also aware that someone might walk in and discover what he is doing. He has already invented a lie for anyone who finds him to say he is checking that Tom's research papers have all been submitted, in case anything is pending that the Department of Galileo could help to get published posthumously. It takes a while searching and clicking through countless files, but then he spots what he is looking for, a document titled, 'An Evening of Stars on

Stourbridge Common'.

Professor Crowhams tuts, and then clicks on what looks like a mailing list. He starts to compose an email, while still listening out for anyone coming. He capitalises the words 'all events cancelled until further notice' and makes them bold before hitting 'send' to the mailing list. He shuts everything down and wipes the keyboard of his prints then stands up to go. He sees a photograph of Sarah, Tom and some horses in the background and cannot help himself. He pushes it off the desk and watches it smash on the floor, before turning and closing the door behind him.

29
CYANIDE

Elizabeth just makes it in time as she walks into the Department of Sciences lecture hall on Downing Street. The University auditorium is already packed. Year Four undergraduates sit squished in, some on the stairs up at the back, to hear Professor Elizabeth Green talk about poison. More specifically, she is delivering her fifth lecture in the series on toxicology. This is always popular with the students, who have other important but often drier lectures on things like how to map ribonucleic acid, which to some is more like computer code than anything they can relate to in real life. Most all students are aware of Professor Green's relationship with the police, so hope to hear some titbits of crime stories.

"So today we are going to talk about cyanide. This isn't on the curriculum but nevertheless is a poison derived from plants, a natural poison rather than anything manufactured by chemists. Although you can get synthetic cyanide, we won't be talking about that today. Mother nature does it best. Can anyone tell me where one can find the cyanide in a concentrated form in nature?" A sea of hands go up, Elizabeth looks at the students all keen to show her how intelligent they are. One young man in the front row is laughing with his friends. So she points to him. "You!" she says firmly.

"I never put my hand up?" He looks around, confused, to his friends, shaking his head.

"Nevertheless, you are, are you not a final-year natural sciences undergraduate who has chosen to specialise in plant science?" Elizabeth replies, walking closer.

"Yes," he says nervously.

"So this is basic A-level stuff, Mr Panfrey."

"Apples?" he offers.

"It's true. Apples contain a compound called amygdalin in their seeds, a cyanide and sugar-based molecule. If chewed, the apple seed can split the sugar from the cyanide. If enough cyanide is consumed, and a fatal dose for humans can be as low as 1.5 milligrams per kilogram of body weight, then symptoms will start including stomach cramps, headache, nausea, vomiting, ending in cardiac arrest, respiratory failure, coma and death." Elizabeth smiles at Mr Panfrey, adding, "Well, there are many plants in truth that have cyanide levels in them which are non-trivial. Don't ever be in an enclosed space with cherry laurel leaves, as they can emit high levels of cyanide and, as you well know from this poison, one doesn't have to ingest to be affected. Just breathing it in can be enough to prove fatal."

The students emit sighs of surprise, thinking they knew everything about cyanide, but never having heard about the room and cherry leaves. "Cyanide is found in the pits of green plums, which some studies have shown have the highest amygdalin, followed by black plums, peaches, apricots, red cherries and then apples." Elizabeth continues, "References to those studies are in your notes handed out for this lecture. Please do read. Mr Panfrey, I have some cherry stones cut open up here. Would you like to sample them?" She beckons Mr Panfrey up on stage, and he climbs up and picks up one of the stones. "What are you doing? Sit back down! These are poison. Here, have chocolate instead." The lecture room erupts with laughter at Mr Panfrey's idiocy. He then plays the fool, completely unphased. Elizabeth throws Mr Panfrey a bar of chocolate, which he holds up and baits the crowd with before biting into it.

"Is it true you are working on the case where they found those horses poisoned by cyanide?" Mr Panfrey asks.

"I'm not a vet, but I've seen the news reports just like you," Elizabeth replies.

"When I grow up I want to be just like you, investigating murders." Mr Panfrey shouts, so many can hear, then bites into his chocolate.

"Mr Panfrey, if you ever grow up it will be a miracle." Elizabeth raises her eyebrows, adding, "But should it ever happen, make sure you read more than four books a year, listen to your wife as she will most certainly always be right, and perhaps get a dog, as you will need someone wise around you."

30
PROFESSIONAL ENEMIES

Elizabeth has just got back home from her lecture this afternoon. There is no Godric, and no message on the answerphone from him requesting something or other. In fact, Foxes Haven feels very quiet. Inspector Abley is fast asleep on the sofa snoring. And Hector and Monty are also asleep, breaking wind and hardly lift a head when she stands at the door. So she decides to leave them all and head out to the bakery. But she is hardly out the door when she bumps into Ed, the Lock Keeper, running towards Stourbridge Common.

"Hey, what's the hurry?" she asks from the other side of the river.

"It's the boats. They are adrift. I've been called to go and see if I can help get all the boats back to their moorings. Sorry, can't stop." Ed rushes off, but Elizabeth catches up with him as they hurry now along the river path. By the time she gets to the boats, there is a police car, and Lemon is there again, scratching his head.

"We got a call that all the boats had been let off their

moorings and that there were a couple of sunken dinghies. Ordinarily I wouldn't have come, but—" Lemon tells Elizabeth.

"Is anyone on them?" But as soon as Elizabeth asks she sees the Constable rowing out to the boats to check. "Sad news about more horses being poisoned isn't it?" she says.

"We've checked with the vet, and his tests confirm cyanide again, in high concentrations like before too," Lemon adds. "But they were all administered with medicine and are going to be okay."

"I think it is murder and attempted murder." Elizabeth says and looks at Lemon. "I've also seen the Inspector. He came to my house after he'd seen the Super, who is trying to sack him."

"What?" Lemon is shocked, his eyes watching as the police Constable climbs out of a dinghy onto the first canal boat and picks up the tow rope and throws it to another Constable on the bank. The first Constable then disappears down into the boat. Both Lemon and Elizabeth can see him walking from one end to the next. Then he climbs up on deck and shouts, "It's empty, apart from a cat."

He throws the other rope then jumps back into the dinghy to row to the next canal boat. There must be about eight boats adrift, and some have gone far down the river. It takes the police over an hour to tie each boat to moorings, most probably in the wrong place. The policeman checks every boat and they are all empty.

"I would not have thought that they are at work, but perhaps everyone's just busy," Lemon says.

"What's the point?" Elizabeth asks. "Of releasing them from their moorings. A warning?"

"I don't know. In fact, I have no idea. I'm stumped," says Sergeant Lemon. They both look at the plant pots from the boat decks that have been chucked in the water. Geraniums are bobbing and floating nearby, apparently having been dislodged from their containers, which have long sunk. A closer look at the canal boats also reveals that mud has been wiped all over the windows. Perhaps from the plant pots before they were flung. It maybe an attempt to vandalise the boats and leave a message.

"No broken windows," Elizabeth says. "Where are Sarah, Joe, the other boat dwellers?" But Lemon just shakes his head. He has no idea. "They were just here. I was here earlier," Elizabeth explains to Lemon. "Something about this is not right. I think someone was trying to hurt them, arrived and there was some kind of skirmish. Perhaps they ran?" Elizabeth says to Lemon.

"The Super wants to see me. I think he's going to put Pober on the case with me." Sergeant Lemon sighs.

"We can't let that happen." Elizabeth says. "Don't go in. Stay busy. Raynott's got it in for Bob."

"I can't do this on my own," Lemon shrugs. "Apart from anything else, I can't be in two places at the same time. I got a call from Professor Crowhams about some office break-in, someone has been on his computer in his office apparently. He ordered me to go in."

"You're not on your own, but perhaps you can go and see him alone. I'm going after this to take my results into Leedham to check," Elizabeth says. "I found high concentrations of cyanide. And this second horse poisoning is possibly the same thing. One minute everything points to the horses. No one appears to have been harmed this second time. Then this happens to the boats, which has nothing to do with the horses." Elizabeth is confused.

"Aside from seeing Professor Crowhams about his computer, I have to question everyone at the Department of Galileo." Lemon is hardly listening, he's so tired, "The Super left me a message and asked why I hadn't done this yet. But I've still got to talk to all those who have been poisoned on the boats. Every time I come here, they are gone, and they're not at the hospital. Where are they?"

Lemon thinks out loud, sharing his concerns with Elizabeth.

"They're watching a lunar eclipse night tonight on the Common. The one Sarah was talking about. Do it then. I'll help you," Elizabeth offers. "They'll all be here, stuck in one spot for hours."

"A lunar eclipse?" Lemon asks.

"When the moon passes into the Earth's shadow," Elizabeth replies. "Yes, it is a particularly busy week as there is a Blood Moon later this week too."

"Oh, right." Lemon replies, thinking that's just one more thing he has to attend. That's all he needs.

31
LEMON IS TOLD

Sergeant Lemon has tried Inspector Abley's phone over a dozen times now and left umpteen messages, but heard nothing. A few of the Constables admitted to Lemon that they had seen the Inspector in the Free Press and had sunk a few pints just yesterday evening. And one or two admitted they'd gone back to the bed and breakfast where the Inspector was staying and had shared some beers with the Inspector until the early hours, and how worse for wear they were feeling, but begged Lemon not to tell Inspector Pober.

They said the Inspector was in fine fettle, telling quite a few anecdotes about Superintendent Raynott, but they were sworn to secrecy about sharing them and couldn't if they wanted to, as they were far too drunk by that point and couldn't remember the details. They did remember how Constable Petticoat had fallen off the stool and hit his head, however, and how the Inspector had made him wear a silicone baking mould he'd found behind the bar over his head packed with morello cherries and slices of lemon. Petticoat had screamed and started to cry when the lemon juice had fallen into his eyes, so the Inspector had sung him some of his back catalogue of Northern Soul. That's when they all stuffed olives into their ears. Lemon should have been there.

Sergeant Lemon presumes the Inspector surely must be back home by now, not being told by Elizabeth Green to the contrary, so decides to give him a knock. Park Parade is quiet on this nippy Monday afternoon, and one or two curtains twitch when they see a squad car outside, even though they know a police Inspector lives at the home with the front garden full of winter roses.

Lemon is just wiping the mud off his shoes from Stourbridge Common when the front door opens. It is Mrs Abley. Sergeant Lemon has met Maureen often, usually at staff Christmas parties, the odd retirement party, and sometimes as the sad funeral of a police officer or fireman. Police wives often show up at such events and somehow make them more palatable. He always remembers Maureen for her baked goods and for running the stall or organising the kitchen at these police events. So he is not expecting to find a tanned, slimmer woman, wearing a short dress and with a new bleached blonde haircut standing in front of him. He hardly recognises her.

"Oh hello, Mrs Abley," he says.

"Sergeant Lemon," she replies. Lemon expected her to ask him in, to wait in the kitchen and have a coffee while her husband finishes something upstairs, or watches the end of the golf on the television. He knows Bob Abley has more sports channels than most, probably more than the whole of Park Parade put together, and there is always some golf on somewhere. He's had to sit through a few shots himself while waiting. But one quick glance through the crack in the front door and the house seems empty.

"May I speak with the Inspector?" Lemon asks.

"He's not here," Maureen says.

"Oh," Lemon replies, not sure what to say next.

"He's not staying here," she offers.

"He mentioned he wasn't here last night. I just wondered if he'd returned?" Abley says.

"No." Maureen tries to close the conversation down.

"May I ask, when do you expect him back?"

"I think you should just be in touch through the station."

"Oh," Lemon says again, unsure what to say next.

"If you must know, I'm hoping he gets the message," she says.

"Oh." Lemon starts to feel terribly sad for the Inspector, but cannot tell Mrs Abley just how much his boss was looking forward to getting back together with his wife. How much he'd missed her, was lost without her.

"I'm glad he's not here. Please don't tell him to come. I'll only send him away," she says.

"What?" Lemon is surprised and unsure where to go with their conversation now, "Are you not—?"

"No, we're not," she replies firmly.

"Oh," he says.

"Yes, well, I don't see what business this is of yours." Maureen gets a little shirty.

"Right." Lemon smiles, completely gutted for his boss and feeling like he wants the ground to swallow him up.

"You know, he might be your hero, but he's not mine," Maureen says. "He stopped being that a long time ago when his priorities shifted. Now if you don't mind, I want to shut the door."

Lemon doesn't know what to do. He just looks surprised as the door closes on him.

32
HORSES DOWN BUT NOT OUT

Walking back from Stourbridge Common, having left Sergeant Lemon by the boats saying he'd drop in on Inspector Abley, Elizabeth felt terrible. But she couldn't let Lemon know that right at this minute Bob was sleeping off a hangover at her home. If Lemon turned up, it would just make Bob feel even more shame than he already did and probably cause him to run again to god knows where. And she hopes that when she gets home, Bob Abley may have even rested up enough to talk to her about this case right on her doorstep. She knows these Commons like the back of her hand, the trees, boathouses… How can something so terrible have happened again so close to her home?

Sergeant Lemon's words about Inspector Pober being put on the case too are like a nasty taste in Elizabeth's mouth. She needs to solve the murder and quickly, as she most certainly cannot work alongside the most unpopular Inspector in Cambridgeshire, perhaps the whole of East Anglia. It's not that she's fearful of Pober, more that he's so disagreeable that he makes Elizabeth want to scream. She knows something about how the current internal politics at the station are working. Raynott rewards results. No, if she wants her friend back and working, then she needs to get on with it.

Elizabeth can hear Gerald's voice in her head, telling her to be careful, don't be a hero and not to walk alone on the Commons. Gerald would be happy that she normally has the dogs to keep her company. What she would give for just one last walk along the river path, arm in arm with him. But he has gone, and although she knows he is never coming back, she cannot stop believing that he is with her. He is here to talk to her about the case, here as she thinks about things.

Elizabeth starts to walk towards Professor Crowhams' home on Brunswick Walk, a long parade of houses with just a railing between their front gardens and Midsummer Common. Elizabeth wants to speak with Professor Crowhams as she increasingly wonders if there was a burglary and attack at all up at the Department of Galileo at the old telescope house. Could Crowhams have faked his own injury? It feels a little too convenient that he saw nothing the night he was hit on the head, and that Lemon said the police had found no prints other than those from people in the department. Nor was there any sign of a struggle, nor anything missing. Not even among the Professor's papers.

Add this to the fact that Crowhams seems the least moved by the death of his colleague, despite all of his peers mourning and having started a funding page to continue Tom Mirren's stargazing nights. Crowhams also appears to be the only person in the department to have spoken ill of the boat people. Maybe he had been trying to poison Joe all along, for it was clear he held unkind feelings towards the man.

Then there was Ed the Lock Keeper, as well as Joe, who had been adamant that the person they knew who was most vociferous against the right of these animals to roam the Common was indeed Professor Crowhams. No, Crowhams seemed to have the strongest motive among those interviewed. Elizabeth regretted not having gone up to the Department of Galileo with Lemon to hear all about the Professor's computer.

As Elizabeth walks through the black wrought iron gate separating the grass of the common from a private pathway she realises she has no idea which house is Professor Crowham's. She knocks on the first door. No answer. And another. Elizabeth's first encounter is with a young man who looks like an academic. She can separate town from gown in a second with a series of judgements and is rarely wrong. It might be the tweed jacket, or the books piled up in every corner of the room behind him. But nine times out of ten it is what comes out of their mouths. This academic, however, didn't even know Professor Crowhams was his neighbour, too caught up in his own world. Though he was pleased to hear the news that he has an esteemed neighbour, had heard good things about Crowhams' papers and must pop round with some port soon, he says. Then Elizabeth knocks on the next door. This time a mother with two small children. They don't know Crowhams. Then Elizabeth knocks on the next door. This time an elderly smiley man opens.

"Yes, I know Nigel, he lives next door. You're the lady with the lovely dogs. I see you on the Common a lot. Where are they now?" he asks.

"I was hoping to talk to Professor Crowhams, but he doesn't appear to be in." Elizabeth tells a bare faced lie.

"Come in, I have some dog treats you can take back for your dogs. Are they allowed?" Elizabeth nods at the question. "Lost my Eddy a month ago, kept the treats. I miss them so much," he says of his dog. Elizabeth feels his sorrow.

"You can borrow my two anytime," Elizabeth offers, in case it brings solace to the elderly man.

"Oh yes, I'd like that. What are their names?" the man asks.

"Hector and Monty," Elizabeth replies. "Sleeping off their morning walk as we speak." She pauses just a short while and then asks, "Do you get along with Professor Crowhams? He's a friend of mine," Elizabeth lies, "only, I hope you don't mind me asking. I've always wondered what with his head being in the stars, whether he made friends with his neighbours? I'd hate to think he's alone over here, you know if something happened," she says.

"Oh yes, I understand completely." The elderly man seems quite lonely to Elizabeth, but continues, "it's a nice little community here, we all fit in rather well, and he's very friendly. Always chatting over the fence at the back."

"What about?" She asks.

"Horses mainly. He hates them," he says. "Always conjuring up new ways to keep them away from our properties."

"Hmm, they're beautiful creatures," Elizabeth replies, a little depressed by the man's words. But the man doesn't hear.

"He's an angel keeping them vermin out of my back garden too," the elderly man continues.

"Vermin?" Elizabeth doesn't like the sound of this.

"Cats. Nasty creatures. Digging up my petunias, pooing all over my chamomile." His face starts to screw up.

"How does he keep them at bay?" Elizabeth dares to ask.

"Oh, you're going to laugh at this," he replies. "He has a water pistol. One with a pumping action you know, like the children have these days. Powerful." The man chuckles.

"Water pistol?" Elizabeth is shocked.

"More like a water cannon." The man now has built up to a laugh. "But when it doesn't work, he has the pellet gun. Got one right on the backside. Oh, how it jumped!"

"And what about the horses?" Elizabeth asks.

"Oh, I wish he could shoot those. They only thing they are good for is to place a bet on. Why on earth they're allowed to roam around here. What's the sense in it?" The man shakes his head, exasperated.

"Yes, Nigel says he doesn't like them." Elizabeth baits the man.

"Oh, he loathes those horses as much as me. Send them off to the glue factory." The man's face has turned so hateful.

"Right, I'd better get home back to the dogs." Elizabeth says, making her excuses.

"Ah, a pair of darlings. I'll take you up on those cuddles. Walk them for you if you like?"

"Right, thank you. I'll bear that in mind," Elizabeth says, but she privately thinks when hell freezes over.

As Elizabeth starts to walk back home, it's a surprise that she bumps into Professor Crowhams walking towards her across the Common.

"I've just knocked for you, Professor," she says.

"Oh, you found my attacker?" Crowhams sounds bored.

"We are still looking. Hopefully, it won't be long. Do you think it is related to the attacks on the boat dwellers?" she asks.

"What, you mean the horse attacks?" Crowhams asks. "Well, I don't know about that. If they will feed the horses, then perhaps they got too close to whatever killed them."

"Oh, I'm sure they were all poisoned," Elizabeth says.

"Good," he replies.

"The only thing is, Professor, it's strange, don't you think? I mean to poison some horses, and then do it all over again. Poison more horses? Surely if someone meant ill to the horses wouldn't at least one of them be dead, rather than Tom Mirren? And you're the only one in your department who doesn't like the horses. Yet all the attacks this week have been to people in your department, and—"

"And I'm ruddy well one of those people attacked!" Professor Crowhams interrupts. Elizabeth thinks how he looks so guilty and continues to study his face as he talks, "I'm not happy someone is dead, but Tom was a proverbial pain where the sun doesn't shine, he was always pushing for change for change's sake."

"I'm not sure who you hate the most," Elizabeth asks Crowhams. "Is it Tom for being a rival in your department, or Sarah or even Joe for feeding the horses?"

"Who said anything about them?" Crowhams replies.

"Why, you. You said that Joe may have sabotaged your telescope. Is there a vendetta against him, or him against you?" she asks.

"You'll have to ask him. I don't know his comings or goings, just that he's a most unpleasant man." Crowhams replies.

"And what of Sarah?" Elizabeth asks.

"What of her? If pushed I'd say she needs a good bath." Crowhams looks at Elizabeth and raises his eyebrows. "Well really, living on a boat and coming in stinking of a wood burning stove and dirty clothes? She stinks out the lecture hall. She's as bad as Tom. Both of them trying to make the public understand the stars. As if."

"Perhaps you see them as rivals. Perhaps Tom was your first victim?" Elizabeth pushes Crowhams.

"Hang on. What? You can't go around accusing people of murder!" Crowhams is cross at Elizabeth.

"I'm only asking you what Sergeant Lemon would ask if he were here."

"I've already seen him, and he most certainly didn't ask me that and if I'm not much mistaken you are a Fellow at Granta and not a police officer so that I will bid you a good day." Crowhams walks off.

"I will see you later. Going to be eating in your college tonight." Elizabeth shouts to him.

"Well, I'm sure you will enjoy the swan the kitchens are

preparing for supper," he shouts back at her.

And with that Professor Crowhams walks off, leaving Elizabeth reeling as she looks at Jesus Green and can just see Victoria College through the foliage. Are they really going ahead with that?

33
AN APPLE A DAY

Elizabeth cannot believe that Inspector Abley is still sound asleep on her sofa when she gets home now so late in the afternoon. She is very tempted to wake him up. In fact, she puts the radio on to see if that will do it, but nothing. She even lets the dogs lick him again, but he just mumbles something and snuggles into their hair. In the end, she throws a blanket over him, grabs her bicycle from the back porch and peddles over to the Cambridge Police Head Quarters.

It's getting dark now, especially as the clocks have recently fallen back and autumn's claws have replaced British Summertime. Elizabeth pedals over Magdalene Bridge down Bridge Street, along Sidney Street and on to St Andrew's Street. Not the fastest route and three of the busiest streets in the City centre, but she wants to stop to buy herself some food, as without Godric at home she forgot her lunch. At this time of year, the tourists are beginning to thin out and be replaced by frightened looking freshers and local shoppers hopping from door to door, laden with bags.

Elizabeth leaves the buzz of the shops behind as she swings off the road onto Parker's Piece and cycles past the University Arms Hotel, all the grand houses and towards a secondary school which shared the Piece with Cambridge Police Station and Cambridge Fire Station. Elizabeth parks her bicycle in a rack and uses her consultant pass to make her way into the pathology lab, where she'd already biked across the results from her laboratory earlier.

Elizabeth is thankful that Leedham isn't in the room at the moment, so she has some peace to herself to double check her work and the samples she looked at in her laboratory. She opens the samples again and a link to the data results. She doesn't need to look under the microscope, as she already has what she wants. It's true, the apples which had made the pie, the apples on the floor beside Tom and Sarah's boat, had huge concentrations of cyanide in them. She can now see from the results here in the Pathology Department here that the stomach contents from Tom, and blood samples from him and the other boat dwellers who had fallen ill, all had huge concentrations of cyanide. It was natural cyanide, and from the report on the apples, it was conclusive that they had been injected with it into the flesh of the apples themselves. Now it's time for Leedham to confirm her findings and take a look at these medical reports from Ripplewater.

"Professor Green." Elizabeth jumps as Sergeant Lemon comes in behind her and greets his friend.

"The vet was right. It is cyanide, injected into the flesh of the apples," Elizabeth tells Sergeant Lemon, adding. "It was lucky that Joe was awake to tell the hospital of his suspicions. I'm sure that's what Joe cottoned onto, given they were around his feet and perhaps he saw the horses as he was carried into the ambulance, seemingly the only one awake at that time." She continues. "Otherwise, how would he know the pie had been the contributing factor? This was murder, not accidental poisoning." Elizabeth knows she already has the green light from Superintendent Raynott, following her recent success solving the murder of the porters at All Saints' but doesn't want to step on Lemon's toes.

"I need all the help I can get." Sergeant Lemon replies, "Don't even know where the Inspector is. So you're sure it is murder?" he asks.

"Put it this way... this was no accident. The amount of cyanide was deliberate. Add that to that all the vandalism on the boats. Then whether the killer intended to scare or to murder the victim, they did end up killing them. So if we are getting technical, I guess it could have been manslaughter. But I think it is murder." Elizabeth stares at Lemon.

"Right," Lemon sighs, none the wiser. "We need the Inspector now. This is getting ridiculous. I went to his house, and his wife hadn't seen him. Do you have any idea where he is?"

Elizabeth doesn't want to give Bob's whereabouts away, not while he is in such a fragile state. Best not tell Lemon that he's probably still lying on her sofa watching the golf as he tries to come to terms with Maureen's rejection. They need to hatch a plan to convince Raynott that Bob deserves his job back. Right now, she can't think of a good argument.

"Maybe Professor Crowhams is guilty." Elizabeth tries to throw Lemon off the scent.

"Huh." Lemon raises his eyebrows and picks up a test tube and holds it to the light.

"Careful." Elizabeth takes a sample tube out of Lemon's hands "Cyanide." Lemon wants to drop it but knows this would be a mistake; now he holds it like it is a bomb. "Just place it gently down," she says.

"Poor horses," Lemon finally says, when the tube is back safely in its stand on the desk. "What is it about horses? They neigh?" Lemon thinks. "People ride them," he says. Elizabeth nods for him to keep guessing, so he continues, "They like mints." She continues to look at him for more reasons. "They're in kids' books, they eat hay, they're big, they—"

"Exactly." Elizabeth picks up a report on the desk. Lemon is confused. "They're big," he says. But he still doesn't get it, so Elizabeth puts him out of his misery. "They are so big in fact that the concentrations of poison, as anyone who knew about cyanide would realise, were not in high enough concentrations to kill horses."

"So this was meant for the people?" Lemon asks.

"Or person. I think we might be looking at murder. Sarah cooked the pie, so was it meant for Sarah and Tom. No one knew that all the other boat people would eat it. Someone wanted to kill Sarah and Tom," Elizabeth says, as Lemon stares back at her. They now have more of a case, but still with no motive.

34
PYJAMA PARTY

"I'll kill him," Abley says to Elizabeth as she opens the front door.

"Have I come home to the wrong house? I could have sworn this was mine, but then recently…" Elizabeth looks at the address plaque 'Foxes Haven' on the side of the wall outside, making the point as she looks at Bob Abley who is standing in a pair of Godric's pyjamas, having just come downstairs holding a plate and fork.

"I had a bath, well you told me you'd be back for tea, but then you weren't, and I was tired." He shrugs.

"Has it occurred to you that just because you are officially not working for the Cambridge Police Force, you could still be working for them. There's a computer in there, you could have spent the afternoon doing some research on Professor Crowhams, or found out some more about Dr Tom Mirren or Joe Grader from the boats. Nobody made you eat strawberry cheesecake in the bath." Elizabeth raises her eyebrows.

"He went round there to see Maureen. Made it ten

times worse." Bob Abley cannot hear anything but his own thoughts, swirling around in his head.

"Who went round there? And where?" Elizabeth is confused.

"Bloody Lemon." Abley huffs.

"Why are you in my grandson's pyjamas?" Elizabeth asks.

"Because my clothes smell, so I put them in the wash. They are already in the drier, s'okay?" he asks.

"But you could have worn some of—"

Bob Abley looks at Elizabeth and smiles, interrupting her.

"No, these are fine," he replies.

"Well, put the kettle on then and make yourself useful," Elizabeth says.

"He's sent everything backwards," Abley continues, walking into the kitchen, scratching his head.

"Of course he hasn't." Elizabeth is irritated by his complaining.

"She called my phone. I was in the bath. I didn't hear it. She left me a message. She was fuming. Listen." Abley pulls his phone out of Godric's pyjama pocket, and presses play on the voicemail, "Here listen to this." And the phone message plays: "It's me. Can you not send your fan club round? I think I know you better than they do. They don't know how hard you are to live with. Just stop pressuring me, alright? I need time to think. I don't know. I just don't know anymore." And Maureen hangs up.

"I don't know what she's talking about." Elizabeth fronts it out.

The Inspector plays message two: "Oh and tell Elizabeth that I don't need her advice, and she can't have the lemon tree back if that's what she's angling for. It's mine. She gave it to me for my birthday. If I want to kill it, I will."

"What? She can't do that!" Elizabeth says. Abley shakes his head at her. So she adds, "I didn't ask for it back. I asked her if she'd brought it in from the cold. I left you explicit instructions with the tree, but I'm not sure of your wife's care for such a precious plant. It's a fine specimen. Brought that back all the way from Capri. Growing lemons every year. Oh no," Elizabeth says, "how can she kill that?"

"It's our plant now, it was a present. You gave it away," Abley replies.

"Are you ready for bed, or not dressed yet… it's hard to tell." Elizabeth tries to force herself to stop thinking about the tree.

"How's she going to see me now? I'm banned from home. I don't have anywhere to go, no job. I can't exactly walk up and down outside our home."

"Forget about it tonight." Elizabeth privately thinks her friend is well shot of his wife, but can't tell him that just yet. "Come with me to see the stargazing on Stourbridge Common."

"I can see the stars out the window. My clothes are drying," he replies.

"I think you need to get out," she says.

Elizabeth takes Bob upstairs. There she opens Gerald's wardrobe. Everything is as it was. Some of his suits are in covers to protect them from mothballs, but she picks out a pair of midnight blue fine lined corduroys, and a big grey jumper, far too big for even her to wear.

"I can't," he says.

"He'd want you to." And Elizabeth takes down a shirt. "Come on, come and help me on this case."

35
STARGAZING

The moon looks ten times bigger tonight, lit up in the sky with reds and oranges as if it was on fire, which is why the *Cambridge Herald* has the headline 'Blood Moon Soon'. The blood moon will be here in a few days. In preparation, the Department of Galileo has put on a stargazing event, the first of two with the second in Grantchester later in the week. Little children have come out to gawp at the wonders above their heads in the sky. To see with the naked eye the many impact craters on the Moon's surface and the lines where the ancient lava flowed, their young minds imagining interplanetary galactic battles and war scars. Their parents, meanwhile, taking a breath from duty and responsibility to gaze at its remarkable beauty.

The River Cam is sparkling in the night, capturing the moon's fiery image below until broken by the glide of a swan, dispersing reflections across the surface until they hit the canal boats, the river bank and sleeping moorhens. Bicycles, not generally out at this time, swish and ting along the river path, heading to the gathering. People wrapped up in coats and mittens congregate on the grass, laughing and chatting. An industrious food stall has parked up by the children's play area, and is selling candy floss, toffee apples, roasted chestnuts, jacket potatoes, hot chocolate, as those milling around it agree it is 'just like the old days'.

Holding a stargazing event on Stourbridge Common just two nights before the county's biggest firework display and bonfire celebrations on Midsummer Common was probably not the department's best record of proper planning. But then they could not exactly plan the timing of the Blood Moon later this week either and wanted to offer public open nights on both sides of the city. Barriers and temporary fences for the big firework and bonfire night are already impeding the Stourbridge Common stargazing public from easily finding their way. However, with his priorities being to look after Sarah now, earlier on Joe had plastered lampposts with posters of arrows and stars to make sure the event went as smoothly as possible tonight.

By the time Elizabeth and Inspector Abley arrive there is a crowd of at least a hundred people wandering between ten or so portable telescopes, all roped off for protection with everyone taking turns to look at the already huge Moon. Other members of the Department of Galileo have also brought very powerful binoculars, especially for the little toddlers. They are not so interested in listening to the dry facts about Jupiter and its Moons until told that there are also galaxies far, far away.

Elizabeth has done her best to catch Inspector Abley up on the case on the way over and on arrival she wastes no time in looking for those involved. She spots Sarah, Tom's girlfriend, helping someone stargaze and nods to say hello. Sarah is standing with her friend who Elizabeth remembers was at the hospital, Talya. Inspector Abley follows behind.

"A very popular event." Elizabeth offers her

observation to Sarah, "I wonder what the Common will look like after so many people have trampled it tonight?"

"Professor Green." Sarah smiles and passes a gentleman a pair of binoculars and points upwards at something. "Hello, glad you could make it." Sarah still looks white and sickly. Talya gives the man a seat so that he can relax.

"Is it usual to get this number of people out to look at the stars?" Elizabeth asks Sarah.

"Oh yes, sometimes more." Sarah replies, "These events are growing in popularity. We're doing another one this week down on Grantchester Meadows too. It is darker down there. But this one is more popular, closer to a larger residential location I suppose."

"Are you okay?" Elizabeth notices Sarah's sweaty hue.

"I've told her she should go and lie down," Talya replies. Sarah strokes Talya's arm, catching her jumper in Talya's bracelet, one of those bracelets with charms attached. There are little stars, a moon, unicorns, and she spots the letter T on it.

"We're joined at the hip, Professor," Sarah says clinging onto Talya. Sarah feels something in her hand. "Nice bracelet," she says to Talya, feeling the bracelet around her friend's wrist and watching it sparkle in the night, detaching her jumper.

"Why do you need to show people the stars? Surely they can just look up at night?" Elizabeth interrupts the friends.

"We have some powerful telescopes, so people can see much more than they could themselves. Without knowing very much, it's hard not to get caught up in the beauty of a nearly full moon. Look at it, Professor, isn't it breathtaking?" Sarah offers a very silent Inspector Abley a pair of binoculars. He takes them and smiles, looking through them at the stars.

"It is, as you say, lovely. But I wonder, should you be working?" Elizabeth says.

Talya looks at Inspector Abley now, wondering who he is. Realising Elizabeth hasn't introduced him.

"Inspector Abley." He introduces himself to Talya and Sarah, as Elizabeth has no time for names.

"Oh, hello." Talya is a little surprised.

"Yes, the Inspector here has been looking at the case which we are pretty sure is murder." Elizabeth says matter-of-factly to Talya. Inspector Abley looks at Elizabeth, in no doubt that she is testing these two women, but also not wanting to join in any of Elizabeth's games.

"Cambridge Police are investigating the death of Tom Mirren thoroughly, as you would expect," Abley adds, "and will need to speak with you both again I am sure at some point, to go through the events of that night. Just to check statements."

"Of course," Talya replies. "If it means you catch Tom's killer. Whether they meant to kill Tom or not, the fact is he is dead. So that's murder in my book," she says.

"It might be manslaughter if it was unintentional," Abley corrects her.

"But we have enough evidence to suspect it was murder," Elizabeth adds.

"Do we?" the Inspector unhelpfully replies.

"Yes." Elizabeth glares at him.

"Where's Joe?" Elizabeth asks Sarah.

"He's around here somewhere," Talya replies. "I keep telling Sarah she needs to rest. We can look after this evening."

"He's been so lovely to me, so kind," Sarah says of Joe. "I couldn't have got this to happen, especially not so close to T—." She pauses, "he's been a real shoulder to lean on." Sarah takes a breath and looks away from Elizabeth and up at the moon for a moment, then continues, "He's not even technically working, and shouldn't be spending all his spare time helping me. He doesn't get paid for this. He's more—"

"Messing about with plants?" Elizabeth finishes

Sarah's sentence.

"Bit like you." Abley turns and smiles at Elizabeth, then he spots Maureen, and his heart skips a beat. Elizabeth sees and pulls him towards her.

"Just ignore her," she says. "She's just having a lovely evening, with her head in the stars." Then to Sarah, "We have it confirmed that you were poisoned by cyanide. Very nasty indeed by fruit in the apple pie. At first, we thought it was meant for the Stourbridge horses, but the apples you ate had much higher concentrations of cyanide than the amount in their stomachs. Where did you get the apples you used to cook the pie?" Elizabeth asks.

"From Tom—" Sarah is interrupted by Joe, who sees Elizabeth talking to Sarah and rushes over.

"What am I missing? Hello Professor Green," he says.

"I was just saying that the apples Sarah used had higher concentrations of cyanide than those the horses ate," Elizabeth says.

"Wow, how can you know that?" Joe asks. "You said the dish—"

"We found the dish." Elizabeth interrupts him. "You're not the only ones with talent on the water. Police frogmen found a dish as well as two bicycles and a shopping trolley."

"I can't believe it," Sarah says. "Those horses have been left to graze under common rights since at least the twelfth century. And it is only now that they have been poisoned? I'm glad they didn't die."

"Well that's as maybe, but didn't you hear me?" Elizabeth replies "Although someone was happy to hurt them in the process, it looks like the apples left by the boat were much more lethal and were intended for you."

"I thought at first that Tom had picked up the fruit scattered for the horses and I cooked a pie as they looked fine, like cookers," Sarah says, "but he did say later that he'd got them from the barrel. I just presumed it was one of the other boat people who'd been doing a bit of work in the fields. Did I kill my boyfriend? I killed him. I killed him." Sarah looks at Elizabeth in shock. "Oh my god." Sarah is comforted by Talya, who holds her.

"There, there. Who could have known that the apples had been tampered with? Who does that? C'mon, shh, you'll make yourself ill," Talya says, hugging her friend.

"Do you live on a boat too?" Elizabeth asks Talya.

"No, but I might as well do," Talya replies.

"Talya's one of us, always down here. We had an autumn fire that night," Joe chips in. "I thought you brought the apples, Tal?"

"I wouldn't bring cookers… coxes, nice and sweet. And not so many." Talya replies. Elizabeth is curious, so Talya explains. "I have a large property up at Fen Ditton, with an orchard."

"You have an apple orchard?" Elizabeth asks.

"I do indeed, a fruit orchard, but there are no apples left on the trees. I don't eat them myself. I don't actually like apples. Give them all away to neighbours and charities for the homeless." Talya smiles. "I also have blackberries, cherries, raspberries which I do like very much, not so good at keeping the birds off the strawberries. They all see me through the winter, full freezer. Are you okay now?" Talya rubs Sarah's shoulder.

"What am I going to do?" Sarah is in her own world thinking of Tom, "We had to put this on, for him."

"Yes, you mentioned Tom was keen on public events," Elizabeth says to Sarah.

"Professor Crowhams did everything he could to stop him," Joe says, speaking on Sarah's behalf.

"And he doesn't like horses either," Elizabeth reminds everyone.

"Is that right?" Abley asks Elizabeth. "Actual evidence?"

Elizabeth glares, knowing Bob doesn't like her sharing information unless it is a fact.

"Professor Crowhams went into my room this

afternoon and sent emails to those coming today to tell them that it was cancelled," Sarah says. "Only he wasn't smart enough to realise perhaps that people would email me asking if it was going to be on another date. That's how I knew." She then adds, "Tom thought these events are so important, to give something back and share this state of the art equipment. Not just to keep it for the few." Sarah looks up and stumbles a bit on her legs, "They show us where we've been. And, when we rush around at a thousand miles per hour here, so caught up in our own lives, they remind us how small and insignificant our lives are."

"You're saying Professor Crowhams was trying to sabotage the event?" Elizabeth asks.

"That man needs shooting," Talya chips in. "Well, it hasn't worked. The field is packed."

"Tom said he did it all the time. You probably know that as Deputy Head of the Department Tom was always a threat to Crowhams. Crowhams is old school, likes the old ways," Joe says.

"Why did we not know Tom was Deputy Head?" Elizabeth asks.

"I think it was very new, not announced yet even?" Sarah adds.

"Oh, that's right." Joe looks at Talya. "We were celebrating it, in fact, the night he—" Joe trails off, not wanting to say the word 'died' in front of Sarah.

"Tom, Tom's a genius. I—" Sarah's voice starts to break just as Professor Nigel Crowhams strides over.

"You have gone over my head on this. You were not supposed to organise this event using this equipment or using the Galileo's name. You do not have permission!" Crowhams shouts.

"Tom was just trying to share the joy of the universe," Sarah says quietly.

"I'm shutting this down now before any damage occurs to the telescopes. Do you know how much these cost?

How many research grants we have to get to keep us going? Do I have to do everything to protect the department? You must put a halt to this immediately. Get everything back in the van. Give me the key." Crowhams holds out his hand for the key to the university truck, which has in it the generator powering the big screen and some of the electrics for a couple of the telescopes as well as for the sound system powering the speakers.

"I don't have the key. And I'm not going to shut this down. Over my dead body," Sarah replies.

"You're worse than him, yet you're still here. Where's the justice in that?" Professor Crowhams pushes Sarah and grabs her bag and tips it upside down to find the key.

"Hey!" Inspector Abley wades in to pick up Sarah, who has now fallen despite not being pushed that strongly.

"Get lost. I only nudged her!" Professor Nigel Crowhams shouts back at Inspector Abley and pushes him too. Inspector Abley then shoves him again, and Nigel lashes out and accidentally hits Inspector Abley with a flailing arm. Inspector Abley then retaliates by pushing the Professor backwards away from him. The crowd gasp and turn from the almost full moon to watch human blood as Abley and Professor Crowhams now scuffle, not letting go of one another as they fall and start to roll around in the grass until Sergeant Lemon rushes over and breaks it up.

"Hey! Hey!" Lemon shouts at them. Both men stand up and struggle to catch their breath.

"Typical ignorant copper." Crowhams scoffs.

Inspector Abley feels his lip and considers his options and then, despite Lemon's attempts to separate them both, punches Professor Nigel Crowhams in the cheek so hard the Don falls back to the ground. Abley looks up and sees Maureen watching. Unimpressed with his gorilla antics Maureen turns and leaves.

"Maureen!" Abley shouts after her.

"Don't," she says, but he chases after his wife, catching up until she shoves his arm away and takes the arm of her friend instead

"Leave me alone."

Abley stands and watches her walk away for a moment, his hands on his head in despair.

"That helped everyone, Bob," Elizabeth comments as he walks back. Elizabeth offers a hand to pick up Sarah who looks very frail now. "I think you should be resting. It's too soon to be out in the cold." And Elizabeth starts to walk Sarah towards her boat. Sarah stops and throws up.

"What's the matter?" Joe worries, having followed behind.

"I think you should take Sarah to hospital. Just to be on the safe side," Elizabeth says.

"But the night?" Sarah protests. "People have come all this way."

"Ah, most of them have walked fifteen minutes at most. I think there will be other moons," Joe says, "but there's only one Sarah."

"I expect you got more of the cyanide than the rest." Elizabeth says to Sarah, then turns to Joe, "You are looking remarkably well Joe."

"Am I?" he says.

Behind Elizabeth, Inspector Abley is still wiping his lip, watching Maureen walk off with her friend through the gate onto Riverside. He can't stop her now.

"Never change?" Abley says. "I've changed. I've forgiven her affair. I never thought I'd do that. What more does she want?" he says to himself.

"Oh, ignore her. She's just angry." Elizabeth turns, trying to hold two conversations.

"What have I done?" Abley asks Elizabeth, completely wrapped up in himself.

Elizabeth is about to tell Bob Abley that he's a man, so everything is his fault, but behind them, Sarah collapses down the bank beside her canal boat.

"Has anybody got a phone? Can someone call an

ambulance?" Elizabeth shouts. Elizabeth looks at Abley, who takes out his mobile but the battery is dead from having not had his charger since he left home. But Sergeant Lemon hears and rushes over and dials it in. At this moment Cynthia arrives with Ed following behind her.

"I was a nurse many moons ago, always like to help if I can. Where's the patient?" But when she sees Sarah on the floor, she is in shock. "Sarah? Sarah! Oh my goodness!" Cynthia rushes after Elizabeth down the bank to reach Sarah, who has fallen perilously close to the water between the canal boat and moorings.

"Are you okay Inspector? Did you get all my messages?" Lemon says behind them. Inspector Abley shows Lemon his dead phone.

"It's dead." Abley shakes his head, aware what he must look like, aware he has been avoiding Lemon.

"Are you coming back?" Lemon asks.

Cynthia looks back up at Inspector Abley.

"Are you an Inspector?" Cynthia asks.

"No," says Abley attempting to walk off.

"Yes," replies Lemon quickly. "Yes, he is."

"Will someone tell me what's going on?" Cynthia says about her colleague.

"She's probably been poisoned again." Elizabeth replies to Cynthia matter-of-factly, "Can you get out of the way?" Then she kneels down to Sarah. "Sarah, do you feel sick?" Sarah shakes her head.

"I feel dizzy," Sarah replies.

"Again?" Talya says quietly, frozen to the spot.

"You are so sparkly. You are my best friend. Best sparkly friend with your moons and stars," Sarah mumbles.

"We need to get you to the gate. An ambulance will be here soon. Can you walk?" Elizabeth's face is urgent. "I think you might have been poisoned with cyanide again. What did you eat?" But Sarah starts to drift in and out of consciousness. "Sarah?"

"Nothing, I've only had the chestnuts." Ed throws

down his bag of chestnuts he's halfway through eating.

"Stop them selling the chestnuts," Elizabeth shouts over her shoulder to anyone who will listen.

"We are giving them away for free," Cynthia says to Elizabeth, then spots the Professor. "What are you doing here? You hate these things."

"Exactly!" Crowhams shouts. "I'm shutting this bloody thing down if I can find the key to that van!"

"Stop, Nigel. Can't you see you've lost?" Cynthia says.

"Stop people eating the chestnuts!" Elizabeth interrupts Cynthia, frustrated by her slow response.

"Right ho, yes." Ed says, listening to Elizabeth. And for a moment Elizabeth sees him talking to the closest bunch of people, who then throw their chestnut trays down.

"We need to get Sarah to the ambulance," Elizabeth says, hearing the ambulance siren getting closer. "They should have some amyl nitrate she can inhale and intravenous sodium nitrite to get into her. Sarah, Sarah, stay with us. Sarah." Elizabeth starts to slap Sarah's cheeks as Sarah begins to slip into a coma. Talya grabs the other arm of Sarah, and together Elizabeth and Talya begin to walk Sarah towards the gate.

Professor Crowhams stands and watches, the full moon behind him and the public touching the telescopes. Cynthia, having previously mentioned her nursing skills, stands and watches Sarah being carried off, failing to help. Lemon notices but says nothing, his eye on Inspector Abley. The moon illuminates all the people now looking up to the sky, oblivious to what is happening with another academic from the Department of Galileo.

36
MOURNING TOM

The next morning and Sarah is still in the hospital recovering from possible second time poisoning. Joe has been up all night at her bedside. But the nurses told Joe he could go and get some sleep himself as she is out of intensive care. Cynthia phoned Joe and offered to see Sarah this morning. So Joe has returned to Stourbridge Common.

Tom's old boat that Joe has been staying on is next to Sarah's where Tom had been living. Joe decides to check Sarah's boat it to see if it is okay. Having been given a spare key a couple of years ago, he soon gains entry and is down in the depths of the living room. The central heating is on, so the boat is nice and toasty. He decides he will get some sleep here as his boat will be cold. But as Joe lies down on the sofa feels a little short, so he heads for Tom and Sarah's bedroom. He opens the door and is surprised to find Tom's clothes on the bed. Joe remembers Tom's white flowery shirt and lemon trousers. Then he sees the framed photo on the wall. These are his wedding clothes.

They got married in some barn, and no one wore formal clothes He realises Sarah has put the clothes out to bury Tom in. He can't lie down on the bed now.

As he's feeling the cuff of a flowery shirt on the bed Joe's body jolts sideways. The boat has been struck. It feels like another boat. Joe runs through the rooms to get out up on deck, and that's when he sees them, two scullers, Wallis and Brad rowing by. He looks down at the side of Tom and Sarah's boat, and there are weeds and mud all stuck to the side, fresh and sliding down.

"What the hell do you think you're playing at?" Joe shouts.

"It was a swan. We've not touched it," Wallis replies then looks at Brad and sniggers.

"If I could reach you I'd swing for you," Joe says.

"Yabba, yabba, yabba," Wallis replies and laughs.

"You know this man is dead?" Joe says.

"What are you on about? Ghosts?" Brad chips in.

"The man who lived on this boat is dead, and you are throwing stuff at his boat," Joe says.

"It was a swan," Wallis says. Brad has been drifting towards the boat, and his oar hits it.

"Why you—" It's enough to make Joe's blood boil, and he leaps onto the scull, causing it to tip, and tries to punch Brad. The scull rolls and Brad goes under the water, his legs caught in the footrest. He tries to come up for air but the boat won't right itself, so he slips back under. Joe, has his oar and is hitting his scull, but Wallis can see Brad is in trouble.

"Stop! Can't you see he's caught?" Wallis slips out of his scull to rescue his friend. Joe holds onto a dinghy, not sure what to do then sees Brad freed by Wallis so shouts.

"Serves you right. Stay away, or it will be worse next time." Joe jumps into the dinghy. It looks for a moment like Wallis is going to swim over and fight him, but Brad stops him. The scullers swim to the other side and collapse on the bank.

37
TEA ELOPING

Cynthia has had enough of the subtle dance of Ed's affections. She has brought him to Victoria College for tea and crumpets and hard talk. She wants to know what he has planned for the rest of his life and whether that includes her. At her age, Cynthia doesn't have time to mess about with 'ifs, buts and maybes'. She's done with commitment-phobes. Cynthia is on a mission, and if there is one man she thinks she can still conquer, it is Ed.

Cynthia loves Ed, more than she thought she would. His mannerisms, which at first she found mildly irritating, are now subtly reassuring. The way he kicks his boots against the side of a door before walking into a room, to loosen the mud is a case in point. Ed walks over to Cynthia, still wiping his jacket down for any possible twigs or leaves, another unnecessary habit until finally he pecks her on the lips and sits in a chair opposite, grunting as he lands. Cynthia has grown to love his grunts, which come when he gets up as well.

They sit in her quiet College office, not immediately

speaking. Cynthia may well now be Project Manager at the Department of Galileo, with research duties, but for thirty years she was a Don in the Physics Department where she used to research many topics related to gravity. She was a very popular lecturer, and her talks would fill the biggest halls in Victoria College. The college has rewarded her with a sunny modest office overlooking cricket fields. Cynthia's room is lined with books on every wall, while papers and stationery fill her desk.

Now as they sit, the only gravity Cynthia seems to care about is what she's waiting for Ed to say to her but is taking far too long to spit out. Ed has often told her how Victoria College and her room make him feel like some academic preying mantis is eating him. Not her, he qualifies, just the place. Cynthia thinks perhaps they should leave and find a more conducive environment. Anything to make him ask her that question he has never asked.

Ed stares at Cynthia somewhat blankly. It has been an eventful couple of days, and the stairs he just climbed to get to this room have left him out of puff. He knows his angina will only get worse and he's not looking forward to opening and closing the lock this winter, that's for sure. Ed looks into Cynthia's eyes and notices her smile, but seeing Cynthia in College, surrounded by smart people has always put him at unease. In Ed's opinion academics are a particularly unfriendly and pompous bunch with no time for small talk. Cynthia is his ray of sunshine in the midst of the gloom.

"You shouldn't have checked yourself out this morning. I told you I was going to bring you brunch. I was just leaving. It's all in my car." Cynthia says. "This is just College morning tea and crumpets. We can leave this."

"I have to walk Clive," Ed replies.

"I would've done that. Once I'd dropped in your food. I had it all planned out."

"You're allergic," Ed smiles, "and anyway there's nothing else they needed to do. I'm fine. The doctor says these pills will keep my ticker going for years."

Cynthia looks at the beads of sweat on Ed's forehead.

"Sorry, it's rather too hot in here. I lit a fire earlier. Shall we go home to mine to eat something?"

"Talking of eating, is it true?" Ed has to ask.

"Is what true, darling?" Cynthia asks, rubbing Ed's knee and leaning in for a kiss.

"Swan. Are they really cooking swan here tonight?" Ed asks.

"I believe so, but don't think about it. The bird will be long dead by now." Cynthia changes the subject as she has more important things on her mind. "Do you know I've just had a visit from Professor Crowhams?"

"That man makes my blood boil." Ed turns bright red.

"Calm down, don't stress yourself out. He won't be back. The strange thing is, he never comes over this side anyway. His offices are in the buildings across Jesus Lane. I think the Bursar put him there so he wouldn't upset anyone."

"That Bursar should lock him in and leave him there to rot." Ed waits for Cynthia to tell him what Crowhams wanted, but she says nothing, so he presses, "Well?"

"He wanted to know if I'd like a promotion," she says. Ed's heart sinks. He thought Cynthia was almost ready to take early retirement with him. He is not sure if he can hold on and wait much longer. He's always thought he'd wait until she retires – which she says she wants to do – and pop the question, ask her to move into the Lock Keeper's House with him and live happily ever after. As he's thinking about his dreams slipping away, Cynthia continues, "but he made it clear I'd have to stop working on the public understanding of science project if I wanted it."

"So what did you say to him?" Ed asks.

"I told him to stuff it," Cynthia replies.

Ed is relieved and laughs out loud.

"I bet he was cross," Ed asks.

"He was furious, angrier than I expected. He turned purple."

"Why is that man so intent on spoiling everybody else's fun?" Ed wonders out loud.

"Well, he's not spoiling mine. I've always wanted to up sticks and go back to my roots." Cynthia says tentatively.

"What roots?"

"When I was a little girl when we used to live in Wells."

"Next-the-Sea?" Ed hasn't heard this plan before.

"The very same. I've decided, I want to run away to the sea and take you with me!" She claps her hands. If Ed is not going to propose, then she will ruddy well do it for him.

"What, and leave the Lock Keeper's House? What about my job? It's the perfect retirement. They pay me a stipend for just keeping an eye on things. We won't find anything like that by the sea."

"What about the lifeboat house? You could volunteer." Cynthia is a little disappointed by Ed's reaction.

"I have my stipend with the Lock Keeper House. It keeps me in corn for the chickens, and food for Clive. And, I think I'm too old to move into the middle of nowhere," Ed says, disappointed their dreams are not aligned.

"Oh, I have money, have lots of savings. I've got the flat in Ely. I'll sell it! And it's not the middle of nowhere it's the seaside. It's wonderful there." Cynthia is too happy for Ed to spoil this moment. He hasn't said no, so she's taking it as a yes. Ed, on the other hand, is in shock and feels like his heart is about to stop.

38
CHANGED THE LOCKS

Inspector Abley has decided to ignore Elizabeth's advice to leave Maureen well alone and has come round to see her this morning at Park Parade. He didn't mean to punch that Professor last night at the stargazing event, but he was asking for it. Now Bob Abley knows he has to perform hasty damage limitation if he is going to salvage his marriage.

Bob Abley thought he'd leave it until around elevenses before he surprised his wife and is armed with a bag of Maureen's favourite macaroons. He puts his key in the front door to creep in, in case Maureen is out or upstairs in the bath. He figures if he can perhaps dump his bag and put the kettle on it will feel like he's not intruding, like a normal day. But the key won't turn. It takes him a while, but he realises Maureen has had the locks changed, a little chipped paint around the edges of the lock confirming this. All of a sudden this storm of anger wells up, and he starts to bang on the door.

"Maureen! Maureen, let me in! Maureen!!" He doesn't

care that curtains twitch, doesn't care that Maureen might be mad. His wife has locked him out of his home. As he bangs the bag against the wall, macaroons split and fly and smash below his feet. How dare she! "Maureen!" He lifts up the letterbox slit and sees her putting on a cardigan and walking to the front door. She is wearing the slippers he hates and looks very cosy in the warm.

"All right, all right. Don't break the door down." Maureen flings open the door and folds her arms, blocking Bob Abley's entry.

"I'm coming in, and we are going to talk," Abley says brushing past her, dumping his bag in the hallway. He looks around, and everything seems polished and clean. There is no dust, and there are vacuum lines on the carpets. He used to like seeing this. Now it just makes him feel uncertain. He stomps into the kitchen, opening cupboards, opening the fridge. He takes out a bottle of beer and puts it on the side, then sees his wife's face so fills the kettle instead and clicks it on.

"You haven't drunk my beer at least." He turns and glares at Maureen, clearly about the locks, but he's too fuming to say anything, and she says nothing. He continues, "A day, you said."

"I say a lot of things to try to keep my life on track these days," Maureen replies.

"So you were lying." Abley stares at her.

"You think what you like. You will anyway."

"What's that supposed to mean?" Abley questions, annoyed.

But Maureen is quiet again. Abley opens another cupboard and finds some biscuits. He breaks open the packet, and they fall all over the counter. "For god's sake," he says. He loses it with the biscuits. Maureen shakes her head and turns to look at the garden. Bob Abley tries to compose himself again.

"Let's go out for tea, eh? My treat, somewhere nice. How about The White Pony on Hill's Road?" Abley says, now trying to mend things.

"You know I always wanted to go there," Maureen replies.

"So let's do it." Abley tries to fake enthusiasm.

"You were always too busy. There was always a case, then another case."

"So let's go now? Nothing to stop us." Abley tries to persuade, reaching out for Maureen's hand, but she pulls it away.

"So we only go when you look like a tramp, have been drinking this morning and have lost your job?" she replies. "Huh, thanks for the offer but I think I'll pass."

"Maureen." Abley looks at his wife. She has shared decades of her life with him, but in her eyes, he sees a stranger.

"And stop telling people to come round and tell me to take you back. It's so unpleasant. I never liked Professor Green in the first place. One of the great things about splitting with you is not having to put up with them anymore."

"Come on, they were just trying to help, want to see us both happy," Abley pleads.

"I'll be much happier when you realise—"

"When I realise what?" he asks. The kettle clicks itself off.

Maureen can't bring herself to say the words 'it's over' but everything is screaming this in Abley's ears. He starts to shake his head.

"Everyone goes through tough times. I refuse to accept it." Abley says quietly. But Maureen starts to touch her wedding and engagement rings. Abley shakes his head, to stop her from doing what she is about to do, but it is no use. She pulls the rings from her finger and puts them on the side. Abley picks up the beer and walks out of the kitchen and through the front door. There are no words. He can't breathe.

When he gets outside, he looks up at the sky. For once

it is not blue, but a heavy white cloud. In front of him, a group of students are playing Lacrosse on Jesus Green. People are walking their dogs, or cycling across… life goes on. But for Inspector Abley his life has changed, significantly in one direction and never to be the same again. Everything starts to spin, the lack of sleep, the lack of good food, and now the devastating blow that his wife no longer loves him. He stands paralysed outside his front door, unable to take a step forward, unable to know what to do for the best. He pulls the top off the beer and takes a glug.

Without thinking, Inspector Bob Abley turns and heads for the place where he feels most safe. A place that he knows if his wife now found him there it would be over forever. He is past caring.

39
ART

The boats are quiet. To a stranger walking by, it is difficult to tell if the dwellers lead regular routines and have gone off to work this Tuesday afternoon, or if they have such different lives to the passers-by that they are not even awake yet, more like the nocturnal owl perched not far in the hedgerow on the far side of the Common. Only smoke coming out of a chimney emits a clue as to the answer. Then the doors burst open on the one closest to Riverside gates, Sarah and Tom's, and out steps Joe.

Joe stands at the stern watching the world go by. The Common is relatively quiet. A mother behind a pushchair wheels her little darling over to the swings in the far corner, passing Joe on the way. A cyclist, coming back from the City now loaded up with grocery bags on handlebars, heads towards the Green Dragon Bridge and home, dodging the horses on the way after his food. Another bicycle goes by, but nothing looks suspicious. Of all the boat people, Joe seems the most 'boaty' for this part of Cambridge. For this is not St. Katharine Docks, there are no deck shoes and jumper around the shoulders here. Joe's red hair, beard and tie-dyed T-shirt fit right in.

Just when everything is quiet Joe stands up and takes hold of the stern plate. It is a beautifully carved piece of wrought iron in the shape of a fish. Tom made it for Sarah many years ago. Joe pulls it out of the hole in the floor and chucks it in the river. It came out much more easily than anticipated as he watches it submerge and the bubbles on the surface show the only trace. That's when he notices an Afghan hound in his peripheral vision, then another one running up to him.

"Wrong season for a spring clean, isn't it?" Elizabeth Green shouts over to him, having seen what he's just done.

"Oh, Professor Green." Joe looks around confused as to where she's come from.

"I was hoping to speak with Sarah. Is she back yet from hospital?" Elizabeth asks.

"I don't think so," Joe replies.

"Isn't this her boat?"

"Yes, but it is a big boat. She might have snuck in," Joe answers.

"Do you often make a habit of being on other peoples' boats?" Elizabeth asks.

"Oh, we're always on each other's boats," he says.

"When the other person is not there?" Elizabeth is curious.

"Yes. All property is theft," he replies.

"And what about the vandalism? Do you often do that to each other's boats?" Elizabeth raises her eyebrows.

"Sorry?" Joe asks.

"You just threw something into the river," she presses.

"Just a buoy. Look." And Joe picks up a buoy from the side of the boat. "What are you doing here?" Joe asks Elizabeth.

"Knocking for Sarah." Elizabeth climbs onto the

boat and pushes past Joe and knocks on the door. There is no answer, so she walks down into the boat.

"Hey, that's trespassing. Do you have a warrant?" Joe asks.

But Elizabeth is already below deck, followed by Hector and Monty, and wandering past the bedroom into the kitchen and through to the living room. Once she is inside, she starts to look around. It is a very tidy boat, and homely. There are flowers, now looking a little sad, fruit in a bowl. Monty finds a biscuit and leans over the table surface to reach it, licking it. But Elizabeth stops him in time.

"No, that's chocolate. No good." Then reaches into her pocket for a dog treat for them both, after which she brushes the biscuit and puts it back on the plate. Joe is behind, huffing at her cheek.

Elizabeth sees a black cat asleep on a cushion on a shelf. She strokes the cat. Then spots a wallet on the table. She thinks it reckless that the wallet is in broad daylight visible through the windows, and that the boat is not locked, until she opens it and sees that it is Tom's wallet and that it is more or less empty. But a burglar wouldn't know that and it might spark them to break in. She flicks through the contents. Some loose change, no notes. In fact, there are no cards either. The only thing which identifies it as Tom's is the picture Elizabeth saw in the first place, a photo of Sarah. Inside there is a voucher from a takeaway for two for one pizza, a receipt to the boatyard for a new crankshaft, some other receipts from the supermarket, a dinner at The Plough in Fen Ditton, and one for banana milkshakes at The Milk Bar in town.

"Do you always wander into peoples' property and go through their things?" Joe asks.

"Only when there has been a murder. As I say, there are no dead horses, only a dead Tom. Perhaps the whole thing was to kill a boat dweller. Did you like Tom?" Elizabeth turns to Joe.

"What? Yes, of course. I've said that already, countless times. Everyone loved Tom. He was the best," Joe replies, picking up Tom's wallet Elizabeth has now placed back on the table and fiddling with it.

"So you don't know anyone who might have wanted to kill him, or had a beef with him?" Elizabeth looks at Joe with her beady eyes.

"No, I don't. You've asked me this. Like I say, he was the most popular guy I know."

"Perhaps he wasn't the target. Perhaps it was Sarah, and she was meant to die instead." Elizabeth continues to look at Joe straight in the eye.

"No, that makes no sense. We all love Sarah. It was the apples for the horses. That's what everyone thinks apart from you." Joe shakes his head.

"Apart from me and the police. Sarah made the apple pie for you all. Maybe she was trying to kill everyone?" Elizabeth lifts other things on a shelf: a little wooden duck, a bookmark, and a packet of mints. She puts them back down.

"Oh my god, maybe we bumped him off together!" Joe replies.

Elizabeth continues to look around. She squeezes into the seat behind the table. Everything is stuck to the floor, making her have to bend to do this. Once she is sitting, she looks around. The dogs jump up and sit down too.

"I don't know how you do it," she says to Joe.

"What?" he asks, now scratching his head, confused by her questions. "Do what?"

"Live on a boat. My husband wanted me to go on a boat trip once, up the Rhine," Elizabeth says. "Apart from the fact that I didn't want to stare at mountains for days on end and eat cheese, I've never been able to fathom the dream. Why would one choose that as a permanent lifestyle?"

"Are you for real? You come in here and accuse me of murdering my best friend," Joe says, "and now you talk about holidays?"

"Why do you live on Tom's boat?" Elizabeth asks.

"Freedom. Off the grid. We're our own masters," Joe replies, irritated. "We don't pay any landlord and can leave at a moment's notice if things get tough." Joe stops. "But all this, now. I don't know. I've been telling Sarah that we should just go, run off to Mexico," he adds sarcastically.

"Where they're celebrating the Day of the Dead right now?" Elizabeth looks at Joe.

"What are you talking about?" Joe asks.

"You mention running off there and yet profess to not knowing about one of the biggest festivals for the dead that there is?" Elizabeth shakes her head.

"Coincidence." Joe looks shocked and tries to change the subject. "You should go. If Sarah gets back, I don't want you upsetting her."

"But you said she doesn't mind it when you come into her boat, that she's easygoing. All property is theft, you said," Elizabeth replies.

"She is. But not you sitting here, looking through Tom's things."

"It's just a wallet and a duck." Elizabeth continues to look around.

"Please go," Joe asks. They both feel the boat rock, and realise that someone has just stepped onboard. "Great, and now here she is." Joe waits for Sarah to walk in. But it is Talya, dressed in a beautiful purple coat down to her feet.

"Oh, I was just coming to see if Sarah needed anything." Talya is surprised to see Elizabeth, Joe and two Afghan Hounds crowding the living room of the boat.

"She's not here. Don't you knock?" Elizabeth asks.

"Oh, she must still be at the hospital, Talya. You can wait in my boat, come and have a cuppa. Then we'll go and see if she's well enough to come home," Joe offers.

"Sounds like a good idea." Talya smiles at Joe.

"Did you eat apple pie that night, Talya? You weren't ill, were you?" Elizabeth asks.

"You've already asked before. No," Talya replies. "I told you, I don't like apples."

Elizabeth is struck by how different Talya looks to Joe and Sarah. She reminds her of Emily, classily dressed, not someone who is friends with boat people.

"How do you know Sarah again?" Elizabeth asks Talya.

"We went to school together. Best friends since then," Talya replies and then looks at Joe. "I brought her some food." Talya points to a very posh looking hamper by the door in the boat. "She's a fussy eater, but I know all her favourites." Talya explains to Elizabeth.

"Perhaps whoever killed Tom is also trying to kill Sarah." Elizabeth states then walks through the boat and picks up the hamper. She opens it.

"Hey, what are you doing?" Talya says.

"Just double checking nothing has been tampered with," Elizabeth replies.

"I'm not going to poison my best friend. I'm trying to be nice!" Talya says.

Elizabeth picks up the jars of preserve and pickle and inspects their lids. Then she looks at all the meat and turns up her nose. It all seems vacuum sealed. And the wine also has a plastic covered cork. Everything looks pristine and shop-bought. She sees some rare olive oil and picks that out of the basket.

"Who said anything about you poisoning your friend? I will just have to take this for testing, however, as I think the security cap is broken." Elizabeth says.

"But that's the most expensive thing in the basket, hand-picked and pressed." Elizabeth holds the bottle of ultra-premium olive oil in her hand up to the light of the window and admires the olive oil.

"Where were you when your friends were being poisoned?" Elizabeth asks.

"I was with them. You already know that. I have the clothes stinking of smoke still to prove it if you want them," Talya replies, irked at Elizabeth for taking the olive oil.

"That won't be necessary. What did you eat if you didn't eat apple pie?" Elizabeth pockets the olive oil.

"I brought some crème caramels," Talya says. "They went down a treat. Shop-bought, I didn't poison them."

"Apart from Sarah, who doesn't eat dairy," Joe added, helpfully.

40
AFTERNOON TEA

When Elizabeth finds that Inspector Abley has left Foxes Haven, she decides to go and find him to talk about him coming back on the case. It is very chilly driving with the top down in the Talbot, but the sun is peeping out behind some white cloud. The journey out of the city is broken by local traffic around the Our Lady and the English Martyrs Church on the corner of Gonville Place. But she is soon gliding down Hills Road then up the Babraham Road to Bob's favourite haunt, the Gog Magog Golf Course. Turning into the golf course is like a trip down memory lane. Many an evening after she had finished up in the laboratory she would bring herself up to the bar to join Gerald after he'd played a round. They would sip their drinks as they watched the sun go down on the nineteenth hole.

Parking the car, Elizabeth spots Inspector Abley's BMW in the car park with its golfing blanket on the back window and unmissable 'Kiss my Putt' sticker above his rear bumper. It isn't long before she finds him inside sat in a chair in the clubhouse bar, staring out the window at the beautiful lush course. He looks messy and upset, even from the back.

"Surprised you're not out there, taking advantage of the free pass." She knew he'd be here.

"Free pass?" Inspector Abley turns around.

"From work, from marriage. It's a lovely blue sky day." Elizabeth stares at him.

"That it is." Bob Abley looks up at the sky, the clouds parting even more to reveal a beautiful afternoon.

For a while Elizabeth says nothing, she looks at the view.

"Maybe I'll give you a game." She says.

"Don't be ridiculous. You're a terrible player," Abley replies.

"Yes, but you're not on form. So I stand a good chance. Let's get some sticks."

"No."

"You have afternoon tea here, very civilised." Elizabeth looks at the scone crumbs and teapot.

"No beer, no sticks," Abley replies.

Elizabeth just sits with Bob Abley for a while, saying nothing. Two golfers walk up and past the window and sit down outside. They have their golf clubs and are still wearing their muddy shoes.

"Two more heart surgeons are taking the afternoon off," Elizabeth says.

"How do you know?" Abley replies.

"Gerald used to play with him. I forget his name, isn't that terrible? Can't remember anyone's names unless they've done something bad," she adds, thinking about her husband again.

"Sounds about right," he says.

More silence ensues between them. Elizabeth struggles not to look at her watch, as she knows Bob is now running on empty. So much is at stake for him. He can save his career if he just puts up more of a fight with the station.

He's got a terrific track record behind him. What man wouldn't go to pieces about family life going south? Something tells Elizabeth that her usual talking tough will only drive him further away. So instead she does something she's not a fan of, hates doing, and believes is the worst tactic in life. She decides to be extra-friendly.

"You know, you can stay at mine for a while. Not just on my sofa. Must have been uncomfortable." She refers to last night, having seen the bump on her sofa from his body before she left. "Godric seems to have stormed out yesterday. He hasn't come back. He's in love with an idiot. What a mess. Just because of hormones." Elizabeth realises what she's just said. "I mean him. He's always got a different man on the go, how do youth cope these days?" There is another silence. One of the golfers outside on the terrace hands over some golf balls to another golfer, pats him on the back and walks off. The remaining man then pockets the balls and leaves in the same direction. The view is unobstructed again outside. A bird lands on the decking and starts to peck at crumbs.

"It's over." Abley stares ahead.

"What she's doing is pretty rich if you ask me," Elizabeth says, "She's in the wrong and should get out of your house too!" But Elizabeth can tell that Bob doesn't care and doesn't want to hear it. "The sooner you can stop thinking about her, the sooner you can get on with the rest of your life. Get back out on the course, get back to work."

"Why didn't I see it coming?" Abley's words are flat. "I feel like I've been hit by a train."

"You're still here after the collision, so you're stronger than you think," Elizabeth replies.

"I'd like to stay with you, thank you." Abley stares at Elizabeth. "But on one condition." Bob Abley looks at his friend.

"We'll see about conditions," Elizabeth replies tentatively.

"We never mention her name again."

"Whose name?" Elizabeth replies.

"I'd beat you at golf, blindfolded." Bob tips his head back and shuts his eyes.

41
COLLEGE

Godric is too mad to go back to his nanna's. He's determined to stay out this Tuesday evening and find somewhere else to put his head down. Perry Sidcup's is always good for one night, but his friend's snoring could equal any tuba solo at the Albert Hall proms. He hasn't bothered to try his own College as he knows there are never any spare rooms. Bene'ts is always full of visiting Fellows and religious types. So he's come to Victoria to see if he can find Wallis. But now Godric is here, despite knocking for his lover and looking in both bars, Wallis is nowhere to be seen. So Godric walks into the dining hall deciding to eat alone. Smells swirl into his nostrils of gravy and carrots, which lift his spirits. He pops his head into the JCR and does a circuit. No Wallis, but then he hears a shout from across the room.

"By George, it's Cartwright Green. God! I say Goddy!" Godric spots his old friend Toby Pinkham and walks over to his dearest, most dramatic friend. He finds Toby holding court with a rather loud group of acquaintances.

Toby pours Godric some champagne, and before too long Godric is in the arms of a very handsome man called Ben. Godric feels Ben's muscles through Ben's bright green and black striped sweater. Unlike everyone else around Toby's group, Ben is the only one not wearing his gown ready to go to dinner. Godric smiles through his blonde fringe at Ben, who smiles back.

"Shall we go and get some robes for you?" Godric suggests.

"Toby never told me it was a formal." Ben replies.

"Huh, Toby. That's rubbish." Godric says. They both laugh as they walk out, Ben pulling out his pockets to see if he has money to hire.

"I'm skint. I may have to owe you." Ben says.

"Never let it be said that Godric can't help a man on with his clothes." And they leave for the Lodge to organise the key for the hire room.

Once out in the courtyard, Godric sees Professor Crowhams from his physics lectures on astronomy shouting at a woman. The woman has a piece of paper in her hands and is trying to give it to the Professor. Standing next to the woman is a man Godric recognises. It's Ed, the Lock Keeper. Ed puts his hands up to Professor Crowhams to stop his tirade. But the Professor smacks Ed's hands out of the way. Ed falls back a little on his feet and puts his hands on his knees. Godric cannot hear what the Professor is shouting about but feels the need to slow down to listen.

"We'll miss the starter," Ben says.

"I've had him for astronomy lectures. Professor Crowhams. What's he doing having a go at that woman? Can you hear him? What is he saying?" Godric asks.

"Everybody heard that," Ben replies, continuing, "you don't often hear pistols at dawn and 'I'm going to kill you' on an average day at Victoria. But then Professor Crowhams is notoriously unpopular. Now we know why." Godric slows down even further, but Ben grabs his arm and pulls him towards the Lodge.

When they are on their way back to dinner, Professor Crowhams, Ed and the woman have now gone. But Godric walks over to where they were arguing, as he can see the paper the woman was holding on the floor. Godric picks up the paper and puts it in his pocket. Then Ben says, "So how come we've never met before?"

"We're meeting now. That's good enough for me," Godric replies, and the two walk off into Formal Hall for dinner.

42
A REAL SWAN

Elizabeth and Bob Abley head back from the golf course to Foxes Haven, with him following in his car. Leaving the Talbot safely tucked away they go straight upstairs. There is something lovely about Elizabeth's corner guest bedroom. Apart from the fact that it is en-suite it probably has the best view of the garden. She wonders why she doesn't use it herself anymore but knows she prefers the balcony at the very top loft, where she can sit outside and breathe fresh air while watching the sunset. Godric has already complained that this most substantial bedroom in the house is far too light for him as there are four windows and he needs somewhere pitch black when it's time to sleep. So for the foreseeable, this is Inspector Abley's home.

Elizabeth watches as Bob Abley drops his bag and sighs. He knows he has walked into the old master bedroom that Elizabeth must have evacuated when Gerald died. This makes him feel uncomfortable. Little tell-tale signs make it evident – a wardrobe full of Gerald's clothes, his shaving equipment still in the en-suite. Even Gerald's reading materials left on the chest of drawers, Elizabeth can't bring herself to throw away his golfing magazines, "You never know if a guest might like to read them. There is a lot of grass between their pages. It can make one feel happy," she tells Bob as she shows him the towels.

Elizabeth leaves Bob to settle and takes a while in her boudoir, adjacent on the landing. She comes out having sprayed far too much hair lacquer on her curls.

"Ooh, get you." Bob jiggles his shoulders and purses his lips as he leans in the doorway of his new temporary home.

"Stop it."

"No, you look good. Blind date?" Abley asks.

"Don't." Elizabeth doesn't even entertain the idea.

"Well, have a lovely time." He says.

"Thank you, there's lots of healthy veg in the fridge if you feel like cooking, or the board in the kitchen has our local takeaways," She offers. "Use a plate." Her words are sounding like a reprimand before the fact.

"They come with a box which is a plate," Abley replies.

"Which has oil all over it." she counters.

"I'll use a plate. Go, you'll be late, wherever you are going on your date, non-date," he says.

"There's some rather special olive oil on the side I picked up earlier," Elizabeth says. "Try it with some bread. It will be a very Italian experience."

"Yum, bread and oil for tea. Chefs can stop inventing new dishes now."

*

Elizabeth has just walked across Jesus Green and is now standing outside Victoria College. She takes a deep breath. It is obvious from Emily's remarks that Elizabeth might come face to face with a dead swan at supper. But for now, Elizabeth will honour her friend's invitation. It isn't long before Elizabeth is walking through the corridor of one of the oldest Colleges. Tourists are often found in static stupors, drooling over the wood panels, the old light fittings from when electricity was first invented, and the richest parquet flooring.

"Hello, Liz, lovely of you to come." Emily gets up, just as soon as Elizabeth spots her best friend and best friend's husband sitting by a fire in the Senior Common Room.

"Hello, Elizabeth," Cuthbert nods and also stands.

"Hello, hello. Brrr, I'm hungry. It looks like it will be packed tonight," Elizabeth replies.

"Yes, Formal Hall is always packed here apparently. The chef spent twenty years in a cordon bleu restaurant in London before she came here. She's one of the best in the country," Cuthbert replies.

"Ah, I love my Granta. They always have a special and different vegan option for me," Elizabeth says.

"Well, we've told Aubyn that you are a vegan, and you told me that you've already spoken to the chef," Emily chips in, "so it should all be fine."

"Aubyn?" Elizabeth asks. At this point, Aubyn peeks from behind a third chair, with a big smile and large hands. He stands up and offers one of them to Elizabeth.

"I've heard so much about you," he says to Elizabeth. Elizabeth looks bemused at Emily.

"We have wanted to introduce you to Dr Aubyn Sutcliffe for some time," Emily says to Elizabeth. "Aubyn works in the Department of Geography, with research on the glacial structures in Svalbard. Isn't that right?" Emily turns and smiles at Aubyn.

"Yes, some people call me ice man." He laughs, showing a broken tooth, which Elizabeth guesses he must have lost biting down on the fur of polar bears.

"Well Aubyn, hello," Elizabeth says.

Cuthbert and Aubyn turn as the dinner gong strikes. Elizabeth pulls Emily back.

"This had better not be a setup." Elizabeth grabs Emily to make her acknowledge her words.

"He's very nice and very lonely," Emily says. "His wife left him because of his research. He's away a lot. Perfect for you."

"Emily stop," Elizabeth says. "I have nothing against older men, but that beard has creatures in it, I can see them moving."

"And you like animals, so it's perfect." Emily replies and she and Elizabeth follow the men into the Formal Hall supper, joined by other Fellows as well as a sea of undergraduate students at Victoria, all with the purple velvet stripes along the line of their gowns, to distinguish them from the graduates with their gold striped trim. The Fellows wear black velvet. Elizabeth adores her own Granta gown which has green velvet trim, her absolute favourite material. So it is with some disappointment, having had to bring her spare gown this evening from the back of the wardrobe, that she then spots her own gown draped over the shoulders of her errant grandson now sitting just a few rows away from the top table. Elizabeth is in two minds whether to shout at him for the crime of theft, but instead bores holes into his back with her eyes. It doesn't seem to work as Godric appears to be having so much fun that he doesn't notice. Elizabeth can't see Wallis, so at least there are small mercies.

Elizabeth is now beginning to dread the length of the evening, stuck with Aubyn and his moving beard sitting to her left.

"What do you do then? Cuthbert tells me you are a force to be reckoned with." Aubyn interrupts Elizabeth's train of thought. "And I hear you're one of those, you know, vegans? Don't you miss protein?" There it is, Elizabeth thinks. But he continues without any encouragement. "You have a drink with ice in I can see, with countless bacteria and life forms in the ice you know, so you're not actually a vegan. You do eat living things, there in your glass. You won't complain about me eating swan will you? You're not one of those angry vegans. I've been looking forward to the swan tonight as well. I would kill anything with my bare hands. I have to catch my food up in Svalbard. Fish mainly, but I've eaten polar bear. Caught by the locals. That's vital for their culture." Aubyn looks at her and smiles.

Elizabeth focuses on her starter which has just arrived and tucks into her warm avocado, walnut and pomegranate pastries drizzled with balsamic vinegar, with roasted carrots and parsnips. She glances at Aubyn's slice of ham on toast and knows she had the tastiest food as well as the kindest and smiles to herself. Without speaking at all, she then turns her back on Aubyn and engages with the person sitting to her right.

"Hello." The handsome young man smiles, noticing they are both eating the same food. "Looks like they've put us all together." And he points out his friends are all eating what Elizabeth is eating. She also notices how beautiful these people all look.

"Are you studying here?" Elizabeth asks this handsome man.

"One of us. The others, well, we're just here let's say, to make a point." He smirks. Elizabeth looks at his face and notices how at peace he seems. Elizabeth hears Godric's laughs over the noise of the dinner hall. She looks up and sees a man kissing her grandson's cheek and looking adoringly at Godric's face. This may be a good thing, she thinks, as it is not Wallis. But then she sees Godric wipe greasy food fingers on her gown. Her gown!

"Liz. Liz! Elizabeth!" Emily calls to Elizabeth. "Tell Aubyn about your work on endangered plants up in the Arctic." Emily tries to pull her friend back into the conversation.

"They are not my favourite plants I must admit, though I do send money to charity for polar bears." Elizabeth is irritated by Emily's attempt to set her up with Aubyn, and also resents the fact that she had just started a conversation with an altogether more interesting man who also appears to be a vegan.

"You should stop supporting polar bear charities." Aubyn says. "They just spend all their money on skidoos. They don't know what they are talking about," Aubyn adds, wobbling his head.

"They say the ice is melting because of climate change and they are saving polar bears and moving them back to where there is more ice," Elizabeth replies, irked that this man is telling her what to do.

"Yes, but then there will be too many polar bears." Aubyn laughs. "You have to let nature take its course. They are not from the region they are moving them to." Aubyn again fails to see just how irritating he has become.

"Would you say the same to refugees?" Elizabeth asks, her blood now starting to simmer, tipped over the edge by hearing the gong clang followed by four butlers proceeding to enter the hall carrying a huge swan, dead and ready to serve up on a platter. Another man behind them is carrying the largest knife, while waitresses scurry to take away the starter plates before Elizabeth could even finish. Elizabeth stops talking to Aubyn, in shock and horror at what she sees. This majestic bird sacrificed so some selfish and mostly overweight diners can tick something off their list.

There are gasps and cheers, but at the same time, Elizabeth starts to hear scuffles and chairs being moved back. At first, it appears people are beginning to stand to burst into applause, and Elizabeth is preparing for the worst nightmare of all her decades of dining years at Cambridge. But she can never have guessed what happens next. It is so quick and swift that in the moment she knows it will forever be burned into her mind as an act of such elegance and beauty as it speaks to the room without a word being uttered.

Four young men in white suits, much taller than the butlers holding the tray, simply lift the swan out of the butlers' grips and glide silently out of the room with the swan. Another woman, who has discarded her robe to reveal a ballerina swan costume rather like one from 'Swan Lake' starts to film everything. Another woman also dressed like a ballerina in a swan outfit sprays 'swan killers' on the wood panelling at the back of the Hall, right behind where the Master is currently sitting, not far from Elizabeth. Elizabeth can hear a pin drop in the room, as diners are in shock.

In concert with this activity, more students involved in the protest stand up and start to remove their gowns. Elizabeth hears the Master shout, "Put on your gowns!" but they ignore him, and underneath their gowns are beautiful swan wings. The room starts to turn from black to white as dozens of students, previously like black chrysalises, reveal their white T-shirts and white wings underneath. They start to open their wings, which seem to be attached to their hands with string or wire as they start to flap the wings. For a magical moment, Elizabeth feels like she is with her people. Some "Ahs" and "That's beautiful" and "Wows" start as for a minute everyone soaks up the thirty or more students flapping their swan wings, beating like Elizabeth's heart. That is until the first young man's wings are pulled off by a disappointed swan eater.

Then another, then a kerfuffle turns into a bit of noise, then into a small disturbance. And suddenly, the whole room is awash with smashing glasses, flying rolls, falling chairs, punches and mayhem. Elizabeth spots Godric, who is currently pushing someone into a dish of butter. The victim picks up the butter and grabs a chunk and spreads it all down Elizabeth's beautiful green lined velvet gown. Godric then stands on the table and beckons the diners nearest him to try and take him on if they think they are hard enough, at which point he is pelted by cranberry sauce, gravy and red wine. Elizabeth looks at her gown, now with butter and half the food from the tables trickling down it on Godric.

"Ah, no. No swan." Aubyn looks at Elizabeth with a mock disappointed look on his face. "Were you behind this?" He stares at Elizabeth. From out of nowhere, the contents of a pot of mayonnaise are sent hurling towards and splat across Aubyn's face and chest. Elizabeth tries her hardest not to smirk. He looks at her and some cranberry sauce hits him from the side.

In the midst of this mayhem, Elizabeth spots Cynthia leaving. She is not the only person to notice Cynthia's departure, as Elizabeth sees Professor Crowhams rush towards Cynthia and pull her back, to try to talk. Cynthia slaps his face. Elizabeth spots Ed at a table, whose eyes are also glued to the pair. Professor Crowhams grabs Cynthia and kisses her. But Cynthia pulls away and rushes out of the hall, closely followed by Professor Crowhams. Ed and Elizabeth are left staring at the door.

43
CAREFUL PROFESSOR

Despite rushing out of the swan supper after Cynthia, Professor Crowhams cannot see her anywhere. He is desperate to speak with her and starts to head for her home in Fen Ditton. Crowhams doubts he will find her now, however, as ahead of him is only an empty expanse of Midsummer Common, all but those wretched horses. By the time he realises his search is a lost cause, he is heading for Stourbridge Common.

Professor Crowhams marches on. He cannot face going home. He is so disappointed he didn't even get to eat swan. He has never had it before, despite having spent time as a post-doctoral student many years ago at St James's College, the only College in Cambridge allowed to serve swan with the Queen's permission. He has no idea how Victoria managed to bend the rules tonight, though they may as well have not bothered due to those good-for-nothing students causing pandemonium. If he had his way he would expel them all, but unfortunately he is not very popular in Victoria College and his views are, in the main, ignored.

The air is very still tonight. The stars are sparkling, a good time of year to gaze at their wonderment. A large part of him now wishes he were at his telescope. But on he walks, giving him time to think about the only woman he ever really loved. What on earth does she see in that Lock Keeper? Maybe she has already double backed to that eel of a man who has no place at a College dinner. Professor Crowhams always rationalised that the women who had left him over the years were just shallow and uneducated. His mother had called them mice, and told him it was because they couldn't deal with his intellect. Ed most certainly is not a clever man, Crowhams knows, but neither does he possess muscles or good looks. For Cynthia to choose Ed over himself was incomprehensible. Cynthia is the first woman he knows he could learn to love. She had gone out with him on a few dates many years ago, and had paid half for the meals as well. She told him he put his work first and ended it.

Before he knows it, Professor Crowhams has arrived at Stourbridge Common and the trees reach out towards him, the mud under his shoes throwing up earthy scents as he wanders down the bank to the boats. There are no lights on inside any of them, and he wonders where all the people must have all gone. He climbs aboard the nearest boat. He knows it is Tom's as he can see Tom's bicycle still up on deck, with its unmissable bright red frame with stars on the spokes.

Crowhams' boat breaking and entering is interrupted by the cantering of over half a dozen horses, heading straight for him. It is cold out there on the Common, and they often get a midnight treat from the boat dwellers, and mistake Crowhams as a feeder. He feels cornered as he has no food and cannot leave the boat for fear of being bitten or kicked. He walks down through the unlocked front door.

He passes the wallet on the table, which Elizabeth had

opened before. He flicks through some papers on the table and frowns. Crowhams then sees a brochure for a very smart hotel, The Star Boutique, in Northumberland. There are printed details, a trip for two to see 'Dark Skies'. Perhaps Tom was going to surprise Sarah; he sees Tom's name at the top and also the department address. Was Tom going to charge this through the department? Crowhams frowns. He picks up the brochure and letter-headed booking and stuffs them under his arm to check out what else Tom has put through on department money.

On the next boat, Joe has opened his doors, having seen the horses outside. He steps up with some carrots, broken up into small pieces he scatters them on the ground, and the horses start to feed. He spots Professor Crowhams coming out of Sarah's boat.

"Hey! What are you doing?" Joe says.

"You are good at that." Crowhams looks at Joe feeding the horses. "Poisoned them before have you? I should thank you." Crowhams looks into the darkness at the horses munching carrots.

"What are you doing?" Joe asks more quietly. "Only to most, it would look like you've just broken in."

"Hold your horses," Professor Crowhams says, trying to be light and lying on the spot, "I came to see Sarah. Saw the door open and showed my face. But she's not there. She really should lock her boat."

"You think?" Joe replies.

"Where is she?" Crowhams asks, trying to keep up the pretence.

"Just go. It's too late to be calling on people," Joe says.

"I can't go because of these ruddy horses," Crowhams replies, waving his hands about and clapping.

"They know you're frightened," Joe scoffs.

"I'm not frightened. It's reasoning. They bite." Crowhams continues to clap and gesticulate.

"They know the truth," Joe replies

"Did you feed them apples? Did you poison them? They've come over for food," Crowhams repeats.

"I feed them, yes, of course I do. It's freezing tonight. They should have coats, should have cover," Joe replies.

"So you think they shouldn't be here either?" Crowhams is curious.

"I think it's strange to find you at this time of night on Tom and Sarah's boat," Joe says, "I think it's worrying that Sarah's door is open and you have some papers under your arm." Joe spots that Crowhams had taken something. "I'll let Sarah know don't you worry. Papers, I see them."

"Do you think Tom was murdered?" Crowhams tries to change the subject.

"I hoped not. But don't have to think, the police have confirmed it now," Joe replies, matter-of-factly.

"Well, I'd keep quiet about these, if you want to keep your job that is," Crowhams warns Joe.

"I think you should get off Sarah's boat and go," Joe says.

Professor Crowhams huffs and climbs onto the riverbank where he is jostled and chased by the horses until he gets back through Riverside gate. Joe laughs. Professor Crowhams turns once through the gate and gives Joe the evilest look.

"You'll be sorry," Crowhams says.

44
WHAT BERTIE NEARLY SEES

Elizabeth is nearly home after Victoria College's disastrous Formal Hall swan supper. She walks alone across Jesus Green, something Emily is always telling her not to do. But the emptiness of the space makes Elizabeth feel free. Past nine in the evening in autumn and there are no tourists, no children screaming in the playground, no tennis balls bouncing, no footballs being kicked or bicycle bells dinging. Just the very large silvery moon and the dark shadows, wispy mist and fresh wet air. For at night Jesus Green comes alive with the shadows of hundreds of years old trees, which stretch as high as the heavens and hang down lower than the ankles. Elizabeth feels as if at any moment a branch might pluck her up into the leaves where she will disappear forever.

The River Cam running along one side of Jesus Green sparkles, a solitary swan asleep perilously close to the Jesus Lock Weir, something Elizabeth knows not to worry about, having never seen them fall. Tonight she also feels strangely buoyant, having witnessed the beautiful protest.

She crosses Jesus Green Lock Bridge and walks the few hundred yards to the left before putting her key in the lock. Opening her front door she is confronted by the sound of the television. The volume is high, and the canned laughter travels all the way to greet her, swiftly followed by Hector and Monty, Bertie on the top stairs, and behind him Soot.

"Have you been fed?" She looks at the dogs, then calls out, "Hello!" Elizabeth remembers she had offered Inspector Abley somewhere to stay. It has been such a busy day for a second it had slipped her mind, but it all comes rushing back.

"Cooee," he shouts back. Elizabeth walks in and sees curry takeaway boxes all over the table and floor. "I used a coaster," Abley replies observing his own mess. Sure enough, Bob Abley has found table mats from somewhere and laid them out like a patio on the dining room table. "Would you like some pop?"

"Not drinking?" she asks.

"Nah, I didn't feel like it," he replies. This is a big moment for them both and the words hang in the air until Abley breaks the silence, "Though I did try some of that olive oil on my naan bread. Really good." They both look at the bottle of olive oil that Elizabeth took from Talya's hamper.

"Oh, I hope you left some for me," she smiles.

"Yes, here," he replies.

"Elizabeth takes a seat next to Bob Abley on the sofa. She turns the television off, and they sit in silence for a while. Elizabeth pours some oil into a bowl and dips a naan bread in. She can taste the peppery oil and the tumeric of the naan and shuts her eyes.

"So did you hit 'send' on that email? Have you heard anything yet?" she asks through her chewing.

"Nope. Maybe he thinks he can just hit 'delete' and hope I change my mind and don't fight him," Abley says. "Take early retirement or something. I mean, they haven't got any dirt on me to investigate."

"That is ridiculous. He can't make you do that," Elizabeth replies.

"No, he can just try to trip me up at each hurdle," Abley huffs.

"Even you said you are not suspended anymore from today, you can come back and just ignore him then," Elizabeth says.

"I've said, I need Raynott's agreement, and he hasn't given it, quite the opposite. I'm in limbo," he says.

They hear the doorbell ring.

"Who can that be?" Elizabeth wonders. "Godric has keys and won't show his face after what he's done to my robe that's for sure." Elizabeth half hopes she's wrong, and would forgive the robe shenanigans just to see Godric. She is unnerved by his lack of communication since yesterday lunchtime. It's not like him. And why hasn't he been back or phoned, he looked perfectly well at the Formal Hall tonight? He didn't even come and say hello. Maybe he didn't see her. Of course he saw her. She was on the top table.

"It's not going to be for me," Abley replies. Elizabeth gets up and walks to open the door.

"Is he here?!" A big man, in his forties, barges past Elizabeth and walks straight into her drawing room, coming face to face with Inspector Abley. "Abley? You look older than the picture in Maureen's bedroom." The man looks Abley up and down, and Abley has no idea who this man is.

"Who the hell are you?!" Abley puts down his pop and turns to look up at the huge man.

"Excuse me! You can't just storm in here like you own the place. This is my home. I've a good mind to call the police," Elizabeth booms, cross at the intruder for upsetting her animals and treading in dirt from his shoes.

"He is the police," the man replies, confused at Elizabeth. He turns to Bob Abley and points his finger.

"Now listen here, Maureen is distraught. She said there were words. And I don't want my Maureen upset."

"Who the hell are you?" Inspector Abley repeats, still none the wiser about this intruder.

"Whoever you are, get out! Get out!" Elizabeth shouts.

"I've no beef with you lady," the intruder replies. "I've just come to warn this gorilla off harassing his ex-wife," the man says back to Abley. "She could report you."

"Excuse me. He's done nothing of the kind," Elizabeth replies angrily.

"What do you call pulling the 'for sale' sign off the front wall today and leaving chocolates in the shape of hearts on the window sill then?" The man looks at Elizabeth and then back at Bob Abely. Elizabeth looks at her friend confused.

"It's my house too. She can't just sell it a day after moving back in. My name's on the deeds. She needs my permission!" Abley shouts, then stands up. "Get out the hell out!" Inspector Abley nearly bursts a blood vessel. The dogs are now barking. There is a pause where the three of them all stare at each other. Then finally the man says, "I just came to tell you to leave her alone!" The man pushes Abley on the collar.

"I have a message for you to send to my dear wife." Abley spits out the words.

Elizabeth looks at the two men, and around at all her lovely priceless things in her drawing room, pleading with her eyes to Abley not to start a fight. Abley sees Elizabeth's concern and throws himself back down on the sofa.

"Tell her I'm done," Abley says quietly.

"I'll tell her you're going to leave her alone," The intruder replies.

"Oh yes." Abley picks his pop back up and takes a slow glug. "Well and truly. She's all yours, whoever you are."

The man stares at Abley and then decides he's made his point. He changes his manner and tone.

"I'm Mike, we met at the airport." Mike feels a little guilty at coming in heavy-handed, clearly having been told by Maureen that Abley is a terrible man.

"Would you like a naan, Mike?" Abley picks up a tray of naan breads and passes it to Mike.

"No, you're alright." Mike's demeanour changes completely until he says an awkward goodbye. Elizabeth follows Mike out to make sure he shuts the door, and the dogs don't run out the front. Then she goes back into the drawing room and sits down. Both of them say nothing for ages. Then Abley breaks the silence.

"No more wallowing." He looks at her and continues to drink his pop. Elizabeth waits, letting the silence hang. After a while, she stands up.

"I find in situations like these a good cherry cheesecake works wonders." Elizabeth goes to fetch two pieces from her fridge then finally sits back down. Inspector Abley regains composure. The last thing he needs is cherry cheesecake. Elizabeth, however, is hungry after only getting a starter this evening before everything kicked off at Victoria College, and doesn't fancy finishing Bob's now cold curry. "Not bad, if I do say so myself. It's the Bing cherries, so juicy." And Elizabeth takes another large bite of cheesecake. "Try it." She pushes a plate under Abley's nose. He doesn't want it, but then Elizabeth cuts a piece with a fork and prongs it ready to eat. She picks it up and holds it in front of his nose.

"No. I've had the Indian, I'm stuffed," Abley says, turning his head.

"Go on." Elizabeth makes like an aeroplane for a small child. "Don't worry, I didn't make it. I bought it from the bakery. After hearing those words, Inspector Abley opens his mouth. He starts to chew and immediately begins to feel better. "There, all better," she sighs. "Sugar."

"What's up yourself?" Abley notices Elizabeth is also

not her happiest.

"Swans – don't ask. And Godric. Been a funny day," she replies.

"Thank you," he says.

"What for?"

"For this," Abley replies. Elizabeth smiles.

"The strawberry tart tomorrow night's on you," she says, with a mouth full of cherry cheesecake herself.

"Will Godric be okay with me staying?" Abley asks.

"I haven't seen him for over a day, and he's not answering his phone. I think he's going to live in College," she says.

"You're inseparable." Abley wonders what's going on.

"He's perfectly entitled to a life." Elizabeth hides how upset she is from Bob, but he knows.

Abley looks at Hector and Monty, both eagerly waiting for dropped crumbs, having already managed to grab one of the curry takeaway boxes, which Elizabeth can now see under her dining table, all the juices licked clean. Bob Abley finishes his cheesecake then leans back on the sofa and shuts his eyes. Elizabeth does the same. After a while, he turns his head sideways and stares at Elizabeth.

"We're more like each other than you know," he smirks.

"Are you out of your mind?" Elizabeth pulls a face as she finishes her cheesecake with her eyes still shut.

"I'm a copper and with your obsession with solving crimes. I just think we have more in common," he says.

"Your obsession with getting a hole in one makes you more like Gerald." Elizabeth continues to talk and eat. She can feel Bob looking at her, but doesn't mind. In fact, it feels warm and friendly. She knows how Bob knows her better than most and she likes his easy company. Gerald was like Bob in some ways. He would tell Elizabeth that if you cut him open, you would find that he was half hedonist. She would enjoy Gerald's passion for jazz, golf, rowing and picnics. 'Not everything has to be so serious,' Gerald would say to her and take her out to see a show or some comedy.

As Elizabeth thinks of Gerald, she can feel Bob moving closer. Maybe he is going to rest his head on her shoulder like Gerald used to. She can feel Gerald with her right now. Somehow their heads touch as they both rest on the back of the sofa. She can smell Bob's shampoo. She can feel the dogs at her legs and a wave of relaxation travels through her. But before Elizabeth knows what is happening, Bob Abley moves very quickly to kiss Elizabeth. In the same moment she had moved her head and so the kiss landed on her neck. It makes her jump out of her skin. Was he aiming for her neck or where? She can also see Emily standing in front of both of them.

"And to think I was worried about you storming off." Emily says, "that I'd apparently pushed some man on you when you weren't ready to date? And look at you, canoodling with this good-for-nothing! Of all the people, Liz. Of all the people." Emily folds her arms, waiting for an explanation. Elizabeth sits up. Why didn't the dogs bark? How did Emily get in? She looks at Monty finishing her cherry cheesecake from the plate in her lap. Then back to her friend, who has got the wrong end of the stick entirely. How the hell did that nearly happen? She can see Bob Abley's moccasins, and he is wearing Gerald's trousers from when she lent them to him. This has gotten out of hand. Everything is wrong. Elizabeth feels sick from the sugar rush. She doesn't know herself. Has she become so obsessed with solving crimes that she wants to bed the Inspector? No, no, no. "Well?" Emily says.

*

Elizabeth refuses to get into a discussion with Emily. She makes her excuses mumbling something about how she was about to take the dogs out for their last ablutions after the supper in College, and how awful the swan sacrifice was, then leaves. She leaves Emily feeling a little awkward, and in front of Bob Abley, who remains on the sofa where Elizabeth left him. Bob starts to flick through the television channels looking for golf until he finds one which isn't a match but someone giving golf chipping lessons. He watches the gentle undulation of the greens in the background as the professional walks the viewer through some tips to get out of bunkers. Anything other than having to speak to Emily.

"Why can't you leave her alone?" Emily starts to confront Bob after Elizabeth shuts the front door behind her. Emily looks down her nose at Bob Abley's curry take-outs still strewn around the place. "Didn't you think to tidy up?" Emily picks up as many cartons as she can carry and takes them through to the kitchen. She comes back into the drawing room.

"Nice to see you again too," Abley says.

"Huh." Emily starts to pick up cushions from the floor and then both empty plates from the cherry cheesecake, and a bottle of pop and Abley's half-drunk glass. "You should go home now."

"Liz says I can stay here," he says.

"And you try to kiss her? You should go before she gets back. You're taking advantage. And like all men, you don't know what you are doing, or the damage you can cause. She is just getting over the death of her husband. Haven't you thought about that?"

"Nothing happened," Abley finishes his pop.

"Only because I came in," Emily replies.

"Nothing happened. Nothing will happen. We're just friends, Emily," Abley says, a little irked at having to have this conversation.

"Friends with benefits? Not on my watch. Get your stuff and go and stay in a hotel. Have some dignity man. Stop wallowing and using Liz. She told me you lost your job because of your drinking. Stuffed everything up. That you are weak. Have no fight left in you. It's not her job to buck you up. Get a backbone, stop leaning on her and using her," Emily says.

Inspector Abley is quite shocked by that. He didn't think Elizabeth would have bad-mouthed him so spitefully. He hasn't quite lost his job, but if Elizabeth believes that? It's enough, in his fragile state to defeat him. A cloud passes across his mind, and all of a sudden his mood drops through the floor.

"You're right. What am I doing?" Inspector Abley turns and walks up the stairs. It isn't long before he's back down with his bag. "Will you stay here until she gets back? I don't know if she took a key."

Emily shuts the door and smiles to herself. Thank goodness for small mercies. Bertie comes down with Soot to say hello.

"Neither of you liked him either, did you?" And Soot brushes up against Emily. Emily smiles. She has sorted out Elizabeth's life again. She turns the golf off and spots the coasters across the table. She gets up and tidies them away too, and then dusts the coffee table, so it is spotless again. She wants to clean away all traces of that dirty man from Elizabeth's life.

45
VANDAL

A couple of miles away at the Department of Galileo, Joe stands outside the old wooden telescope building. He looks at the broken police tape hanging from the door. Joe knows all too well how that Professor Crowhams has tried to monopolise this place and scowls at the sign on the door – 'No students permitted without being accompanied' – another way Crowhams isolates his pride and joy. The door is locked, but Joe knows where Crowhams leaves the key, for emergencies. Crowhams hates that Joe has this access. Joe walks over to a box on the wall and uses his garden key to open it. Inside are a few keys for the greenhouse, the shed, and one for the telescope house. He takes it and opens the door. He walks into the circular space, looks up at the telescope, the ceiling is closed tonight which he thinks is a shame given the stars are out in force. But no matter, Joe has brought something with him this time to entertain himself. He climbs the ladder to reach the viewing platform and opens the sack he's carrying. He puts on gloves and then starts to smear horse manure over the telescope. When it begins to get too pungent, Joe climbs back down and scatters the rest on the floor. That will teach him.

"What are you doing?" Sarah stands at the door.

"Sarah." Joe looks guilty as hell.

"This beautiful piece of equipment survived a World War? What would Tom say if he were here?" Sarah steps in a little further, trying not to stand on manure.

"I did it for you and Tom. He does nothing but pick on you." Joe puts down the now empty sack of manure. "He was on your boat earlier. I don't trust him. He's up to something. He stole some papers you know. Looked like a brochure or something."

"Do you know me at all? I want nothing to do with this shameful behaviour. You know I could have slipped on this." Sarah says, now standing still and looking at the mess. "You must get a bucket and clean this up now. Two wrongs don't make a right."

Joe looks at Sarah, hurt by her reaction.

*

A short while later, Elizabeth is still walking Hector and Monty on Jesus Green before bedtime. She spots Sarah and Joe walking home from the Department of Galileo.

"Good evening. Is everything okay?" Elizabeth asks.

"It will be. Once Professor Crowhams is not walking on this planet!" Joe replies ominously.

"Take no notice of him, Professor Green," Sarah replies. "I think everyone is walking on eggshells at the moment. We just left the department. Saw Professor Crowhams arriving as we left. Didn't speak to him. He looked angry. Mind you, he always looks angry."

"I'm angry, at him," Joe shouts at Sarah.

"Yes, well shoving horse manure on his favourite telescope isn't going to resolve anything is it," Sarah snaps back, immediately regretting her words in front of Elizabeth. “He didn't mean it, Professor. We're both just tired.”

“And probably ill. You really should rest,” Elizabeth stresses.

“Well if she had been resting she would have bumped into Professor Crowhams breaking into her boat a couple of hours ago,” Joe tells Elizabeth, then turns to Sarah. “Maybe it was you he wanted to confront rather than the brochure he stole?”

“What has he got against me? I’m a lowly staff member. I’m sure he doesn’t give me a second thought.” Sarah shrugs.

“Maybe you have something of Tom’s that he wants?” Joes replies. “Like I say, he left with those papers under his arm?”

“There’s nothing of Tom’s left on the boat, apart from his clothes.” Sarah says. “He kept all his work documents in his office at work. Which reminds me, I have to go and sort through them all. There must be some important research findings which should be published.” Sarah turns to Elizabeth “What do you do when an academic dies? He had so many ideas, so much research. I can’t let it all go to waste.”

“I don’t know, perhaps contact his closest research partner, someone working on his projects with him, or close to him.” Elizabeth suggests, remembering how she had to do the same for Gerald.

“Good idea. Cynthia did some research with him. I'll talk to her.” Sarah nods.

*

Professor Crowhams had indeed turned up at the department late and had seen Joe and Sarah slinking away. He wondered what they could be doing there so late? He had a few notes to write up in his office. They were a huge nuisance, but he wanted to make sure he wrote to every member of staff in Galileo about his misgivings about the stargazing events. He had to put a stop to the next one, as it was due to be even bigger and was a complete waste of department money, money that could be spent on getting more historic telescopes to preserve. He finally sits back in his chair once he's hit 'send'. So it is with some delay that he walks out to check on his beloved telescope. When he opens the door the smell of manure hits him.

"Horses!" He climbs the ladder and can see horse manure in the cracks of the telescope, where Joe didn't make much of an effort to clean before. "Edward!!" Professor Crowhams screams.

"Why are you screaming Edward?" Elizabeth stands at the door with Hector and Monty, having walked from Jesus Green.

"God damn it, woman, are you following me?" Crowhams says.

"Should I be? You look so angry, are you about to commit a crime?" She asks.

"Wouldn't you be angry if your prize research equipment was covered in horse manure? And get those dogs out."

"It does smell of dung in here, yes. But surely this isn't your telescope? It belongs to the department, for all to share," she says.

"You're beginning to sound like that Tom Mirren, and look what happened to him," Crowhams replies. "He wanted to open this to the public, for stargazing nights. Can you imagine? Huh. No thank you. I can achieve everything I need to with her here. That's if we're left alone."

"I wanted to ask you why you stormed out after Cynthia earlier this evening, from the Victoria supper?" Elizabeth asks.

"So you are following me. Didn't think swan would be for your palate?"

"It turns out it wasn't for most others either," she replies. "I hope that is the last time the College decides to pull such a ridiculous culinary stunt."

"I love meat. Can't get enough of it. Bury me with rump steak and veal." Crowhams looks at Elizabeth, hoping his words cause upset.

"Why was Cynthia running away from you?" she asks.

"What business is that of yours?" Crowhams brushes manure off the telescope.

"This is an official murder enquiry." Elizabeth stands carefully so as not to tread on any manure.

"Who are you, the cat's mother? When the police get here, as I will be calling them about this vandalism, I will talk to them," he says.

"You have something to hide." Elizabeth raises her eyebrows at Crowhams. "That's okay, I'll speak with Cynthia. To hear her side of the story."

"Good luck with that. She won't tell you anything. She doesn't want it to come out," Crowhams says.

"Doesn't want what to come out?" Elizabeth asks. But Professor Crowhams doesn't say anything more. He just shakes his head. "From where I was sitting she looked rather repulsed by your kiss, and wanted nothing to do with you."

"I was telling her to keep that boyfriend under control," Crowhams replies.

"Ed?" Elizabeth asks.

"Edward has been around my house. Keeps breaking in and leaving manure everywhere. Likely he did this too! If I catch him in the act, he won't know what's hit him. She's the same. Wanted one thing does another. Women, you're all the same." Crowhams shakes his head and continues brushing off the manure, now with his handkerchief.

"That's a sweeping generalisation. Is that why you were breaking into Tom and Sarah's boat?" Elizabeth asks.

"I wasn't breaking in. I went to talk to Sarah about

Tom's public stargazing project. It's got to stop. She seems intent on keeping it going, for his memory. But she'll regret it."

"Why?"

"The public doesn't want to understand science," Crowhams replies. "They want to fear it, jeer at it. They just watch their idiots' lanterns every night, eating pizza, burger and chicken, growing more obese with their diabetes-ridden carcasses. Let's leave them in their soporific stupor to keep out of the way of our critical work."

"Don't let Inspector Abley hear you say that." Elizabeth can picture Bob's face as if he were here now.

"What, who?" Professor Crowhams shakes his head, irritated adding, "Tom's dead, and it stops with him. That's the end of it."

"Everyone I talk to about you says you are a difficult man, that you don't have any friends. Why d'you think they say that?" Elizabeth asks.

"Just get out. Meddling irritant, go on," Crowhams says, raising his voice.

Elizabeth can't say she's surprised that he baulks at her last question. She isn't quite sure why she said that. It isn't very professional or kind. The truth is, she has no idea who has murdered Tom and isn't at all sure that it was Professor Crowhams.

46
A TRUE FRIEND

A good while later, Elizabeth comes back home. She is surprised to find that coats have been picked up in the hallway, and when she comes through to the drawing room, all the takeaway has been tidied away. Perhaps Bob has done it before he's gone to bed. She's tired herself and thinks she will go up now but decides to give the dogs a midnight treat first to settle them. She wanders into the kitchen and is surprised to find Emily still here, sitting at the table alone with a cup of tea. The kitchen is also spotless. All the washing up has been done and put away.

"I wanted to wait until you got home. The Green is not a safe place at night." Emily says.

"Nonsense Emily, it's fine. It's just empty. The way I like it." Elizabeth reaches up into the cupboard where she keeps all the pet treats and takes out two for the cats for upstairs and two for the dogs. She makes Hector and Monty go and sit in their beds and then gives them a treat each. "Good boys. Now sleepy deepy time. Sleepy deepy time."

Emily has got up and fetched another cup and is pouring Elizabeth a peppermint tea from the flask of hot water on the table.

"You were a while?" Emily asks.

"Yes, well, I went for a walk. You won't be interested," Elizabeth says.

"No, go on. I'm all ears." Emily tries to get Elizabeth to talk, wondering what had happened before with the Inspector.

"I went to speak to some of those close to the murder," Elizabeth replies, but can see Emily deflate and ever so slightly shake her head.

"Why do you get caught up in these things?" Emily asks, "They never lead to any good. Is it definitely murder? What about the horses?"

"Tom Mirren is dead." Elizabeth looks at her friend. "He was a Reader at the Department of Galileo. No horses are dead. And, although he is a particularly unpleasant man, Professor Crowhams was hit on the head in the Department of Galileo. The back of the head, mind, and he didn't see his attacker. So that could have been attempted murder. They both have the department in common."

"It could have been a coincidence?" Emily suggests.

"On the same night?" Elizabeth replies.

"Well who did it then?" Emily asks.

"I have no idea. I've been trying to work out a motive for three days now."

"Is it a feud?" Emily can't believe she is continuing this conversation about police work, but is trying to get Elizabeth to open up, still wondering what on earth she walked into earlier with the Inspector. "What does Inspector Abley think?" Emily asks.

"What? Oh, I don't know. I've been working on this with Sergeant Lemon. The thing is, it could be related to these stargazing nights. Tom ran them, Professor Crowhams hates them. Could they have tried to hurt each other on the same night and Crowhams just got in there first?" Elizabeth says.

"I don't know what you're talking about." Emily replies, "So the Inspector hasn't been helping you?" Emily brings it back to Bob Abley.

"Why did you take me to a swan supper?" Elizabeth knows what Emily is doing but decides two can play at this.

"Don't change the subject," Emily says. "What did I stumble into tonight?"

"And as for that unpleasant man." Elizabeth shakes her head at her friend about Aubyn, refusing to answer.

"You mean the one I found you nearly kissing tonight?" Emily again brings it back to the Inspector.

"Shh, he'll hear your nonsense, be quiet, alright?" Elizabeth puts her fingers to her mouth. "That awful man at dinner, Aubyn. What were you thinking?"

"He's gone," Emily says.

"Good, I think I'd poke pencils in my ears if I had to listen to him again." Elizabeth replies.

"No, your Inspector. He realised he shouldn't be burdening you with his problems. He's a car crash, Liz." Emily takes a sip of tea.

"What? Where's he gone? He's got nowhere to go?" Elizabeth can feel Emily is behind this, and isn't happy.

"He's a grown man, Liz. There are hotels." Emily replies putting down her cup, not pleased with Elizabeth's tone.

"And how did he come to this conclusion, might I ask? With a little help from you?" Elizabeth says.

"He's a bad influence." Emily puts her foot down.

"Oh, thank you for waiting and for caring, but what have you done?" Elizabeth storms off, surprised by her anger at her dearest friend.

47
LINE ON THE RIVER

A silver blanket covers Stourbridge Common, tucking in everything under its cold grip. Still, in the early hours of Wednesday morning, a solitary sculler breaks through the mist on the River Cam, with oars dipping and dripping past the narrow boats with their curtains pulled tight behind huffed up portholes. Ducks, with heads tucked under wing, nestle in a nearby boathouse under the Green Dragon Bridge. But this peaceful winter landscape is interrupted by a sudden gurgling scream, followed by splashing in the water behind the canal boats. Despite the early hours it isn't difficult to see that the water is turning another colour around the rower who continues to cry out and flap until finally a boat dweller, Joe, opens a roof hatch on one of the boats and looks out.

Joe can see the horrific accident, climbs out of his boat and throws a rope into the middle of the river. He recognises the shadow in the water as Brad, a post-doc from his department he was arguing with just the other day. He grabs the rope and holds on for dear life. Joe slowly pulls Brad to the murky bank but there Brad lolls and dips, unable to climb out. Joe lays flat on the bank, his arms outstretched to help Brad out of the chilly waters. It is a huge struggle, and Joe is covered in Brad's blood in the process, but finally after a lot of grunting both lie still, one too ill to move, blood pouring out of a line across his neck and falling onto the concrete ledge and dropping back into the water, the other too in shock, that is until Joe notices red blood oozing far too quickly from Brad's neck. Joe the holds on and never lets go of Brad's wound, pushing against the pumping blood as he dials for an ambulance.

A short while later more people are awake and watching as an ambulance drives onto Stourbridge Common, and two paramedics jump out and rush to the victim. Not long after they have stabilised Brad, one calls for the police. They can see what others can see clearly, now the sun has risen above the horizon on this cold morning. A wire, no more than five millimetres thick is stretched right across the river from one side to the other. With one end tied to a street lamp and the other to a tree, the wire looks for all intents and purposes placed deliberately to cause injury to rowers. Someone in the background is shouting at another rower to slow down.

Not long after, Sergeant Lemon arrives with his Constables. They borrow a dinghy from one of the canal boats and put tape across either side of the wire on the river, as well as drape 'Closed' signs, to stop boats or rowers. Then the SOCOs come in white suits. Sergeant Lemon is taking no chances, not after a murder not twenty feet away from this spot the weekend past.

"Did you see who did this?" Sergeant Lemon asks Joe.

"No," Joe says, standing over rower Brad who is being given a drip to replace all the lost blood. "I heard screaming and a lot of noise on the water. I was asleep. It sounded like an injured swan. But when I looked, it was this man in the water. I didn't know what to do. It's cold in there," Joe replies, stressed.

"Quite. And nothing else? You didn't see who attached this wire?"

"No, of course not. He could have been killed. The rowers can be travelling quite fast by the time they get to our boats. I should know, they hit us enough. It could have severed his neck right off. Is he going to be okay?" Joe looks at Brad with an oxygen mask now on his face and a foil blanket over his body, with paramedics about to carry him off to the ambulance.

"Are you alone, or with anyone else?" Sergeant Lemon continues to question Joe for any details.

"My friends should be on the boat behind, and Sarah there." Joe points to Sarah's boat.

"It looks dark," Sergeant Lemon replies, looking at Sarah's boat.

"Yes, it does. Maybe she's asleep? Maybe she's up staying with Talya. Her friend in Fen Ditton. She's been up there a bit since Tom, you know, was killed. I don't think I could sleep on that boat either."

"Talya Febland, who was at the hospital?" Lemon asks, looking at his notebook.

"Yes. Crowham's broke into her boat last night. Maybe he did it? I think that injured man, Brad, is one of his post-docs too?"

48
AN OLD FLAME

Sarah and Talya are sitting by a roaring fire in the grand hall of Talya's substantial Georgian home in Fen Ditton eating breakfast of toast and coffee. They are both in fluffy dressing gowns and slippers belonging to Talya. Talya inherited money from her American father and bought this house, which she then fitted out with the most expensive of interiors. Tom often told Joe that he used to walk into Talya's and melt with a warm fuzzy glow, then cry inside when he knew he had to go back to the cold, damp boat. Joe spots Sarah almost lost in a vast purple velvet sofa. He sits down beside her and hugs her. Talya watches them and smiles. Then spots the blood.

"What is that?" Talya asks.

"Oh yes, sorry. It's dried, it won't come off on—" Joe replies.

"Is it yours?" Sarah interrupts, looking worried.

"No, this rower was injured on the river. Badly, I just helped him out. He's gone to hospital. It was—"

"Who?"

"I think his name is Brad?" Joe replies.

"Oh, Professor Crowhams' post-doc?" Sarah asks.

"Yeah." Joe doesn't know what to say. They all stare blankly, unsure what is going on.

"Well, take those off, I'm sure I have another dressing gown." Talya says, standing up. Joe picks up a pain au chocolat and dips it in Sarah's coffee.

"There." Sarah says, lifting up her cup so Joe can dip more easily for a second time.

"Boats are all safe. I've moved them up closer to here, get them away for tonight," Joe says. "You two look like you've been putting the world to rights," he adds, looking at Talya. "I wanted to check Sarah was feeling okay." He turns to Sarah for her to confirm. "Did you tell Talya about Crowhams breaking into your boat?"

"I swear that man searches horses out, darling," Talya replies, adding, "You should come and live here, just until everything settles down." She looks at Sarah.

"No, I couldn't possibly," Sarah replies, "Thank you so much, I don't mean to sound ungrateful, but I want to stay near Tom." She replies, a little embarrassed. "My bed still smells of him."

"Course honey, but Joe's right. It might not be safe. I mean, if that Professor is wandering all over your boat," Talya says, about to leave to get Joe some clean dry clothes.

"I can show you where I put your's and Tom's boats," Joe offers.

"Can I get you coffee honey?" Talya asks after Joe, who nods before she leaves to replenish the drinks.

"I came to see if you'd like to stay with me from now on, on Tom's old boat?" Joe says, looking deep into Sarah's eyes. "I mean, I'm close to your boat. But you'd be safe."

"I'm sorry Joe, it was lovely but I think we both know it was a mistake that can't happen again," Sarah says.

"It meant the world to me. I love you." Joe stops

breathing, waiting for Sarah to melt. Sarah, however, squirms instead.

"I'm sorry Joe." Sarah turns away. But Joe pulls her back round to face him.

"That's not what you said before when we—"

"It was a one-off, I was upset," Sarah interrupts.

"I said I'd do anything to get you, anything." Joe now stares a bit more aggressively. Sarah is nervous about what he will do next.

"Don't." Sarah untwists her arm from Joe. The fire crackles and spits behind. Talya walks back in, unaware she has interrupted something.

"There." She has brought in a fresh coffee pot and cups, as well as custard tarts. And a dressing gown for Joe.

"Sarah? Tart?" Talya asks.

"No thanks," she replies.

"Sugar will do you good," Talya says.

"Milk doesn't agree with me," Sarah says.

"Oh god, sorry I forgot. Joe?" Joe nods. Talya holds the plate of custard tarts for Joe and continues, "You must feel awful that it was your pie that killed Tom?" Talya looks at Sarah, shaking her head.

"What?" Sarah looks confused.

"Your apple pie," Talya says.

"Yes, but I didn't do it deliberately," Sarah says, upset.

"You deliberately cooked the pie—" Talya replies.

"Talya?" Joe interrupts.

"I'm only asking," Talya says. "I know it would be on my mind all the time. Would torture me, darling. I feel for you. I've always loved your cooking."

"You didn't eat any apple pie," Joe says to Talya.

"You know I don't like apples. I brought the crème caramel?" Talya replies.

"I do think about it," Sarah says, looking into the fire. "I encouraged him to have seconds. If I hadn't done that, maybe he'd have survived like we did." Sarah then looks at Joe with real horror in her eyes.

"It's okay. Shh," Joe says to Sarah. "Why did you bring that up?" he hisses to Talya.

"It's good to let the boo-hoos out. That's all. Better out than in my old ma used to say. I'm glad I didn't eat the apple pie too. What's it like, the poison?"

"Really?" Joe asks Talya.

"What? I've never been poisoned before that's all. I'm just wondering what it felt like?" Talya replies.

"Like I was dying. That's the worst thing about it. That I know what Tom must have felt like. The panic, the not feeling ready to die." Sarah starts to cry.

"I'm sorry, I didn't mean… I meant the physical symptoms. But forget it." Talya realises she's gone too far. "Look, Tom knows you loved him. We all loved him. He was a wonderful man and has a special place in all our hearts." Talya gets up and hugs Sarah. Joe scowls at Talya.

"I think Tom knew about you two." Talya drops a bomb. Joe looks at Talya, and Sarah almost stops breathing. "Just the things he said to me."

"There is no us two," Sarah replies under her tears. "You're wicked this morning."

"Come off it." Talya stands up and laughs. "Everybody knows that Joe is head over heels in love with you Sarah." Talya looks at Joe. "Am I wrong?"

"Stop shit stirring," Joe says, "What Tom did or didn't know has nothing to do with this tragedy, and I know he knew Sarah loved him deeply."

"No one else knew. It was once. Joe hasn't told anyone," Sarah says, looking up at Talya.

"You were spotted," Talya replies.

"Who by?" Sarah asks.

"Me. I might have accidentally told Tom. I didn't say you were sleeping with one another. Just wondered if Tom knew that Joe was so crazy about you."

"You little bitch." Joe gets up and is about to grab Talya, to shake her or something.

"Oh, keep your hair on. He's dead. It's up to you two if

you get together now. I don't care. In fact, I think it would be pretty healthy, after a period, to admit your feelings for one another. He's not going to stop you unless you believe in ghosts and being haunted from the grave." Talya says, walking away to the fireplace.

"It was a mistake, and Tom and I were on a break at the time," Sarah says quietly.

"Well, that's fine then. No harm done. No need for secrecy," Talya replies, stoking the fire.

"Come on Sarah, let me take you back to the boats. This is toxic." Joe pulls Sarah up out of the sofa and grabs her coat, leaving Talya smiling.

"Suit yourself. You came to me. To be honest, I think you both need to have baths before you come back and sit on my sofa. I don't want nits or bed bugs. Thank you." Talya walks with them until they leave and then slams the door on them, her face full of anger as she shuts them out.

Outside, Joe and Sarah are left completely shocked by what has just happened. Joe helps Sarah into her coat.

"Someone's rattled her cage. C'mon, there's a reason we went to live on boats in the first place," Joe says as they walk off. "To get away from people."

49
INSPECTOR ABLEY

After kissing Elizabeth's neck and being taken down a peg or two by Emily, Inspector Bob Abley had gone to The Green Magician to nurse his away his ego. He wasn't a big fan of the establishment, as it was always changing hands and he was forever busting it for one reason or another. But it was central, warm, had a very late licence and he could blend into the background until the early hours. But when everyone was asked to leave at four o'clock, as they had to close, Bob Abley had had enough of being chased from one seat to the other. After walking the city at night for a while, he decided to try somewhere at the other end of the scale. Somewhere he could be sure to be treated well and sit in comfort. The night staff at the University Arms Hotel had taken pity on the Inspector, knowing him well and liking him a lot, and had left him on a sofa in the Brasserie waiting an hour for first breakfast, not questioning his snoring as they set out the immaculate linen table cloths and polished the cutlery. A kind waiter then woke the Inspector by wafting some fresh coffee under his nose.

Bob Abley is now sitting at a table overlooking Parker's Piece, reading the tabloid sports section and devouring the delightful breakfast. With a full belly Inspector Abley decides to check himself into a room here at the hotel. If Maureen wouldn't let him go home and if he couldn't go on holiday abroad then he can still live it up in luxury. Abley is shown to a room, a suite in fact. He thanks the porter, kicks off his shoes and falls back into the soft pillows on the bed. After a few stretches and sighs and a serious thought to fall asleep, he props himself up and looks out onto Parker's Piece. He hears a police siren leaving the station and immediately thinks about Elizabeth and Lemon working on the case. He feels ashamed. He knows they are trying to solve the murder before the Super puts Pober on it, thereby closing the window even more to his return. Elizabeth had told him as much. The Super is hardly about to let a Sergeant run a case, not now it has been confirmed as a murder investigation. Pober is probably already on his way.

Inspector Abley puts on the television. He flicks through channels until he gets to a drama where they are showing a murder mystery. The detective in this show is very clever, and Abley has always identified with this particular character. He notices how well the detective on the television is dressed, how everyone is listening intently to his every word. The detective on the television takes out his little notepad, licks his pencil and writes something. Then he looks up with a thoughtful gaze, speaks to his Sergeant and writes something else. He rips off the piece of paper and gives it to his Sergeant. The Sergeant nods and says something about 'right away'.

Inspector Abley has slouched down on the bed. He mutes the television but leaves the detective show on. Staring at his feet, he notices for the first time that he is wearing odd socks. He can see himself in the mirror on the opposite wall. He is a mess. Inspector Abley sits up. He turns to the bedside table and sees a notepad and pencil on the side. He lifts it up and plumps some pillows behind him and starts to think.

For the first time in ages, Abley's mind is on the case. He starts to draw an apple to help him think. If someone poisoned Tom with apples, they had to know he would eat apples. Then he scratches out the apple and turns over the page of the notepad. From Elizabeth's sharing what she knew over cheesecake last night, Abley thinks that Tom Mirren's death did seem highly suspicious. As Elizabeth said, no horses died. Surely that was evidence enough together with the break in and attack of Professor Crowhams. Abley writes the word 'telescope' on the notepad.

And although not calling Lemon back, he had listened to the answerphone from him about the injury to the rower on the river with the wire. It was strange that, although everyone seemed linked to the department, two of the assaults were down by the boats. Abley writes the word 'rower' on his notepad. What have the boats to do with it? Abley adds 'canal boats'. And poisoned by an apple pie? He adds 'apple pie' to his list, and 'horses'. It was such a random and unreliable way to murder someone.

So the murderer has to be someone either in the department or someone Tom knew. 'Department of Galileo' and 'friends' are added to his list. It cannot be a stranger. But maybe it isn't any of them. Abley thinks that perhaps Elizabeth and Lemon have missed the main clue. The fact that all the boat people were poisoned. Maybe no one meant to kill Tom. Perhaps they just wanted to make the boat people ill to teach them a lesson, or even kill them all. 'Everyone poisoned.' He has to talk to Elizabeth about it. He must find her straight away. He picks up the phone and calls Foxes Haven, but there is no reply.

"Get a mobile, woman!" He shouts in frustration at his friend who cannot hear. Inspector Abley writes down

'Professor Crowhams' but in even bigger capitals he writes down 'Cynthia Hatman' on his notepad.

*

When Elizabeth gets back from walking Hector and Monty this morning, the last person she expects at her front door is Sergeant Lemon. It seems like everyone is popping round, apart from Godric that is.

"I heard from Mrs Abley that the Inspector might be here," Sergeant Lemon says. "She seems angry."

"You went to see her again?" Elizabeth raises her eyebrows.

"No, I went to find him. I was hoping he might have gone home by now." Lemon shakes his head

"Oh. Well, don't believe anything that woman tells you. He's not here." Elizabeth smiles a little, feeling for Lemon's wasted time.

"Have you seen him?" Lemon asks.

"Come in, I'm making tea. It's cold out there." Elizabeth dodges the question again, hoping her lack of response will be read that she has not. For Abley's sake.

"Thank you." Lemon shuts the front door and walks through into the kitchen.

"That's a lot of birds." Lemon looks up at one of Elizabeth's many bird feeders and spots a dozen or so on the bird table and hanging off, picking at the dangling feeders.

"Yes, well. They like my seeds. But you haven't come to look at the birds. Why are you looking for the Inspector today? What's happened now?" Elizabeth expects Lemon is going to tell her about how the Inspector has been found in a ditch in a drunken stupor. Or worse after having been chucked out of Foxes Haven by Emily.

"So Inspector Abley called me, that's why I went to his house. About half an hour ago. Didn't say where he was," Sergeant Lemon replies.

"And?" Elizabeth is glued to Lemon, not quite

believing her own ears. "He called you, and?"

"He left a message. I couldn't believe it. He actually spoke about the case?" Lemon half laughs. Elizabeth cannot help herself cracking a smile. Lemon continues, "It was a bit rambling. I don't think he's been sleeping."

"Yes, yes. What did he say?" Elizabeth asks impatiently.

"To find that Cynthia woman, Cynthia Hatman."

"Have you got the message? Play it." Elizabeth says. Lemon takes out his phone and presses 'play', and Inspector Abley's voice starts.

"Hello Lemon, yes well, er, you know. Anyway, I think it's someone who might want to hurt the boat people. Where are you? Are you still asleep? Yes. You should try the breakfast at the University Arms Hotel. Oh my god, I have to have that again. The Jap Fancies too, in the rooms." They both hear Abley clear his throat and acknowledge he's clearly been living in luxury last night. "No, I mean I'm sure you're busy. Too busy to answer your phone. I just wondered, have you questioned this Cynthia Hatman? I think you should.

Professor Green mentioned she ran away from Professor Crowhams at dinner last night. What was that about? I think she might be hiding something. She worked with Tom Mirren – Professor Green said that in one of her messages. And that she knows both the boat people far better than Professor Crowhams from what Professor Green told me. Well, they are the facts. We may have a motive. Jealousy.

I hear from Professor Green that she was working on research with Tom Mirren." Abley continues on his long and winding message, "That Cynthia had mentioned this herself when you went to attend Professor Crowhams' attack, right at the start she admitted he wanted to see her paper. You left that message, Lemon. She may have been the only one who can continue Tom's work. They were in it together, but now Cynthia Hatman will get the glory, get the accolade. She's no spring chicken I hear. She was there at the stargazing event on Stourbridge Common. I saw her. This could be her last chance. Cynthia Hatman, you even told me on one of your messages – I've listened to them all now Lemon, thank you – you mention she also doesn't like her boss, Professor Crowhams. I think she has most to gain from both of their deaths. Bring her in and question her. Don't wait for me, but I will try and get there. Well, they're my notes on it. Keep up the good work. Over and out."

"Over and out?" Elizabeth says.

"I think he's trying to be funny," Lemon replies. Elizabeth pulls a face.

"This is great. We can get him back in his job and on the case." Elizabeth says, looking for Lemon's help to make this happen.

"The Super has been away on a police course yesterday afternoon but is back today, so will probably put Inspector Pober on this morning for sure." Sergeant Lemon replies.

"Surely this means Bob's going to come back in and fight for his job?" Elizabeth says about Abley. "He told you to question Cynthia Hatman, which was an instruction. He said to start without him, but this implies he's going to join later." Elizabeth is convinced this is a good sign, but Lemon just shrugs, not sure what to say about his boss.

"Thank you for your message by the way." Lemon says, "I caught the one about the Professor on Sarah's boat, and him acting strangely at the College feast was it?"

"Yes, and the Professor's telescope has been vandalised again. Did he not call that in?" Elizabeth says. "With manure."

"I don't think so. We had to go down and get an ambulance for a sculler who rowed straight into a wire earlier this morning. The incident occurred alongside the boats on Stourbridge Common. A tree right next to Tom Mirren and Sarah Robertly's boat. We hadn't even removed the police tape."

"What?" Elizabeth is surprised to hear about the sculler.

"One of those trip wires, like you see in old Western movies. You know, when the baddies ride into town on their horses shooting up the place, but the sheriff who is all alone has trailed a wire across two buildings in the main street. And the baddies fall straight off their horses, caught by the wire." Lemon pulls out a pretend gun, fires it and then blows the smoke from the barrel.

"You're too young to watch Westerns," Elizabeth says.

"No one is too young to watch Westerns," Lemon says, pocketing his pretend gun, but not before pretend twirling it around his finger.

"Tell me if you think we should bring in Cynthia Hatman? I'd be interested in your opinion. And stop playing sheriff and maybe you'll be a real one, one day." Elizabeth watches as Lemon starts to take out another imaginary gun for his other pocket.

"Funny you should say that," Lemon replies. "Only, I was also looking for the Inspector to tell him my news."

"What news?" Elizabeth asks.

"I was hoping to tell him first," Lemon replies, but Elizabeth stares at him. "If you can keep it to yourself for now." Lemon looks for any acknowledgement from Elizabeth to promise that she will, but she is silent. "I've been offered another job, but please don't say anything if you see the Inspector. I want to tell him. It's with the Thames Valley Police."

"Why would I do that?" For a second Elizabeth's face displays disappointment, but she stops herself from congratulating Lemon.

"I can't stay here with Pober. He'll drive me nuts." Lemon says, "I'm not a huge fan of the Super either, and with the Inspector away, my hours have been just mental."

"And you think everyone is like a sweet bobby and the hours are short in Oxford? Seriously?" Elizabeth says.

Lemon takes something out of his pocket to show Elizabeth. She frowns and shakes her head.

"And? It's a beer mat?"

Lemon just gestures for Elizabeth to look more carefully. Elizabeth holds the beermat between her fingers. She can now see Bob's handwriting scribbled on the front and back. She shakes her head, she doesn't understand. "My first appraisal by Inspector Abley. He did it in the pub." Lemon smiles. Elizabeth looks more carefully and reads just a few words from the many on the beermat: 'I don't care what everybody else thinks. I think you're a bloody good copper'. Lemon smiles at Elizabeth again. There are no words. Elizabeth can see that Lemon is exhausted.

"Congratulations." Elizabeth says eventually, half smiling at Lemon. "You know he's coming back." Elizabeth isn't sure if she believes it herself.

"Rumours have gone mad at the Station. Word is, he's blown it. Shown no teeth to Raynott, just rolled over. Raynott is walking around with a spring in his step, seen it myself. Never seen him so happy. He thinks he's got shot of the Inspector for good now. This is the first call I've had in days from the Inspector." Lemon puts the beer mat back in his wallet.

"He's blown nothing. I'm sure the Super can't just sack him. He will have to go through a proper process. And as for you, for what it's worth—" Sergeant Lemon interrupts Elizabeth. He doesn't want to hear her telling him he's good at his job and stay.

"They say you have to go away to come back and get a promotion. And the girlfriend is keen." Lemon says.

"When do you start?" Elizabeth realises there is no debate left.

"After this case, or in two weeks. Depending what comes soonest. Mrs Abley eh? She really has—"

"People always forget about the ripples," Elizabeth interrupts, stopping Lemon from saying something he'll regret. But in her head, Lemon's words have sunk in. What if Abley has blown it? She is worried that perhaps the Inspector is not helping himself. One of Bob's qualities she likes so much is that he has never been one to sweat the small stuff, always knows that things turn out for the best in the end, is ever the optimist. But this could have got him into trouble. She had better go and see if she can do something at the station. Speak to someone. She's hoping it isn't Raynott, but she has a feeling in her stomach that she may just need to confront the man head-on.

"Well anyway, I'm on the hunt for Abley. So please call me if you see him. Raynott wants to see me, to see if I know anything. You know I've been trying to avoid that meeting. But I can't put it off for much longer," Lemon says.

"If I knew where the Inspector was now I'd hit him around the head and frog march him to the Station," Elizabeth replies, "But we both know he'd probably say something to Raynott that we'd all regret." See you later at the station?" Elizabeth says to Lemon, who nods.

50
THE ARREST

When just after lunchtime, Professor Elizabeth Green and Sergeant Lemon turn up at Cambridge Police Station for Lemon to show Elizabeth the photographs of the earlier attack on the River Cam this morning, they are both surprised to learn that Inspector Pober has arrested Professor Crowhams.

Not waiting for anything or anyone, Pober had ordered that Professor Nigel Crowhams be pulled out of bed this morning. Crowhams has now been sitting in a cell for a couple of hours waiting for his interrogation. Inspector Pober was going to start without Sergeant Lemon but is pleased, if only for continuity, that Lemon has now arrived and can be present while the chief suspect is questioned.

"I think Inspector Abley wanted us to bring in Cynthia Hatman to question, Sir?" Lemon says to Inspector Pober.

"Who?" Pober shakes his head in the corridor. Then he looks at Elizabeth. "It's okay, luv, I've got this from here. Thanks for all your help." Then Pober turns his back on Elizabeth. Elizabeth doesn't bat an eyelid but glances quickly at Lemon who nods. She turns and walks to the pathology lab in the Police Station ignoring Pober's dismissal. "Glad she took it so well," Pober says to Lemon, when Elizabeth is out of earshot. "These amateur sleuths. Watch a bit of police procedural crime drama on the telly and think they're all that." Pober indicates for Lemon to follow him into the interview room and they both head in and sit opposite Professor Crowhams.

"So you hate people, they're a nuisance. I get it." Pober starts to speak to Professor Crowhams, having left the tape running and door open hearing Lemon was on his way. "You want them nowhere near your precious department, yada yada. Motive. And because of your enlightened ex-colleague, one Dr Tom Mirren—" Pober reads from his notes on the desk, "who was trying to bring astronomy into the twenty-first century, and perhaps has more in common with the man on the street. Well, you saw red. You also hate horses. Just say yes for the tape." Pober is frustrated by this posh academic.

"I'm not answering these ridiculous questions. On what grounds have you arrested me, for not being a hippophile?" Crowhams replies. Picking up Inspector Pober's notes and starting to read them.

"Hey!" Pober snatches his notes back. "I've said nothing about hippos. Stick to answering the questions. You murdered Dr Tom Mirren because he was turning your world upside down. I also hear he was popular in the Department of Galileo. Perhaps you were fearful that he was going to take your top billing? That's what you lot argue about, isn't it? Petty squabbles over research grants. I've had my fair share of academic crimes. Some of you are worse than common criminals, huh." Pober looks at Lemon and nods, waiting for Lemon to nod back. But Lemon looks away.

"As much as I'd like to hear hypothesis riddled with hyperbole, I have places to go," Crowhams says. "So if you are not going to charge me, then you had better be very careful, as I will find a lawyer to sue you for time wasted."

"Calm down Einstein," Inspector Pober replies, smirking at Sergeant Lemon again. "We know you did it. You have a motive, for both human and equine attack. You had a vendetta against this… " Pober looks back at his notes, "… Dr Tom Mirren. You have no alibi."

"I was being attacked apparently when they were found?!" Crowhams says.

"Yes, but not earlier. A-ha!" Pober now points a finger at Crowhams. "Think you are being clever, eh? Earlier you said you were in your office. But no one can verify your whereabouts. You could have been purchasing apples and leaving them on Stourbridge Common. Mark my words."

"Do you have a receipt for the apples?" Crowhams asks Inspector Pober.

"What?" Pober leans back in his chair. "They're apples!"

"Anyone could have left apples on the Common." Crowhams knows the best form of defence is attack.

"We know you had an argument with Sarah Robertly on the night of the stargazing, while she was ill. You shouted at her, not content with murdering her boyfriend," Pober says.

"You have no evidence whatsoever," Crowhams replies, as cool as a cucumber.

"We have witnesses, who have seen you shout at the horses." Pober leans forward and picks up his notes again.

"Sir, may I have a word?" Sergeant Lemon interrupts, and Inspector Pober frowns, but eventually gets up.

"Don't you go anywhere," Pober says back to Crowhams and winks at the Constable standing in the corner. Sergeant Lemon walks into the corridor far enough away before Pober follows and shuts the door.

"What the hell?" Pober says to Lemon.

"With all due respect, Sir, we don't have enough evidence to charge this man."

"Are you questioning my authority? I've been put on this case now, and as your superior… are you my wingman, or not?"

"Respectfully, I understand I'm still working on this case, Sir, but I do not believe we have enough evidence to convict Professor Nigel Crowhams for the murder of Dr Tom Mirren, or we would have done it already."

"That's why I'm trying to squeeze a confession out of him," Pober says rolling his eyes, "You go and drum up some evidence. He's our man. Leave him to me." Pober orders Lemon to leave with a hand gesture.

51
KNIFE IN THE BACK

Sergeant Lemon has tried his best to avoid the Superintendent while at Cambridge Police Station. He's only gone in when he has to. He has ducked out the car park exit every time, avoiding the main entrance, so as not to be spotted. And he has also kept strange hours, really only filing critical documents and reports late at night when everyone is supposed to have left.

So Lemon is taking a risk but isn't expecting the horror of being tapped on the shoulder as he walks into Inspector Abley's office in the middle of the afternoon. At first, he wonders for a split second whether it might be Abley himself. But he knows that Abley doesn't have pokey fingers, and wouldn't tap his shoulder like the grim reaper. If he took him by surprise much more likely, he would throw a soft indoor golf ball at him, and even then only to catch. No, he recognises those spindly fingers.

"Hello, Superintendent."

"Lemon. I've been looking for you." Raynott rocks up on his toes so as to appear a little taller in the presence of one of his tallest Sergeants.

"Sorry, Sir, been a bit busy with this poisoning case. Got Professor Green on it though. We are getting somewhere."

"I shall need a full report immediately on my desk. I take it you haven't heard from him?" Raynott asks, still rocking on his toes. Lemon has already decided what he'd say if he ran into the Super like this, so the first lie rolls off his tongue pretty easily.

"Yes, we've been speaking. Why, have you not seen him?" Lemon says.

"No, I have not." Raynott stares with his huge eyes at Lemon, looking for a chink in his armour, and knowing full well his Sergeant is bare-faced lying to him.

"Oh, well this case has kept us pretty busy—" Lemon goes on.

"He's suspended. He's not supposed to be working on your case." Raynott frowns.

"Oh, I thought that was just for two months. It ended this week, didn't it, Sir?" Lemon replies.

"Technically, but I need to speak to him about it. He's avoiding me," Raynott says.

"Would you like me to give him a message, Sir?" Lemon asks.

"Tell him I want to see him. It's ruddy simple. He can't carry on as if nothing has happened and hope that works for him. Well, it won't wash," Raynott says.

"Of course. I think he's over at the department now, looking to speak with Dr Cynthia Hatman." Lemon regrets his lie as soon as it leaves his lips, worried it might have got the Inspector into deeper trouble. "I'm sure he's only dipping in to help, Sir. Nothing he shouldn't be doing."

"He's either in, or he's out," Raynott says, "and quite frankly, he doesn't have permission to be in. He should be here, sorting things out with me at the station. Not fiddling about around the edges of some investigation."

"We have a murder case, Sir," Lemon reminds

Raynott.

"Don't get smart with me Sergeant. That is exactly why I have brought in Pober this morning, as you well know," Raynott replies.

"Really no need, Sir. Professor Green and I nearly have it wrapped up. Inspector Pober arrested Professor Crowhams. There is no evidence for that, Sir," Lemon replies.

"What? Not *the* Professor Crowhams. Head of the Department of Galileo at the University?" The Super is shocked. Lemon nods.

"What about Inspector Abley? What shall I tell him, Sir?" Lemon says. "He doesn't think we have enough evidence on Crowhams either by the way, Sir."

"Tell him to stop if you see Abley and come and see me straight away." Raynott glares at the corridor, deeply unhappy that this case seems to have taken a wrong turn.

"Right you are, Sir." Lemon tries to hide a smirk, knowing Raynott will not be happy with Inspector Pober right now.

"Do I detect a slight resistance to follow orders in your voice, Lemon? That would be most unwise," Raynott states.

"No Sir."

"Good," Raynott says. Lemon has this sudden urge to tell Raynott what he thinks. Perhaps it is because he is leaving and has nothing to lose, perhaps because he doesn't think Abley has anything to lose by him sticking up for him either. Things seem pretty bad all round. Lemon pauses in the doorway, unable to get the first word out.

"Spit it out, Sergeant," Raynott says impatiently.

"It's just that Inspector Abley is a good man, that's all. I think he wants to come back, but—" Lemon replies. The Super's eyes open wide like plates. Raynott can't believe that Lemon has the audacity to question his authority. But Lemon doesn't care. He will fight for his boss, the man who has been most loyal to him since he joined as a junior

Constable all thosc years ago. "And, well, he's the best policeman I know, Sir. He taught me everything. The lads agree. We all miss him at the station, Sir, his reassuring presence, his guidance, advice." The words spill out of Lemon.

"All right, all right, Lemon. Enough." Raynott puts his hands up. He doesn't want to hear it.

"It's not the same without him, that's all Sir," Lemon adds, unable to help himself.

"Enough!" Raynott doesn't want to hear another word. But Lemon can't stop.

"Just so long as you know that's how we all feel. There's been a whip-round in the canteen, still going. I don't know if you know, but the Inspector isn't at home. So the lads, well, we have got together with some items for his next place, just to show we care. We know separation is never easy in relationships. I wondered if you'd like to contribute?" Lemon asks tentatively.

"The man's not broken!" Raynott is now flabbergasted with his team's actions and that he is having to listen to another word of this drivel.

"It's more to show we care, Sir." Lemon says, finally hoping the message has sunk in. Superintendent Raynott says nothing and turns his back to the window. He rocks up and down on his heels. "He's made mistakes, but we are all human. And, well, the place just isn't—"

"I hear you, Sergeant. Enough. It's too damn late to get sentimental," Raynott says, adding, "Anyway, surely you'd like to take his place one day? You have your ambitions. Young man like you. Need to cut the apron strings at some point."

Lemon can't quite believe the Super would go as far as Inspector Abley warned he would. It's clear as day to Lemon that the Super is already banging in the nails of Inspector Abley's coffin. He has to persuade Abley to get back in the station and fight for his job. But how?

"I've put in for transfer Sir. Been offered a position

with Thames Valley. Perhaps the paperwork hasn't made it up here yet?"

"You're not blackmailing me are you Sergeant? No one is irreplaceable."

"Oh no Sir. Inspector Abley has taught me well. Just stick to the facts." Sergeant Lemon's mobile rings. He listens and after a while says, "There has been an incident at Jesus Green Lido, you will have to excuse me, Sir?"

"It'll have to wait, whatever it is. We need to discuss this further!"

"It's another death, Sir."

52
POOL OF BLOOD

Cynthia is a 'Christmas day in the sea' type swimmer. Although she hasn't yet swum the Channel, it is a childhood dream that one day she will. For now, she'll have to stick to using Ed's key and swimming in Jesus Green Lido, before it gets too cold in the winter that is. Cynthia hopes that her talk with Ed the other day about moving back to Wells-Next-The-Sea has sunk in, for she's pinning her hopes on early retirement. Cynthia won't be bullied by Professor Crowhams any longer. If only she didn't need his signature, if only she had a better Head of Department. What was he thinking last night? As if she would still see him in a romantic light. She knew him far too well for that now.

She knows Ed will come and bring her a snack soon after she has done her two hundred laps of the pool. It is a very long pool, Olympic-sized, so she will have the chance to swim off all her worries first. These days, Cynthia certainly finds swimming more therapeutic than working in the Department of Galileo.

So when Cynthia turns up and opens the Jesus Green Lido gates, she greets a different kind of morning. For in the water is a woman's body floating on the surface. The woman looks blue, and Cynthia knows full well that the water isn't warm. Ed has often warned Cynthia as much many times. The woman is lying face down in the water and not moving. Cynthia shouts out, but no movement so she jumps straight in. When she gets to the woman and turns her over it is clear she is stiff and cold as if she's been here all night.

*

Soon after Sergeant Lemon and Professor Elizabeth Green arrive.

"I haven't told Pober, but he will be here any minute I'm sure," Sergeant Lemon says to Elizabeth. "Talk fast." Elizabeth nods and walks over to Cynthia who is sat on a sunbed in the cold, wrapped in a towel. Elizabeth tries to get some sense from her.

"So you always swim in here even though it is shut?" They both look at Talya's body, floating in the water, as Lemon calls the SOCOs.

"Yes, I'm not causing any harm," Cynthia realises the irony of her words. "It's just before it gets too cold."

"So other people could have known you were using it. Do you think she might have come to swim in here too?" Lemon asks.

"She's not wearing a costume," Elizabeth says.

They all look at Talya's soaked velvet dress, clinging to her body.

"This is such a wonderful place. The changing rooms. Everything is spotless," Lemon says.

"You swim here?" Cynthia asks.

"When it is open, and you're allowed to," Lemon replies, raising his eyebrows. "It's my favourite place to swim in Cambridge." He looks up at the trees blocking out the chill. The sun shines down in the Lido, and despite the death, it is hard not to agree that the place is like a little oasis. Lemon says to himself quietly, "I shall miss it."

"This is Talya Febland. She was at the hospital when the boat dwellers were poisoned, visiting them," Lemon says.

"She was at the stargazing event." Elizabeth adds.

"That's right, she's a friend of Tom, Sarah and Joe's. She often helps at the events. I think she has a lot of time on her hands. Doesn't work. I live in Fen Ditton and she lives in the biggest house there. Wealthy family." Cynthia stares, upset, at the body still floating.

"What's she got to do with the Department of Galileo?" Elizabeth asks.

"Nothing," Cynthia replies, curious, "Why?"

"She didn't live on a boat either then?" Elizabeth adds.

"No. Like I say, she would be the last person to live on a boat," Cynthia replies.

Elizabeth cannot work it out. The three things linking Tom's death so far had been the boats, the horses and the Department of Galileo.

"Does she own horses?" Elizabeth clutches at straws.

"She has no horses, no. Though she does have a beautiful outdoor pool. It's heated. She's let me use it a couple of times when she's thrown parties for the people who live in the village."

"So she'd not likely have come to swim here then, that's for sure," Elizabeth says.

"No," Cynthia replies. "Shouldn't we get her out?"

"The SOCOs will do that shortly," Lemon says.

"I wonder who is her next of kin?" Cynthia asks. "She never had family to visit that any of us noticed."

"We'll find her house and go and check things out." Lemon says to Professor Green. They both hear the sirens. That means only one thing. The SOCOs and Pober are just minutes away.

"So tell me. What were you rowing about with Professor Crowhams at the Formal Hall in Victoria College the other night?" Elizabeth asks.

"I wasn't arguing," Cynthia replies.

"I saw him kiss you," Elizabeth says.

"He shouldn't have done that. Why did he do that?" Cynthia says.

"You tell me," Elizabeth replies.

"He wanted me back. Not that I've ever been his," Cynthia adds.

"Wanted you back?" Elizabeth asks.

"Yes, he wanted me to be his, you know—" Cynthia doesn't finish her sentence. "Hell would have to freeze over."

"So why did you disappear?" Elizabeth asks again.

"Because I didn't want a scene," Cynthia replies. "Ed, he's jealous. And with his heart."

"You are going to get all the acclaim from Tom Mirren's research we hear?" Lemon remembers Inspector Abley's telephone message.

"What are you talking about?" Cynthia shuffles her feet in her flip-flops as they are now getting cold.

"That's right, isn't it? You were conducting research together? Now you will get all his grants, you will get to publish the papers under your own name only?" Lemon continues.

"Where did you hear that? Yes, I suppose, if I wasn't trying for early retirement. If Professor Crowhams will allow it, which he won't."

"We'd like you to come down to the station later today please, and answer a few questions and make a statement," Sergeant Lemon asks Cynthia.

"Okay, but I've told you a lot here already," Cynthia replies.

"We need you to write it down and sign it," Lemon says. "And I'd like to ask you a few more questions."

*

A dozen or so SOCOs arrive. Divers in the pool search the bottom for clues, while Talya Febland's body is pulled up and out of the water onto a stretcher. As Elizabeth quickly slinks back out through the gate before Pober spots her, she sees the crass Inspector Pober laughing to himself as he mimes the backstroke as Talya's body is placed on the side of the pool.

53
BONFIRE NIGHT

Professor Elizabeth Green doesn't like firework and bonfire night. There is nothing that redeems it. She doesn't like fireworks because they terrorise dogs, cats, birds, you name it. Bonfires are also high risk to hedgehogs and other small mammals, so this is a particularly traumatic time for animals and Elizabeth Green on the whole. If fireworks are necessary, then what is wrong with having gentle Catherine Wheels, or a Gold Fountain. Why do they all have to sound like bombs going off? Elizabeth remembers all too well the night she burnt her hand on a sparkler. From her kitchen window at Foxes Green, she looks through the window to the corner of Jesus Green on the other side of the river and can just see children waving sparklers around with abandon. No thank you, not again. Elizabeth knows she is in the minority.

Emily stands beside Elizabeth. All the dogs are shut up tight inside, cat flaps locked. The pet calming spray plug ins have been going since this afternoon and the television and radio are on in both the drawing room and in the kitchen too to try to drown out any noise to come.

It isn't long before Elizabeth and Emily are wandering across Midsummer Common to get a good spot far back from this Wednesday night's fireworks. Elizabeth has to come here tonight because she knows so many of those close to the murder victims will be here. Emily has agreed to join her, feeling a little guilty about sending Inspector Abley off into the night. There is still no sign of Godric, and Emily knows how sad this is making Elizabeth, even if Elizabeth refuses to admit it.

In the darkness Elizabeth spots Ed, looking a little more frail, holding onto the arm of Cynthia.

"Apparently, he has angina," Emily says. "It was a warning sign Cynthia told me earlier."

"Sergeant Lemon visited the hospital after his collapse, just to check he hadn't been poisoned. Yes, angina," Elizabeth adds.

"Bumped into Cynthia in College. She came into St Andrew's this morning. She's just letting people she knows know that she's taking early retirement," Emily says. "She's off to the coast. I don't blame her. Sometimes this place feels too crowded. I do prefer the winter. It's so empty."

"Well it's not empty now and it feels pretty cold to me." Elizabeth looks at the huge crowds beginning to jostle on the Common.

"I'm sure finding a dead body in the Lido probably prompted it. That would change my view I think." Emily says. "Was it murder?"

"Oh, I'm sure of it," Elizabeth replies, "and I'm sure it's connected to the other poisonings."

"Well, she was pretty shaken up and says she's off as soon as possible. I think she's hoping Ed will go with her," Emily says. "Maybe she's worried she'll be the next victim. She knew Tom quite well."

"She never said they were friends," Elizabeth says, "only research partners. I hope she's gone into the Police Station. Sergeant Lemon wanted her for questioning and she hadn't turned up yet last I checked."

"Didn't you say Ed found the boat victims?" Emily asks, adding, "Didn't Ed go to the hospital to see how they were?"

"Yes, but he doesn't like them," Elizabeth replies. "Said they were a menace to the wildlife. All that diesel and disruption to the riverbank. Can't say I disagree," Elizabeth adds. "And he is the one with the keys to Jesus Green pool too."

Just then, Elizabeth spots Joe and Sarah saying hello to Ed.

"Perhaps they're asking him how he is, after his heart condition? Hardly a suspect, is he? If he's likely to keel over at any moment." Emily watches the trio and looks to Elizabeth for her opinion.

"What's he doing out? He should be at home in the warm. Not standing out here surrounded by thousands of people packed in like sardines, spreading their cold germs," Elizabeth says, putting her scarf to her nose. "If Cynthia is moving, is she taking Ed too? Maybe they are talking about that. And I presume that means she really is stopping all of her work. I wonder what that means for Tom's research?" Elizabeth adds, "Professor Crowhams will be pleased. But then he does appear to have a crush on her, so I don't suppose he will be pleased she's leaving either."

"He does? And what's wrong with the public being helped up a notch or two?" Emily wonders, taking Elizabeth's arm and leading her to a more open and less jostley space.

"Crowhams says he's going to do whatever he has to do to stop the project. So I guess ultimately with Tom's death, he's got his way now," Elizabeth says, as she is pulled even further away from the bonfire the size of a house.

"Let's not get our hair singed. That monstrosity could send smoke signals to Ely," Emily says, "and I've just had a cut and set," adding, "I've never understood that.

Scientists who think they know better. I mean, science is just trial and error. There's no genius involved." Emily smirks at her scientist friend.

"Says the classicist. What are they still talking about?" Elizabeth replies, watching Joe and Sarah listen to Ed from her vantage point under the trees back up by Brunswick Walk. Then she sees Cynthia join them and start talking.

"Maybe she is telling them about her retirement to the seaside. So is Ed going with her?" Emily says.

"No idea. I hope he hasn't left Clive in the Lock Keeper's House while the fireworks are going on," Elizabeth says.

"No, Cynthia was telling me that she has the dog in her home in Fen Ditton," Emily replies. "She was complaining as she is allergic to dog hair and said he is shut in the downstairs utility room with the radio. She was joking that she hopes Clive likes Radio 4, and she knows Ed listens to Radio 2."

"It must be nearly time for the fireworks soon. Why do they always have the overly jolly DJ playing music for half an hour?" Elizabeth complains.

"It's to allow everyone to squeeze in in time. Not everyone lives ten minutes away like you, Elizabeth." Emily reminds Elizabeth of her privileged lifestyle as Elizabeth watches the candy-floss and hotdog stands do a roaring trade and glances over the happy and excited faces of families and the elderly, small children and groups of teenagers. She cannot see one face of disappointment like she knows her own face shows.

"What are they talking about?" Elizabeth's gaze switches back to Cynthia, Ed, Joe and Sarah who haven't moved, and yet are frustratingly too far away to hear.

"Cynthia is a woman after your own heart you know. She told me earlier that she argued with the Bonfire Society for a modern hologram light display to take place instead of the fireworks. You can do this thing, apparently, with 3-D lighting, to make it look like there is a bonfire.

They can even add in smell."

"What's the point of that?" Elizabeth looks at Emily, adding, "Surely the advantage of lights is to get rid of the sound and the smell?" Elizabeth says, "I seem to remember that Cynthia was arguing about it with Professor Nigel Crowhams when Ed collapsed."

"Let's hope there is not a repeat," Emily replies, nodding towards Professor Crowhams, who is marching up to Cynthia, Ed, Sarah and Joe and wastes no time in shouting.

"Are you responsible for this?" Emily and Elizabeth can hear him over the bustling crowd. "They are going to be bloody delayed because someone has sabotaged the fireworks," Crowham's thunders.

"Exactly why we should have gone for illuminations. There is a beautiful display of E-luminations in the spring. We could just have had the same, only on Midsummer Common," Cynthia shouts back.

"So you are responsible for this?" Crowhams's nose is right up against Cynthia's.

"Of course not. Calm down. No one has done this on purpose. It is probably just a dodgy circuit or something. I'm sure the experts will have it fixed in no time." Cynthia is still raising her voice to match Crowhams' anger. Elizabeth and Emily start to sneak under the trees and closer to the group, so they can hear better.

"If I find that one of you did this, there will be trouble!" Crowhams shouts.

"Professor Crowhams, you need to calm down and stop accusing us of things we haven't done." Joe says. "If it hasn't escaped your notice, you are standing with three people who are recovering. Two from poison, one from an angina attack I have just learned. We don't have the energy to be sabotaging anything. Now please leave us to enjoy our evening. We hope to be watching the fireworks shortly."

"Joe, I think I need a hot chocolate," Sarah says.

"Just leave us alone," Joe adds to Crowhams, turning to Sarah. "Come on. I'll get you one. You stay with Cynthia and Ed."

Elizabeth is slightly relieved when Crowhams leaves in one direction and the others wander off in the opposite, as she can't see Sergeant Lemon anywhere. As she scans the crowd she spots Wallis and Brad, the two rowers, though there is no Godric. Elizabeth knows Godric loves the fireworks and hopes he is somewhere in the crowd, but wonders why he's not with his boyfriend. It's not like Godric, as when he falls for someone he doesn't usually let them out of his sight. She recognises Brad as the young man who rowed into a wire from the huge scarf wrapped around his neck. She notices that both Brad and Wallis start to head off in the direction Professor Crowhams left. Before long she can't see them anymore as the crowd swallows them up. Then from nowhere, and without announcement, the fireworks start.

The noise is deafening, with explosions high and multiple. Emily starts to "ooh" and "ahh" along with hundreds of other people. Small children sit on their parent's shoulders and scream in delight, while Elizabeth notices couples lean their heads into one another or turn and kiss. Elizabeth remembers how much Gerald loved the fireworks. They would make him laugh, while she would complain about the smoke which always blew in her face. Elizabeth turns to look up into the sky which is filled with pretty explosions of colour and light zooming and zipping in every direction. Then Elizabeth feels her body being knocked from her feet to the ground.

*

Paramedics are by Elizabeth's side when she wakes, lying on the grass on Midsummer Common.

"I think you were hit by a firework." Emily leans over, looking very worried.

"What?" Elizabeth sits up on one elbow and sees her lovely new duffel coat still smoking. There is no ambulance, just two emergency response workers having seen the stray firework shoot past Elizabeth and knock her over. The firework has ended up in a tree, and is still burning with flames now shooting out its end.

"You were lucky." And Emily looks at the burning tree to highlight to Elizabeth what nearly happened. The paramedics stand up confident that Elizabeth was only grazed. They receive another call on their walkie-talkies. They start to run towards Jesus Green.

"Busy night," Emily says to Elizabeth.

"Bunny!" Godric appears. "What happened?" Godric looks at Elizabeth's coat, which is still smoking. In that moment he regrets having left Foxes Haven, regrets having let his nanna out of his sight. She looks so small on the ground.

"I'm okay, just knocked off my feet," she replies. "I told you fireworks are dangerous." She says, so pleased to speak to her grandson after two days. He lifts her up and with his friend standing next to her and without introduction, he says "Let's get you home." As he hits Elizabeth's coat to make sure it is out, Elizabeth doesn't protest. But partly also because home is in the same direction as the paramedics are now running, and she wants to see what all the fuss is about, especially as she can now hear a police siren on its way.

"Where have you been hiding?" Elizabeth asks Godric.

"Hello Emily," Godric beams.

"Hello Godric, lovely to see you." Emily picks up Elizabeth's hat from the mud and starts to brush it down.

"Ben here put me up in St James's," Godric answers his nanna, giving her a big squeeze, and then beating her duffel coat some more. "Ben has got digs over the river. Pretty cool," Godric says to his nanna, smiling back at Ben.

"Very pleased to meet you Ben," Elizabeth says to Ben,

then to Godric, "I won't mention my robe, but will expect it back from the dry cleaners by tomorrow." Elizabeth wants to ask if he's been okay and if he misses Foxes Haven, but somehow she cannot find the courage. Scared in case she hears something she doesn't want to know.

"Sorry, I'm coming back too, if that's okay?" Godric replies, "I should have called. You can't keep me away from my cosy Foxes Haven." Godric hugs his nanna again, tears in his eyes so worried about her. Elizabeth doesn't want to say anything, as she doesn't want to break Godric's mood, especially delighted that Godric's departure was only temporary. But she can't help herself.

"Wallis?"

"I'm here, with Ben," Godric says quietly, widening his eyes to try to make it clear that all talk of Wallis is inappropriate in the light of new things, new people unfolding in his life. Elizabeth has enough and is proud that her grandson does have some judgement and appears to have binned Wallis. She glances at Ben, standing a little way behind Godric. Ben looks kind. She's relieved. "You know Wallis has apparently been throwing things at the boats. Why?" Elizabeth says quietly, so Ben can't hear.

"I think they fight with them over space," Godric replies, "The rowers are always hitting the boats. You know that," Godric whispers, then more loudly for Ben to hear, "I never hit the boats. How can you imply that my rowing is not accurate to a pin?" Godric is fake affronted at his nanna.

"You're such a toff," Ben laughs. Elizabeth is in a little pain from her fall and has lost sight of the paramedics. She isn't listening to Godric anymore as he jokes a little with Ben.

"Concentrate on your nanna," Ben says, Elizabeth catching Ben's words. She approves of him already.

"I will make us all cocoa, and we can have some of the cheesecake if there's any left after the Inspector came to visit," Godric says.

"My roof, my choice of guests. But yes, he's left. Emily scared him away."

"He creates such a mess," Emily says to Godric, "whereas you are nice and tidy Godric." Emily squeezes Godric's arm.

"Good." Godric looks at Elizabeth more carefully. In the lamplight as they walk along the path now on Jesus Green, he can see his nanna has mud all down one side of her coat and a big black mark where the firework hit. Godric looks at Emily's beautiful gloves now black from patting down Elizabeth's coat. Godric squeezes Emily back and says "Thank you" quietly in her ear. He can see that his nanna looks cold and tired. "I can carry you," he offers.

"Don't you dare!" Elizabeth marches after the paramedics, and it soon becomes apparent to Godric and Emily that Elizabeth isn't going home.

"Bunny, you need to rest. The bridge is up here." But as Godric tries to steer everyone to walk towards Jesus Green Lock Bridge, so the police sirens drive up Victoria Avenue, stop to open the gate, and turn onto Jesus Green. Elizabeth has already seen why. She now starts to walk more quickly following the car. She has spotted Sergeant Lemon in it, which means this might have something to do with the case. "What are you doing? Slow down. A firework has just hit you!" Godric worries.

"Your nanna's spunky," Ben says, joining in the speedy walk. Emily is lagging behind due to her beautiful pencil skirt and heeled boots holding her back."

The police car pulls up to a stop in the middle of Jesus Green, just in front of the avenue of London planes which are hundreds of years old. Most people are still more interested in watching the fireworks to look back and notice. But Elizabeth can see the torches now shining up into one of the trees. She sees Lemon jump out of the car and another two policemen follow him. The Constables start to tape around an area a few hundred yards square.

Another has already started to divert the pedestrians.

Lemon points a powerful torch up into the branches of a two hundred feet tall London plane tree, and in the beam Elizabeth thinks she sees someone's shoes, dangling in a branch. Elizabeth starts to run. Why would anyone throw their shoes up into a tree on a cold November evening? In stark comparison to Midsummer Common with its sky lit up with fireworks, it is so dark on this part of Jesus Green. The bangs, cracks and fizzes of the fireworks are still in full force, but all behind Elizabeth, her grandson, his friend and Emily. Ahead of them, Elizabeth sees the two paramedics who treated her just moments ago, now standing below the shoes, and then she sees what Godric, Emily and Ben must also have spotted… Wallis and Brad.

Wallis and Brad are standing looking up into the tree at the shoes still inside the cordon, together with Sergeant Lemon and Inspector Pober. This is going to be awkward for Godric, Elizabeth thinks.

"You go home, put the kettle on for cocoa like you promised. I'll meet you there soon," she shouts back to Godric who follows her with Emily through the cordon. Godric looks at Wallis.

"What are they doing there?" he shouts back. Elizabeth hears the paramedics calling for an ambulance. Then finally, it becomes impossible to escape the macabre view above her head. Dangling from a branch isn't just a pair of shoes. But attached is a pair of black trousers and above that a black coat, and at the top a neck hung from a rope. Hanged dead, fifteen feet up it is clear to see that the man is Professor Nigel Crowhams. Elizabeth, Godric, Emily and Ben stand aghast at the sight, as Crowhams' body sways a little on the rope.

"Can't someone cut him down?" Elizabeth shouts.

"We're getting the fire brigade." Lemon answers Elizabeth and walks over to stand with her.

"We can't cut him down yet. Need to examine the evidence." Pober corrects Lemon in front of everyone.

Lemon rolls his eyes at Elizabeth. The SOCOs arrive and Pober shouts at them too, "Get something around this pronto. Where have you parked? I hope not on the grass." Pober adds, speaking to the SOCOs.

The SOCOs erect a large tent with scaffolding poles to hide the body, which is still dangling inside but thankfully now out of sight of the thousands of members of the public who are soon to be walking back into the city centre after the fireworks shortly finish. Police tape shuts off half of Jesus Green now, from the London planes up to the river, only allowing the public to walk along the lower path by the Victoria College. Lemon tries to call Inspector Abley's phone again. Nothing.

"He's not picking up." Lemon says, showing Elizabeth his phone and Inspector Abley's number.

"I wouldn't be surprised if he hanged himself because he was feeling guilty about committing double murder, and knew he'd be caught," Pober says to his police officers listening. Lemon looks at Elizabeth as if it could be possible, but she changes the subject.

"Oh dear. We need to slap Bob around the face." Elizabeth peeks up into the pop-up tent tower, and watches a SOCO on a ladder taking photographs. "Could this really be a suicide? Though how could anyone force someone up a tree? I mean, these trees are hardly easy to climb anyway."

"I don't think we will know for a while," Lemon replies. "Leedham is assigned." Both know Leedham is not the fastest when it comes to examining all the evidence.

"It's hard to see in the dark, Sir, but you might want to take a look at his chest." The SOCO shouts back down to Pober. But as Lemon is nearer he wastes no time in climbing the ladder inside the tent. Elizabeth watches Lemon's legs disappear out of sight, the fireworks in the background still lighting up the sky. Lemon comes back down.

"Well, what is it?" Pober has now walked over, curious.

"He's been stabbed, Sir," Lemon replies. "Won't know if it's the cause of death until we get him on the slab, but given all the blood all over his coat—" Lemon adds, looking at Elizabeth.

"I'd hazard a guess that he was dead already before he was winched up here." Elizabeth points to the rope, the other end of which is tied around the bottom of a tree.

"It was suicide," Pober replies confidently. "He's a murderer."

The sight of Professor Crowhams swinging is too macabre for Elizabeth to watch anymore. With the Professor's shoes just inches from her face, she feels a little sick, but she can't help herself talking with Lemon. She walks away, encouraging Lemon to leave close proximity to Pober.

"First there was Tom Mirren killed by eating poisoned apples. Then Talya Febland found drowned in a pool and now Professor Crowhams hanged from the tallest tree on Jesus Green," Elizabeth ponders quietly, "Perhaps his hit over the head was really attempted murder after all?" She studies Lemon's face in the dark, flummoxed by this latest death.

"Could be," Lemon replies. "Don't forget that student standing just yards away, near your grandson. Brad Brick. He was nearly killed by a cable across the river. Is it a coincidence that he's standing watching this?"

"Brick?" Elizabeth hadn't heard his surname before. "Isn't he a post-doc at the department?" Lemon nods to answer Elizabeth's question.

"Inspector Abley is right, we should question Cynthia Hatman. She has links to them all." Lemon waits for Elizabeth to respond, still whispering so that Inspector Pober can't ruin his and Elizabeth's already advancing investigation.

"One thing we know about this murderer. They are killing people in different ways every time. Poison, drowning, stabbing. And the attempted wire garotting, and hitting on the head."

"A serial killer?" Lemon asks Elizabeth whether she really means what he dreads to hear.

"The facts would seem to suggest so, but I don't think this is random. I think there is a strong motive for each killing. We just can't see it yet. But we will." Elizabeth glances around, noticing Godric, Emily and Ben staring at all the police and getting a glimpse of Elizabeth's life.

"Whoever is doing this must be very clever, not to be seen. I mean, to lift this body up on a night like tonight? How on earth? This place is heaving?" Leedham walks over and chips in, having just arrived and much preferring their company to Pober's. "Maybe they did it when the fireworks started. Everyone would have been looking the other way. That's clever." He answers his own question.

Elizabeth and Lemon look at each other, then Elizabeth closes her eyes. This is all too much without Inspector Abley. She can see Lemon is out of his depth, suggesting a serial killer. What is she doing? She's interested in helping when she wants to know the poison, but this is bigger than she thought she would ever get involved with. Multiple people are now dead in a very short space of time indeed. If they don't solve this, and quickly, Elizabeth can imagine there will be more. Despite not feeling comfortable with this case, she can't abandon Lemon now. But a hand reaches hers and grabs it. It is her grandson's. She can see his anxious face and Emily getting cold.

"Okay, let's go and get cocoa." Godric blows warm air in Elizabeth's little hand. She reluctantly nods, then turns to Lemon.

"Call me later, if anything happens. Perhaps with a night's sleep things will be clearer?"

"Sleep, what's that?" Lemon says back, looking tired.

"See you bright and breezy. You never know, Inspector Abley might show his face. His message sounded positive. I agree, we should speak with Cynthia, in the morning.

*

It isn't long before Ben has laid the fire in Elizabeth's drawing room, and the dogs and cats are all sitting beside it, thankfully oblivious to the loud bangs outside having spent the past couple of hours watching a bird video for cats on the television.

As Godric and Emily sit either side of Elizabeth. Elizabeth looks at Ben and wonders how Godric manages to find such lovely boyfriends, apart from Wallis. She wonders what Wallis and Brad were doing calling in the murder of Professor Nigel Crowhams earlier and getting the police to arrive. Lemon had told her. Was Brad responsible for Crowhams' death? They did follow him when he left the fireworks. And by calling it in no one would ever suspect him?

"What was Wallis doing under the body of Professor Nigel Crowhams? Did he have anything going against him?" Godric asks his nanna.

"Not that I know," Elizabeth replies. "They were both at Victoria, as you know."

"Yes, I saw you at the swan protest. Nice wings, weren't they?" Emily chips in.

"Could Professor Crowhams and Wallis have been friends?" Elizabeth hadn't joined the dots that College connected them.

"Definitely not. Wallis hates authority. He thought all the professors were a bore. Wallis is a bit of a bore. He has so many chips on his shoulders, a bit of salt and vinegar and he could open a shop," Godric replies. This is music to Elizabeth's ears. Wallis has been given the boot, in one way or another.

"Wallis?" Ben asks.

"Oh just some really unpleasant man that studies at Victoria, Ben. No more than that." Elizabeth tries to help

Godric out of his latest sticky patch. "What subject are you studying?"

"English Literature." Ben smiles.

"How lovely. Lots of reading and writing essays," Elizabeth says. "Can you get Godric to do a bit more work?"

"Bunny, please," Godric replies, turning to Ben. "Can I get you a drink?" And Godric and Ben go into the kitchen, leaving Emily with Elizabeth.

"I can't believe you chucked Bob out." Elizabeth goes back to that.

"What, so you could talk about the case with him now?" Emily asks, "I know you."

"Well, yes, that would have been nice. But no, I'm just worried. No one has seen him or knows where he is," Elizabeth replies.

"Perhaps that's for the best. He's a grown man, don't worry about him so much."

"Where is he? What if he's sleeping rough and drinking again? What if he's left Cambridge and never comes back? He could be in trouble. There are a lot of ex-convicts I'm sure who'd like to see him ten feet under. He said he was coming back. Left this message on Lemon's phone. Then nothing. Something has happened."

"Don't be silly Liz. He's a man who plays golf and likes his creature comforts."

"He was in a state when he was here. I mean, rock bottom," Elizabeth says.

54
LONDON PLANES

Elizabeth has brought Hector and Monty out very early this Thursday morning before she steps into the department to give two more lectures to her students. She has woken up still unsure about a lot of things. She is so pleased that Godric has returned and with a much better man. In fact, Elizabeth was even happy that Ben stayed over, pushing back any worries about the speed of her grandson's changing passions. Elizabeth can't help but worry, however, about Inspector Abley, about whom she has no idea either of his whereabouts since Emily kicked him out of Foxes Haven, or his motivation or lack thereof. And now Lemon leaving Cambridge? How could he, especially at this time?

Elizabeth is cross this morning, sad about Lemon. He's like a rat deserting a sinking ship. If Lemon leaves, she's sure as hell can't work with Pober. It will be the end of her experience with Cambridge Police. If all this isn't enough, she has to strongly question Emily's efforts to try to set her up with another man, and what a man she chose. Does her best friend know her so poorly? No, of course not. So why does she think such an awful man suitable? Elizabeth is baffled, and despite trying to forget, the whole thing is still lingering with her days after. Elizabeth's walk is helping to calm her mind. Cambridge runs through her veins, a city she loves dearly with all her heart. She can feel it beneath and around her, supporting her. It is quietening her anxieties.

Up ahead Elizabeth can see Brad and Wallis. They are all the more noticeable as the Green is still empty, bar two other dog walkers. She assumes they are either on their way to or way back from rowing. Nevertheless, it is a little odd to stop as they have, drop their bicycles down and look once again at the spot where Professor Crowhams was found hanged last night, like they are looking at an art installation in an exhibition. Elizabeth watches them pointing and staring, trying to look up into the tent. But they are too far away behind the cordon. Hector runs ahead and spots them and goes to say hello. Elizabeth follows.

"Oh look, it's Godric's 'Bunny', aren't we lucky?" Wallis says to Brad, then laughs.

"What were you doing right by Professor Crowhams last night?" Elizabeth asks.

"None of your beeswax," Wallis replies.

"Ah, but it is. I'm helping the police on this case," Elizabeth says, waiting for an answer.

"Yeah, Godric told me about how you like to meddle with the cases." Wallis laughs. Elizabeth knows Godric is very proud of her work, so ignores Wallis's comments. "But you're not a police officer though, are you. You're just some hired help when they get stuck on poison. And I don't see you in a laboratory, and there aren't poisoned horses lying about the place."

"Who told you the horses were poisoned?" Elizabeth asks.

"Er, the internet," Wallis replies.

"What are you both doing?"

"Looking at a crime scene?" Wallis says, now bored of sparring with Elizabeth.

"Was he murdered?" Brad asks Elizabeth.

"Yes, Elizabeth says, with extreme confidence. "He was murdered. Now we have three murders. And I come back to the fact that you were right below the last murder victim before anyone else turned up." She continues to give Wallis her most beady stare.

"What were we supposed to do, not phone it in?" Wallis asks, sarcastically.

"What were you doing here in the first place?" Elizabeth repeats.

"Er, it was the fireworks," Wallis replies.

"On Midsummer Common, not Jesus Green," Elizabeth corrects Wallis.

"Stretching my neck – back was hurting, so we decided to move back," Brad replies, a little tired of Wallis's contrary responses.

"How is your neck?" Elizabeth asks Brad.

"More painful than I thought possible. Drugged up to the eyeballs. Though I think I was lucky. If I'd been rowing faster that could have been the end of me," Brad replies, lifting his chin and lifting his shoulders in pain.

"Do you have any idea who might have done that to you?" Elizabeth asks.

"I hate to point fingers, but yes. I do. In fact, I'd state my life on it," Brad says. Elizabeth was not expecting that.

"Go on."

I think it was the old Lock Keeper, Ed. He hates us. I mean, he's always shouting at us and complaining that we annoy the birds. We don't. They are part of Cambridge's heritage just like the rowers are, and have rubbed along together for decades without any trouble." Brad looks at the river nearby, "But no, he has to shout and gesticulate at us every single time we pass. And the other day, he threw stale buns at us. He said he'd get us if we didn't stop harassing the ducks. I'm sure he threw my oars in the river that time. I mean, what is the old boy on about? We just tease him now, that we are going to hurt them, but we don't."

"Threw your oars in the river?" Elizabeth asks.

"He also hates, or hated Professor Crowhams." Brad looks up at the SOCO tent.

"I found it hard to find anyone who liked Professor Crowhams," Elizabeth admits.

"Professor Crowhams hated the horses. Ed loves the horses," Brad continues. "I think Ed tried to injure me. And, who knows, maybe he's the killer. Didn't he also have a key to Jesus Green pool where that woman was found floating? I've seen him opening it for Cynthia to swim there. Even though it's shut up for winter."

"So you really think Ed's a murderer? Heart condition and all?" Elizabeth asks.

"The man has no heart," Wallis scoffs.

"Have you got a better theory?" adds Brad. Elizabeth isn't sure that she has but certainly didn't leap to the same conclusion that this young post-doctoral student has.

"What connection have you got to Professor Crowhams? Aren't you a post-doc researcher up at the Department of Galileo?" Elizabeth asks, "I heard he was pretty mean to his students working for him."

"I've heard that too. But I don't work for him. I worked for, or rather was supervised by Dr Tom Mirren," Brad replies.

"What's happened to your research now?" Elizabeth asks.

"As it happens, I'm not too sure." Brad kicks the path below his feet.

"Hmm." Elizabeth wonders if that gives Brad enough of a motive. "Wallis, you have been heard shouting at Ed, at the boat dwellers. Why are you so curious about this crime scene?"

"Get over yourself old lady. Come back to me when you're an Inspector. Otherwise, nose out," Wallis replies.

"Okay, well it was good speaking with you both. I am seeing the Superintendent later today, so I will be sure to mention your cooperation, Wallis."

"Whatevs," Wallis replies. "Maybe we're just placing our bets as to who is next."

As Elizabeth calls the dogs to walk on and continues across Jesus Green, she wonders why both Brad and Wallis were just standing at the crime scene. But the markings of the fireworks on the grass of Midsummer Common soon replace her thoughts.

She is never surprised by just how well organised the fireworks event is, as it is almost difficult to tell that anything at all occurred last night, all apart from the still burning bonfire and its staked-out perimeter. Litter pickers have already been out working in the early hours. Hector and Monty run and play, finding other dogs to jump and race.

As she stands in the middle of the Common, looking up at the sky and breathing the fresh autumnal air, she wonders just how much Brad has to lose. It must be very expensive to come from America and study in England, and with Tom gone and no one to supervise his project, his ambition and academic future hang in the balance. Never underestimate the ego and ruthless nature of the young academic, Elizabeth thinks. Under a charming exterior is often a fireball of determination and sweat to make it to the top of their profession. Why would someone try to kill Brad if he weren't involved? He has to be. Though why someone hasn't killed Wallis yet is a complete mystery to Elizabeth – he is the most unpleasant young man she has met in a long time.

Resolved in her mind that she has to speak to Lemon this morning for him to dig into this particular post-doc's backstory, she starts to head back. It is then that she passes the beautiful and very old oak tree on the corner of

Brunswick Walk. The very spot where the firework which hit her last night lodged into its trunk and burned for a while. There is no firework lodged there anymore. Perhaps the police went back and removed it, perhaps a member of the public saw the tree alight and took matters into their own hands. Whichever way, in its place is a large black hole, almost a foot wide. If that firework had hit Elizabeth, it was likely that she would be severely injured or worse. There were tens of thousands of people at the fireworks last night. The more she thinks about it, the more she is convinced. Whoever let off the firework did not have good things in mind. Perhaps it was Wallis.

The poor tree on the corner is damaged forever. She hopes it will not die from this injury. She makes a promise to keep an eye on this tree, and feed it in spring. A pedestrian hears Elizabeth talking to the tree and hugging it. But Elizabeth doesn't care. The hug with the tree offers temporary respite from concerns about this case which are just growing and growing.

55
NO ESCAPING IT

Inspector Abley slept well last night. It could be that the University Arms Hotel knew how to make a comfy bed, or that perhaps just for the first time in ages Bob Abley had just stopped thinking about his own life. He'd stopped thinking about his wife, stopped thinking about the future. He began to think about the great game of golf he'd have this morning too. Yes, it was sunny and beautiful outside, albeit a little crisp no doubt. No more having to excuse himself to go and play. A bachelor again, free to do whatever he wanted, when he wanted and with whom.

He goes down to sit in the Brasserie and picks up a paper to read on his way in. A waiter immediately appears. Coffee comes almost immediately, piping hot. The world is good. That is until Abley opens the folded paper to see Inspector Pober's ugly mug on the front page. Next to him was a photo of the avenue of London planes on Jesus Green with the headline 'Hanged, Drowned And Poisoned – And That's Just The New Murders In Cambridge This

Week…' Abley stops reading.

56
SUPER ELIZABETH

Elizabeth is feeling guilty after giving her morning lectures as she now cycles into the centre. She should be heading to the Department of Plant Sciences, or to Granta College to pick up her mail and give her supervisions, which she knows she has to do next or there will be some very unhappy graduate students adrift in a sea of invasive species essays. But instead, Elizabeth heads in a different direction. She has been mulling over for some time whether to visit this particular man and give him a piece of her mind. She's been putting it off for a while, as she doesn't want to go in too hot-headed, or say anything she'll regret and make matters worse. But it seems that things really couldn't get worse now, and something has to be done.

As Elizabeth enters the front door of the Cambridge Police Station on Parker's Piece, she is greeted warmly by the receptionist, who tells her to go straight up and that he's waiting to see her. Elizabeth never understands why buildings like this are always so clinical. There is no reason that the stairs have to be white and the walls so grey. It's a police station, not a prison. If she ran this place, she would put paintings on the walls and bring in lots of plants. It might make a few more people think twice about reoffending. Instead, her boots squeak up the stairs, and light disappears into the corridor as she gets closer.

It's not that Elizabeth is scared of Raynott, far from it. It's more that she detests him and will find it hard to hide. Superintendent Raynott is an unpleasant man at best. He seems recently to Elizabeth to be a vindictive, grudge holding and spiteful to boot. The only upside is his limited intelligence. He seems to pick away at something but not notice what else is going on around him. So Elizabeth's tactic going in is to bamboozle him as much as possible then leave.

"Superintendent." Elizabeth greets him as she walks into Raynott's office, as local radio blares out around the room.

"Morning Professor Green. Good of you to come in and see me. A lot going on."

"Quite." Elizabeth lets him talk.

"It can't have escaped your attention that we have a triple murder on our hands," he says, walking around his desk to shake her hand. Doesn't Raynott know she's helping Lemon, she thinks? But he continues, "And with Inspector Abley otherwise engaged, well I'll not beat about the bush… we are stretched."

"I hear Lemon is doing a fine job, and you have Inspector Pober helping now?"

"Yes, Lemon. I thought he'd go far." Raynott says, "It seems he's not as attached to us as we thought. And Inspector Pober is far too busy, which may be why he might have arrested one of our most prominent and now deceased academics by mistake." Raynott raises his eyebrows.

"I think Sergeant Lemon's missing Inspector Abley, Superintendent. Perhaps that's why he decided to leave,

now you have put Pober in place?" Elizabeth suggests.
"I'm not sure exactly what part of Abley he would be missing? It can't be the drinking or the wandering off to the golf course. Anyhoo," the Super replies, walking over to his coffee pot and gesturing to Elizabeth if she'd like some. She shakes her head. She stays silent, waiting for the reason the Super brought her in. She knows he is going to ask her about Bob. She knows he will want more ammunition to sink Bob, but she's not going to give it.
"You're probably wondering why I asked if you'd be so kind to come in and see me?" he continues, when she says nothing. "Well, as I say, we're stretched on this case. Lemon is a wonderful Sergeant, and one day he will make a fine Inspector. But, he's just too young, too inexperienced to leave this case to him. And as I say, I assigned Inspector Pober." Elizabeth nods, resisting saying that Pober is the worst Inspector she's ever met. Raynott continues, "It now turns out Pober is going to be in Audley for another few days. A bank heist and he's getting closer to catching the criminals. Been working on it a long time. So, not to put too fine a point on it… would you consider stepping into Inspector Abley's shoes until we recruit another Inspector?" Raynott pauses to let what he said sink in. And sinking in it is, for Elizabeth doesn't know where to look. She is speechless. So Raynott continues, "I don't say this lightly, as I appreciate you are a busy woman. And it would be for more than a few days. Lemon told me you've been very helpful in the past. Don't think these things escape my notice."

This is not what Elizabeth is expecting to hear. Did the Superintendent just offer her a job with the police force, as an Inspector – albeit temporary but still? Is she dreaming? Elizabeth's stunned but remains mute, leaving Raynott nonplussed and convinced she needs persuading.

"Right, well, you see because we would be creating this just for you I can relax some of the rules. You won't be an official Inspector, but for all intents and purposes—

”

“Can you do this?” Elizabeth asks.
“I can do anything I want. I’m the Super.” Raynott smiles a sickly smile.
“I have dogs. I can't leave them for long periods of time.” Elizabeth is surprised this is the first thing that comes out of her mouth to illustrate the insanity of making her a temporary Inspector. “I'm also an academic, and a busy one at that,” she adds.

“Bring them in. Take a sabbatical. You’ve been an academic for many years I understand. Surely that pulls in some favours? Just take a few weeks off?” Raynott replies.

“In here? The dogs could come in here?” she asks.
“Yes.” Raynott laughs. “I'll give you Inspector Abley's office. They'll love it in there. Lots of balls, though dogs shouldn't play with golf balls should they?” Raynott becomes sidetracked in his head about the dangers of golf balls. “We can clear all that out before you come in. Of course, you'll have a car, or you can use your own and claim, but the parking will be free.”
“Right,” Elizabeth replies.
“You'll get a siren,” Raynott continues to pile on the perks, seeing that Elizabeth is giving nothing away. “I suppose you'd have to put that in the front seat or something if you keep your own. I'll assign Lemon to you. He's off soon but assured me he'll see through this case. So, hopefully, we can recruit a replacement for the Inspector before he leaves. I've even had a word with the chef in the canteen, and he assures me he can rustle up some what do you call it? Vegan food?”
Elizabeth is now dumbfounded for a second. She knows she's being played, knows that the Super is happy with her track record for solving cases. But this is more about getting rid of the Inspector than employing her. If he doesn't even have his office, how can Abley fight to come back? But then another thought crosses her mind. If she says no, will Raynott just ship in a new temporary

Inspector anyway, from another force, or promote another Sergeant a little older and wiser than Lemon already in Cambridge Police? Is her saying yes to this offer a good way to leave the door open for Bob? Raynott can see her thinking, so adds.

"Oh, and Leedham would have to do what you ask." Raynott hopes this might clinch it.

"If it happened at all, it would have to be part-time. I have lectures, tutorials, which cannot be put on hold," Elizabeth replies. "Though I have to ask, why is Inspector Abley not coming back? I understand he was suspended for drinking, but I also hear that he now has this under control. He's served decades at the force. Surely this isn't grounds to sack him?"

"He's not been sacked. Whatever gave you that idea? But where is he?" Raynott looks around the office. "His suspension was over and yet he doesn't come in to talk to me? I waited for days after it was lifted. Then we just had a tense conversation, I won't go into the details with you. Suffice it to say that I saw no change in his behaviour, so he left me no option." Raynott shakes his head.

"I don't want to step into his shoes," Elizabeth replies.

"Trust me, I don't want that either." He says. "His shoes have left the building." Raynott checks around his floor to see if he can see any shoes. Very uncomfortable about the conversation, Elizabeth decides to cut things short.

"May I think about it?" she says.

"You will appreciate I can't wait long, with three murders and one being a Head of Department at the University, we need to close this down quickly," Raynott replies.

"Yes, yes of course." Elizabeth watches Raynott pick up some papers and hand them to her. "When do you need to know?"

"Yesterday," he says, "but for you, I will wait until tomorrow morning. Need it wrapped up before the end of the week."

"I will let you know then. Thank you for thinking of me. I certainly enjoy my consultancy here," Elizabeth says, walking towards the door.

"You are our best. You get results. And in no other profession do results matter more," Raynott replies.

Elizabeth thinks surely being a heart or brain surgeon results matter more? But she lets it go, as she knows what he means.

On the way out, Elizabeth feels like she's about to suffocate. Why doesn't this feel good? She could be an Inspector of sorts. In her wildest dreams, she never thought such a thing might happen. Wondered about being in charge of a case. And what a case – three murders! As if Raynott needed to remind her. She needed to solve this one, and yet it kept slipping away from her. Elizabeth wanted to find Bob, but no one had any idea of his whereabouts. She has to talk to him, tell him to come back now. Where is he hiding? The last thing she wants to do is replace Bob, her friend. She thinks about the kiss and is confused as to why he did that. Could that be why he is keeping his distance? No, he is her friend and nothing more. The only thing she can think to do is to solve the case before she has to decide about the police position. That way it might buy Bob some more time to come back before Raynott appoints his replacement.

57
FIRE ON THE WATER

Having moved the boats back to Stourbridge Common after the fireworks, Joe and Sarah walk back from the local shop in Chesterton, where they went to buy some bread and coffee, and food for Midnight. They are in shock, having also seen the local *Cambridge Herald* this Thursday morning and heard about Professor Crowham's death. They had only just been called before to ask to come into the station to give statements about where they were when Talya was murdered. Having stayed up late last night talking about Tom and Talya's deaths, especially as they were with Talya just before she died, they now feel closer to each other than they did before. They are going to go back to the boats, make breakfast and close the door to the world.

It is a beautiful crisp autumnal morning, and despite it being close to eleven now, there is still a mist over Stourbridge Common. The horses are grazing, some just standing looking off into the far distance, as if they know something, as if they know the secrets that people just cannot understand about this world. Everything is still, save for a mother with a pram slowly progressing along the river path towards the city centre. Ducks and swans are still sleeping. As Joe and Sarah climb to the top of the Green Dragon Bridge, they can smell smoke. Perhaps a house backing down to the river is having a bonfire. But the smoke seems to be coming from the other side of the river. Joe eats an iced bun, offering Sarah one, but she says no.

"Are you going to be okay?" Joe asks Sarah. "I mean well enough to go to work this afternoon? You should take compassionate leave."

"I feel dead inside, so it can't get any worse," Sarah replies. "Without work, I'm not sure what I'd do."

"Okay, but remember in all of this you've got me." Joe wants to tell Sarah that he's madly in love with her, that he'd do anything for her, that he just wants to get out of this city now, but he can't find the courage. He knows she doesn't love him, that she sees him as a friend. Even though they had that one-night stand a couple of years ago. He has dreamt of being with her ever since.

"I'm in some nightmare and I can't wake up," Sarah says, "like someone has cut open my chest, stuck a knife in my heart, twisted it and now they are scraping it out onto the floor while I watch, and I'm helpless to stop them. I'm just watching all the blood run out."

"Come here." Joe hugs Sarah as they walk.

"This is never going to go away, is it?" Sarah looks at Joe, "not something like this." Joe hears Sarah's words as if for the first time. Perhaps he thought she would get over Tom quicker than this, for him. Perhaps he hoped too much that his shoulder to lean on would be enough for her. But looking at the anxiety in her face, perhaps he was wrong.

As they walk further, they begin to realise that the smoke is coming from one of the boats, and now they are closer it looks fierce, with strong flames shooting up into thc sky.

"Oh no." Sarah starts to run, and it isn't more than a couple of seconds longer before Joe sees that Sarah's boat is on fire and adrift in the river. Someone has untied the mooring ropes, making it hard to get on board to put out the flames. "No!" Sarah screams, watching her home go up in flames. Already now quite advanced the flames smash another window. People have gathered on the riverbank. Someone is in a dinghy, trying to get a rope from the boat to pull it back to shore, but the flames are too strong, and the ropes burnt. All they can do is watch the flames take hold. Sarah sobs and screams, as Joe, watches another window pop.

"Midnight!" Joe runs towards the flames, but from behind him Tom's black cat appears and rubs his body against Joe's legs. Joe picks up the cat and kisses him. "Thank god." Then turns to Sarah, "Stay with me for now." Sarah turns and cries into his chest. He strokes her hair as the sirens sound for the fire brigade and the police near Elizabeth Way Bridge. But it will be too late.

"Who did this?" Sarah asks.

Joe shrugs and watches the boat burn. The first fire engine arrives at the end of Riverside. Firefighters start to unravel their hose. This one is easy for them, as they have a close source of water that they can turn on the boat, and within minutes they are dousing down the boat. When the police turn up, Lemon is among them. They rapidly move the people away and stake out yet another cordon around the riverbank, to protect everyone's safety, and Lemon also points to set up a cordon for the crime scene. For it is clear to Lemon as he watches that it is highly unlikely this was an accident. The flames lick up from inside the boat, as part of the roof caves in around the roof hatch. But the firemen slowly begin to win the battle. Police and firefighters borrow a dinghy, and as the gathering crowd watch, now behind the police cordon, they see them pull what is left of the boat back into the moorings. Joe and

Sarah move Joe's boat back along the river a little, so as not to be in the way or inside the cordon.
"What happened?" Lemon asks Joe.
"Everything was fine. We just went to get some bread." Joe lifts up the loaf. "And when we came back—" Joe scratches his head, Sarah's eyes are red with tears, and she just looks at Joe and her boat.
"We can offer you police protection," Lemon says to Sarah. Sarah looks nonplussed and can't speak. She has no home, no boyfriend. From somewhere she finds the strength to reply finally.
"They can't win. Whoever did this is trying to stop me from putting on the public displays. I can't let them win."
"Don't worry. I won't let anything stop you," Joe says.

58
POLICE PATHOLOGY

Before Elizabeth leaves the police station after speaking with Superintendent Raynott, she sneaks in to say hello to Leedham. She knows that Leedham is the slowest police pathologist in all history, but hopes for some news. She had investigated the poison cases herself when the boat people and horses fell ill, but wants to check Leedham has verified her work. So she is pleasantly surprised when she finds that Leedham is far more advanced than usual, though he is looking thoroughly exhausted and like he hasn't slept. His normal pristine lab coat is saggy and a little bloody, his glasses foggy and his laboratory, usually immaculate, is a mess. Everywhere there are pieces of equipment left out, doors open, pipettes dropped, notes on every bench.

"Yes, he died from the stab wound," Leedham says. "That's why there is profuse bleeding, which was present around the back of his body. The Professor was wearing many layers, perhaps because he knew he was going to stand in the cold and watch the fireworks. Ew, I hate standing in the cold. Always have to wear three pairs of socks, so I don't get cold feet. A friend of mine has one of those houses overlooking the Common, so I can watch from her living room these days. Toasty!" Leedham rubs his hands, then continues. "Anyway, all the blood soaked into his T-shirts and jumper. He fell, as a lot of it had pooled around his back. He was then hanged by the neck after he was dead."

"So he was definitely murdered?" Elizabeth asks.

"He died from the stab wound. That's all I can say. You do the rest. Motive and all that," Leedham confirms.

"Yes, I got that." Elizabeth looks away from Professor Crowhams body on the slab.

"And as for the woman in the swimming pool. A simple case of being drowned." Leedham lifts the sheet to reveal Talya, but Elizabeth looks away.

"She was a good swimmer apparently," Elizabeth says, looking at Leedhams messy desk.

"Not if she was being strangled." Leedhams says, adding, "She was most probably facing her killer, by the shape of the bruising around her neck, windpipe and back of her spine. The killer must be a good swimmer, as this victim was strangled while she was inhaling water, so she must have been under the water too. Nice," he says.

"This is quick if I might say. And what's with all the—" Elizabeth looks at the mess and back at Leedham.

"Anything to close this case as quickly as possible, so we can get Bob Abley back. Been working around the clock." Leedham shakes his head. "Have you seen him? I saw Pober's face in the paper. I get my news from here, always the last to hear." Leedham shows Elizabeth the front page of the local paper. "I can't work for that man. Please, do something."

"It won't be Pober." Elizabeth doesn't share Raynott's offer for her to take up the reins.

"Thank God for that. Is he coming back then?" Leedham asks.

"Did you verify my results, on the poisonings?" Elizabeth changes the subject.

"I'll tell you if you tell me." Leedham is adamant he wants to know more.

"The results?" Elizabeth isn't about the tell Leedham anything, she knows far too well he is one of the biggest gossips in this place.

"What I don't understand is why so many different types of murder? A poisoning, yes, a drowning and a stabbing, slash hanging? Normally these serial killers have a modus operandi."

"So you did find poisoning too. I don't think it's a serial killer. I think there is a strong motive. We just need to find it."

"What about trying to wipe out the Department of Galileo?" Leedham offers as a motive.

"Perhaps. At first we presumed someone didn't want horses on Stourbridge Common. That they were the target. Yes, I will admit to sometimes having been nudged by them myself a little too close towards the river. But they are beautiful, and thankfully it looked like they weren't the target. That it was the people on the boats."

"Thankfully?" Leedham replies. "Wouldn't it be better if it had been horses people were trying to kill?"

"Would it?" Elizabeth replies. "Sometimes I wonder. I don't see killer horses roaming about the place."

"What?" Leedham is confused. Elizabeth doesn't care if Leedham can't keep up with her thoughts. But maybe Leedham being wrong has helped her unlock a thought.

"Maybe it has nothing to do with the Department of Galileo at all. The woman who died in the Jesus Green Lido. She lived at Fen Ditton, on the river, didn't she?" Elizabeth asks rhetorically.

"I don't know their life history, just about their bodies. And she had a good one, very curvy." Leedham replies.

Elizabeth can't believe what Leedham has just said, but

her mind is on the puzzle, so she shakes her head dismissively and continues.

"And even Professor Crowhams, he lived on Midsummer Common. So they have all lived either on or very close to the river. And then there was that post-doc who was injured on the river."

"I know nothing about him. Presumably he's therefore still alive." Leedham shuts the trays holding the dead bodies of Professor Crowhams and Talya Febland.

"He was a fortunate man." Elizabeth fills in Leedham, then continues with her train of thought. "All of these deaths and injuries have either been on Stourbridge Common or Jesus Green. It makes me wonder if the next will be on Midsummer Common."

"So you think geography is key? A Commons murderer?" Leedhams asks.

"Have you seen Bob?" Elizabeth replies with a question.

Leedham shakes his head and sighs.

"You know what the Inspector would say about this case?" Leedhams says. "Do you?"

"Oh, will you just spit." Elizabeth frowns.

"There's the Professor Green I've missed." Leedham smiles at Elizabeth. "He'd say only look at the facts. Don't try to surmise. Facts, baby. Three dead. One injury. Different ages, different types of death, different locations, different days. Things in common, river deaths, department deaths. Someone doesn't like department people who live by or on the river. Lemon was telling me that Inspector Abley told him to bring in someone called Cynthia? But that the woman is being evasive. I'd say get onto that."

"Thanks, Leedham. Thanks very much. That's helpful." Elizabeth has everything she can get from Leedham, and this is wasting her time. She needs to find Bob, and quick.

"Just find Bob and get him back quick," Leedham shouts.

59
FOXES HAVEN

Godric makes himself a cuppa and looks out of the kitchen window down to the river. He can almost feel winter's fingers curling around the edges of his nanna's garden. He is still in his pyjamas. It feels good to sleep in a proper bed and not on the floor of friends in college. He toyed with the idea of moving out, leaving Foxes Haven for the excitement of College, but knows which side his bread is buttered. Washing is done, fresh sheets twice a week, comfy sofa, television and snacks. Godric isn't a usual Cambridge undergraduate. He likes holding onto the apron strings and is more than happy for them not to be cut from his nanna. He knows deep down it is because his mother is so bloody cold that now he feels like he's now receiving the childhood he never had. Bunny makes his afternoon tea with all the trimmings. She folds his socks, picks up his magazines.

And then there is the garden, where she lets him sunbathe nude, so he can get an all-over tan. She has the most amazing summerhouse where he can pretend to work, but really sleep. And now it is autumn; whenever he returns there's always a fire crackling and a box of cakes from the vegan bakery. But more than anything, he enjoys living with his nanna. He likes her company. It's worrying then, that someone had lit a firework which had hit his nanna.

She hasn't told him what was going on. People dead on the river. And he's already heard through College about the rower nearly getting garroted. He decides the best thing he can do to pay his nanna back – apart from working harder at university, which she is always telling him to do and he isn't about to start – is to go and investigate what's happening on the river. He decides he will get dressed now and take the dogs out and have a sniff about with them. Hector and Monty don't tell Godric that they have only just been for a walk with Elizabeth, while Godric was sleeping. They are happy to accompany Godric if they must.

60
HEART OF GOLD

Godric steps out across Jesus Green and strides away from the Weir, so the dogs are safe from the deep and thrashing water. The leaves have turned a beautiful reddish yellow on the London plane trees. He decides to walk along the river path towards Midsummer Common, but before he gets very far, he comes across Ed, the Lock Keeper of Jesus Green. Ed is leaning against a tree out of breath. His dog, Clive, wags his tail at Godric.

"Hello, fellow. Are you okay?" Godric asks Ed.

"Just a minute," Ed says.

"Come and sit down then." Godric points to a bench, worrying that Ed looks clammy and pale.

"You're alright son. I'll just catch my breath. Clive here needs a walk this morning," Ed says. Godric waits and strokes Clive while he subtly watches Ed. Ed looks up at the sky and stands again. "There, just needed to catch my breath. All's fine now." And Ed starts to walk towards the Lido and children's playground. "It's the cold air. It gets into my lungs."

"It does feel like winter today, not long to Christmas," Godric replies.

"We've only just had bonfire night!" Ed says, not pleased with how time rushes by so quickly.

"Terrible about that Professor, isn't it?" Godric makes conversation as they begin to walk on the path.

"Karma, that's what that is," Ed replies.

"Sorry?" Godric isn't sure he heard properly.

"He was a miserable bastard that nobody liked. Now he's dead. I call that karma," Ed repeats.

"Surely you wouldn't wish him dead?" Godric asks.

"Wouldn't I?" Ed replies.

Godric isn't sure how to answer, but knows he will tell his nanna when he gets back. He watches as Clive, Hector and Monty run down towards the river, as if to jump in.

"Hector, Monty, get out of there." Godric shouts, but the dogs ignore him. They both watch them get dangerously close to falling in, so Godric gets out the treat packet, rustles it and gives them all a biscuit.

The two men walk further, down under the Victoria Avenue Bridge, just talking about the dogs when eventually Godric spots Wallis with another sculler, rowing up towards them. A couple of swans and some ducks are now stuck between the riverbank with the dogs and scullers. Wallis hasn't seen them yet, with his back to them, but he can't believe the venom with which Ed starts to shout at the rowers.

"You shouldn't be up this far. You do not have permission. Get back. Go back I say! Get off the river!!"

Godric sees Wallis stop rowing and lift his oars, then turn around to see who is shouting. Godric doesn't know where to hide at this point and waves at Wallis, who frowns at him, not having heard from Godric in a while but having heard that he has been seen getting cosy with a man called Ben.

"Not you again old man. Haven't you died yet?" Wallis says.

Godric can't believe Wallis is so mean. He hadn't seen such continued hatred for one man. What was it about these two?

"Bugger off! If you so much as touch one of those ducks I'll jump in and do for you!" Ed shouts.

"You sad old man, go home and shout at the television instead you silly old duffer," Wallis replies.

"You think this is funny, but poor innocent ducklings and cygnets are losing their lives because of your display of selfish arrogance. Acting like you're god on the river!" Ed replies.

"We are god. We can kill as many ducklings as we like. It's not illegal. Anyway, it's autumn. There are no flipping duckings!" Wallis scoffs.

"Yes, it bloody well is illegal. I could report you!" Ed shouts frantically.

"Get your dog under control!" Wallis shouts back. Godric sees that Clive is standing by Ed obediently. It is Hector and Monty who are curious about the swans, now trapped.

"Shut up Wallis, you know they're mine," Godric says.

"Well get that old man under control. Take him to the nursing home," Wallis replies. "And, we're done."

"Yup," Godric says, raising his eyebrows and pulling in his lips in disappointment at his poor judgement on Wallis. His nanna was right.

"Get back! Just leave these poor creatures alone!!" Ed screams at Wallis. He's had enough as Wallis starts to row again, dipping his oars perilously close to the ducks and swans. Godric slips down the bank and puts Hector and Monty on leads, but when he pulls them back up the riverbank, he drops the leads immediately as he sees Ed clutching his chest and falling to the ground. Ed's now grey and writhing in agony. Godric pulls out his phone.

"Ambulance please."

Another dog walker has seen Ed collapse and runs over

to see if they can help. Everything goes into slow motion as Ed shuts his eyes. The dog walker rips open Ed's coat and listens to his heart. Then starts to pump at his chest. For a minute Godric stands there, talking to the ambulance emergency caller at the other end, watching CPR being performed on Ed. What has just happened? Godric looks back at Wallis and the other sculler, seeing that they are now facing the right way on the river to see everything that is happening on the river bank. So he is shocked to his core to see that they just row away. Godric looks back at Ed and sees that the four dogs are all sniffing him, curious as to what is happening. Godric, still with phone in hand, catches Hector and Monty's leads.

Two other people have now stopped on their bicycles. One announces he is a doctor. He places his bicycle carefully by a tree and bends down to help the person already carrying out CPR. Godric wonders where his nanna is; she'd know what to do.

61
DEPARTMENT BUSINESS

After hearing Superintendent Raynott tell her that Inspector Abley is through, Elizabeth looks everywhere for Bob. She is desperate to find him and drag him to the station to bang his head together with the Super's. She must have spent hours traipsing to all his haunts. The golf course, his favourite bars, she even knocked on his house again. But Maureen sent her packing again and told her that she wasn't getting the lemon tree back. No one knew where he was.

Elizabeth is now worried that he's done something stupid. What if he's just left Cambridge, decided without his wife, home or job just to do a runner. He'd told her earlier that he'd booked a holiday for himself and Maureen. What if he'd gone without her, just buggered off with his head in the sand? In the end, it was Sergeant Lemon who jolted Elizabeth out of her search by suggesting they visit the Department of Galileo to see what people were saying about Professor Crowhams. Perhaps someone would reveal something, a clue to help them unlock this case.

But when they got there, they found none of the familiar faces. The acting Deputy told them that many of Professor Crowhams's colleagues were off today, in shock, and that his lectures and seminars had been cancelled. Elizabeth watched some of the undergraduates — without televisions or interest in the local news — now reading the notes on the doors about Professor Crowhams's death for the first time and then huddling. Eventually Lemon and Elizabeth tracked down Joe, who was in the gardens, raking up leaves on one of the side lawns.

"Where did you get to last night?" Sergeant Lemon asked him "After the fireworks?"

"What do you mean?" Joe says.

"The boats, moored. They were there this morning when we came to the fire. But during the fireworks, they were not by the river?" Lemon says.

"Oh, we moved them. They were at Fen Ditton. You always get so many people trying to climb aboard during fireworks night." Joe replies. "It's so packed. We always move them the afternoon before everything starts. And Midnight, Tom's cat, I couldn't put her through it. That would be cruel," He adds.

"Where is everyone?" Elizabeth asks about the empty department.

"I guess some have stayed away, having heard the news about Professor Crowhams. Probably feel a little unsafe," Joe says. "Do you blame them?"

"It clearly doesn't bother you," Elizabeth replies.

"I'm not scared of anyone. Bring it on. If they come for me, I'll give them the same back," Joe says.

"Is Miss Sarah Robertly with her police protection officer?" Lemon asks Joe.

"No idea. She's gone to Grantchester Meadows for a stargazing night of the Blood Moon." He shrugs.

"What?" Elizabeth asks, surprised that is still going ahead.

"Oh, the local astronomy club has been inviting the

university for donkey's years. Tom said 'yes' this year, so Sarah is honouring his acceptance. Cynthia's with her. So they should be okay together," Joe replies.

"Sarah told me about the second public event. But I presumed it would be cancelled after Professor Crowhams' and Talya Febland's deaths? You don't seem worried about her safety?" Elizabeth asks.

"Yes, well, maybe my offers to protect her have fallen on deaf ears," Joe shrugs. "She made it quite clear that she doesn't need my protection. She needs 'space' apparently."

"Do you think she needs protection?" Elizabeth asks.

"The police think so," Joe replies, bemused by Elizabeth questioning this. "Anyway, she's far away from Cambridge. What could happen on Grantchester Meadows, eh? You can see anyone coming from miles away. The least likely place for surprises. And, as I say, they are together, Cynthia and Sarah. I think they should be okay."

"I wish you'd told us about this earlier," Elizabeth says. "It does seem poorly timed. With so many dead, to be doing something with so many people about at night, in the dark," she adds.

"Oh, they're well organised. It would be pretty hard to kill someone in front of so many people too," Joe replies.

"You seem so sure. Are you going?" Sergeant Lemon chips in, watching Joe's body language.

"Like I said already. I'm not going." Joe shakes his head and picks up his rake to continue his bit of light border tidying.

Elizabeth says quietly to Lemon, "Have you seen the Inspector?"

"No, I was hoping you had," Lemon replies. "His phone must be switched off. Either that, or he's still ignoring my calls. Not sure which is worse at this point. He's left it too late now. The Super has called a staff meeting tomorrow. I think he's going to announce a new Inspector. That's the rumour. At least Pober is too busy to take on the role."

Elizabeth and Lemon walk a little way from Joe, so as to be sure not to be heard. "Talking of rumours, there is a rumour that the Super has offered you Inspector Abley's job?" Lemon says, looking at Elizabeth for the truth.

"Where on earth did you get that from?" Elizabeth tries to shrug this off, knowing full well and not being best pleased that the Superintendent must have spread this rumour himself.

"Canteen, where all the rumours are usually true." Lemon replies, "I don't know if the chef has his ear to the air vents in the Super's room or something, but he always seems to get it right. Is it true?" Lemon gives Elizabeth a hard stare, so much that she doesn't know where to look or what to say. She knows that it won't be healthy if this is confirmed among the officers back at the station, so in a split second, she replies.

"That's crazy. We will find Inspector Abley and I'm sure will also find that he has just been recovering from what has been a very stressful period in his life. And we will support him in his role as Inspector. I am very sad you are leaving us Lemon."

"Me too," Lemon sighs.

When Elizabeth looks back at Joe, he has gone. His rake is on the ground and his tea still steaming in the cold air.

"I've put out the nod for our drivers to keep an eye for the Inspector by the way," Lemon adds.

"Do you think they'll find him?" Elizabeth asks.

"If he's in Cambridge."

"I might just drive down and watch the Blood Moon in Grantchester," Elizabeth says.

"Is that wise? We have a murder case here in Cambridge. I could do with your help here." Lemon's phone rings. He listens for a while. "Okay, I'll come now."

Elizabeth wonders what the call in was and stares at Lemon.

"Old Ed, he's had a heart attack," Lemon says

"Oh god no." Elizabeth waits for more information, sad for Ed. "Apparently he was with your grandson and in a bit of a verbal spat with a couple of rowers?"

"So he wasn't attacked or anything?" Elizabeth asks.

"No, but given this is another thing on the river, I want to rule out foul play, just to be sure. Will you check for poisons for the same reason?" Lemon asks.

"Yes of course, when I get back. I will go over and tell Cynthia in person," Elizabeth explains to Lemon.

62
THE DRIVE

Elizabeth returns to Foxes Haven to fetch the Talbot. As she is pulling out of the drive, Godric is coming home with the dogs. She stops the car in the driveway, dressed up in her burnt duffel coat, hat and scarf, with a hot water bottle on her lap and a blanket over her knees. He can see her breath in the air.

"Did you see the message I left on the table?" Godric asks.

"What message?" Elizabeth says.

"When are you going to get a phone? Ed the Lock Keeper, he's had a heart attack." Godric leans on the car door. "I was with him when it happened. Wallis was riling him up, and his heart must have burst with all the stress."

"Are you okay?" Elizabeth is concerned that is not a nice thing for Godric to have to deal with. She makes a note to talk about it later.

"Yes, I think so. It was truly awful. Where are you going?" Godric asks, watching the car's headlights beaming ahead in the dusk.

"Grantchester. Will you watch the dogs, they need their tea now? There's another astronomy event. Bearing in mind someone was punched at the last one and killed at the fireworks. I want to be there. Seems the night sky brings out the worst in people."

"Want me to come with you?" Godric says. "Not sure I like the idea of you going alone."

"Dogs, tea, and feed Bertie and Soot. And you need a rest yourself after Ed, I'm sure. There's some cannelloni, bought it from Gino's today for you. Needs eating." Elizabeth puts the car in gear and starts to drive away, looking at her grandson in the mirror behind her. She is in two minds whether to stop and ask Godric to get in after all, unsure what she is driving into. But there is a break in the cars going by and she turns out left into Chesterton Lane.

63
THE MOON AND THE STARS

After Professor Green and Sergeant Lemon leave the Department of Galileo, Joe tries to continue working the gardens, but it is getting late now, and there isn't a lot more he can do in the light. And much of the autumnal going into winter gardening work is about mending fences, oiling locks, raking up leaves and mending nest boxes for birds for the spring. Joe has done most of this already by now. Often November, December and January are all about trying to look busy without really being too busy. As well as attending meetings with the Director of Gardens, to discuss what would be planted in the borders for the coming year, he would be making sure all the seeds are purchased and soil in the greenhouses ready to get going with gusto at the end of January. There are big greenhouses at the back of the department, and often Joe hides in them. He is in there now, drinking soup with the radio on.

The news comes on, reporting Professor Crowhams' death, not mentioning anything about it being murder, though mentioning the murder of Talya and Tom. It is enough for Joe to put down his potting up of early annuals and lock the greenhouse before heading to his car. He rushes out of the car park and drove towards Grantchester. It is clear only to Joe why he is heading for the astronomy event at Grantchester, where Sarah is probably already setting up, even though she told him not to come, that she needs space. It is clear only to Joe why he has brought a spade with him from the greenhouse.

64
A WOMAN IN MIND

Lemon is sitting on the bed next to Ed the Lock Keeper at Ripplewater Hospital. Ed looks very pale and is attached to drips and machines. He isn't conscious, so in no state to be interviewed. But Lemon is thinking about the case. No one else is in the room, and the only distraction is the beeping of the heart monitors. It is clear to Lemon that he's in above his head. He didn't predict the murder of Talya Febland, nor Professor Crowhams. He sure as hell can't work out who is doing all the killing, but as soon as he catches the perpetrator, he is leaving Cambridge.

"It's all a bit of a mess, isn't it?" he says to Ed, who can't hear. Just as he speaks a nurse walks in who frowns at him.

"Has a woman been in, Cynthia Hatman?" Lemon asks the nurse. The nurse shakes her head. Lemon feels the need to explain himself. "She's his partner. We contacted her and left her messages, but haven't heard from her either."

Lemon smiles at the nurse who is tending to Ed's pillows. He finds it odd that Cynthia would choose to attend a stargazing event rather than come to Ed's bedside. There must be something very important happening, he thinks, for that to happen.

"Did you find her number?"

"His phone has a lock on it. We couldn't find next of kin in his wallet." The nurse shrugs.

"We called her a few times to see us." Lemon takes out his phone and dials Cynthia Hatman's number again. But it goes to answerphone. Nothing. What person doesn't answer their phone if they are organising an event?

Then something dawns on Lemon and, making excuses to the nurse and knocking over some water on the bedside table, he leaves abruptly.

65
GOLF

Sergeant Lemon arrives at the golf course. No harm in seeing if he can catch Inspector Abley in his most likely of hiding places. On arrival, he spots the Inspector's car. He lifts his arms to the air and drops them by his side in frustration, shaking his head. He'd been here earlier to look for him and it wasn't there. Perhaps hoping he was wrong about his boss, Lemon takes no time in walking straight into the lounge bar, where just three women are relaxing with G&Ts, having just finished playing. Lemon coughs as he walks up to them.

"Hello," he says.

"Hello," the women purr as they all look up and stare at Lemon. They have the same sunburnt leathery creased faces Inspector Abley has from hours spent walking the holes up high on this hill. They look somehow happier than those down in the city. Perhaps they have fewer cares. Perhaps they have rich husbands. Lemon can't put his finger on it, but is only interested in finding his boss.

"I wonder, do you happen to know Inspector

Abley?" he asks.

"Bob? Yes of course. We all know Bob. Our lovely Bob," one of them offers, now flirting a little with Lemon.

"Right, well, I don't suppose you've seen him recently, have you?" Lemon asks, trying to keep away from one woman trying to stroke his arm.

"Yes, he's on the old course. On the seventeenth," one answers.

"Gosh, that's specific. And where might that be?" One of the women give him her scorecard. Lemon frowns.

"Turn around darling," she replies.

Lemon turns around to face the window and thinks he can see Inspector Abley taking a putt on a green a way away. He rushes out the doors to the terrace and spots Abley's bright pink jumper in the distance. A rush of anger wells up inside Lemon as he marches across. A man taking his shot on a putting green shouts "Hey!" at him, but Lemon can only see the Inspector. Bob Abley has his back to Lemon and is on the seventeenth green taking a putt.

Lemon has a good mind to run up and kick Abley's ball. The other player, who has walked the course with Abley and looks like he lives here, in his green slacks and orange top, spots Lemon first. He says something to Abley, as Bob stops eyeing up the hole and his ball and twists around to look behind him. As soon as he sees Lemon, he stops what he is doing and looks guilty.

"Inspector." All the anger inside Lemon hasn't left him as he rushes up to his friend, but he is trying his hardest to contain it. It comes out in just a hard, cold stare instead.

"Can you give us a minute?" Abley says to his playing partner. The man nods and walks over to his ball to take his own putt, not wanting to hold up those behind them on the sixteenth. Abley and Lemon walk off the green, Abley following Lemon perilously close to a raked bunker. Lemon starts to flail his arms around, trying not to raise his voice.

"Have you been playing golf all this time? I've been up here umpteen times looking for you. Have you got them covering or something?" Lemon asks, in disbelief. Abley says nothing. Lemon continues, "Only, we have a triple murder, and the Super is planning to replace you. You know that."

"I heard," Abley finally replies adding, "I hear you've been doing brilliantly without me. Well done lad."

"With all due respect Sir, that sounds a little patronising," Lemon says trying to hide his bitterness.

"You'll be an Inspector soon," Abley says, maintaining his normal kind tone.

"No I won't," Lemon pauses, "but I'm leaving." Lemon says, wondering what Inspector Abley will make of that.

"What?" Inspector Abley's manner changes immediately from one of ease to sounding anxious. "You can't do that. You love Cambridge."

"I've been offered a job with Thames Valley. Better job, more prospects," Lemon replies. "Inspectors who turn up for their jobs."

"Ouch. Well, I have to say I'm disappointed. I thought you were a loyal man," Abley replies. Lemon is catatonic inside – the audacity of this man, to accuse him of loyalty. He has nothing to say, and knows he now made the right choice to go. Abley continues, "Why aren't you with Elizabeth, you should be with Elizabeth now. You should go, she needs you." Lemon cannot believe what he has just heard. It might be in the knowledge that he is leaving or perhaps that he has been pushed to the limit, but something inside Lemon explodes in a way it has never done so before.

"You complete selfish bastard, Sir," Lemon says, with a mix of anger and deference.

"Right," Abley replies. Lemon waits for Abley to say more, but his boss just shrugs his shoulders and starts swinging his club to get back into the rhythm before his putt, so Lemon continues.

"You know, I used to admire you. You were the copper I

always wanted to be. Got results, always had time for the little man, inside and out of the station." Lemon says, "But now, it seems I don't know you at all."
"You know me. I play golf, what can I say?" Abley shrugs.
"You're a flake!" Lemon can't believe he's letting the words tumble out of his mouth, but is so angry he can't stop himself. "Hiding up here playing an idiotic game that no one in their right mind would play, not giving a flying ferret what's going on down in your City." Lemon just about manages not to swear, then stares at Abley and can see Abley wince a little but try to hide his feelings then continues to practice his swing in the air. "That's it, concentrate on what's important, not on trying to solve these murders before someone else is killed." Lemon adds.
"Are we done?" Abley replies.
"We are doner than done," Lemon spits out bitterly.
"It's just that I only have the eighteenth left after this then I was going to leave to go to this Grantchester stargazing. I don't want to be late. Elizabeth phoned me, told me she was picking up her car at to meet her there at six. She said Cynthia Hatman was there. Did you interview Cynthia, like I told you to?" Abley asks Lemon while looking at his golf companion putt a long shot right into the hole. Abley signals to him that he'll be over in a minute. Lemon is angry at the Inspector for asking him about Cynthia Hatman, especially as he hasn't managed to get her into the station to question. She has been ignoring Lemon's calls.
"Not yet. But Professor Green left a while ago. I've been to the hospital since I left her and she was going straight there. So she must be there by now." Lemon says.
"What?" Abley's manner changes immediately. "No, no, no, no. She said six," Abley panics.
"Yes, she will have been there a while now." Lemon replies, confused as to why an hour makes a difference.
"What? She said she'd be there at six, at six," Abley repeats, his mind racing. He drops his golf clubs and runs

to the clubhouse, leaving Lemon in shock before he chases after him.

66
DEAD MAN'S CORNER

It hasn't taken Elizabeth much time at all to drive out to Grantchester. The lanes are very eerie now it is dark and surprisingly empty, all but the huge blood moon rising on the horizon. As she creeps slowly into the village, pumpkins smile and frown from front gardens and strings of winter lights drape trees and porches, already prepared for winter. But doors are shut up tight, and curtains closed. Grantchester village is quiet. There is no one milling about, perhaps because the temperature is dropping quickly into the night. You can almost hear the church mouse's whiskers twitch as Elizabeth pulls over in the Talbot and walks across the village green.

From Joe's directions earlier, Elizabeth surmised the stargazing is going to take place down by the river, where the village is at its darkest. Elizabeth walks past The Green Man pub with its smells of chestnuts and jacket potatoes roasting on a brazier out the front. Despite the cold, two people are standing eating and chatting. They nod a greeting as she walks past.

But as Elizabeth steps out onto the field behind, and despite the stars out in force tonight, the difference between the dimness of the village streets and the darkness across Grantchester Meadows is stark, with the huge moon shining even a little brighter than before between the trees. If she didn't know these meadows well, she would risk falling into a number of boggy ditches, small streams, and land locked puddles. But Elizabeth is overly familiar, and the moon is illuminating watery reflections on the grass beneath her feet, making light work of the next hundred yards which take her down to the river's edge. There in the distance further up the path, she can just make out a wooden platform with silhouettes of telescopes and a big screen erected beside.

"Hello Professor Green." Elizabeth hears a voice and recognises it as Cynthia Hatman's. Elizabeth turns and Cynthia is already standing close behind, holding a large wooden post with a spike at the end. "You made it. I thought you might." Cynthia adds. Elizabeth can see that Cynthia's face is a little dirty.

"Did you fall?" Elizabeth asks, wondering how Cynthia got into such a state, mud down her coat.

"How did you guess? You look startled," Cynthia says.

"You kind of crept up on me there," Elizabeth replies.

"That's the dark for you," Cynthia says, swinging the post from side to side.

"Is anyone else here yet?" Elizabeth enquires, trying to avoid the post spike swinging about in front of her.

"Sarah was here earlier, we brought the telescopes down together, but she told me she's just popped away to get something to eat. So it's just us," Cynthia replies staring at Elizabeth in the darkness.

"What time does the event start?" Elizabeth wonders when others will appear.

"Oh, not for another hour-and-a-half." Cynthia looks at her watch. "We have plenty of time. You want to interrogate me? That's your thing, isn't it?" Cynthia huffs.

"I'd like to ask why are you ignoring Sergeant Lemon's requests to come in to the station?" Elizabeth remarks.
"Why, does he think I'm the murderer?" Cynthia asks.
"I was curious about that. Do you have something to hide?" Elizabeth replies.
"You're a very annoying woman sometimes, Professor Green," Cynthia says, "Always with the questions. Sometimes people don't appreciate your questions. You could end up getting yourself into trouble. You know that?" Cynthia lifts her spike post up onto her shoulder and the spike points right at Elizabeth's face.
"Sergeant Lemon wants you to tell him where you were when Professor Crowhams was being killed," Elizabeth says, trying to keep her cool.
"Does he now," Cynthia scoffs.
"Where were you during the fireworks?" Elizabeth asks.
"I don't remember," Cynthia replies, shifting the post from one shoulder to another.
"But it was only last night?" Elizabeth isn't accepting Cynthia's reply.
"Oh yes." Cynthia is about to say something but treads on a wet patch of mud and slips. The post she is holding nearly hits straight into Elizabeth as Cynthia falls onto her and they both trip to the ground. Elizabeth is stuck under Cynthia and starts to struggle to get away, but the weight is pinning her down, so she slaps Cynthia round the face instead, attempting to get her to move.
"Hey! What did you do that for?" Cynthia looks at Elizabeth. "I'm so sorry I slipped. But no need for that." It is clear from Cynthia's demeanour that she is really sorry as she rolls off Elizabeth, rubbing her red cheek. Cynthia begins to stand up, offering Elizabeth a hand which Elizabeth takes. The two of them are now very muddy, having fallen into a boggy puddle. Elizabeth's duffel coat has turned brown. They take a moment to catch their breath and check they haven't broken or bruised anything. Then Elizabeth asks, "Why are you not with Ed?"

"We are not joined at the hip you know. He's been ill. It's far too cold to be out here so I said he shouldn't come," Cynthia replies, straightening her hair.
"Hasn't someone rung you? He's in the hospital," Elizabeth replies. "He's had a heart attack."
"What?" Cynthia looks at Elizabeth for a second as the news sinks in. "What?" She is in complete shock. "My phone, it's in the car. I must go." Cynthia panics and starts to run towards her car. "Is he okay?" She shouts back "He's going to be okay?"
"I don't know. Where were you last night?!" Elizabeth shouts, but Cynthia isn't going to reply, already with her back to Elizabeth and now running as fast as she can across the field and back up to the village.
After a while of standing and catching her breath and checking that she hasn't lost anything from her coat pockets from the fall, Elizabeth decides to go and inspect the telescopes. Perhaps out of a sense of duty to the university, someone at least should be here now Cynthia has left, so they are not stolen. She climbs the few steps up to a large wooden platform. She looks into a telescope, but she can't see anything. Perhaps it is not switched on she thinks. Elizabeth is mildly irritated by telescopes. Like an impressionist painting what she can see with the naked eye is beautiful enough without needing to look closer. She is a little stuck here, however, now that she has decided to guard these huge metal beasts, so looks into another. This one works and she sees what must be the moon up close. She pulls away as it is so bright and shakes her head.
"Hello, Professor Green," Sarah says from behind.

"Ooh, hello. You made me jump. That's twice now tonight," Elizabeth says, laughing to herself a little. "Cynthia mentioned you'd gone for a bit, and all this equipment was left out, so I thought I'd better stay."

"I only went back to my car for a sandwich?" Sarah replies, carrying another smaller telescope to set up on the pontoon.

"This a big stage. How many will fit up here?" Elizabeth looks around at the half a dozen telescopes of all sizes.

"We hope around twenty at a time. People will take turns. We have binoculars as well for others in the meadow," Sarah replies, placing the telescope down and spreading its legs. "What are you doing here?"

"Well, Cynthia had to leave in a hurry. As I say, I was watching these." Elizabeth looks to the telescopes. Curious, Elizabeth asks, "In the circumstances aren't you worried? It's dark now. There is no one else about. Given all the murders." Elizabeth looks about in the dark and the big moon above.

"There is the odd dog walker. It's not completely isolated. I can still see the lights from the village too, which is very annoying. I don't understand people who don't love stargazing, who'd rather sit in a pub and drink alcohol," Sarah says, adding, "and Cynthia was supposed to be here. Where's she gone?"

"I'm sorry to hear about your friend, Talya," Elizabeth comments, not wanting to go into the details about Ed.

"Are you sorry?" Sarah replies.

"What do you mean?" Elizabeth finds this a strange response.

"You didn't know Talya, did you? So how can you be sorry?" Sarah says matter-of-factly.

"I'm sorry when anyone dies," Elizabeth replies. "Aren't you?"

"If they didn't we'd have a full planet." Sarah looks up at the stars. "We come from the stars, we return to the stars. We're just amino acids."

"Hmm." Elizabeth says, again finding Sarah's reply a little strange. "Who do you think killed Talya?" Elizabeth asks.

"I have no idea. I'm still in shock." Sarah looks at Elizabeth disapprovingly for bringing up the graphic image. "She was my friend. My boyfriend and now my friend. Who will be next?" Sarah shakes her head.

"I don't know, but d'you think it's the same person who killed Professor Crowhams?" Elizabeth asks, studying Sarah's face.

"I honestly don't know," Sarah replies. "I just hope you catch the killer soon before they do it again, or before I catch them."

"You think they will strike again?" Elizabeth asks.

"I don't know," Sarah says, sighing. "And I seriously don't think I'm cut out for this anymore." Sarah looks around at all the telescopes awaiting the swathes of public. "It's Tom's project. And to make matters worse, Cynthia just told me that she's retiring. I can't do this on my own. I'm so tired." Elizabeth observes in the moonlight that Sarah looks exhausted.

"You seem good with the public. And from what I've observed are determined to see things through, just like this evening."

"I'm beginning to wonder if Tom cared as much as I did about these events?"

"Did care?" Elizabeth asks.

"Oh, I don't know. It's all such a mess," Sarah says, turning from Elizabeth to look up again at the stars. "Is Cynthia coming back?"

"You may have to start this one without her," Elizabeth replies, adding, "When Professor Crowhams spoke about these public events he only ever spoke as if they were Tom's project, not yours. I thought you were just seeing them through after Tom died from what you've said before?" Elizabeth notices Sarah pick up a mallet and some small luminous signs on sticks and start to walk down the steps again from the platform with telescopes. "Can I walk with you?" Elizabeth asks but doesn't wait for an answer.

"Where did she go? I have to put some signs out, so people don't fall into the river," Sarah replies.

"People aren't stupid," Elizabeth comments, not wanting to get into the whys and wherefores of Cynthia leaving.

"Of course, but it's dark, and some come all the way from London to see this and haven't been here before," Sarah says.

Elizabeth watches as Sarah hits a 'Danger Deep Water' sign into the ground with a mallet.

"So was it your project too?" Elizabeth continues.

"We talked about it for a while before Tom set it up. I've always thought people should get the opportunity to learn as much as the privileged. No disrespect, but Cambridge is so bloody elitist. Just my way of connecting I suppose, putting something back. I think in the end I've loved this project more than Tom. He sometimes got irritated by the level of ignorance confronting him. He was a public schoolboy you see, Professor. And Cynthia was a privately educated boarder. Scratch the surface. No understanding of the everyman and woman."

"Ah, and so you're the rebel?" Elizabeth asks.

"Hardly a rebel." Sarah bangs in a second sign with a mallet. It is very dark so Sarah pulls out a torch to walk to the next spot to place the next sign. "It's nearly time. The public we are talking about will be here in less than an hour. I need to get a move on. It was nice talking to you, but I can't be talking anymore as I have so much to do. Cynthia was supposed to help me with this. Will you excuse me?" Sarah says walking off.

"Are you sure there is nothing more you want to tell me?" Elizabeth asks following.

"About what?" Sarah frowns a little.

"About Tom and Talya, about Brad, Professor Crowhams?" Elizabeth raises her eyebrows.

"Brad?" Sarah shakes her head and frowns a little.

"Brad Brick, the rower. Great name, isn't it?" Elizabeth watches Sarah stand up, now holding the other signs in one hand, mallet in the other and starts to walk away again.

"I don't know what you're talking about?" Sarah replies over her shoulder. Elizabeth follows and they arrive at Dead Man's Corner.

"Funny isn't it, the name, Dead Man's Corner," Elizabeth says, looking at the murky river with trees leaning into it.

"Surely there are no dead men in it?" Sarah replies.

"Punts lose their poles here because it's so deep, and novice punters get stuck in this basin, sometimes for hours, until a professional punter arrives and can fish them out. I don't believe it has claimed many lives."

"Yet," Sarah replies. Again, Elizabeth feels a little surprised by Sarah's answer. She observes her tapping in a sign, watching her for clues. Sarah is taps away and then starts to move off, so Elizabeth decides to move things along.

"It was a genius move, to poison the apple pie." Elizabeth decides to speed up this conversation, now looking directly at Sarah.

"Excuse me?" Sarah turns, surprised, still holding the mallet and remaining signs.

"You cooked the pie. You used the apples." Elizabeth accuses Sarah, waiting for her expected denial.

"Which were left for us in a barrel." Sarah frowns.

"Ah, yes, but you ordered the barrel of apples online. We traced the purchase back to a computer in the department. A computer that you use, the one in your room in fact," Elizabeth says waiting for Sarah to deny it.

"What?" Sarah looks stunned, she wasn't expecting this. "Anyone could have used my computer. I don't lock it. It's University property. Remember, it's likely Professor Crowhams cancelled our last stargazing event from it."

"But they didn't, did they? It was you. You poisoned Dr Tom Mirren." Elizabeth stretches out each word.

"Like I say, everyone has access to that computer. Professor Crowhams, Joe even. That's insane, I wouldn't hurt my own boyfriend," Sarah says, angry at the accusation.

"Not hurt, more premeditated murder. You didn't murder him on the day you ordered the apples. Professor Crowhams was out. Joe was out. Cynthia was out. Even Tom himself was out. You were the only one in the department at that hour when that order took place. Oh, it was you alright." Elizabeth is disappointed that such a seemingly kind person, the last person she would have suspected, is a cold-hearted killer.

"That means nothing. I didn't order any apples." Sarah is beginning to look uncomfortable.

"Then you went on to bake a pie so lethal that with two slices anyone could have died from eating it." Elizabeth says, "You had to get the doses accurate mind, but then I'm sure you gave Tom an early slice. Joe mentioned that he would have eaten more pie if there had been more left. There were eight of you. At first, I thought that meant you all must have had a slice each, you were all ill, and that Tom had just been unlucky. But I guess you only had a small piece, and you cut Joe a sliver and the others too. So that he and the others wouldn't die, just be ill enough for it to look like an accident. And poor Tom, with his two large pieces of pie, maybe more, made by his loving girlfriend." Elizabeth pauses. She finds it beyond a tragedy that someone could murder their loved one. "Genius that you made yourself ill," Elizabeth carries on. "Didn't suspect you for ages, and making a pie Talya didn't like so she didn't have any threw the suspicion onto her immediately. Well played, just should have ordered somewhere else."

"I don't know what you're talking about. This is crazy. I have to organise a public event and you, you are getting in the way!" Sarah raises her voice for the first time.

"Very clever to poison yourself for a second time. I must admit, I was worried for your safety for a while there, trying to work out who could have poisoned you," Elizabeth says. "But to poison the horses again too, to draw attention away from yourself. That's unforgivable."

"This is madness." Sarah waves the 'Danger Deep Water' signs about in her hand.

"So when Talya was murdered, that made me suspicious of you. Up until then it had still been in my head that this was about Professor Crowhams' and Tom's departmental rivalry and Crowhams' hatred of the horses. But when I found the receipt for the milk bar in Tom's wallet, it just made me curious. There were clearly two drinks on the receipt… Joe said you don't drink milk. It was the day before he died." Elizabeth lets the words sink in. Then continues, "And that thing you said about Talya's bracelet at the stargazing on Stourbridge Common, something about 'the moon and the stars'. Tom must have given her the bracelet." Elizabeth pulls up Sarah's sleeve and sees the bracelet. "You took it from her body?"

"This is mine." Sarah says, but Elizabeth spots the letter 'T' charm and looks at Sarah. They both know it's over. This is enough in Elizabeth's mind to be sure. But she continues, telling Sarah what she knows, waiting for Sarah's confession.

"Then Professor Crowhams found Tom had booked a 'Dark Skies' weekend. Picked the brochure up in your boat, didn't he? One of those weekends where you watch the stars in the darkest place you can find. Very romantic I suppose, if you like staring at stars. Up outside Durham, one of the darkest in Europe apparently. We found it on Professor Crowhams' body, the night he was killed. And you knew Professor Crowhams had taken the brochure. Joe told you. I heard him." Elizabeth continues, "Professor Crowhams was just annoyed that Tom had booked it using a department credit card no doubt. But you thought he now knew about Tom and Talya's affair. Tom was going away with Talya on this trip," Elizabeth says, adding, "I didn't realise for a while, as Tom had left his plus one blank. But if it had been you, there would have been no need. It was enough to make me suspicious. It wasn't to hide it from the department. Tom was hiding

it from you. Had Professor Crowhams told you he had the brochure?" Elizabeth looks at Sarah, who is now floored by Elizabeth's knowledge. There is no hiding place. Her face changes from innocence to anger.
"She stole my boyfriend. She had everything, could've had anyone," Sarah says bitterly. Elizabeth listens to her excuses, "She was my best friend, and she betrayed me, and so did he. They deserved it. Carrying on behind my back, the dirty slut."
"So you dished out your own form of retribution," Elizabeth replies. "Pretty ruthless aren't you? Cynthia had told you that she sneaked into the Lido every lunchtime. You knew, living so close by, that Ed opened the Lido a little earlier than when Cynthia arrived. A perfect place to bring Talya where she wouldn't suspect your motives, where it was quiet, where you could kill Talya and then get away quickly before Cynthia arrived. She must have got undressed, as must have you, and got in the pool. You could have taken her by surprise. That's why she was strangled in the water. I wonder how frightened she must have been?" Elizabeth ponders.
"She was pathetic." Sarah spits out her words. "Thinks she can do what she wants and get away with it."

"Hmm, well she didn't, did she?" Elizabeth says, staring at Sarah to see if she can understand just how Sarah could have sunk so low. "Only, you didn't bank on Professor Crowhams seeing you leave the Lido that morning, did you? He didn't see you murder your friend, or he would have called the police straight away. No, he must have just seen you leave. That was enough in your mind. Eventually, he would have put two and two together, with the Dark Skies brochure and worked out that you were there at the time of the murder. Maybe he'd already called you to ask what you were doing there? We're checking the phone records," Elizabeth says.

"What would that prove? That a colleague called another colleague? So what?" Sarah replies, shaking her head and gripping the mallet tighter. "I did the world a favour, finishing him off."

"How did you get him in the tree so quickly?" Elizabeth asks.

"Have you never heard of a pulley system? Thought he deserved a dramatic send-off," Sarah scoffs.

"Positively Shakespearean. You won't get away with all this." Elizabeth raises her eyebrows, looking at Sarah now lifting the mallet.

"You have no proof. What can you do? I'm sure you haven't told anyone yet or the police would be here. You stupid woman." Sarah begins to leer over Elizabeth.

"We have some proof. We'll find more." Elizabeth replies, trying not to show any fear. "You kept sabotaging your own boat. Letting all the boats off their moorings, chucking in the plant pots. All to make it look like Talya was responsible, trying to shift the focus away from you. I'm sure we will find evidence to prove that it was you who burned your own boat."

"I didn't!" Sarah now shouts.

"Yes, yes you did. Why do you even try to deny it?" Elizabeth shakes her head. "Probably to destroy evidence of Talya on your boat with Tom. But it didn't burn completely, we saved it. So I'm sure we will find traces of Talya in your bedroom, won't we Sarah?" Elizabeth looks up into Sarah's eyes, and can see her raising the mallet and tries to jump out of the way. But it is too late before she is lowering it down on Elizabeth, who struggles to stop a second blow. Elizabeth feels the full force of Sarah's body against hers as she launches at Elizabeth, the sheer weight catapulting them both into the waters of Dead Man's Corner. As they come up for air, and before Elizabeth can recover Sarah jumps on top of her, holding her under the water. No matter how much Elizabeth struggles, Sarah is stronger and pushes Elizabeth under every time she comes up for air, gasping to survive.

The water is cold, and the trees hang over Sarah, hiding

the heinous act behind the foliage. As Sarah holds Elizabeth down in the murky water for a little longer, noticing that she has stopped struggling, she looks up at the Blood Moon, shining through the branches and closes her eyes. Sarah isn't expecting the thud to the back of her neck as a huge splash behind her and a large man jumping on her causes the water to dip and sink. In a split second, she is thrown feet away back into the water and hits her head on a tree. Inspector Bob Abley dives down into the dark water, now searching for Elizabeth. He comes back up for air with nothing, but dives down again. Nothing. He dives down again.

Sarah rubs her head, then starts to swim away. On his third dive, Abley retrieves Elizabeth's lifeless body, swims to the bank and pulls her up and out. Bob Abley puts Elizabeth into the recovery position, then listens to hear for breathing. Nothing. He immediately starts mouth-to-mouth and chest pumping. Nothing happens. Elizabeth looks blue under the blood red moon. Bob Abley refuses to stop, getting more and more desperate. He hears sirens and boots running across the field. Wallis and Brad arrive, having broken through Lemon's cordon at the top of the lane with Joe behind them, with his shovel.

"There is a huge crowd trying to get down here. Waiting to see the moon, which is in the sky?" Brad says, a bit nonplussed, having come to sink a few pints in the Red Lion with Wallis and noticed all the commotion.

"Just grab that women. Don't let her get away!" Inspector Abley shouts to Brad and Wallis, who sees Sarah having climbed out of the river now running in the direction of Cambridge.

"That's Dr Robertly?" Brad says.

"Sarah?" Joe looks horrified.

"Get her. I'm Inspector Abley. Do it!" Brad and Wallis nod and start to give chase.

"Call an ambulance!" Abley shouts to Joe who dials for one immediately.

"You should show your badge you know." Joe says.
"Too busy!" Abley spits out, knowing full well it is inside Raynott's drawer back at the station. Joe then takes off his coat and puts it over Elizabeth's legs as Abley continues to pump Elizabeth's chest. Nothing. He holds her nose again and breathes air into her lungs. As he does this time, she coughs out river water right into his mouth. He pulls a face and wipes his mouth and leans over her to stare at her as she coughs and splutters, then rolls her over again into the recovery position.

"Don't tell Emily that I kissed you." He whispers as Elizabeth opens her eyes, trying to lighten the mood. Elizabeth says nothing, feeling half dead.

"This chap has called for an ambulance," Abley says of Joe. "Will be here soon."

"I don't want an ambulance." Elizabeth whispers, her head still on the ground, her body not moving at all.

"Are you kidding?" Joe shakes his head. "Secondary drowning. You can die from that." Joe takes off his jumper and puts it under Elizabeth's head until the ambulance arrives. Elizabeth looks at Joe. "Hospital," Joe says, looking at her and finally smiling, while shivering now himself. He looks up at Sarah being taken away, realizing what she has done.

*

A short while later, already wrapped in warm blankets, Elizabeth is being tied onto a trolley and lifted into an ambulance at the edge of the meadows. Sarah has been caught by Brad and Wallis and is being led off into a police car by two Constables. Inspector Bob Abley climbs in and sits in the ambulance next to Elizabeth, watching her as she has her eyes are shut, while a paramedic takes her pulse. She looks small and frail.

"I thought I'd lost you there," Bob says quietly.

"I thought I'd lost you," a little voice pipes up, and Elizabeth's beady eyes open.

"Never." He smiles.

"Thank you for coming," she says.

"A very sneaky tactic telling me you were meeting Cynthia in the dark by the river meadows to have it out with her. How could you be sure I'd come?" Abley says.

"Because I told you I was going to make a citizen's arrest of the murderer you suspected at five o 'clock in the dark, by the river meadows on my own. That it was all about jealousy. But not the academic jealousy you are always banging on about. We should have seen earlier that this wasn't about Professor Crowhams' jealousy of his colleagues. Or Cynthia Hatman's jealousy of Crowhams' career and power. It was the jealousy of a woman who had been cheated on," Elizabeth says, trying to avoid saying that she knew Bob would come because he knew she was in a vulnerable position.

"The oldest story in the book, a women lover scorned. And you said six." Abley corrects her smiling, glad Elizabeth seems to be recovering.

"I said five o'clock and no sexist remarks in this ambulance please or the paramedic will need to give you a sedative," Elizabeth replies.

"You said six and you may have drowned had it not been for Lemon telling me it was five!"

"Where is Lemon?" Elizabeth asks.

"He drove me here. I asked a Constable. Don't worry yourself," Abley pauses before he breaks the news. He looks out at through the open backdoors of the ambulance. He can see a number of stargazing members of the public who appear to have broken through the cordon, while other Constables are taping around the telescopes and ushering them back up towards the lane. "He's gone."

"Gone?" Elizabeth looks sad. They both know what it means. Abley looks at her and then back at the night sky. Shining into the ambulance is the huge Blood Moon,

illuminating everything, causing the equipment to glint.
"It's my fault," he says quietly.

They both know that this is true. Elizabeth doesn't know what to say, as it is an open wound. After a while, and between the paramedics fussing around her, she replies, "Thank you for saving me." Elizabeth smiles as much as she can, then coughs a little.

"Back atcha," Bob Abley says, taking Elizabeth's hand.

"How did you know she'd push you in and try to do that?" Abley asks Elizabeth.

"I didn't," Elizabeth replies, but Abley just looked confused. "I just had a sense that she might try to hurt me. But you came in time. You solved the case." Elizabeth smiles as much as she can.

"I didn't," Abley looks at her and can see what she's doing.

"It was you that said you thought Cynthia Hatman would be dangerous and you wanted to protect me if I was coming here." Elizabeth opens her eyes widely to make her point.

"Yes, well. She's not here." Abley raises his eyebrows.

"She was. We tell Raynott you're back and you solved the case." Elizabeth says as forcefully as she can. Abley shuts his eyes. Inspector Abley takes Elizabeth's hand as the ambulance door shuts and it pulls away.

67
CLIVE

Elizabeth is propped up against a bank of pillows on the sofa in her drawing room. She is peeping out from under her favourite blanket.

"Scratchy old thing," Emily says, tutting. "I wish you'd have kept the lovely blanket I bought for you."

"I don't have wool in the house. You know that Emily." Elizabeth replies.

"Another stray. How many are you going to take in?" Emily plumps a pillow behind Elizabeth's head.

"Clive is not a stray. He's part of the family," Elizabeth says, "and Ed can come and visit him whenever he likes."

"Where's he gone again?" Emily asks, wiping under Elizabeth's water, and moving the fruit bowl closer and within reach.

"Wells-Next-The-Sea. After his heart attack, he can't have the dog for a while as Cynthia is allergic and he can't get out. But when he's on the mend, he can come for Clive. I said I'd look after him until then, that's all."

"Your beautiful home is starting to smell of dog," Emily

replies, opening a window a little, but it is so cold she shuts is straight back up, shaking her head.
"Good, it will keep away all the people who don't like animals. And for the rest of us, we will be as happy in mud as can be." Elizabeth smiles at Clive and pats him. Clive eyes Elizabeth's sandwich that Emily made her earlier, resting on a side table. Godric walks in and rubs Clive's head. He is carrying a huge lemon tree and plonks it right next to Elizabeth, so that she's almost hidden behind it.
"Who's a lovely boy? C'mon. The doorbell rang and this was just standing there when I opened it," Godric says. "There it was in all its green glory." Godric sits next to his nanna, bouncing the sofa so that she is propelled a little into the air, as Clive jumps up onto Godric.
"Ah, my lemon tree." Elizabeth is delighted that she has her grandson back and now her lemon tree too. She beams.
"I thought you gave that to Inspector Abley."
"Yes, well, it found its way home. It didn't like Park Parade. It wanted to sit just there." Elizabeth points to a spot and looks at Emily. Emily rolls her eyes, picks up the lemon tree with a struggle and puts it by the window. "Left a bit." Emily huffs and pulls it left a bit. "Right a bit." Emily pulls it right a bit.
"I'm only doing this because you are to be monitored carefully for twenty-four hours. Hurry up and get better," Emily says.
"Thank you," Elizabeth says, smiling for the first time, "for tucking me in with the blanket." Godric gives his nanna a great big hug.
"Next time you are on your investigating capers, I'm coming. Get it?" Godric kisses her cheek.
"Well actually, I have to admit, that annoying Wallis and his friend Brad were not as annoying after all. They caught the murderer. I don't like what he does to the birds on the water. You should have a word with him about that. Maybe he will finally stop."

"Okay nanna."

"I'm not saying date him. No."

"It's okay Nanna, I'm sticking with Ben. He's taking me hill-climbing."

"You've lived in East Anglia all your life and now you want to go upwards?"

"Der." Godric looks at his nanna. "Who tried to kill Brad? That could have been me."

"Not if you're hill-climbing, Goddy."

"Yes, but could they strike again?"

"No, Sarah Robertly did it. Thought it would draw attention away from her murdering Tom. Same reason she poisoned the horses for a second time," Elizabeth replies. "I must admit, I feel a little sorry for Joe. He didn't actually do anything wrong. Unless you count stealing a stern plate off a boat and throwing it in the water. He was just in love with Sarah Robertly. He wanted to lose it as Tom made it. He was trying to move into Sarah's life and I suppose it was staring at him all the time. He has to leave his boat as it was Tom's and when Tom died he lost the right to live on it." Elizabeth says, "But he's taken Tom's cat Midnight you know. So he is a good man for that. Inspector Abley says Joe's going to stay with a friend in Italy. Midnight will have a different life!"

"So you are not going to be an Inspector then?" Godric asks.

"What Inspector job?" Emily is surprised.

"Oh, I think Godric has his wired crossed." Elizabeth opens her eyes widely at Godric for letting the cat out the bag. "Yes, I think Superintendent Raynott was very angry that Inspector Abley solved the case." Elizabeth smirks. "I couldn't have done it without him, was consulting him all throughout the case." She says to Emily. "He arrested that woman with Lemon in Grantchester. He was magnificent. Such a good man."

"Why do you lie for that man?" Emily shakes her head. "No, don't tell me. I know." Emily realises something has been going on, but would prefer Elizabeth just got her rest. However, she can't help mutter to herself, "Because he reminds you of someone…. Golf, big laugh, big shoulders." Emily interrupts herself. Elizabeth says nothing. She doesn't even want to think about it, think about her feelings. Emily just raises her eyebrows and smiles.

"Well, I think it must be time for elevenses." Godric says, "My turn this time, popped to the bakery." Godric jumps up and brings in some plates a knife and a vegan lemon meringue pie. Elizabeth reaches behind her pillows and brings out some pet snacks. Monty and Hector rush in, as she shakes them, along with Bertie and Soot. She gives them all a treat, Clive getting the most.

Godric throws himself down again on the sofa next to Elizabeth, causing the cushion below her to bounce up into the air raising Elizabeth off the pillow for a split second, and spilling all the treats from the packet all over the floor. The dogs run for the treats in a frenzy which makes Godric laugh so hard he falls into Elizabeth. Emily laughs and shakes her head. Elizabeth tries to pick up the remaining snacks but Godric gives her a big hug instead. Clive jumps up on the sofa and licks Elizabeth's face.

THE END

Thank you so much for reading 'BLOOD MOON'. If you would like to read more by this author, please check out www.charlotking.com or you can follow the author on Twitter @queencharlot or Instagram @charlot_king_cambridge

Printed in Poland
by Amazon Fulfillment
Poland Sp. z o.o., Wrocław

50186185R00197